HANNAH ALEXANDER

SILENT PLEDGE

BETHANY HOUSE PUBLISHERS
MINNEAPOLIS, MINNESOTA 55438

Silent Pledge
Copyright © 2000
Hannah Alexander

Cover by the Lookout Design Group, Inc.

Published by Bethany House Publishers
A Ministry of Bethany Fellowship International
11400 Hampshire Avenue South
Bloomington, Minnesota 55438
www.bethanyhouse.com

Printed in the United States of America by
Bethany Press International, Bloomington, Minnesota 55438

Library of Congress Cataloging-in-Publication Data

Alexander, Hannah.
    Silent pledge / by Hannah Alexander.
        p. cm.
    ISBN 0-7642-2444-1
    1. Emergency medical personnel—Fiction. 2. Women physicians—Fiction.
3. Physicians—Fiction. I. Title.
    PS3551.L35558 S56 2001
    813'.54—dc21

                                                        00-011335

God was in Christ, reconciling the world to himself,
no longer counting people's sins against them.
This is the wonderful message he has given us to tell others.
We are Christ's ambassadors, and God is using us
to speak to you. We urge you, as though
Christ himself were here pleading with you,
"Be reconciled to God!"
For God made Christ, who never sinned,
to be the offering for our sin, so that we
could be made right with God through Christ.

(2 CORINTHIANS 5: 19–21, NEW LIVING TRANSLATION)

———

In memory of our beloved cousin,

Mark Mercer Patterson,

December 24, 1954 to April 14, 2000,
Cheryl's childhood playmate and defender.
May his courage and tender heart live on
in the character of Clarence Knight.

Books by
Hannah Alexander
FROM BETHANY HOUSE PUBLISHERS

Sacred Trust

Solemn Oath

Silent Pledge

HANNAH ALEXANDER is a pseudonym for the writing team of Cheryl and Melvin Hodde. Their previous fiction includes *The Healing Promise* and *Ozark Sunrise*. When not assisting Cheryl in the writing process, Melvin practices emergency medicine in a Missouri hospital.

ACKNOWLEDGMENTS

We continue to thank our editors, David Horton, Terry Mc-Dowell, and Jeremy Greenhouse, for continuing to point us in the right direction. We thank Jack Cavanaugh and Dr. Michael Block, whose pastoral insights helped us with difficult theological questions, and also Mr. Erwin Hodde, an excellent writer who was willing to share his heart.

For tireless help with publicity and rewrites we thank Lorene Cook, Ray and Vera Overall, Jackie Bolton, Barbara Warren, Grant, Bonnie, Jessica, and Megan Schmidt, Jerry Ragsdale, Brenda Minton, and scores of brothers, aunts, uncles, cousins across the country and around the world.

For professional insight, we thank Sergeant Jerry Harrison and Sergeant Mike Abramovitz for advice on police procedure—any mistakes found within these pages are purely our own.

PROLOGUE

Odira Bagby sat on the edge of her great-granddaughter's rumpled twin-sized bed, soaking a thin washrag with water from an old leaky mixing bowl. She squeezed out the excess and applied it to Crystal's hot tummy. The rag warmed quickly. Odira winced every time seven-year-old Crystal coughed.

The hoarse crackle and wheeze sounded loud in their small three-room apartment, and the little girl bent double with the effort to breathe. Her pale, blue-veined face was flushed, and her mouth opened wide as she gasped for breath. The sound of her struggle was worse than any nightmare. Odira caught herself automatically trying to breathe harder and heavier, as if she could take in extra air for Crystal.

The room smelled like Vicks, even though Odira knew that rubbing the ointment on Crystal's bony chest probably wouldn't help. It'd never helped before, except to ease Odira's arthritis for a while and make her feel as though she was at least doing *something*. Her hands always stayed sore and swollen from the thumping she did on Crystal's back and chest. Crystal had cystic fibrosis.

"Gramma," Crystal whispered, stiffening her neck to push the bare sound from her throat. She reached up and pressed her hand against her chest. "Hurts."

"I know, little 'un." Odira felt the tears in her eyes that Crystal never cried. "We'll get help." Heaving herself up, she lumbered the few feet across the room to her own bed.

She peered at the numbers on the secondhand alarm clock. It was almost midnight on a Saturday night. What was she supposed to do? Crystal's mom, Odira's granddaughter, had disappeared last year— Greta had never been married, and they didn't know who Crystal's daddy was. And Millie, Crystal's grandma, was dead. The grandpa "didn't want nothin' to do" with the whole mess. There was nobody else.

Bedsprings cried out in alarm as Odira sat down and picked up the receiver of her old black rotary phone. She leaned forward and peered at the list of emergency numbers on the bedside stand. There was no ER in Knolls, not after the explosion last fall. Odira couldn't afford a car on her social security, so she couldn't drive Crystal to another ER. Besides, on the hills and curves of these Ozark roads around here, the drive would take an hour. She didn't want to wait.

She did all she knew to do. She dialed the home number of Dr. Mercy Richmond.

———

Buck Oppenheimer woke to the shock of silent winter darkness in the bedroom he shared with his wife, Kendra. The room felt like the inside of the unheated tool shed out back, and for a moment he wondered if the pilot light in the central heating system had gone out again.

But as he listened to small sounds gradually creep to him through the house, he heard the furnace popping, and he felt warm air coming from the vent on his side of the bed.

So why was it so cold?

He listened for the soft sigh of his wife's breathing but didn't hear anything. He reached toward her and felt the emptiness of icy sheets.

"Kendra? Honey?"

He didn't hear any sounds coming from the bathroom and no sound of drawers clattering or silverware clinking in the kitchen— sometimes when Kendra couldn't sleep she'd go in and make some toast.

And sometimes when she couldn't sleep . . .

Buck threw back his covers and scrambled out of bed, switching on the bedside lamp. The bedroom door hung open, but there was no light coming from the rest of the house. He didn't like the feel of this. He pulled on the jeans he'd worn home from the fire station just a few hours ago. They smelled like smoke.

"Kendra?" he called again.

No answer.

She hadn't said much when he came home two hours late from his shift tonight. There'd been a flue fire out in an old home north of town, and he couldn't get away any sooner. Not that she got mad anymore when that happened, but ever since the arson and the hospital explosion last fall, Kendra was scared. Which was understandable—her fireman father had been killed a year and a half ago in the line of duty. Kendra said she knew that would happen to Buck someday, too.

He went into the kitchen. Kendra wasn't there, but the door to the back porch stood wide open. Icy January wind blew in, nipping at the bare skin of his chest and shoulders. He stepped to the screen door and looked out, curling his toes up from the cold linoleum.

"Kendra?"

Quiet. Had she gone out again? He fought back the memory of two months ago when he woke up at 1 A.M. to find her coming through this very back door, a sweater slung over her arm, her makeup smeared, and the sound of a car motor heading off down the street. She'd acted high on something—not booze, but something. And, man, did they ever have it out that night!

Now he was hearing a car again . . . the sound of a motor, its *chug-chug-chug* reaching him through the dark. Music drifted faintly through the icy air. He felt the familiar pain rip through him.

Was she doing it again? After all he'd done for her, didn't she even love him enough to be true?

He let out a deep breath and watched the white puff drift from his mouth. The air was as cold as he felt inside. How much was a man supposed to take?

Kendra wasn't the woman he thought he'd married five years ago. Over the past few months she hadn't been the same, and her mood swings were getting worse. If she wasn't hiding out at home crying, she was laughing too loudly and flirting with all the guys down at the fire station, going to shows in Branson with her girlfriends, and buying things he couldn't afford on his fireman's salary, like lots of jewelry and expensive clothes. There was no middle ground.

He pushed the screen door open and stepped onto the back porch, bracing himself in case she came walking in drunk, or maybe even with another guy.

He still heard the car motor idling, but the sound didn't come from the road. And he recognized that idle. With a deepening frown, he looked toward the small garage where Kendra kept her five-year-old Ford Taurus. The music was clearer now. Clint Black. Kendra's favorite. The doors were all shut. The idle continued steadily.

But that was stupid. She knew better than to leave the motor running with the—

"No," he whispered, then more loudly, "Kendra, no!" He reached inside and flipped on the porch light, then turned and raced down the wooden back steps and across the grass to the side entrance to the garage. Through the windowpane he could see the glow of the car's interior light, but he couldn't see around the shelving by the door to tell where she was.

He grasped the knob and tried to turn it, but the door wouldn't budge. "Kendra!" He banged on the pane. "Open up! What're you doing in there?"

No answer. And she had the only key to the garage—she'd lost the spare one last month.

Buck bent over and grabbed a broken piece of amethyst crystal about the size of his fist from Kendra's rock garden. He swung the chunk of rock against one of the windowpanes and shattered the glass, avoiding the shards that flew in every direction.

He reached in and unlocked the door from the inside, then shoved his way into the garage. "Kendra!"

His worst nightmare came true as he caught sight of her golden brown hair splayed across the backseat, the car door open, her pale skin illumined by the overhead light in the car. The heavy fumes tried to drive him backward.

Choking, eyes tearing, he rushed over and knelt beside her still body. He touched her face, her neck, felt for a pulse, and raised her eyelids to check her pupils. She groaned. She was still alive!

Gagging from the filthy air, Buck reached between the bucket seats in front and switched off the motor, then gathered his wife in his arms. He had to get her to help fast.

Delphi Bell peered out the small front window of the cluttered living room and saw her husband's hunched, brooding form on the porch steps, silhouetted by the moon. All he had on was an old pair of holey jeans and a white T-shirt with a pack of Marlboros rolled up in the right sleeve. Like a fifties greaser—dirty, stringy hair falling down over his forehead and into his eyes.

He might freeze to death. A girl could always hope. . . .

She saw the glowing tip of a cigarette, then saw his shadow move as he turned and looked at the window. She knew he saw her, and she stepped backward fast.

He'd been like that all night, quiet and glaring. She got scared when he acted like this. Sometimes the air around him seemed dark, just like it got outside before a bad storm that tore trees up by their roots and blew the shutters off houses. And he didn't even drink much anymore. He wasn't drinking tonight, but that didn't make much difference, not since he got out of the hospital. And that whole thing had been her fault. He kept reminding her of that.

She thought of the duffel bag under her side of the bed. Inside were a jacket and a sweater, and she'd been saving her tips from her job down at—

A thump on the porch startled her just before the knob turned and the door swung around and crashed into the side of the coffee table. Delphi cried out and jumped backward.

Abner loomed in the threshold. "What's the matter with you?"

She hunched forward with her arms over her chest, afraid to breathe. She shook her head.

He looked around the front room, and his face twisted in disgust as he stepped in and allowed the cold air from outside to swirl around him. "Why don't you get busy, then? What a pigsty. Get me some food." He kicked a pile of dirty clothes out into the center of the floor and got his foot tangled in one of Delphi's two pairs of jeans. "What's this stuff doing in here? Can't you do anything right?" He grabbed up a handful of clothes and slung them across the room, then turned on her again, arms out to his sides like a fullback getting ready to block a move.

"I . . . I been working, Abner," she sputtered, averting her gaze from his purple red face and those devil's eyes she saw more and more often lately.

"So've I!" He swung around and slammed the door shut, looked over his shoulder at her and gave her an evil leer, then deliberately snapped the door lock.

Delphi's thoughts scrambled. That was what he did the last time, just before she ran to her so-called friends from work and begged them to take her in. He'd smacked her a good one then, cut her lip and blacked her eye and nearly broke her arm before she could get away. And they'd turned her back over to him as if she were some annoying stray dog they didn't want around.

"Come 'ere," he muttered, pointing to a spot on the floor in front of him.

She took a step backward.

His expression didn't change. "I said come 'ere."

Delphi thought again about the duffel bag beneath her bed. She would take it after he went to bed—if he went to bed tonight; sometimes he didn't when he got like this—and then she would head to another town and never come back.

"You been talkin' to that Richmond doctor, haven't you?" His voice deepened and his words slurred, though there was no smell of booze. *"Dr. Mercy,"* he mocked in a singsong voice. "She been telling you to leave me again?"

Delphi knew the surprise showed on her face before she could stop it. She'd run into Dr. Mercy at the store the other day, and they'd talked a few minutes.

Abner snorted, his lips pulled back in a snarl, and his yellow brown eyes gleamed with a crazy light. "She don't know nothin'! She know you're the one who banged my head into the garage floor last fall?"

"Yes." Delphi felt that rush of guilt she got every time he reminded her of what she'd done. He'd been drunk and yelling at her and hitting her. When he fell and passed out, she'd tried to make sure he'd passed out for good. She couldn't help herself. But he was smart. Or at least tricky. Maybe he hadn't really been passed out at first. Maybe he'd been testing . . .

Suddenly his eyes narrowed, and his whole body surged toward her like a black cloud. His right arm raised, and she ducked as his hand came down on her shoulder. She winced and cried out and tried to get away. He grabbed her by the back of her shirt and jerked her toward him. She wrenched away and tried to run, but he stuck out a foot and tripped her.

She fell face first onto the wood floor. Pain hammered her right cheekbone and elbow as she closed her eyes tight and gritted her teeth, waiting for a kick in the side or a smack in the head.

Nothing happened. He grabbed a handful of her hair and jerked back. Hard.

She flinched, but by now she was used to pain. As he lifted her, she drew her feet under her and swung up and around with her left elbow and slammed him in the jaw.

He grunted and let her go.

She stumbled and nearly fell, but she caught herself and kicked him hard, low in the gut. Without waiting to see what he would do, she ducked past him and ran for the kitchen, holding her hand over her eye.

He screamed a curse and came for her. There was no time to grab a coat, let alone the duffel bag. She just ran on out the back door and down the steps and kept on running. She didn't care where to.

CHAPTER 1

The crunch of tires on gravel echoed across the unpaved parking lot as Dr. Mercy Richmond drove into the apartment complex where Odira Bagby lived with her great-granddaughter, Crystal Hollis. A bare lightbulb glowed over the small concrete front stoop at the door nearest the alley so she'd know which apartment was Odira's.

Mercy pulled as close to the steps as she could and reached over to turn up the heat in her car. The curtain at the window beside Odira's front door was open, revealing a front room with an old threadbare sofa and a straight-backed chair crammed into a ten-by-ten-foot space, along with an old TV resting on a nightstand. An off-white lace doily topped the TV. Mercy had never been here before, but she knew the sixty-six-year-old woman supported herself and seven-year-old Crystal on social security. She couldn't get a place at Sunrise Villa, the retirement apartments, because the new management didn't want children.

Before Mercy could shift the gear into park, the front door opened and out lumbered Odira, all two hundred seventy pounds of her, with wraithlike Crystal beside her, bundled all the way to her nose in a thick quilt.

As Mercy stepped out of the car into the icy wind and hurried around to open the door for them, Crystal started coughing again— the same hoarse, dry sound Mercy had heard in the background when Odira called a few minutes ago. It was typical of a child sick with bronchitis, maybe even pneumonia, brought on by the specter of cystic fibrosis.

"Hope you didn't have to leave your own little girl at home alone for this," Odira said in her booming baritone voice that always seemed to shake the walls when she came to the clinic.

"No, I dropped Tedi off at my mom's on the way here." Mercy got Crystal and Odira settled in the car, stepped back into the driver's seat, and pulled onto the quiet street for the five-minute drive to her clinic.

At the first stop sign, she noticed Odira sniffing, great, heaving sniffles. Tears, which she obviously could not contain, paraded down her cheeks. Combined with her loud, worried breathing and Crystal's wheezing cough, Mercy knew she had been right to come for them. Odira was known to talk more than she breathed, a counterpoint to Crystal's silent watchfulness. But not tonight.

Mercy cast a second concerned glance toward the woman, where the dash lights illumined her broad, heavy face and rusty-iron hair that looked as if it had been cut with a pair of scissors as old as Odira. Beside her, Crystal's face was thin and pale, filled with a sad knowledge. She raised her hand to cover her mouth when she coughed, just as Odira had taught her to. Her stout, clubbed fingers demonstrated the effects of oxygen deprivation to her extremities throughout her battle with CF.

"Are you two warm enough?" Mercy asked.

"I'm plenty warm." Odira looked down at Crystal and wrapped a thick arm around her. Worn patches at the sleeves of her thirty-year-old coat had been carefully mended. "You okay?"

Crystal nodded and ducked her head into her great-grandmother's side.

"What's Crystal's temperature?" Mercy hadn't bothered to inquire about that over the phone because she knew that if Odira was desperate enough to call for help, Crystal was sick.

"Hundred and two." Odira's voice sounded like a solid mass in the confined space. "Couldn't get her temp down, and the coughing just kept getting worse. Think she might have that pneumonia again." She sniffed and wiped at her wet face with the back of her hand. "Sorry . . . just couldn't figure out nothing else to do but call you."

"You don't have to apologize, Odira." Mercy laid her heater-warmed hand on Crystal's face. Yes, it was hot. Crystal's underdeveloped body was always fighting some kind of an infection. She'd had bronchitis and pneumonia since Odira took over her care last year. Who knew what nightmares the child had suffered before that? She talked more now than she had when she first came to Knolls after her mother disappeared. She was healthier, too. That didn't surprise Mercy. Love and kindness had great power over illness, and nobody could envelop a little girl in love the way big, awkward Odira Bagby could.

Mercy shared the hope with Odira that they would see Crystal live to adulthood, maybe even into her forties, with the new treatments and increased knowledge about this debilitating genetic disease. And by the time Crystal reached her forties, maybe they would have a cure.

As Crystal's coughing and wheezing increased, Mercy turned onto Maple, the street that fronted Knolls Community Hospital and her clinic. The hospital came into view, glowing a dark rose color in the security lights set strategically around the grounds. Mercy slowed to the required fifteen miles per hour as she passed the property, set in a scenic residential section of town, with plenty of open lawn and evergreens. Bare branches of oaks and maples jutted out from between humps of burlap-protected rose plants.

She looked up to see, without surprise, that the administrator's office was illuminated on the second floor. Mrs. Pinkley had opted to move her operations into an unused storage area rather than take the time to repair her own suite, which had been damaged in the explosions when the ER was destroyed. The ER was Estelle Pinkley's first priority. Knolls Community usually employed about two hundred fifty people, many of whom would be out of work until they had the west wing rebuilt with an emergency department. Estelle's sense of civic responsibility had impacted her career as prosecuting attorney for thirty years. Why stop just because she'd changed careers? At seventy, she was a more powerful force than a whole roomful of attorneys.

Odira sniffed and wiped her face again. "Sure do miss Dr. Bower." Her heavy voice had an unaccustomed catch of sadness. "Bet you do, too. Bet you get all kinds of calls like this since there ain't an ER."

Mercy reached over and patted Odira's fleshy shoulder. "You know I wanted to come." But what the woman said was true. Mercy's practice had been overwhelmed the past three months. She missed Lukas a lot, and not just for his professional ability.

Lukas Bower, the acting ER director, was working temporarily at a hospital on the shore of the Lake of the Ozarks, a three-hour drive from Knolls. Patients and hospital staff members continually asked Mercy when he'd be back. She wondered, too. Nobody missed him more than she did.

"Don't seem right he should be out of work just because some monster wants to set fire to the ER." Odira pulled Crystal closer. "Don't seem right we should all be suffering like this."

"I feel the same way." Mercy looked down at Crystal. "How are you doing, sweetheart?"

"My chest hurts."

Mercy bit her lip and prayed silently, the way Lukas had taught her to do. *God, please help me with this one. She's so young. Why is she suffering like this?* The question came up often lately in Mercy's mind, and after all the talking she and Lukas had done about the subject, she still hadn't found a satisfactory answer. Every time she found herself questioning God about it, she felt afraid. Sometimes it seemed as if all those great, profound truths she and Lukas had discussed last summer and autumn had deserted her, and that her new belief in Christ was just a fairy tale.

She turned into the dark parking area of her clinic, less than a block from the hospital. "Let's get inside and get a breathing treatment started."

Clarence Knight just happened to be in Ivy Richmond's kitchen, raiding her refrigerator and practically swallowing three frozen chocolate chip cookies whole, when the phone rang for the second time Saturday night.

He jerked backward and knocked his head on the overhead compartment where Ivy had been hiding the treats from him. He thumped his elbow on the door and spilled crumbs down the front of his size 6XL T-shirt in his rush to get to the phone before the ringing could wake Ivy. If she came in and found him eating, she would roast him whole over an open fire, all four hundred twenty pounds of him.

He jerked up the receiver, then realized his mouth was still full. He chewed and swallowed. "Mmm-hmm?"

"Hello? Who is this?" It was a man's voice. Sounded familiar. Sounded upset. "Clarence?

"Mmm-hmm."

"Is Dr. Mercy there?"

Clarence swallowed again. "Hmm-mmm."

"Do you know where she is? This is Buck. I just tried her at home, and I couldn't get her. I need her bad. Kendra tried to—" His voice broke. "She needs help. I've got to get her somewhere . . . got to get her on some oxygen." There was another crack in his voice. "Clarence? You there?"

Clarence swallowed again. "Hol' up, Buck. Ith's okay." One more swallow. There. "Mercy dropped Tedi off here a little bit ago, 'cause she was on her way to the clinic for some emergency. What's the matter with Kendra?"

Buck took a breath. "She tried to kill herself. Carbon monoxide poisoning. She was running her car motor out in the garage when I found her. The doors and windows were all shut."

Clarence grunted as if he'd been hit in the gut with a football. "Oh, man." Poor Kendra. And poor Buck. "She okay? Where are you?" He knew they were still having trouble in their marriage, but was her life bad enough for her to want to die?

"We're still at home. I've got to get her to Dr. Mercy's," Buck said. "There'll be oxygen there."

"Yeah, Dr. Mercy'll check her out. Want me to call the clinic and see if I can let her know you're coming?"

"Yeah. Thanks, Clarence."

There was so much relief in Buck's voice, Clarence went even further. "You'll be coming right by here on your way. . . ." He hesitated. He'd just started getting back out into public after losing all that weight, and he still had a long way to go. Could he do this?

Yeah, he'd do anything for Buck. Buck had been there for him when he was in trouble. "I could meet you out at the street. All you'd have to do would be stop and let me get in and ride with you. Then you wouldn't have to do this all by yourself." And maybe he could talk to Kendra some. He knew firsthand what depression could do to a person.

There was a pause, and he braced himself for Buck to turn him down. He'd lost over a hundred pounds since last spring, but he'd still draw a big crowd at a circus sideshow. He was big and clumsy and took up two seats wherever he went, and strangers stared and laughed, and he knew the few friends he had were probably ashamed to be seen—

"You'd do that for me, Clarence?" came Buck's relieved voice. "It would help."

Clarence blew out a bunch of air he hadn't realized he was holding in his lungs. "Sure would, pal. Look at what you did for me last fall. I'll be waiting out front when you get here."

He hung up and glanced toward the hallway that led to Ivy's bedroom suite. Good. No lights, and he thought he could hear her snoring over the hum of the refrigerator. Mercy's daughter, Tedi, had gone straight to sleep in the spare bedroom without waking her grandma. He guessed neither of them had heard him on the phone.

Ivy had once compared his voice to a derailed locomotive running loose through the house, and she really griped when he woke her up in the middle of the night. Especially when she caught him eating.

Clarence and his sister, Darlene, had come to live with Ivy Richmond—Dr. Mercy's mom—three months ago when their health got too bad to live on their own. And Ivy had bullied him every day since then to eat right, exercise, take his vitamins, exercise, take his medicine, drink a bucket of water a day, and exercise. She'd even tried to make him go to church with her. He'd done everything but that.

Since he couldn't bend over and pick up all the crumbs he'd scattered on his way to the phone, he shoved them aside with his foot. Though sloppy and crude, it might save his life. He had to hurry and brush his teeth and get out to the curb. He wanted to be there when that pickup truck came rolling by.

Shouldn't've taken that Lasix a couple of hours ago. He knew from Mercy that the medicine kept him from retaining fluid, but it also kept him running to the bathroom all night long.

———

Crystal Hollis lay on Mercy's softest, most comfortable exam bed in an overheated room, with a pink teddy-bear sheet draped over the lower half of her body. Some of the color had returned to her face, and the sound of her breathing was not as labored, nor her lips as blue, as a few moments before.

Mercy pressed the warmed bell of her stethoscope against the little girl's chest. "Take a breath for me, honey."

Seven-year-old Crystal had the body weight of a five-year-old, with stick-thin arms and legs and a slightly protruding abdomen— clearly the cystic fibrosis affected her pancreas as well as her pulmonary system. Which meant Crystal could eat as much as an adult and still not put on weight. It was a constant battle. She had an aura of maturity in her long-suffering expression and sad gray-blue eyes that befitted someone seventy years older.

Her chest sounded a little better, but not enough. She coughed and Mercy grimaced. The breathing treatments weren't going to cut it this time.

"How's she doin', Dr. Mercy?" Odira's deep voice rumbled from her chair four feet away. She leaned forward, her puffy, wrinkled face filled with tense worry.

Mercy sighed and placed the stethoscope back around her neck. She tucked the sheet back up over Crystal's bony shoulders and took the little girl's hand in her own. "I'd like to see her breathing better, Odira." She perched on the exam stool beside the bed and faced the child's great-grandmother. "The x-rays don't show what I suspected, but this could be early pneumonia. I'd like to have her checked out by a pulmonologist in Springfield. I could transfer her to Cox South, and . . ." The expression of sudden fear in Odira's face halted her words.

"But you're her doctor," the older woman argued. "You're the one we trust. Couldn't you just do one of those consults they talk about on TV? That big place up in Springfield would be so scary for Crystal, and they might not even let me stay with her. You know how those big places are."

Mercy patted Crystal's hand and released it, then stood up and walked over to the chest x-rays placed in the lighted viewer box. The films most definitely indicated bronchitis. Time to blast those lungs with high-powered antibiotics. Odira always made sure Crystal received the nutritional support Mercy suggested, including the pancreatic enzyme supplements and vitamins, but Mercy would increase the caloric intake even more for a while. Crystal's fever had dropped a little, but Mercy didn't want to take any chances.

Accompanied by the unrhythmic sound of Odira's loud breathing, Mercy checked Crystal's heart once more. With severe disease, right-sided heart failure could occur, but there was no sign that the CF had progressed that far. Would it be possible to keep them here?

Mercy turned around. "Odira, are you feeling okay?"

"Don't worry about me, Dr. Mercy. I'm just worried about keepin' our girl in Knolls. You people know how to take care of us right."

"I'll try," Mercy said. "I'd like to get her temperature down before I decide."

"You need me to be your nurse?" Odira asked. "I know how to follow orders, you know."

"Yes, if you would." Mercy gave her instructions to go to the staff break room and get a Popsicle out of the freezer for Crystal. It would be a special treat for the child and would be a painless way to help drop her temperature and add a little fluid.

Odira struggled to get to her feet and finally succeeded. "I sure do appreciate your heart, Dr. Mercy."

Mercy knew her patients hated the thought of leaving Knolls for a hospital stay, even to places like Cox or St. John's, two of the top-rated hospitals in the country. Mercy didn't blame them. They liked a small community hospital with down-home caring, close to where they lived. Their indomitable hospital administrator took pro bono cases and occasionally paid for them from her own bank account. This would probably be one of those cases.

"Please, Dr. Mercy," came Crystal's soft, hoarse voice. "Can't I stay here?"

Mercy sighed and looked over into the little girl's solemn eyes. Her softheartedness always got her into trouble. But she supposed she could call Dr. Boxley as a consult. He was an expert on CF patients, especially children, and he'd given her advice on Crystal's care before. And Robert Simeon wouldn't mind checking her out as a favor. With his specialty in internal medicine, he'd had some experience with this, and he lived and practiced right here in town. And the

ICU staff at this hospital was the best anywhere. Maybe . . .

She looked once more into Odira's hopeful face and sighed. "I'll set you up for an admission."

The strain of worry gradually eased from the older woman's heavy expression. She walked out into the hallway toward the back. "That's our doc," she called over her shoulder.

CHAPTER 2

Deep-voiced curses and shouts careened down the short hallway of the Herald, Missouri, emergency room, followed by the whiff of stale beer and marijuana smoke. The hospital was in for another exciting Saturday night on the shore of Lake of the Ozarks.

Dr. Lukas Bower stepped to an uncurtained window in the ER staff break room and stared out at the glimmer of frosty moonlight over the water. Ice crusted the shoreline but didn't reach the center. He could see the bare branches of trees swaying in the wind like the fingers of skeletons, grasping through the air to catch the wispy clouds that drifted past.

He shivered. This place gave him the creeps, and he'd only been here a few days. He couldn't say exactly why the town bothered him so much. Maybe it was just because he missed Mercy and Knolls and the friends he'd made there—the life to which he planned to return as soon as the new emergency room was built and his short-term contract here was up. Or maybe it was the depressing, uncooperative attitude of some of the staff here. Or maybe it was his own attitude.

He frowned at his five-foot-ten image in the reflection from the window, at the harsh brilliance of fluorescent light that caught and bounced back from his glasses. He'd been feeling sorry for himself quite a bit lately with all the temp work he'd been doing the past two and a half months. With so many night and weekend shifts, he'd almost forgotten what the inside of a church looked like on Sunday morning, or how the crisp winter air smelled in the Mark Twain National Forest.

But by no means had he forgotten what Mercy Richmond looked like, the rich alto sound of her voice, the warmth and sweet fragrance of her on those rare occasions lately when they'd seen each other. Why did he have to think about her so much? The thoughts he was having only made things worse.

A shouted epithet echoed through the room once more. He turned from the window and glanced toward the open break room door. All he'd heard for the past ten minutes was the arguing of the bikers who'd engaged in a slug match down the road at the apartments—if the rickety string of rock buildings by the lake could be called that. The only reason the gang members weren't camping out beside their Harleys tonight was the cold front that had moved in earlier this week, sucking all warmth from the air. The front had obviously caught them by surprise.

The shouting grew louder. Lukas grimaced. He'd had too many previous experiences with mean drunks who'd sooner slug a doctor or nurse in the mouth than allow them to take a blood pressure. Should he call the police to come and stand guard just in case? They wouldn't be surprised. With a population of about three thousand, Herald, Missouri, was only about a third the size of Knolls, and the police force had the same number of personnel. In the spring, summer, and autumn they kept busy with vacationing partiers—this area had become a kind of Mecca for bikers. Lukas couldn't figure out why.

He walked back into the small five-bed ER to see if the x-rays were back on the patient who was shouting the loudest. They weren't. Brandon Glass, the Saturday night tech, had to take care of both x-ray and lab, and sometimes he couldn't keep up. He never attempted to disguise his resentment when Lukas gave him more orders. Nobody attempted to hide their resentment around here. Gloom was the password into Herald Hospital.

Lukas shook himself and walked to the sink to scrub. He didn't want the mood to affect him. He didn't like being this way. He was the physician here; he was supposed to make people feel better, not depressed.

"I'm not done with you yet, Moron," one of the bikers muttered to the other through the thin curtain. "If my baby's got a scratch on her, I'll take it out of your hide."

The privacy curtains were open, and Lukas turned around to glance at both men. The mouthy one held an ice pack to his nose, and the skin around his eyes had already begun to darken. Blood matted long strands of his brown hair and stained his black T-shirt. Thanks to his running monologue, everybody within earshot knew that his "baby" was his Harley-Davidson. Thanks to his temper—and that of his antagonist in the next cubicle—and a broken beer bottle, his left forearm had just been prepped for suture repair.

Lukas sniffed. The room even smelled like motor oil and alcohol . . . and pot.

The other biker, who wore black jeans and boots and a black leather vest with nothing else, lay with his head turned away from his adversary. His name was Marin—from which, obviously, his biker buddies had hung the moniker of Moron, like little kids taunting one another. Marin's antagonistic attitude had apparently dissipated with the dwindling effects of the alcohol and other drugs coursing through his veins. His eyes gradually closed as Lukas watched. Good. They were winding down. Maybe the police could concentrate on breaking up barroom fights tonight. And maybe they could spend some time searching for that little girl who had disappeared from the Herald city park last week—if that acre of rusted swings and overgrown grass could be called a park. Lukas had overheard a conversation about that yesterday morning between a couple of policemen who were waiting for their prisoner to be x-rayed. Rumor said it was a kidnapping, and she apparently wasn't the first child to disappear lately in Central Missouri. It made Lukas sick to think about it.

"Dr. Bower, the films are back," came a strong, deep female voice behind Lukas.

He turned to see Tex McCaffrey—no one ever dared call her Theresa—hanging the x-rays up on the lighted panel.

"I had to do them myself. Godzilla's in a bad mood tonight." She cast a disgusted glare toward the open door that led directly into the radiology department, then muttered, "Can't get good help around here anymore."

Lukas wouldn't have dreamed of arguing with her. Tex was the paramedic-bouncer in this joint, and she served as the ER nurse on Saturday nights and quite a few weekdays, from what Lukas could pick up from the nursing schedule. If something came in she couldn't handle, she could call for a nurse from the twenty-bed floor—not that Lukas had heard of that happening. He couldn't imagine efficient, self-assured Tex getting anything she couldn't handle. In just the short amount of time he'd worked with her, he'd been very impressed by her skills . . . and her size. He didn't have the nerve to ask how tall she was, but he had to look up at her to make eye contact.

Lukas checked the films, nodded, returned to the sink. Nothing broken. "Ready to help me with the sutures?" he asked.

"Got it all set up. I cleansed it, then irrigated it with 500 of saline." She paused and grinned in the direction of the glowering patient in question. She blew a couple of stray strands of curly dark blond hair from her face. "Care to guess his alcohol level? Three-twenty." She almost sounded proud of him as she stepped in his direction. "I put the suture tray out of his reach."

Broad-shouldered Tex was in her early thirties and could probably throw the whole biker gang on their kickstands if they got too rowdy. She was also Lukas's next-door neighbor in a duplex at the edge of town. Her first cousin was Lauren McCaffrey, who was once one of Lukas's favorite nurses down at Knolls—until she got him involved in *this* mess.

Lukas pulled on a pair of sterile gloves as he followed Tex's athletic form to the curtained exam cubicle. She had set out 5.0 nylon for the suture and the requested Lidocaine for anesthetic. Good. He glanced at the patient's name on the chart again, hoping he could pronounce the last name properly. Proper name enunciation helped raise the patient comfort level, and he really wanted this particular patient to be comfortable.

"We're ready to start, Mr. Golho—"

"I told you when I came in, don't call me mister!" the muscled, tattooed man growled from beneath the ice pack he continued to hold on his nose. "Nobody calls me mister when I'm on the road."

Oh yeah. Lukas glanced at a note Tex had penciled in on her chart. So much for proper name enunciation. How could he have forgotten? "Catcher." Where did these guys—

"Ha!" came a voice from the other side of the curtain. Apparently Catcher's antagonist hadn't fallen asleep after all. "Why don't you tell 'em where you got the name?"

"Shut up."

"You want to know where it came from, Doc? Huh? They called him that 'cause he used to ride without a shield, and he caught bugs on his teeth and—"

"I said shut up!" Catcher came halfway off his exam bed before Tex grabbed him by the arm and pulled him back.

"How do you feel about another tattoo, Catcher?" she asked, giving him a leering grin as she eased him back onto the exam bed. "Dr. Bower, here, is gonna test your pain tolerance."

While Lukas cringed at her choice of words, Catcher repositioned the ice pack on his nose and laid his head back against the pillow. "No prob. Go to it." He closed his eyes.

Lukas nodded. "Okay, Catcher. Have you ever had an allergic reaction to any anesthetic in the past?"

One eye came open. "Why?"

"Because I'll be injecting Lidocaine into the—"

"No, you won't." Both eyes were open now, and their dark brown-gray gaze held Lukas in a hard stare, which was more than a little out of focus due to his inebriated—and possibly stoned—state.

"Excuse me?"

"No 'caines.' Can't do them."

No Lidocaine? No anesthesia? Lukas did not want to hear this. He did not feel safe sticking needle and Dermalon into the flesh of an already combative drunk. "You mean you've had a react—"

"I mean I've been busting a cocaine habit for almost a year, and I'm not going back to that." Catcher took a firmer grip on his ice pack. "Just do it."

Lukas suppressed a groan, looked helplessly at Tex, and shrugged. Coming to work in Herald had been a big mistake. *Oh, Lord, let my fingers be tender, because any moment I may have to eat them.*

———

"Am I gonna die now?" Crystal's matter-of-fact tone stabbed the silence in the exam room.

Mercy caught her breath at the question and turned from her vigil by the telephone, where she'd been waiting for Dr. Boxley to return her call. Thank goodness Odira was still in the other room. "No, honey." She got up and crossed to Crystal's side and pressed the back of her hand against the child's face. "You're just sick again. Are you feeling worse?"

"No."

Mercy gently stuck the wand of the tympanic thermometer into Crystal's ear. She waited a few seconds to get a reading, then pulled the thermometer back. Relief. The temp was almost back down to normal. "Aren't you feeling any better?"

Crystal tilted her head sideways, seriously considering the question. "Yes."

Mercy sat down on the exam stool next to the bed and took Crystal's left hand in both of her own. "Then why do you think you're going to die?"

Crystal's clear water-blue eyes held Mercy's for a long, quiet moment. Her light brown hair framed her face and stuck in damp tendrils to the translucent skin where perspiration had gathered. She was breathing better. "A girl at school told me."

Mercy winced. "Then don't listen to her."

"But then I asked Gramma. She said I might, but when I do, I'll go straight to heaven and I'll never get sick again." She paused for a few seconds. "I'd like that."

As a mother, Mercy couldn't help imagining her own daughter saying those words, and the thought tore at her heart. She'd never heard a child so young expressing a wish to die. What hurt the worst was the realization of Crystal's suffering, both physical and emotional. From a year of treating Crystal, Mercy knew that the little girl, with her soft heart, worried more about her great-grandma Odira than she did about herself. Odira wasn't in the best of health, with her excess weight and high blood pressure. What would become of Crystal if anything happened to her great-grandmother?

"But, Crystal, we want to keep you here with us longer," Mercy said softly. "I know it might be selfish of us, when heaven is so wonderful, but do you think you could be strong for Gramma and me?" *Jesus, what do I say? How can this be happening?* She tried not to think about the situation, but the questions grew too numerous too quickly. Her faith still felt so fragile.

"Gramma needs me," Crystal said quietly. "I'll stay awhile."

They heard the sound of Odira's footsteps and heavy breathing, and then she came lumbering through the open exam-room door. "I didn't even think about using a Popsicle to get Crystal's temperature down. Here's a red one, her favorite. You've got a nice little freezer in there. Looks like you've got that back room all set up like an emergency room. I bet you use it a lot, what with the hospital—"

They heard the crash of a door flying open out in the waiting room, then the boom of a familiar voice—like a jet during takeoff. "Dr. Mercy! You in here?"

Clarence held the door open for Buck to carry Kendra through, then let it glide shut behind him. He knew the door would be unlocked even at this late hour; Dr. Mercy was expecting them. "Dr. Mercy!" he called again. "Got those patients for you." He tapped Buck's shoulder and gestured toward the open doorway that led to the exam rooms at the back of the waiting room. When he'd telephoned Mercy she'd told him just to bring Kendra to the first exam room. Clarence knew where everything was. He should. He'd been here enough times.

After he'd finally lost enough weight to get around on his feet a little better, Dr. Mercy had made him come to her office once a week so she could weigh him and check him over. He hated going, hated the way the other patients in the waiting room stared at him and whispered. Still, when Mercy asked him to do something, he did it. If she asked nice.

Mercy came rushing down the hallway, her long dark hair drawn back in a loose ponytail, wearing baggy old jeans and a thick wool sweater. Her dark eyes looked tired. "Hi, Buck. Bring her back here. I have a bed ready for her. I'll need you and Clarence to help keep an eye on her." She reached forward and laid a gentle hand against Kendra's cheek, and some of the tiredness cleared from her eyes. "Hang in there, Kendra. We'll get you on some oxygen." She pulled the stethoscope from around her neck, warmed it in her hand for a second, then placed it against Kendra's chest.

Clarence watched Mercy as she guided Buck into the exam room and helped him lay his wife on the bed. He enjoyed watching her work. When she treated patients, she acted as if they were a part of her own family. Of course, that also meant she nagged them like family. At five feet eight, she was four inches shorter than Clarence, but there were times when she seemed bigger than life, especially when she stood over him as he balanced on that dinky little exam bed wearing nothing but his shorts and a sheet.

But the times she made the biggest impact on him were when she saw his depression and bullied it out of him. He didn't get that way as often as he used to, but some days the heaviness of his thoughts messed him up big time. Those were the days he didn't want to diet, didn't want to exercise, didn't even want to get out of bed. That was when her tender toughness showed itself. She could look into his eyes and say, "Clarence, we're going for a walk. Get your shoes on," or "You haven't come this far to give up. Just get through today," and then she would tell Ivy to keep watch. And Ivy could be the queen of mean.

As soon as Buck eased Kendra down onto the exam bed, Kendra covered her face with her hands. Her body shook with sobs that grew louder and more forceful. "Why didn't you just let me die?" She turned her head sideways on the pillow, and her light brown hair, as soft looking as a sparrow's breast, fell across her cheek. "Everybody'd be better off that way."

Buck took a deep breath and bent his head, his square jaw working like a grinding machine. Buck was a big man, lots of muscles, with hair cut so short that his ears, which were already big, looked like doorknobs. He had a big heart, and nobody doubted that he loved his wife. Except her.

Clarence wished there was something he could do to help them both. The pain he felt in this room made even him feel like crying, and he hardly ever cried.

Mercy leaned over. "Kendra, tell me how you feel. Do you have a bad headache?"

Tears dripped across Kendra's nose onto the pillow, and her lower lip trembled. She looked like a heartbroken little girl. "Yeah, real bad."

Mercy gestured to Buck. "Would you please hook up the oxygen? I want her on a 100 percent nonrebreather mask." She reached toward a box beside the bed. "Kendra, I'm going to put this little clip on the end of your finger. It's attached to something called a pulse oximeter, which will tell me how much oxygen you have in your system."

She placed something that looked like a clothespin on Kendra's left forefinger, then went to a drawer and opened it, pulled out a syringe, and attached it to a needle. "And I'm sorry, honey, but I'm going to have to stick you for blood. It's going to hurt, because I have to go deep enough for an artery. We've got to find out how aggressively we need to treat you. Buck, has she been confused?"

"Yes, at first." Buck scrambled around until he found the tubing and mask he needed. "On the drive in I had the windows open, and she cleared up. Now she just keeps crying." He stepped back over to his wife's side.

Mercy leaned over Kendra again. "Are you dizzy? Do you feel sick to your stomach?"

Kendra's face puckered. She covered it with her hands once more and didn't reply.

Buck cleared his throat, tried to speak, cleared it again. "She was feeling sick earlier, Dr. Mercy. She had some shortness of breath."

Mercy turned around and saw Clarence standing in the doorway. "Call an ambulance for me, would you?"

"No!" Kendra cried out. She reached toward Buck, eyes wide and frightened, and tried to sit up. "Don't let them haul me away! Don't—"

"It isn't for you," Mercy said softly as she took Kendra's arm and eased her back down. "I have another patient tonight. I need to transfer her over to the hospital, and I can't leave you right now."

Clarence picked up the telephone in the room, then hesitated and frowned at Mercy. "You want to call an ambulance to haul somebody less than a block? Doesn't make sense to me."

Mercy checked the pulse oximeter box. "Do you have a better idea? I have a sick child in there, and her great-grandmother isn't in much better shape. I can't tell them to walk—"

"Let me take 'em." Clarence spoke the words against his will, as if something outside himself were making the decision for him.

Everyone in the room stared at him in surprise, as if a balloon had just sprouted from his ear or something. "What's wrong?" He demanded. "I *can* drive, long as I can fit behind the wheel. I'm a me-chanic, you know. My driver's license is—"

"Thank you, Clarence. Take my car." Mercy leaned back over Kendra. "My keys are on the desk in my office, and use the south entrance at the hospital. Get a move on. They're waiting for the patient."

For a moment, disbelieving, he could only stare at her. Just like that? He hadn't driven in two years, and she trusted him with her new car?

And then, in spite of the pain that still lingered in the room from Kendra's tears and Buck's stoic silence, he felt a glow of warm satisfaction that he hadn't felt in a long, long time. Maybe never. For once, he was on the giving end.

CHAPTER 3

Tex blotted and held, blotted and held as Lukas finished the last of the twelve interrupted sutures on Catcher's arm. The big biker hadn't even grunted through the ordeal. In fact, Lukas was sure that he himself had been the only one who grimaced every time the needle pierced flesh. Even with alcohol to mask the pain, it had to hurt. This man was tough.

Company had begun to arrive halfway through the procedure, as the first of Catcher's biker friends came clomping into the ER, carrying plastic packs of pimento cheese sandwiches and chips and soda they'd purchased from the vending machine in the waiting room. After an irritable glance in their direction, Tex had shown no reaction to their arrival. Even when one of the buddies came in and handed half a sandwich to Catcher, Lukas didn't make a remark. They weren't supposed to have food in the ER, and if OSHA found out about the infraction, there would be complaints and fines and forms filled out in quadruplicate, but Lukas wasn't in the mood to play hall monitor to a bunch of aging tattoos this early on a Sunday morning. Most of them just came in for a minute to check on their buddies, then wandered out to the waiting room, which was separated from the treatment area by a door and a sliding window where the secretary sat.

One husky woman wearing tight denim jeans and a heavy gray sweater shoved through the dividing door, food and soda tucked against her side by her left arm, holding a pack of cigarettes and a lighter in her right hand.

"Hey, Catcher!" she blared. "They treatin' you okay back here? I'll bash heads if they're not." She took a deep whiff of air. "Phew, smells like medicine and puke back here. Don't you guys have any air freshener?"

Lukas thought he heard Catcher groan, but he didn't move.

The woman swaggered into the room where they were doing the sutures. "There'd better not be a scar, Doc." She let the food and the unopened can of soda topple from under her arm onto the extra chair in the small room, then stepped over to peer at Lukas's workmanship. She sucked in air through her teeth. "Man, that looks gross."

"Shut up," Catcher muttered.

She shrugged and pulled a cigarette from its pack, then raised the lighter.

"Ma'am, no smoking, please," Lukas said automatically. He felt Catcher stiffen beneath his touch and wondered if he was about to get clobbered for his audacity.

The woman leveled a narrow gaze at him and flicked the lighter into flame. "So don't smoke." She held the flame to the tip of the cigarette, and Lukas felt Catcher stiffen further.

"Birdbrain, did you hear the doctor?" came the patient's rough voice. "He said no smoking!" He flexed his muscles, and Lukas nearly lost his grip on the needle driver. "You puff that thing in here, I'll send it up your nose!"

The woman blinked at him, paused for a moment for the information to sink through her inebriated state, and shrugged. She smothered the glowing end against the side of the lighter, shoved the offending objects into the front pocket of her jeans, then gathered her goodies from the chair and wandered back out of the room.

Lukas clipped the nylon thread. "Okay, two more and we're finished poking you, Catcher."

Someone else in leather and tattoos stepped into the ER doorway from the waiting room beyond. "Hey, look, they got a TV! Hey, Nurse, you guys got cable here?" A blare of music screamed through the rooms.

Lukas heard Tex's sharp intake of breath and caught a glimpse of her angry scowl, and he shook his head at her. "We're almost finished here." *Lord, please just hold this all together a little longer. Give me*

patience and compassion. Use me right here, right now, in this situa-
tion . . . and get us all through this alive.

Lukas wasn't supposed to be here. By now he should be working
full-time in a warm, supportive environment, with Mrs. Estelle Pinkley as hospital administrator. By now he would no longer be the acting ER director. Someone else would have that headache.

A loud clank and clatter pierced his concentration. His hands almost jerked the final suture too tightly. Neither he nor Tex could look
up from their work just now, but as soon as he'd snipped the last of
the threads, Tex put her things down and snapped off her gloves.

"If you'll finish up here, I'll check out the crash," she said.

Lukas could almost see her flexing her muscles as she metamorphosed from Tex the paramedic to Tex the bouncer. Uh-oh. Not
only was she about to make a scene, she was also about to make him
look like a coward. Of course, in this particular situation he *was* a
coward. But he did have a little pride left.

"Um, Tex, why don't—"

Catcher groaned. "Oh, Doc, I think I'm gonna hurl—"

With a final glance over his shoulder to see Tex strutting off to
bash heads, Lukas grabbed an emesis basin. "Breathe in through your
nose if you can, Catcher, then out through your mouth. There you
go." He took the ice pack from Catcher's limp hand and placed it
against the man's forehead, then automatically breathed with him, like
a child-birthing coach.

More voices shouted from the other room. Tex's was the loudest.
"I said put that chair back down where it belongs and give me that
coffeepot!"

Catcher's sparring partner and artistic arm carver, on the other
side of the curtain, groaned in harmony with Catcher, which, accompanied by the blaring shouts from the waiting room, made a cacoph-
onous symphony.

Lukas had Lauren McCaffrey to thank for all this. Sweet-faced,
innocent-eyed Lauren. When her cousin Tex heard through the family grapevine that there was an ER physician temporarily without a
job, she'd called Lauren, looking for a replacement for a doctor on
suspension.

"Scenic views, right there on the Lake of the Ozarks," Lauren had

said. *"Small-town ER, probably a lot like Knolls. It'll be like a vaca-tion. How much trouble could a five-bed ER be?"*

And so Lukas had signed on for three months—until the earliest estimated time of completion for the Knolls ER.

More shouts rang out from the waiting room, and then Lukas heard the squall of a siren as an ambulance pulled up outside, lights flashing.

This place needed more staff on Saturday nights. It was time to call the police. And he would never trust Lauren McCaffrey again.

"No!" Kendra screamed the word, her head and shoulders coming up from the pillow, her hands grasping Buck's shoulder in despera-tion. Her eyes widened in fear above the clear oxygen mask. "You're gonna shut me away like I'm crazy!"

Mercy saw Buck's expression freeze in torment as he held his wife.

"No, Kendra," she said firmly. "That's not what this is." She took the younger woman by the shoulders, eased her back down, and re-adjusted the mask. "Listen to me for a moment." She waited until she felt some of the tension release from Kendra's arms, then took her by the hand and squeezed. "Honey, you're in trouble. You have an ill-ness that is causing you to behave the way you are, and we need to get you help." She paused. How would she explain this to a child? Kendra was thinking like a little girl in pain. "We need to protect you until we can get your illness under control with medication. We're going to put you in the hospital for ninety-six hours, which is four days, and the doctors and nurses up there will keep a close eye on you and make sure you're safe."

Kendra held Mercy's gaze for a moment, focusing first on Mercy's left eye, then on the right, with disconcerting intensity. Her whole body quivered, and again tears dripped down her cheeks. "Where?"

"Cox North in Springfield. They're specially trained to take care of cases like this."

"What kind of a case *is* this? What're you talkin' about?"

Mercy tried to pick her words carefully, but she had to be honest. "From what I've heard and seen, and from what I know of you per-sonally, I'd say you have bipolar disorder, but I'm not a psychiatrist, so . . ."

Kendra tightened her grip on Mercy's hands. "Does that mean I'm crazy?"

"No!" Buck snapped in frustration. He closed his eyes and sighed, combing his fingers through his short hair. He stepped back from the bed and flexed his shoulders wearily. "What am I going to do with her, Dr. Mercy?"

"Stop talkin' over my head like I'm a kid!"

"Then stop acting like one!"

The antipathy shot between them like an electric bolt as their gazes held for a long moment.

"This won't help," Mercy said softly. She gave them a few seconds to calm down as she watched the changing emotions play over Kendra's face. She looked like a young Michelle Pfeiffer, with an exquisite beauty that could easily have transmitted itself onto the movie or television screen. But all she'd ever wanted was a husband and children. Lots of children. They'd discovered recently that she couldn't have kids, just a few months after her fireman father was killed in the line of duty.

"I won't go to any psychiatrist." Kendra's soft soprano voice once again held the quality of an angry, hurt child.

"You're going," Buck said, frustration still evident in his voice.

"I'm sorry, Kendra," Mercy said, keeping her voice firm. "You tried to commit suicide tonight, and we can't take the chance that it'll happen again. Too many people love you."

Kendra snorted. "That's a laugh."

Mercy leaned forward. "You feel that way right now because your mind isn't processing your emotions properly. But your condition can be treated. You're sick, and just like we'd do if you had some kind of bacteria in your body that was making you sick, we can treat you with something that will help your brain work better. We're going to keep you safe and administer some medication and give you time to heal."

Kendra glanced around the small exam room as if seeking a way to escape. "Can't you just do that here? Why do I have to go all the way to Springfield?"

"Because our hospital doesn't have the facilities to care for you."

Kendra closed her eyes, and her whole body stiffened. "You mean you don't have a padded room here," she said bitterly.

Mercy understood, and the identification she felt with Kendra right now was disconcerting. Depression was painful, but manic depression must be like standing on a fault line during an earthquake. It was frightening how easily your mind could betray you.

Kendra sniffed and wiped several stray tears from her cheeks with the back of her hand; then she held her hands out in front of her and looked at them. When Buck grabbed a tissue from the exam room desk and tried to give it to her, she ignored him and withdrew from his touch.

Mercy suppressed a sigh. She'd tried several times to explain to Buck why she thought Kendra was behaving the way she had been in the past six months. And Buck had tried, without success, to bring Kendra in to see Mercy for a thorough exam. All he'd managed was to get her checked for strep throat a couple of months ago.

The tears in Kendra's eyes shimmered like blue crystal, and the distress of her crying enhanced the color in her cheeks. She looked like a brokenhearted angel, but with a spirit more fragile than any of those winged, blown-glass figurines they sold down at the Ben Franklin store at Knolls Square.

"What kinds of drugs would they make me take?" Kendra asked finally.

"I'm not sure," Mercy said. "The doctor in Springfield will decide that."

"I don't want a doctor in Springfield. You know me better than they would."

Buck reached over and covered her hand with his. She tried to jerk free, but he held her fast. "Stop fighting this, Kendra." He looked at Mercy. "I know the procedure. If you'll do the paper work and call Cox North, I'll take her up. I'm a trained EMT, so it'll be legal, and I'll see if Clarence will come with me, just to make sure she stays in the truck." He shot Kendra a biting glance. "Otherwise, Kendra, the ambulance will have to take you, with a policeman riding shotgun."

"Why should you care?" she snapped back. "Just as long as you get rid of me. They could be hauling me to the junkyard, just—"

"Cox is a good facility," Mercy said quietly. "I know from first-hand experience. I was there for a ninety-six-hour involuntary stay five and a half years ago, and I remember the time well. The staff treated me with patience and concern."

Husband and wife focused their suddenly silent attention on her. Neither showed surprise at her words, because most people in town knew about the incident.

Mercy had seldom spoken about those days, though, and she did so now with difficulty. During a nasty custody battle over Tedi, at the same time Mercy's father was dying of cirrhosis of the liver, Mercy sought help for her own depression. Unfortunately, the physician on call that night was a buddy of her ex-husband, Theo. They had joined forces, double-crossed Mercy, and had her committed for a ninety-six-hour stay before she could do anything to stop them. When Theo used the incident in court against her, she lost custody of Tedi. She had worked five years to rebuild her practice.

For months after that horrible time in her life, she'd vowed never to "ninety-six" a patient. She'd been adamant about it until the night when a patient she had so kindly released nearly died from a second suicide attempt.

She placed her hand on Kendra's arm. "Honey, I'm sorry, but you no longer have a say in the matter. You're going to Cox North."

Clarence carefully parked Mercy's car exactly where he'd gotten it. He pulled the keys out of the ignition, then leaned heavily on the door and steering wheel to heave himself out. He couldn't get that little girl, Crystal, or her grandma Odira, out of his mind. Because of his help they were tucked safe and warm in a comfortable hospital room with smiling, cheerful nurses. Sure, he'd only driven them a block down the road, and any taxi could have done that, but the taxis in Knolls didn't run this time of night.

A long time had passed since Clarence had been on the giving end. Most people wouldn't understand how he felt being so helpless. They could do for themselves and didn't think much about it. But up until just a few months ago he'd been stuck in his bed most of the time, too heavy and in too much pain from pulled muscles to even walk out the front door. He'd been so bad that even his own baby sister had nearly died trying to take care of him. A guy could feel like he'd lost his manhood in a situation like that, but tonight, in just the past couple of hours—

The squeaky hinges on the front door of Mercy's clinic interrupted Clarence's thoughts.

Buck Oppenheimer stepped out into the darkness. "Clarence, is that you?" He squinted and peered harder, raising his hand to shade his eyes from the glow in the room behind him. "I need a big favor." His hoarse voice cracked with weariness as he stepped farther out onto the concrete walk and pulled the door shut behind him.

Clarence shivered in the icy winter wind. "From me? Sure. What's that?"

"Would you ride shotgun? Dr. Mercy said she'll let me take Kendra to Springfield without a police escort if you'll go along. I don't want to take any chances. Kendra's fighting this, and there's no telling what she'll do. Sorry, pal. I know it'll be a long night for you, but—"

"When do we leave?"

Buck stared at him in silence for a moment. "Thanks, Clarence. You don't know how much you've . . . helped." His voice caught, and he bent his head and turned away. "You can't know what this means to me."

"Wanna bet?" Clarence knew better than to get sentimental or sappy with Buck. "How about when you drove me to the ER when Darlene almost died? You visited me in the hospital when I wasn't a very nice guy to be around." Buck's life had been the pits, too, back then. Kendra had kicked him out, and he'd been suspended from his job with the fire department pending an arson investigation.

Buck turned back around and held out his hand. "Call it even after tonight?"

Clarence took the hand and looked Buck in the eyes. "It's never even, you know. That's what friendship's all about."

———

Lukas hovered closely over seventy-year-old Mrs. Flaherty so he could hear her above the noise of the continuing party in the waiting room and the snores emanating from the sleeping bikers in two of the other exam rooms.

"Can't figure out what happened," Mrs. Flaherty said in a voice barely above a whisper. "One minute I was brushing my teeth at the sink, and the—"

"Catch that before it falls, Boots!" came a shout from the other room.

"—woke up no telling how long after that. I called my daughter, but before—"

"Hey! Get away from that set! I wanna watch—"

"—and you can imagine how she felt when she came in and found—"

Tex walked into the room. "I called the police, Dr. Bower. They're busy with a break-in down at a dock and can't come right away." She glared over her shoulder at the noise. "If I had a stun gun . . ."

Mrs. Flaherty reached up and touched Lukas's arm. "Dr. Bower, do you think I'm having a stroke or something?"

Lukas glanced over at the lady's middle-aged daughter, who sat in the far north corner of the exam room, hands clasped at her knees. "Mom was just lying there when I found her, Dr. Bower. I couldn't wake her up for at least five minutes. When I did I just brought her in. I didn't wait to call an ambulance or anything. Do you think it's her heart?"

Lukas studied his patient's chart—or that part of it Tex had managed to fill out before leaving to call for backup. There were no security personnel at this hospital. Mrs. Flaherty had managed to walk in assisted by her daughter, and she showed no muscle weakness. A quick finger-stick glucose check had revealed normal blood sugar.

Another shout of raucous laughter reached them, and Mrs. Flaherty flinched. She didn't look bad now. Her color was pink and healthy, and perspiration no longer beaded her skin. Lukas would put her on a monitor and—

Another shout. And from the exam rooms where Catcher and his friend were sleeping came loud snoring.

Lukas knew trying to listen to Mrs. Flaherty's chest right now would do no good. He wouldn't hear anything above the noise. This town needed military intervention. He took the stethoscope from around his neck and placed it on the tray table, then took a deep breath. He was stuck with Catcher and friend for another couple of hours, until they recovered from their booze, but he would not allow their crowd of rabble-rousers to endanger the lives of other patients in this facility, not while he was in charge—or at least not as long as he was alive. How long that would be after he'd voluntarily thrown himself to the wolves . . . Oh well, time to get tough.

"Tex, keep an eye on Mrs. Flaherty. Get her on a monitor, do an EKG, check electrolytes, and if you can hear above the noise, get a history. If I'm not back in five minutes, call the county sheriff. Or maybe the ambulance . . . no, wait a minute, Quinn's still on duty. Forget that."

Tex stared at him. "You're going in there?"

"Sure, why not? You did."

"Notice they're still there. And I'm bigger than you."

"Thank you for that observation." Lukas left the room.

He hated confrontations like this. He hated having to deal with bullies, especially when they were drunk or stoned and irrational. But then, when wasn't a bully irrational?

Anger. Work with the anger now. He wrenched open the door that separated the waiting room from the ER proper and flung it back so hard it crashed against the wall. Then the door bounced back and slammed him in the shoulder and shoved him sideways. He felt the pain, which only served to make him angrier. As he stomped into the battered waiting room, he saw at least ten pairs of eyes directed toward him. Silence fell for just a moment, and he made his move.

"Everybody! Out of here! Now!" he shouted in his deepest, most fury-filled voice, but just then a commercial blared on the TV, negating the effect. He continued anyway for a few seconds, taking advantage of the shock on their faces and the impetus his anger gave him to overwhelm the terror he knew was in his mind somewhere, seeking an outlet.

"Look at this mess!" He gestured toward the chairs toppled onto their sides and the pages of newspapers scattered across the floor. The coffeepot was empty, and it looked as if half the coffee had spilled onto the carpet.

He marched over to the TV and ripped the cord from the socket, plunging the room into complete, blessed silence this time. "I said out of here! This isn't your own personal nightclub." So much for patience and compassion.

The partiers stared at him as if he were an alien being. Then three of the biggest, meanest-looking men exchanged nods and slowly moved toward him.

Lukas swallowed and forced himself not to back up or turn and run. *Lord? I could use some help here!*

"We're not goin' anywhere 'til Catcher and Moron can come with us!" a woman shouted back. She was the same woman who had unsuccessfully tried to light a cigarette in Catcher's presence during the suture ordeal.

Catcher? Moron? What was her road name? Birdbrain? What a weird bunch. He glanced at the three men who continued to move toward him, one step at a time, from three different areas of the room, as though they were stalking a wild animal. He just hoped the end wasn't too painful.

He cleared his throat and tried not to flick a nervous glance at the stalkers. Don't act afraid. "I'll gladly release them if any one of you is sober enough to sign them out and take care of them until they can take care of themselves." He looked from face to face—three women, seven men, with grubby, not-quite-in-focus faces—and didn't get a volunteer. "Fine, then. I'll keep them here."

"Fine, then. We'll stay, too," the woman shouted.

"Then you're a brave bunch," Lukas said.

"Why's that?" she taunted. "You callin' the cops?"

One of the men stalking Lukas gave a snort and a low, mocking laugh as he and his two buddies moved in more quickly.

"Oh, they're coming." Lukas braced himself for the inevitable. "But when Catcher finds out you moved your party up here and left his bike alone down by the lake for anybody to carry off, even the cops won't be able to save you."

"My bike!" The loud, gruff voice came from the ER entranceway, and at the sound all attention pivoted in that direction. Even Lukas's stalkers halted their steps to turn and see Catcher, all six feet four inches, two hundred fifty pounds of him, glowering from the threshold, his clothes splattered with drying blood.

He took a step forward, and Lukas wondered if the rest of them could see how unsteady the movement was.

"You left my baby down there all alone!" he thundered. "What kind of—" He broke off and groaned and hunched forward, and

Lukas rushed over to grab him before he fell. But Catcher straightened himself and sent Lukas a warning glance to stay away. He raised his good arm and pointed toward the door. "Get out of here! All of you, get out of here! Boots, you're walking, and I'm taking your bike. If my baby has a scratch on her when I get there, I'll take it out of all your hides!"

Lukas's stalkers were the first ones out the door, followed by Birdbrain and the other women. Catcher turned to bring up the rear of the procession. Lukas let him go.

CHAPTER 4

A t two o'clock Sunday morning Mercy stood on the front step of the Richmond Clinic and watched the taillights of Buck Oppenheimer's big red pickup disappear into the cold darkness. Kendra's condition was stabilized. She had recovered, clinically, from the carbon monoxide poisoning and now sat between Buck and Clarence on her way to four days of forced hospitalization in Springfield.

This was the right thing to do; Mercy knew it.

So why did her heart hurt so badly to remember the look of betrayal in Kendra's tear-filled eyes when the men placed her gently into the cab of the truck? Mercy shivered at the wind and stepped back inside the waiting room, though she didn't shut the door.

As she watched tiny flakes of snow glitter in the light from the front step, other memories haunted her—of seeing her daughter terrified and in danger, and being unable to help; of feeling frightened herself by her own father's alcoholism. She'd lived with past pain for so long she frequently had trouble enjoying the present.

Another gust of wind scattered tiny flakes across her face, and she finally closed and locked the door behind her. "Lord, help Kendra to see the truth of your love," she whispered. "Heal her, Lord. And please complete the healing in me."

Kendra and Buck had been through so much. . . . Would their lives ever be normal? And Odira's struggles to take care of Crystal seemed so endless.

Mercy had begun, in the last few months, to put her patients in God's hands as quickly as possible when her worry for them began.

All she had to do now was learn to leave them there, to stop trying to control every situation. She found that difficult to do.

She went into the front office and fed the fax machine the final pages they would need at Cox North for Kendra's admittance, reading each page as it fed through to make sure she had all her boxes marked and her information correct.

The telephone rang beside her as the final page fed through, and she picked up quickly. Probably the night secretary at Cox North, asking for more information.

"This is Dr. Richmond."

"Hi, Dr. Mercy, this is Vickie over at Knolls Community. I thought you might still be in your office."

"Yes, Vickie," Mercy said in surprise, recognizing the voice of one of her favorite nurses at the hospital down the block.

"I just wanted to let you know that Crystal and Odira are both settled in, and Crystal was already asleep when I left the room. We'll keep a close eye on both of them tonight."

Mercy felt a little easing of tension at the nurse's reassuring tone. "Thank you, Vickie, I'll be over in the morning to check on Crystal."

"If you plan to get any sleep, you'd better get with it. Oh, and, Dr. Mercy, you might want to check Odira out, too, when you come. I saw her press her hand against her chest a couple of times while we put Crystal in bed, and her feet look a little swollen. We'll make her comfortable tonight, but I just thought I'd let you know."

Mercy reached up and massaged her temples, closing her eyes in weariness. "Thank you, Vickie. I'll check her if she'll let me." She replaced the receiver, sighed, and walked back into her office. She'd guessed earlier tonight that there might be a problem with Odira but had to push those thoughts aside while she cared for Crystal and Kendra and completed all the duties that ordinarily her staff would handle.

She stepped over to her desk and plopped down into the leather chair for a moment. She stretched out her arms and flexed her shoulders, rolled her head around, and took a few deep breaths. Odira was always so concerned about Crystal that she seldom took time to notice her own physical ailments. That could turn out to be a real problem. Maybe in the near future. Maybe in the morning . . .

Time to go home, but right now she was too tired to move. Would she ever again get a whole eight hours of sleep in a row? Should she consider getting a partner to take part of the load? At one time she'd hoped Lukas might stay around and help her with the influx until the ER was complete. She'd even dropped a few hints on several occasions, during those few times the two of them had been together in the past three months. He hadn't caught the hint. She hid her disappointment, telling herself that he was, at heart, an emergency physician. Family practice would probably bore him.

But deep down she found herself wondering. . . . Was he, for some reason, avoiding her?

She knew he cared for her. She *knew* it. She could see a tenderness in his eyes when he looked at her and hear a gentleness in his voice. He cared a lot about Tedi, as well, and the two of them spent hours together laughing and talking and working on homework assignments when Lukas was in town.

Mercy couldn't help the doubts that surfaced, memories of last fall when Lukas had told her he couldn't see her anymore. But hadn't all that changed? During the explosions at the hospital, Mercy experienced a more powerful explosion in her own life—she realized she could no longer deny God's power or her need for Him. She had accepted Christ and had announced her newfound faith to a congregation of people at the Covenant Baptist Church. Since then she had witnessed the power of her new faith in many ways. The most obvious was her sudden ability to get along with Theodore—not with perfect ease and not always without resentment, but enough to make Tedi comfortable when they met together.

She glanced at the framed snapshots she kept of Tedi on the credenza—baby pictures, and then school pictures from kindergarten to the most recent sixth-grade shot. Tedi was the joy of her life. Just spending time with that bubbly, outspoken child renewed her, made her laugh, and gave her courage. After everything Tedi had been through, from the divorce nearly six years ago to the near-death experience last year, she was recovering and growing every day. No parent could be more proud.

And then Mercy's gaze drifted to the unframed snapshot of Lukas, the only picture she had of him. She still remembered the day she'd snapped it. He was covered in mud from a hike in the rain. His glasses were steamed up enough to camouflage the blue of his eyes, but not enough to hide the smile that radiated across his face, relieving a habitually serious expression. In the picture, his light-brown hair was darkened to coffee. His slender five-foot-ten frame carried him well, and somehow the way he stood and looked at the camera revealed the gentle, caring soul within. Or maybe his demeanor had impressed itself upon her so much since last spring that she automatically saw it when she looked at him.

She laid her head back and closed her eyes. She would never forget their first hike together in the Mark Twain National Forest in August last year. The spider webs were thick across the narrow, overgrown logging trail they followed. Lukas had insisted on walking ahead of her, watching for snakes, knocking down the webs for her, even though he hated spiders. His thoughtfulness was one of the many traits about him that endeared him to her. She didn't have the heart to point out that she'd been hiking those trails for years and was used to the spiders and the snakes and the ticks and the chiggers. She let him help her over the rough spots, as he had been doing in her life since April. But she was in another rough spot now, and he wasn't here.

Did he know how much she needed him?

———

Lukas Bower paused at the threshold to the ER call room. A big black spider at least an inch in width skittered across the wall and behind the curtain beside the twin-sized bed. Lukas hated spiders. His oldest brother, Ben, had been bitten by a brown recluse years ago and would always bear a deep, ugly scar on his right forearm, just above the wrist. He'd been in the hospital for a week and a half. Lukas was only eight at the time, and the memory had scarred his psyche worse than it had Ben's.

Good thing Mercy wasn't here to see Wimp Bower in action. Of course, if Mercy were here, he would put on a brave front and chase the spider down and kill it, gritting his teeth and shuddering with every move. And Mercy would be laughing because she knew how much he hated spiders. And he wouldn't mind, because he loved to hear her laugh. She laughed so much more now than she did when he first met her.

And here he was thinking about her again.

Ignoring the slight scent of mildew that hovered throughout the call room, he stepped inside and crossed to the student desk placed beneath the wall phone.

And just then it rang. He jumped backward, as if the spider hovering somewhere in the darkness had suddenly growled an attack signal.

Irritated with himself, he grabbed up the receiver. "Yes."

"Dr. Bower, a man just came in by ambulance," said the new, inexperienced secretary, Carmen. "They say he looks like a stroke. He's strapped down, and Tex had just left to go down to the cafeteria to find something to eat, and I'm all alone here, and—"

"Is he responsive?" Lukas hadn't heard an ambulance report, and he'd only walked back here a couple of minutes ago.

"Just a minute and I'll ask."

"Never mind. I'll be right there. Have Tex paged over the speakers." Lukas hung up and returned to the ER to the overhead blare of Carmen's voice. He walked into the cardiac room to find Quinn Carnes and Sandra Davis—the paramedic and emergency tech—transferring a seemingly unconscious elderly man from a gurney to the exam cot. The patient was fully immobilized, arms and all, to a long spine board, with head blocks, C-collar, the works. He had a 100 percent nonrebreather mask over his face. But no IV. No ET tube, so his airway was not protected.

"Hey there, Doc." Quinn said, walking over to the desk in the exam room and tossing his paper work down. He reached up in a habitual gesture and scratched at the thick, wavy brown-gray hair that grew to his shirt collar. "Got you a gomer here."

Lukas flinched. He hated that term. Gomer meant "Get Out of My ER" and was used by burned-out, unprofessional personnel who felt the patient wasn't worth their trouble.

"His wife found him down and unresponsive and dialed 9-1-1," Quinn continued. "Looks like a stroke. Finger-stick glucose was 107 on scene. The wife's on the way in her own car, but no long-playing record here."

Lukas cringed as he stepped over to the side of the bed, and he saw Sandra glare at her partner with obvious disgust. Although Quinn was probably in his midforties, he apparently had only been on an ambulance crew for a couple of years. Lukas believed he never should have been allowed to work with patients in the first place, but there were probably few contenders for the job in a town like Herald. Lukas knew the man was presently working as many hours as possible with the ambulance service and bugging hospital personnel to give him some shifts in the ER. If Lukas had anything to say about it, that wasn't going to happen.

"What's the gentleman's *name*?" Lukas asked, unable to keep irritation from his voice.

"Mr. Wayne Powell," Sandra replied for Quinn. Her voice was hesitant, soft, as it had been the other time Lukas had seen her in here. "His poor wife was almost hysterical when she called."

Lukas leaned forward and squeezed the patient's upper arm. "Mr. Powell?"

"Told you he's out of it, Doc," Quinn said over his shoulder as he sat down to do paper work.

Lukas took the patient's arm in a firmer grip. "Mr. Powell! Mr. Powell, can you hear me?" he called more loudly. "I'm Dr. Bower. Try to open your eyes if you can."

No response.

Tex walked into the room, slightly breathless from her rush back down the hallway. Her large frame and broad shoulders seemed to fill the already crowded little exam room. "Can't leave this place for two minutes without—Uh-oh, what've we got here?"

"I'm still trying to find out." Lukas rubbed his knuckles hard against the man's sternum and didn't even get a groan. "Mr. Powell, can you hear me?" he shouted again, though he knew it was no use. The sternal rub would rouse him if anything would. "Tex, we've got an unresponsive patient with an unprotected airway," he said over his shoulder. "Set up for an intubation, but first let's get the suction set up." He couldn't believe Quinn hadn't intubated this patient, but there wasn't time to explain about the danger of the man's negligence right now. If Mr. Powell vomited, unresponsive as he was, it could kill him, or set him up for aspiration pneumonia—which could also kill him. Every paramedic Lukas had ever worked with knew that.

Tex turned to the cabinets on the left and opened a door to pull out some equipment.

Quinn looked over at them and gave a quick chirp of irritated laughter. "Would you relax, Doc? Don't you think I'd have done that if he needed it? He's not throwing up or anything. His airway's clear."

Lukas grabbed the black box that Tex handed to him. He broke the safety lock and opened the box, pulled out the laryngoscope and endotracheal tube and snapped the blade into place. "An unobstructed airway is not the same as a protected airway. If this is a stroke patient, he's at high risk for aspiration."

Tex came around with the suction. "Got it, Dr. Bower."

Lukas reached over to pull off the oxygen mask just as Mr. Powell retched. "Tex, get the suction catheter in. Quinn, Sandra, help me here." He reached for the grips and turned the patient toward him as Sandra rushed to help. Good. The man's body didn't slip. They'd done a good job of securing him. Quinn ambled over to help.

"Sloppy job, Quinn," Tex snapped above the sound of the suction. "Sloppy, sloppy. Why didn't you intubate this guy on scene? I'd have taught you how if you needed me to. Maybe I could teach you how to do an IV, too, while I was at it, and how to hook up a monitor. And I didn't hear your radio report. I was gone less than a minute. Trying to sneak up on us?"

"No time," Quinn said. "We were busy, and we were just about a mile away. There wasn't time for little nonessentials."

"You call lifesaving and preparation nonessentials?" Tex snapped. "If you'd spend a little more time worrying about your patients and less time whining about your bank account, you *might* make a good paramedic someday."

"*You* try going on scene every once in a while."

Tex returned his glare and shook her head. "I did it for five years."

"Sure, but most of that was years ago," he taunted. "Things have changed. You think being a med-school dropout makes you special."

"I didn't drop out, you stu—"

"Tex," Lukas snapped, "keep your mind on your work."

"Sorry, Dr. Bower." She suctioned for a couple more seconds, then pulled the tube back. "He looks clear."

"Good, let's get him back over. I need an IV now, and give him Ativan, 2 milligrams. Sandra, take over that suction and keep it handy, just in case." He called over to the secretary across the ER. "Carmen, I need an EKG, CBC, electrolytes, PT and PTT—"

Carmen turned around in her chair, eyes widening in panic. "What? Slow down, I can't get all this down." She grabbed a pen and a pad. "Now, what was that?"

Lukas remembered that the new secretary had barely been on the job for a week, and he'd overheard her complaining that the person she replaced had only spent one shift training her. A twelve-hour orientation was not enough. At Knolls they took four weeks.

"Just do a standard cardiac work-up," Lukas said gently. "It's taped on the wall to the right of the phone." He turned back to Mr. Powell and tried to wake him again. No response. He pulled out his penlight and checked the man's pupils. They were sluggish, and the one on the left looked a little dilated. Nothing obvious.

"Dr. Bower," Carmen called from the desk, "do you want a chest x-ray, too? That's listed here."

"Yes, but not until I get the patient intubated." He wanted to verify placement. "And call for a helicopter launch. He's going to have to be flown to Columbia." This did, indeed, look like a stroke, and because of the unprotected airway he was in for aspiration pneumonia, big time. Dangerous stuff.

While Tex set up and completed the IV and administered the drugs he requested, Lukas continued assessing the patient. He had good heart sounds and strong distal pulses, but definite flaccidity of the right leg, as well as the right arm. They had no ventilator at this hospital, so they would have to save the CT head scan for later. Lukas slipped off Mr. Powell's shoe and, with the point of an ink pen, ran the tip up the bottom of the man's foot. The big toe curled upward.

Positive Babinski's. The abnormal reflex was found in stroke victims.

"See? Told you it was a stroke," came Quinn's voice from behind.

Lukas turned to see the paramedic hovering over him, arms crossed over his chest as he watched.

"So you think I should have intubated this guy before we brought him?" Quinn demanded.

"Yes." Lukas saw that Tex had the IV set up, had administered the drugs, and her hands were back on the suction tube to help with the intubation.

"That's not the way I learned it," Quinn said.

Lukas caught Tex's darkening expression and shook his head. There was no time to argue with Quinn now. He bent over Mr. Powell once more.

———

"Dr. Mercy, help me." The gentle feminine voice drifted to her from the dark mist, plaintive and indistinct. A sudden, frantic pounding reached her, and then the voice again, softly, "Help me."

Mercy awakened suddenly with her face pressed against the hard surface of her desk. The overhead light blared down on her, and her right shoulder and arm were splayed across the back of her chair, cramped and stiff. The pounding continued to sound in her head from her dream, but as she listened all she heard were soft puffs of wind against the window and the scratch of branches from the cedar tree against the rain gutter.

She got up, stretched, and walked out of the office, down the carpeted hallway into the darkened waiting room. All was quiet. Was she dreaming about Kendra? Were the worry and stress of the past few months finally taking their toll?

Just in case, she opened the entrance door, and freezing wind rushed in, mixed with a powdery feathering of snow. She shivered and stepped back into the warmth but didn't close the door for a moment.

"Hello?" she called out into the cold. She felt foolish. Of course it had been a dream. "Is anybody out there?"

The snow had barely frosted the walk, and there probably wouldn't be any accumulation. There hadn't been much in the forecast for the weekend. Of course, that could change.

She shivered and started to close the door and lock it when she caught sight of something in the swirling snow, just outside the door—the bare outline of a footprint. Even as she watched, the force of the wind obliterated it.

"Hello?" she called again.

No one answered.

Lukas sat at his tiny work station in the ER, a few feet from the secretary. Carmen muttered under her breath every time she picked up a new chart to code. She had asked him so many questions in the past thirty minutes that he'd almost decided to offer to do the coding himself, but he wasn't sure he knew the routine, either. Every ER had a different office procedure.

He rested his chin on his fist and fought to keep his eyes open, listening to Marin's snores in the curtained exam room across the small aisle from the desk. Tex and Carmen were making bets on whether or not the bikers would return to get their buddy.

Carmen whistled suddenly. "Who'da thought Catcher would have such good insurance? Too bad he left AMA. Now we'll probably be stuck with the bill."

Lukas shook his head and picked up the phone to check on Mrs. Flaherty, who, at his request and upon agreement by the attending physician, had been placed on telemetry on the floor. He knew it wasn't his responsibility, but he wanted to know how she was doing and if she'd had another episode of syncope—unconsciousness.

But no one answered his call.

After ten rings he hung up. Maybe there was a problem.

"Dr. Bower, I can't read your writing," Carmen said. "What's this you put here about Catcher's sutures?"

He spent the next few moments explaining his peculiar—and un- readable—penmanship to the secretary, then picked up the telephone again. If there was a problem with Mrs. Flaherty, he needed to know. This time he allowed the phone to ring fifteen times.

Finally a harried, breathless female voice answered. "What is it?"

"Uh, yes, hello, this is Dr. Bower checking on our telemetry pa- tient, Mrs. Flaherty. Is everything okay there? I tried calling a few moments ago and didn't get an answer."

There was a short silence, then a sigh. "Sorry, Dr. Bower, we couldn't get anybody to come in for the telemetry. Dr. Cain down- graded the admission for us."

Lukas let that sink in for a moment. "Mrs. Flaherty isn't on telemetry?" Nobody was watching her? His request had been ignored? "Dr. Cain specifically agreed with me that—"

"Look, we're operating on a skeleton crew, Dr. Bower. The patient looked fine to us, and she's just a couple of doors down. We check on her when we can. Bringing in another nurse just to watch one patient isn't cost-effective. Mr. Amos wouldn't allow it."

Lukas clamped his teeth down on his tongue for a moment. Since when did the administrator for this hospital have a license to practice medicine? There had been a few guarded remarks about the fact that the man was paranoid about spending money, but when did money become more precious than human lives?

"How many nurses are on the floor tonight?" Lukas finally asked.

There was a pause. "One RN and one LPN."

"That's it? What's the census?"

"We have nineteen patients on the floor."

"And you're the only RN in the whole hospital?"

"That's about the size of it, Dr. Bower," she said, sounding suddenly weary. "And you'd better not let Mr. Amos hear you complaining, or we'll have one less doctor." She hung up.

Lukas groaned. What else was new?

CHAPTER 5

The loud, piercing cry of a hungry newborn baby streaked through the darkness of nineteen-year-old Marla Moore's dreams, echoing through the small room like a ricocheting bullet. It was her baby. Her little Jerod. And only she could stop the crying.

Even as she opened her eyes to the dim room illumined by the night-light, her hands automatically pushed back the blankets and pillows. With stiff limbs and swollen feet, she climbed from bed as if Jerod were pressing a remote control programmed for Mommy.

She stepped once more onto the cold painted concrete floor, but before she reached the used crib that she'd bought at a yard sale, she tripped over the house shoes she'd pulled off when she got into bed. She stumbled backward against the bedside stand. The corner of the stand dug hard into the inside of her right calf, and she cried out. She grabbed the side of the crib for support.

Jerod's cries grew louder and more insistent.

"Stop it!" she snapped. "Just stop it!" She bent over and rubbed her calf, then reached down and picked the newborn up into her arms. Feed him. Then she could get back to sleep for another couple of hours before she had to repeat the routine all over again.

She sat with him on the side of the bed and fumbled with her dirty pajama top. Everything was dirty. She barely had enough diapers for tomorrow, and she hadn't done laundry in three weeks. How could she? Before she had Jerod, the doctor had told her to stay in bed so she wouldn't go into premature labor. Now there was nobody to help her. Marla would have called a church for help, but every time she thought about calling someone, shame kept her from following through.

This little town had turned out to be a setting for a nightmare, and she was living it. She couldn't help feeling she deserved some kind of punishment, but why did this little baby have to suffer for her sins?

Maybe he didn't. There was an adoption agency in Jefferson City that her doctor had told her about. She had the card somewhere in her purse, and she could call them anytime, day or night. But she hadn't even been able to think about asking for help without feeling horrible guilt.

Jerod's cries stopped as soon as he started his early-morning snack, and gradually the pain in her leg began to let up. She'd have a monster of a bruise. She remembered those tight stockings they'd made her wear at the hospital. She was supposed to use them after she got home, too, and she'd done so the first day. But they were hard to put on, and she was so tired she just gave up. If there'd been anyone here to help her . . .

Against her will, Marla thought again about Dustin. She could close her eyes and see his long, lean face. Now that Jerod was quiet she could concentrate—again—on that last argument before she left Bolivar. She remembered the sneer in Dustin's voice when he told her to get an abortion. And she remembered his nasty words when she refused. He'd called her a fat tramp and a lot of other things she didn't want to remember, and then he said he wasn't the father.

Now he didn't want anything to do with her. As far as Dustin was concerned, Jerod didn't even exist. Neither did Marla. With Dad gone, there wasn't anybody else to care.

She sniffed and her face puckered as her body ached all the way from her legs to the middle of her back. "Jesus, what am I going to do? Where are you? Do you hate me now?" They were questions she'd asked into the silence of this room many times these past months. Marla Moore had been a born-again Christian since she was eleven. She'd been raised right.

On the night she conceived, she'd been a virgin, and after that night she'd felt so guilty and so scared that she'd refused to give in again. And when her worst fears came true and the test read positive, she'd told Dustin. He'd dumped her, just that fast. Of course, when she thought about it honestly, their relationship had been going downhill for a long time. Had they ever even *had* a real relationship? What about the rumors about his other girls?

She looked down at the rounded top of Jerod's head, the sparse dark hair shadowed in the night-light. For the past nine months she hadn't planned past this time in her life. She thought about the name of that adoption agency in Jefferson City. It was called Alternative, and these people specialized in helping unwed mothers. The nurse at the clinic had encouraged Marla to give the place a call for help, even if she planned to keep Jerod.

As soon as she could get to a phone, she would make the call. But she couldn't give Jerod to someone else to raise . . . could she? She loved him so much, even if he was driving her crazy right now.

She shivered. The room was cold. She tried to keep the heat turned off as much as possible so the bill wouldn't be so high next month. Her telephone had already been cut off. Her landlord had come by twice looking for rent money that she didn't have, even though the place was cheap, renting out weekly to whoever came along . . . right now her neighbors looked and sounded and partied like a biker gang.

When Jerod finished his meal she didn't take him back to his crib. Instead, still shivering, she climbed back beneath the blankets and drew him in beside her. How much was she willing to sacrifice to make sure Jerod was warm, had clean diapers, and had a home to live where the landlord wouldn't threaten to kick him and his mother into the street?

Monday she would find a pay phone and call that place, Alternative. But she wouldn't give Jerod to someone else. Who could love him as much as she did?

Clarence sat with his overlapping fat pressed against the handle of the pickup truck door, feeling it dig into his side and hoping the lock was a tough one. Too bad Buck didn't have a king cab. That would have made this ride a lot more comfortable, and Kendra wouldn't be squeezed between them like a Beanie Baby sandwiched between two sumo wrestlers. Okay, maybe a sumo wrestler and Arnold Schwartz-his-name. Still a pretty tight fit. Clarence felt like he was being used as a giant plastic lid stuck over the end of a jar to keep the contents from pouring out. Kendra was pretty special contents.

Why hadn't he at least thought to bring his sugar-free breath mints? He always carried them because they were the only thing Ivy let him eat. And why hadn't he taken a shower tonight?

And why, oh why, had he taken that stupid Lasix? The medicine had kicked up a notch, and it was running water into his bladder like Ivy's Jacuzzi faucet.

He shifted his weight against the door and stared out the window, trying not to think about all that. Instead, he watched for lights in the darkness of the midnight forest, revealing farmhouses and an occasional sawmill. A couple of times they passed another car, but mostly there was no traffic on these hills and curves. When they turned onto Highway 60, the curves straightened out and it picked up a little.

Kendra's quiet sniffles continued. "Why do you hate me?" she asked softly, her pretty face highlighted in the glow from the dashboard lights.

"I don't hate you." Buck's grip tightened on the steering wheel.

Clarence wanted to reach down and pat her on the knee and tell her everything would be okay. He wished he could explain to her how much Buck really did love her. Why did women have to talk such a different language from men?

He could tell folks a lot of things they probably didn't realize. It was a funny thing about people who were average weight and height and didn't have any disabilities—sometimes they ignored those who were different. They didn't act that way on purpose, but people said and did things in front of him that they wouldn't do in front of skinny people. When he retreated inside himself and kept his mouth shut, somehow he seemed to disappear from their sight—which was crazy, of course, big as he was. But maybe his size didn't count as much as his silence.

Yeah, it was his silence. For two years he hadn't spoken to anyone but Darlene, and she'd been so busy supporting them that she didn't have that much time to talk. Ever since last spring, when Lukas and Mercy had barged into his life and turned everything upside down, things were different. And ever since then something had been changing in him. The depression that'd helped land him in this mess in the first place lifted, a little at a time. The talks he and Lukas had about God, about meeting human needs, had touched him and stayed with him. Lukas and Mercy both had a special calling from God to help people. Lukas had talked about that once, and for a long time Clarence hadn't been able to get it out of his mind. He and his sister were both alive today because Lukas and Mercy had honored that calling.

And as Kendra continued to sniff and Buck continued to grip the steering wheel too hard, it occurred to Clarence that somehow he was still being touched by this calling. Maybe it was contagious—he felt a gentle urge to pass the healing on to others.

He remembered words Lukas had spoken to him only a few weeks ago during one of their talks. He'd said, *"Trust me, Clarence, God has something in mind for you, too. I think He's calling you, and you're trying to avoid the call because you don't think God has any use for you. But you're wrong. Just listen for Him, Clarence. Just be ready."*

And Clarence had made some typically stupid remark like *"God doesn't need any more tubs of lard in His pantry"* and the subject had been dropped.

Until now. Lukas and Mercy and Ivy were miles away, but Clarence suddenly realized what Lukas was talking about. And he was suddenly as sure of God's presence as he was of the fact that if they didn't stop at a service station soon, he was going to have to ask Buck to pull over alongside the road.

But before he could say anything, the first billboards came into view, and the lights of Springfield burst out over the trees. Kendra bent her head and covered her face with her hands. Quiet sobs shook her shoulders.

"It'll be okay, honey," Buck said, his voice cracking from worry and lack of sleep.

"You don't know." She fumbled in her pocket and pulled out a shredded tissue to wipe her nose. "You don't even know what it's like to feel this way. You save lives and put out fires for a living. Everybody thinks you're wonderful. They just think I'm useless, like some leech attached to you."

"You're the only one who feels that way! I thought we'd settled this a long time ago." Buck slowed as they drew nearer to the city and more cars appeared on the four-lane highway.

"Why did you even bother to take me out of the car? I'd've been out of your way for good then."

Clarence winced at that and glanced at Buck's expression in the light from an oncoming car. She'd cut deep on that one. Muscles tensed at Buck's jaw, and his eyes filled with the quick kind of tears that even the toughest man couldn't prevent when his heart was being mangled. He didn't say a word.

Clarence cleared his throat. "Ain't gonna work, Kendra."

She sniffed and dabbed her nose and looked at him.

"Nothing's gonna make Buck stop this truck and turn around and take you home, because then you might try to kill yourself again, just like Dr. Mercy said. And Buck couldn't stand that. Losing you would tear him up."

The tears on her cheeks sparkled in the city light.

"Try thinking about how that'd make him feel," Clarence said, knowing even that would be hard for her right now. A depressed person had trouble thinking about other people.

And then, as he tried to imagine what might be going through her mind right now, another powerful revelation struck him. *He* was thinking about other people. All those things Lukas told him were true, about loving your neighbor as yourself, about caring for the needs of others, of giving what was in your heart, and how good that could make you feel. Lukas had said living like that was just about the most important thing in life.

Lukas also said there was one thing more important—to love God first. Ivy had said the same thing, and so had Mercy. When you loved God first, everything else fell into place.

And God took your life and made it mean something.

Clarence blinked and looked out his window at the lights of a residential section of the eastern edge of Springfield. The window reflected the outlines of Buck and Kendra and his own dark bulk, as big as both of them put together.

As Buck touched the brake and turned from Highway 60 to Highway 65, Clarence replayed Lukas's words in his mind. Was God really using him tonight to help Odira and Crystal and Buck and Kendra?

The thought overwhelmed him and brought tears to his eyes.

He sniffed. Kendra turned and looked up at him. Oh, great, here was big, bumbling Clarence crying and getting ready to drip all over the place.

"What's wrong?" she asked softly.

The compassionate sound of her voice made his tears come faster, and he didn't really know why. Maybe it was just because all the pain in this truck cab couldn't help but affect him.

Or maybe it was something else. Maybe God *was* here with them. What did Ivy put in those chocolate chip cookies?

"Clarence?" Kendra said.

He shook his head. "I'm okay." He wanted to tell her she would be okay, too, but he didn't know. Who was he to predict how everything would turn out in the end?

But maybe, like Lukas was always telling him, things could be better. With prayer.

Could he pray?

Out of respect for Ivy, he always bowed his head when she said grace over the meal—even though he barely had enough of a meal to pray over. If she could talk to God for his sake, why couldn't he talk to God for Kendra's sake and for Buck's?

He closed his eyes and felt tears slip down his cheeks. He knew, from those preachers Ivy listened to on TV, that all he had to do was think the prayer.

God, let me help them. Let me show them everything will be okay because you're here and you care. You are here, aren't you?

The sudden, soft touch of a hand on his arm startled his eyes open.

"Clarence?" Kendra said. "You sure you're not sick?"

He smiled and looked down at her. "Nope, but I could sure use a bathroom. Buck? Think you could pull over at that station over there? Looks like the place is open."

Marla heard Jerod's tiny baby voice again. She turned toward him on the bed before she even opened her eyes, but a sudden sharp pain caught her in the chest.

She gasped and grabbed at the spot between her ribs. Her breath came in shallow pockets of air, and she could feel her heart beating faster.

Fear washed through her. Was she having a heart attack? Was this what it felt like?

Jerod cried louder. Marla struggled against the pillows and finally pulled herself up.

About five seconds later the pain went away. Oxygen once more entered her lungs, and the sudden relief washed over her in a powerful wave. What was going on?

She took a few more deep breaths and reached for her crying baby, but before she could pull him into her arms, the piercing shaft stabbed her again and forced her backward. She cried out from the shock. "God, help!"

Again the pain subsided and her lungs filled. Was this some weird kind of asthma attack? It didn't feel like one. And there hadn't been the usual warning. Still, her inhalers—the ones her doctor gave her for free because she couldn't afford them—were in the top drawer of her rickety bedside stand. She'd better get them out.

More carefully this time, she reached toward Jerod. He needed changing before she did anything else. She picked up one of the last three clean diapers, and as she did so, she pressed against the new bruise on her right calf.

"Ouch!" She couldn't hear her own voice over the sound of Jerod's squalling. And she barely caught another breath before the shaft struck her chest again, harder than before. She dropped the diaper on the floor and gasped. The pain grew worse, and the dim room went black for a few seconds.

But Jerod's cries brought her back.

She took shallow breaths, willing her heart to slow its beating. She felt weaker now, and she didn't have the strength to pick up the diaper. She pulled open the drawer and took out both inhalers. While Jerod continued to cry, she fumbled with the sprays. She could barely concentrate on breathing.

Someone pounded from the other side of the paper-thin wall at the head of her bed. "Shut that kid up in there!" came a rusty female growl.

The woman must be a part of that biker gang. I think I fixed that now. Marla wanted to tell her to shut up, but she didn't have the courage, or the energy.

Another throb in her leg made her grimace. If she'd worn the stockings they gave her, she would have had some protection.

She reached down to unfasten Jerod's dirty diaper when she felt the hit again. This time the pain shocked her like a kitchen knife jutting through her ribs. She nearly fell on top of the baby before she could push herself away. The room grew blacker. In desperation she slid from the bed to the cold, dirty floor and groped for the telephone, but then she remembered that it had been disconnected.

She had to get help. What if something happened to her? Jerod would be all alone. He could freeze in this room before daylight.

As the pain once more let up, she glanced toward the thin wall. "Help me!" she called as loudly as breath would allow. "Somebody help me, please!"

She heard a muffled groan, and again someone pounded on the wall. "Turn off that TV!"

She closed her eyes in hopeless despair. "No, God, please, don't let this happen." With the last of her strength, and the healthy cries of her cheering section, she shoved the inhalers into the pocket of her pajama top, scrambled to the door of the tiny efficiency apartment, unlocked it, and used the threshold to pull herself to her feet.

That was a big mistake. Everything went black again. She dropped to her knees and pushed the door open and felt the bite of winter wind brace her exposed flesh.

"Somebody help me!" she called out into the night. "Please!" As she said the last word the pain came again, and her baby's cries grew softer as she slumped across the front walk.

———

Clarence shivered as he climbed back up into the darkened cab of the truck. "Sorry about that, guys. Couldn't help it. Mercy has me taking this stuff that—" He broke off when he realized that Kendra was crying again, and Buck was sitting at the steering wheel, facing forward, his hands practically white from gripping so hard. The human emotional pain was thick enough in this truck to cut with a chainsaw.

They'd been arguing again. He felt guilty for making them stop.

While he was gone, they had just hurt each other worse. But maybe he could help them.

"Look, you two, it's really late and you're tired, I know. I've gotta tell you, things aren't gonna be this bad all the time." He reached over and patted Kendra on the arm. "I've been there. I wanted to die, but I don't anymore. There really are people who care about you, and even though you don't see it right now, you're gonna have to trust that I'm telling you the truth."

Buck's hands loosened on the steering wheel, and he shot a glance across the cab at Clarence, then at Kendra. She didn't move. It was as if she felt her husband looking at her, and she refused to give him the satisfaction of reacting.

Clarence hoped he was doing the right thing. "Would you just let me do something to help?" He waited until they both turned to look at him, and then he took a deep breath and let it out. How hard could it be? "I want to pray for you."

He couldn't believe he'd said the words until they left his mouth. Suddenly he thought he might have to go back to the bathroom.

He saw Buck's eyes widen, and he felt a hot flush rushing over his body. Where'd he get the stupid idea he could pray? Who'd've thought that he, church-hater Clarence Knight, would pull something like this at three-thirty on Sunday morning? Had to be lack of sleep.

But then something happened to Buck's expression. Surprise seemed to gradually change to hope. Maybe it was the dim light in the cab or the weird shadows cast by the blinking sign on the front of the convenience store, but it looked real. Clarence remembered Ivy's constant harping: " 'Ask and it will be given to you. . . .' God answers our prayers." And he didn't know of anybody who needed prayer more than these two right now. And there wasn't anybody else in this truck.

"Yeah, I know, sounds funny coming from me, but what could it hurt?" he said at last. "I mean, what've you got to lose?"

Buck sighed and closed his eyes. "Nothing, Clarence. We've got nothing to lose. Go for it." He bowed his head.

Kendra turned and stared at her husband for a long moment. Clarence watched her. For a few seconds some of the pain left her eyes.

Then Clarence bowed his head, like Ivy always did. "God, first of all I need to say that we're praying this in the name of Jesus, just so I don't forget at the end." He didn't understand all that yet because he'd never tried that hard to listen, but he knew Ivy always said these words to end her prayers. "And then I want to ask you to give Buck and Kendra some of the love I think you've been showing me lately. And then I want you to stay with Kendra after Buck and I leave, because I think she's going to need you worse than anybody. And that's all I can think of to say right now." He raised his head and looked at them. "Guess that oughta do it."

CHAPTER

Lukas was drifting to sleep in the call room early Sunday morning when he heard the blare of a siren. He opened his eyes to the sight of orange and red flames racing across the wall, and he sat up with a shout.

And then he realized that the flicker was from an ambulance outside. Its lights penetrated the window blinds in fiery streaks of color. Lukas pushed his blanket back and got out of bed. Sometimes he still had nightmares about the explosions in October, of following Buck Oppenheimer through the collapsing ER and fighting the inferno that nearly engulfed them.

The telephone rang. He reached over, felt for his glasses on the desktop, and picked up the receiver.

"Dr. Bower, this is Tex," came the voice over the phone. She sounded irritated, but with Tex's deep voice it was hard to tell. "Quinn and Sandra are bringing somebody in. Of course they didn't radio us, so I don't know what's going on. I tell you, that man should not be wearing a uniform. Want to join us?"

"I'm on my way." Lukas grabbed his stethoscope from the desk and rubbed at the lenses of his glasses with the hem of his scrubs as he squinted his way out of the call room.

When he reached the ER he saw Quinn and Sandra wheeling a slightly overweight, unresponsive young woman into the ER from the ambulance bay while Tex held the door and helped push. Quinn was doing chest compressions—shoving with both hands over the patient's heart in an attempt to force the heart to beat—and an IV had been established, with a needle and tubing connected to her left arm. The patient had been intubated, and an ambu bag was attached to the tube, which Sandra squeezed rhythmically to help the woman breathe. Sandra was pushing the cot with her free hand. The woman had been stripped to the waist. The odor of sour milk lingered around her.

Lukas rushed toward them. "Carmen," he called to the secretary over his shoulder, "call a code and launch a chopper."

Carmen swiveled in her chair and stared at him blankly. "What?"

Lukas shook his head. "Get me a nurse down here from the floor. Tell her we've got a code. Then call our airlift service and get them here." He grabbed the end of the gurney and helped Sandra and Tex push it inside. "What's the rhythm?"

"V-fib," Quinn said. "I'd just intubated her on scene, and then she crashed." His words came fast, almost as if he were trying to convince Lukas he'd done everything right. "She was unresponsive, and she had inhalers in her pajama pocket. Had to be asthma—"

"How many times have you shocked?" Lukas asked.

"Three."

"Was there any change in rhythm?"

"No."

Lukas turned to find Tex already in the trauma room, snapping the plastic lock from the tool-chest-shaped crash cart beside the exam bed.

On the count of three, they transferred the patient from the gurney to the bed, and Tex immediately replaced the leads to the hospital monitor on the woman's bare chest. The v-fib rhythm continued, with the line racing across the monitor screen above the bed in an irregular steak-knife-edge pattern. The monitor emitted a high, continuous beep.

"Well, you got your intubation this time, Dr. Bower," Quinn muttered. "Hope you're happy, because it's not doing her any good."

Lukas ignored the comment. "What drugs have you given?"

"I just finished the first dose of epinephrine as we pulled in."

"Then we'll have to shock again quickly. Stop compressions but keep bagging." Lukas positioned his stethoscope on the woman's chest, listened, frowned. "I don't hear good breath sounds."

"So? She was obviously in broncho spasm," Quinn snapped. "She had inhalers, remember? Or weren't you listening?"

"And you just took that for granted?" Tex's voice rose like mercury in a hot room. If she saw Quinn's flush of anger or glare of growing resentment, she didn't acknowledge it. "Did you even check the placement of the tube when you did the procedure?"

"What good would it do if she was in broncho spasm?" Quinn's lips thinned and whitened.

Lukas raised his hand for silence and repositioned the stethoscope over the belly. *Now* he heard breath sounds, and he felt a chill of foreboding. "It's in the wrong place. The tube's in the esophagus instead of the trachea." The oxygen was flowing straight into her stomach. She wasn't getting any oxygen. "We have to re-intubate." He turned to the others. "Sandra, stop bagging and take over the compressions. Hurry! Tex, get me a syringe, then get the suction ready."

Tex moved quickly. "It's one thing to miss placing the tube correctly, Quinn," she said as she worked. "That's happened to all of us. But to leave it there . . . unforgivable! The oxygen enters the stomach instead of the lungs and prevents the lungs from receiving even room air. You might as well have placed a pillow over her face and suffocated her! Why didn't you check?"

Quinn's jaw jutted forward. "I *told* you she had inhalers. If you hadn't made such a big deal about that old man's tube earlier, I wouldn't have even wasted my time on this one." He took a step backward, then pivoted and stalked out of the room.

"No!" Lukas shouted after him. "Quinn! You don't walk out on a code!"

"Just let him go, Dr. Bower," Sandra said, her soft voice growing softer as she worked hard to continue chest compressions. "He won't listen to anybody. I tried to get him to check his work, but he was in too big of a hurry. If I can't get another partner I might as well quit. This is stupid."

As soon as Tex handed Lukas the syringe, he attached it to the tiny balloon at the mouth end of the endo-tracheal tube and deflated the air from the gear that kept it in place. He pulled the tube out of the patient's mouth and checked the monitor to make sure the rhythm was still v-fib.

"It's time for another shock. Sandra, bag her again."

Sandra stood at the head of the bed and placed the bag valve mask over the patient's face. Tex charged the defibrillator to 360 joules and handed the paddles to Lukas.

"Clear," he called, and made sure everyone was out of touch with the bed, then pressed the paddles to the patient's chest. The body jerked into an arch with the sizzle of electric current, then fell back onto the bed. Everyone looked at the monitor. The rhythm had changed.

"All right!" Tex exclaimed. The v-fib had stopped, and now the blip danced across the screen with more powerful strokes.

Lukas pressed his fingers against the woman's throat, feeling for the carotid artery, and the hope that had flared within him died painfully. There was nothing. "Oh no. Pulseless electrical activity." This was worse! They couldn't break this new rhythm with a shock. What was happening here?

"Sandra, bag her again," he said.

The nurse from upstairs came rushing into the room, and Lukas gestured to her. "You're just in time. I want you to do chest compressions." What could be causing this? "Let's intubate now, Tex. And let's get some fluids in." What would cause respiratory arrest and pulseless electrical activity in such a young woman?

"Dr. Bower," Sandra said softly, "the bra we cut off of her was a nursing bra." She indicated the young woman. "She's been nursing. She was all alone outside the apartment building."

Lukas felt as if he were on a treadmill going twenty miles an hour. He had to keep up. "Carmen, contact the police," he called toward the secretary as he worked. "They need to check the area for a baby!" He had to focus. If the woman was recently pregnant . . . severe respiratory distress . . . pulseless electrical activity . . . He caught his breath.

"Oh no, Dr. Bower," Tex groaned. "That sounds like massive pulmonary embolism." Lukas nodded. A blood clot in the lung was deadly.

Quinn came rushing back into the room, puffing from exertion and wiping his eyes with the back of his hand. "I'm sorry, Dr. Bower. That won't happen again. I mean it. I'm sorry. I was just so—"

"Can it, Quinn," Tex snapped. "We don't have time tonight for your theatrics."

Lukas ignored the interruption. "Let's get her set up for a pacer, and get me Dopamine." Now he knew what to do. But was there time?

Marla drifted in a dark fog, for a few moments far from the pain and cold and terror. But the drifting didn't last. Her baby . . . Jerod! She could hear echoes of his cries, and she couldn't get to him. He needed changing. He would have to be fed again soon, and there was no one to help him.

And then another voice reached her from some distant place. . . . "We've got a pulse. . . ." Marla's chest hurt again, and somebody was pushing her, hard. Her throat hurt. She felt the pressure in her ribs and heard more people talking around her. . . . "We've got a blood pressure, Dr. . . ." She felt something hard pinch her arm. . . . "The helicopter's landing, Dr. . . ."

Something brushed across her shoulder, and light beamed past her closed lids. But she couldn't open her eyes. She felt the rise and fall of her chest, and the continued sharp pain under her ribs, as if someone was stabbing her from the inside out.

The pain was too much. Even with the echoes in her memory of Jerod's cries, she couldn't force past that barrier of pain. She tried to form words on her lips, but something was in her way. She couldn't speak. *Jesus, take care of Jerod. He's so little and helpless.*

She could almost hear her baby's cries again, wished she were back in the cold, grungy room with wet diapers and neighbors banging on the wall for silence.

And then, as if from somewhere besides the room where she lay, a strong, familiar voice reached her, a voice different from the ones that shot around her with businesslike efficiency. This one was unhurried, calm, even joyful. "It's time to come home, Marla. I'll be here with you."

The sound of the voice permeated her and gave her a feeling of warmth, and she wondered if she were in a coma. But that voice . . . *Dad?* She thought the word and heard her own voice, though her mouth did not move.

"Remember the verses I read for you so often when Mom died? 'The righteous perish, and no one ponders it in his heart; devout men are taken away, and no one understands that the righteous are taken away to be spared from evil.' "

You mean I'm dying? she asked.

" 'Those who walk uprightly enter into peace; they find rest as they lie in death.' "

But, Dad, I'm not righteous, she said sadly. *Look what I've done.*

"Your righteousness has been purchased. It's time to come home."

But my baby . . .

"Dr. Bower, I've lost the pulse," came a brisk voice from nearby.

The wall of pain slipped down and pulled away. Marla felt as if a blanket of comfort were being wrapped around her. She could see again. Her father was holding out his hand.

"No blood pressure," came another voice, this one receding, growing fainter. "Doctor, we've got asystole . . . flat line!"

But the alarm in the fading voices did not disturb her. Dad spoke again. "I have some people for you to meet." And he took her in his arms and led her home.

———————

Lukas called the code long after they lost the pulse and the rhythm flattened, battling his own sense of horror and pain as he'd battled to keep death from taking this young mother. He called time of death for the record, then took a deep breath and willed himself to be composed.

Sandra sniffed with silent tears as she gathered the trash that had collected on the floor. Tex muttered under her breath as she disconnected the monitor from the leads. She paused and glanced at Quinn, her green cat's eyes narrowed with angry disgust. She shook her head and resumed her work.

"What's your problem, Texas, can't take the pressure?" Quinn reached over to remove the equipment from the body of the deceased. "No wonder you couldn't handle your resident training. You—"

"No!" Lukas reached out to stop Quinn's movements. "Don't touch anything on her."

Quinn raised his hands in an exaggerated show of obedience.

"Hey, Doc, lighten up. I'm just trying to help out. After all, she was alive until we brought her to *you*."

Sandra gasped and looked over at her partner.

Tex shoved some trash into a biohazard container and straightened to tower over the man. "Breathing into her belly all the way here was what killed her. We might have saved her if you'd given her a chance in the first place, but no, you didn't even bother to check. You just took for granted that she had—"

"Tex." Lukas was too tired and grief-stricken to break up any more fights on this shift. "Quinn, everything has to stay in place in case the coroner wants to have an autopsy performed. Tex, will you go call him?" Maybe that would get her away from Quinn long enough to get her temper under control. To see that she did so, he walked out with her.

"That man shouldn't be allowed to touch patients," she muttered to him as they left the curtained room.

Lukas shushed her. Her voice carried past the thin barrier of curtain like the growl of an angry crocodile. Even though he agreed with her, he had to look at both sides. "You know an intubation like that can be difficult. Even the most skilled practitioner could have missed it under those circumstances."

"Yeah, but I'd've at least checked her breathing. Couldn't you tell by Quinn's expression that he hadn't?" She lowered her voice at last to a hoarse whisper. "I'm going to talk to Sandra later. That girl's scared of her own shadow, but maybe I can bully her into telling the truth. Quinn's incompetent. It's probably because he works too many hours, but that doesn't excuse his disregard for human life. They need to get rid of him."

"And who would they find to replace him?" Lukas asked dryly.

She grimaced. "Good question. The hospital doesn't want to pay anything. That's why we've got a bunch of losers here already."

"And where does that put you and me?"

She didn't even blink. "You're here to keep busy until the ER is rebuilt in Knolls."

"And why are you here?" Lukas asked. "You're no loser. I've seen you work. You know your stuff. I couldn't help picking up on Quinn's reference. Are you a resident?" He studied her more closely and saw the sudden tightening of her lips, the hooding of her eyes.

She looked away. "I'm a paramedic right now, Dr. Bower. I'm here because this is home . . . or it was." She sighed. "The guy you're replacing? Dr. Moss? He thought he was coming here for a break from family practice. Ha! Now he's on suspension here and his license is in question, and it's not even his fault. You'd better look over your shoulder around here. No telling who'll try to stab you in the back." She glared in Quinn's direction and walked off to use the phone at the nurses' desk.

Carmen swiveled in her chair to face Lukas. "Dr. Bower, a friend of mine from the police department just called. They didn't find any baby, but they called the landlord of the building where the woman was living. He'd gotten complaints from the neighbors for the past two or three days about a baby crying."

"Did he say how many people lived in that apartment with her?"

"Just the woman. Last time he saw her she was pregnant, and that was last week, when he dropped by to try to get rent payment from her, which he didn't get. Looks like she was broke, and the room was a mess, like she'd been sick for a while. The baby was obviously a newborn."

"Did they give you a name?"

"Said the woman was Marla Moore. She stayed inside a lot. I guess the landlord'll have to come down and make identification or something. The police haven't found any relatives yet."

"But the baby," Lukas said, "what about the baby?"

Carmen shrugged. "If it's a newborn, it couldn't've crawled off. Somebody's got to be taking care of that baby." The telephone buzzed again, and she turned back to the desk.

"Hey, Dr. Bower?" came a quiet male voice from behind him.

Lukas turned to find Quinn standing there, head bent penitently, arms folded across his chest. "I shouldn't have given you such a hard time in there. I guess I was pretty nervous."

"You don't walk out on a code, Quinn. We needed you. Where did you go?"

"I . . . I'm sorry. I nearly lost my cool for a little bit. I mean, we were fighting for a young mother's life, and Tex made it sound like I'd really blown it." He shot a quick glance toward Carmen and Tex, who were both on the telephone at their desks. "What are you going to put on your report?"

"What do you mean?"

Quinn shrugged. "I need this job bad, and I can't afford to lose it. What are you going to say about me?"

Lukas felt the fresh weight of grief sharpen his tongue. "The truth usually works." He turned away and left Quinn standing there.

He went into the call room for a moment. He had reports to fill out, work to do, but he knew from experience that if there were no other patients who needed him, it was best to spend some quiet time after a painful event like this one. If there was any time he needed prayer more . . .

And then he realized something. During that whole code, in all the confusion and angry words and difficult decisions, he'd forgotten the most important thing. A habit that he'd developed in his first ER rotations years ago was to pray on the run while treating victims of severe illness or trauma. Praying had become second nature for him; he did it without thinking. But this time . . . this time he'd been caught off guard. He'd allowed his anger at Quinn to divert him from the most important treatment.

Had he made other mistakes, too? A wrong procedure? He thought back over every step, every action, and the orders he had given the staff. He locked the door behind him and sank down onto the desk chair with a groan of weariness as he checked items off his mental list. The drugs he'd used to break the clot in the lungs were standard-of-care. The code had been aggressive, and all the right drugs had been in stock. He'd done the same procedure many times before. He would do a more thorough study of the records later, but now he could think of nothing else out of place. Except for the most critical step.

"Forgive me, Lord." He covered his face with his hands. He knew God didn't need his permission to save a life or to guide the hands and minds of the staff when they were working with patients. Still, he had no doubt that prayer was an energizing touch, a powerful connection between God and the caregivers. Yes, prayer operated on a spiritual level, but weren't human beings as much spirit as body?

And what if the woman—Was Marla Moore her real identity?—

What if she did have a baby? Was there a husband? She was so young. . . .

Just three months ago he'd lost a drowning victim, a young woman like this one. Some fishermen had found her at the shore of the lake and had contacted him by car phone as they raced with her from the lake to the hospital. They'd been devastated when they couldn't save her. So had Lukas. The loss always hurt the worst with the young ones, as if fresh new canvas had been ripped from the center of a painting in progress. With Marla it looked as if an even newer life was involved.

"Lord, please help me to focus on the job ahead instead of what has happened. And please . . . take care of that woman's baby. Please, Lord, when they find her family, touch them with your healing power and give that baby an earthly mother. And, Lord . . . help me not to push you to the side next time."

He paused and took a new breath. He had to return to work, but he might not have a chance to get back here soon, and he needed to eat something to keep his strength up and his mind sharp—he hadn't eaten for eight hours, and he'd barely slept.

Quickly he pulled open the top side drawer of the desk and reached in for the peanut butter sandwich he'd packed yesterday before coming to work. He unwrapped the aluminum foil and pulled it back, then recoiled with disgust. Someone had taken several bites out of his sandwich—he could see the teeth marks clearly. In place of those bites was a dead fly.

He smashed the foil back together over the sandwich and threw the whole thing into the trash can—which had not been emptied in at least a week.

He was beginning to hate this place.

A soft call reached Mercy through the darkness, indecipherable through the haze of the drug she had used so she would be sure to get some rest before returning to the hospital. But in spite of the drug, her eyes flew open. She listened. Had her mysterious visitor at the clinic followed her home? What was—

"Mom?" Her bedroom door slid open, and a glow came through from the hallway night-light to reveal the dark outline of Tedi's sleep-mussed hair. "Can I sleep with you?"

Automatically Mercy scooted over and pulled the covers back. Tedi came forward quickly and climbed into the nest of warmth Mercy's body had generated. She placed her icy feet on Mercy's legs, then giggled when her mom gasped.

"Nightmares?" Mercy asked, grimacing at her daughter's late-night-snack breath. She should have let Tedi stay at Mom's for the rest of the night instead of waking her again and dragging her out into the cold night air to come home. She felt so lonely without her . . . but that was a selfish motive.

"Yeah." Tedi paused a moment, then said more softly, "And I missed you."

"I'm right here." Mercy reached out and gathered her daughter close, bad breath and all.

Tedi snuggled against her. "You're gone so much, though. Can't Lukas just come back and help you at the clinic until the ER opens up and you don't get as many calls?"

"I don't think so, honey." Mercy sighed and glanced at the clock. She'd only slept three hours. This was going to be another tough one. Now she would lie awake and worry that she wasn't giving her daughter enough attention, that too many of her patients were falling through the cracks, and that if she did get back to sleep she might miss another emergency call. Had she done the right thing keeping Odira and Crystal here at the community hospital?

And if she continued to worry like this, would she ever sleep again?

Tedi's rhythmic breathing deepened and her body relaxed. Mercy couldn't even close her eyes. So she started doing what she'd been practicing lately when the nagging specter of insomnia attacked her— she prayed. And she began with a prayer for Lukas to return.

———

Lukas struggled with his frustration as he returned to the ER proper. All his life he'd wanted to be a doctor, although when he was growing up he envisioned himself as the faithful family practitioner who had an office attached to his home, who made house calls, and whose wisdom and compassion alone could make people feel better. He'd watched too many *Marcus Welby, M.D.* reruns. By the time he reached his third year of pre-med, he'd been forced to acknowledge that medical practice wasn't what it used to be. Still, being a doctor was all he'd ever wanted to do.

It wasn't until his first experience in an emergency room during fourth-year rotations that he felt the adrenaline rush of life-and-death decisions. He'd been addicted ever since. He could get high on a successful pediatric code. His heart could break at the death of an elderly nursing-home patient. And it was still all about people.

People were also what made the job difficult. There were so many extremes, and so many burnouts, and he kept in mind that it could also happen to him. His first burnout with people had come before his ninth birthday.

When he was a skinny, shy kid of eight, he'd had to get glasses. His two older brothers picked on him and teased him when their parents weren't watching. Because of that, he remembered backing farther and farther into a shell until he barely spoke to anyone at all, and their teasing only grew worse.

One day Dad took him on a walk, just the two of them, out through their vegetable garden to a small grove of apple trees that always produced the crispest, sweetest apples in the farming community where they lived.

Dad picked an apple from the tree and held it out to Lukas. There was a brown, worn-looking spot near the top. "See this, Lukas? The apple grew too close to the branch, and that branch rubbed against it when the wind blew. Some years these are the apples I like the best, because a lot of times they seem to have the sweetest taste."

Lukas took a bite of the apple, grimaced at the hard bitterness, and heard his dad chuckle.

"Oh yeah, I forgot to mention something," Dad said. "Strange, isn't it? The same rubbing that makes a lot of the fruit sweet some years can also make the fruit bitter and hard other years. Guess it has to do with how much sunshine they've had." He placed an arm around Lukas's shoulders. "Anyway, that's my opinion. People are like that, and you're not too young to learn the lesson. God's love is your sunshine, you know. Just let Him shine through you in spite of the bad weather and the teasing you always get from your brothers. You'll be glad you did."

And so as he approached Carmen at the front desk he forced a smile. This was her first office job, and she was understandably nervous, especially with the unforgiving attitude of many of the staff. Her harried expression always seemed on the verge of panic when an ambulance came in or when Lukas gave orders. She was one of the youngest on the staff.

"How's it going, Carmen?" he asked as he stepped up to the computer where she worked.

She jerked and looked up at him, her fingers fumbling on the keyboard. Her gaze darted quickly to an item on her desk, then away again. "Fine, Dr. Bower. The coroner's on his way, and Quinn and Sandra took off a few minutes ago. Tex finally went to grab a bite because she's starving, and nobody else has checked in." She stood to her feet, eyes wide, movements nervous.

Lukas wished the poor woman could relax a little. If she didn't, she wouldn't last here very long. He frowned and glanced again at an item on her desk that he'd noticed earlier—a blue-and-white tube of surgical jelly.

He shrugged and started to walk away when the phone buzzed beside Carmen's left elbow. She jumped and jerked it up, answered sharply, and listened, catching Lukas's gaze. When she thanked them and hung up, she shook her head. "That was Sandra. She and Quinn went back to the apartments where they found Marla. Did you know that's where the bikers are staying? The police checked the place out. They found baby stuff, but no baby. A couple of the neighbors heard the commotion and came out. They said they'd heard a baby crying for a while, but they'd gotten used to that in the past couple of days. Nobody can find anything now." She shrugged and sat back down in front of her keyboard.

Lukas stared at her bent head. "But they're still looking, right?"

She repeated her shrug. "I don't know, Dr. Bower. Quinn said the police are busy tonight. Maybe they just don't have time to look."

Lukas glanced at the wall clock. It was 4 A.M. Sunday and freezing outside. "Where could a newborn baby possibly be? Surely if someone found a baby they'd call the police immediately!"

"You would think," Carmen said darkly, "but I've already heard some rumors. You know the little girl who disappeared from the park last week? Some people think she was kidnapped. Quinn told Sandra there was a black-market baby ring in the area, and he thinks those bikers have something to do with it. I wouldn't put it past them."

CHAPTER 7

At seven o'clock Sunday morning, Mercy Richmond walked down the second-floor hallway of Knolls Community Hospital. Her stomach growled at the aroma of breakfast. She listened to the clatter of plastic and the clink of china and glasses as the aides collected trays from the fifty-three private-room patients. Census was up. Foot travel was heavier than usual, and the low rustle of charts and papers in the nurses' station and the talk and laughter from televisions in the rooms were more pronounced.

"There you are!" came a deep female voice behind her, and she turned to find Mrs. Estelle Pinkley, hospital administrator, stepping around a tall kitchen cart.

Mrs. Pinkley, a few years past retirement age, had the bearing and vitality of a college student. Her white hair, feathered back from her face in feminine lines, exposed a high forehead. She was as tall as Mercy's five-eight, and she always made Mercy feel dowdy. Today she wore an elegant blue dress with cowl neck. The blue brought out highlights in her lively and intelligent gray eyes. If Mercy made it to church at all this morning, she would wear what she had on—blue jeans and a red cable-knit sweater.

Estelle showed few outward signs of the injuries she had sustained in the October explosion. The general public was seldom aware that arthritis, from which she'd suffered for several years, now concentrated itself on her injured arm and leg during flare-ups. People usually didn't know what took place in her personal life unless she revealed it. For instance, everyone in Knolls knew she was an ethical lady who made intelligent decisions. Everyone knew she was a churchgoer. Few people knew that she and her husband dedicated the majority of their combined income to support three missionaries—one in Minsk, Belarus; one in Guatemala; one in China. And she seldom displayed the scope of her biblical knowledge here at the hospital.

Estelle reached out and drew Mercy with her into the small conference room beside the nurses' station. The heady aroma of freshly brewed coffee filled the room. Mercy took a deep whiff. The smell was wonderful. Coffee was off her diet, however. Lately it had been giving her the jitters.

"I've just been on the telephone talking to our contractor," Estelle said.

"This early on Sunday morning?" Mercy said dryly. "I'm sure he appreciated the call."

"He didn't complain." Estelle reached into her pocket, pulled out a dollar, and deposited it in a collection cup for the purchase of future refreshments for staff. Then she picked up the coffeepot and filled a clean mug. "He has a good head for business. He's polite, and he knows how to get the most out of his workers. I wish more of our directors were like that. We're ahead of the initial schedule by at least three weeks." Estelle's sharp, decisive voice with its gravelly timbre held the familiarity of some of Mercy's earliest memories. Estelle and Mercy's mom, Ivy, had been friends since they attended Knolls Elementary School together.

"He hired three more men last week at my request," she continued.

"Why do that if they're already ahead of schedule?"

"Because I want the job done sooner. I hope to see our emergency department up and running by the end of February if possible."

"You'll probably get what you want," Mercy said.

A pleased smile flitted across Estelle's face and was gone quickly. When she was in fighting form—which was all the time, even right after her near-death experience in the explosion—she could take on an Angus bull.

"I see you're still working out of the storeroom," Mercy said.

Estelle took a sip of the coffee and grimaced. "And that is where our offices will stay until the rest of the hospital is complete. Patients come before carpeting and wallpaper, and if anyone wants to complain, they can come and talk to me."

Mercy laughed. "If that happens I want to be there to see it." Before Estelle became hospital administrator five and a half years ago, she had been prosecuting attorney for Knolls County. A handful of people in the area who had found themselves on the wrong side of the law resented her. The rest loved and respected her, and Mercy was one of them. Estelle represented safety and stability in their small town, and Knolls Community Hospital was now one of the best small hospitals in the state—and would be again, once the damaged areas were rebuilt.

"So," Estelle said with a penetrating look at Mercy, "I don't like the looks of those dark circles under your eyes. Can you get Lukas back here to help us out until then?"

"Me? Estelle, you know—"

"Both of us need him."

Mercy felt the stabbing truth of those words, but she knew her own personal need to have him in her life was not what Estelle meant.

The administrator put the coffee cup down and poured in some powdered creamer, stirred it, tasted again, and nodded, satisfied. "Think of your patients if you refuse to think about your own health. We need our ER doctor available for them. Even with the additional lab and x-ray capabilities in your clinic, you can't do it all yourself. There isn't another ER within an hour of here."

"There *are* other doctors in town."

"Yes," Estelle snapped, "and they're complaining about being overworked, but I don't see any circles under *their* eyes."

"*They* aren't going through menopause," Mercy said.

"Maybe you wouldn't be either, yet, if you didn't have so much stress. We need another doctor, and Lukas should realize that just by talking to you." She paused and gave Mercy a thoughtful, penetrating glance. "You two *are* still seeing each other, aren't you?"

Sometimes Mercy wondered if Estelle had some mind-reading ability. "Mom's been talking to you about me again."

Estelle shrugged. "Ivy knows you're being overwhelmed at the clinic. She worries about you."

"That doesn't give her any right to interfere in hospital politics."

"She's doing what any concerned mother would do."

Mercy could only shrug and shake her head. Her mother was a generous benefactress of the hospital, and sometimes, when she found some strings she wanted to pull, she used her advantage.

"I've taken steps to help with the overload," Mercy said. "I hired Lauren McCaffrey to work at the clinic until the ER is operational again. She's a good ER nurse. She's taking up a lot of the slack."

"She's not on call twenty-four hours a day like you are," Estelle said. "Get Lukas back here, for all our sakes."

"I'm not sure he wants to come back."

"Then convince him otherwise."

"He'll listen to you before he'll listen to me."

Estelle studied Mercy's face for a moment and gave an astute nod. "But he'll listen to you with his heart." She laid a hand on Mercy's shoulder and squeezed. "Bring him home, my dear. It's where he needs to be." She glanced at her watch. "I must get to early service before they start praying for my wayward soul. Then I have a day's work in my office to complete."

"Sounds like you need to practice what you preach," Mercy said.

With a final pat on Mercy's shoulder, Estelle poured the leftover coffee into the tiny sink in the corner, rinsed the cup in the sink, and strode out of the room, leaving the scent of lavender in her wake.

Before Lukas ended his shift at 7 A.M. Sunday morning, he had treated three babies ranging from two weeks to three months. Their cries haunted him and made him think, once again, about Marla Moore's missing baby. Judging by the conversation he overheard from other staff members, most people supposed the child had been kidnapped. Much suspicion hovered over the presence of the bikers so close to the scene of disappearance. The landlord was questioned at length, and the authorities had decided to autopsy Marla.

Lukas had been told by the police that the Missouri Special Crimes Unit had been called in. The delivering physician had been contacted and gave more information about Marla. She was nineteen, alone, frightened. The baby's name was Jerod Andrew Moore. There was no father listed. Maternal grandparents were both deceased.

While treating the final patients of the shift for the usual assortment of January colds, influenzas, and strep throats, Lukas hadn't been able to forget the young woman's deathly pale face. Nor the big question that always haunted him long after a death: What had been her eternal destiny? Was she a Christian?

He was just sitting down at the small work station next to the nurses' desk to chart his last patient when he heard a husky, easily recognizable female voice behind him.

"So . . . have they started initiation yet?"

He turned to see Tex striding toward him from exam room two, her scrubs stretched tightly across her shoulders. She did resemble her cousin, Lauren, in a superficial way, with those green eyes, straight white teeth, and high cheekbones. But where Lauren had a delicate beauty that attracted men wherever she went, Tex had an independent nature about her that said "Back off." Her physical stature added to the impression, with a voice to match, and a glare that could send a strong man reeling. She hadn't aimed her look at Lukas, but he figured Quinn's days were numbered.

"Initiation?" Lukas asked.

She pulled her chair out, turned it around, and straddled it as if she were riding a horse. "We've got some juvenile delinquents on staff here that try to pass for human beings. They like to play practical jokes on the new guys, and you're the newest."

Lukas thought about the peanut butter sandwich he'd thrown away. "What kinds of practical jokes?"

"They let the air out of Dr. Moss's tires and unscrewed the back of his chair so it would fall off when he sat down. They covered his suede jacket with tape, which ruined the material when he pulled it off."

Lukas nodded. He wasn't surprised.

"Dr. Moss was nice about it," she said. "If they'd done that to me, I'd've hung 'em out to dry."

Lukas signed the chart he was working on, added it to the small stack, and reached into the desk for his keys. It was Sunday morning, and tired as he was, he wanted to attend a worship service somewhere. He just hoped he could stay awake long enough not to snore through the sermon.

"Where are the churches around here?"

There was no answer.

He turned his head and ran straight into Tex's hard stare.

"Tex?" What was wrong with her? "Any churches in Herald?"

"Why would you want one of those?" Her voice had suddenly cooled several degrees.

Lukas frowned and glanced at his watch. Yes, this was Sunday morning. "I thought I might pray for Jerod Moore, among other things."

She shook her head in a slow, sad rhythm. "You'd be better off doing that at home by your bedside." She got up from the chair and rolled it back where she'd gotten it. "While you're at it, you might pray for the kid that disappeared from the park last week, and the ones who disappeared in Sedalia and Columbia. Nobody's prayers have been answered for them yet. See you next shift."

———

Clarence woke himself with a loud snore, his head lolling back against the headrest in Buck's truck. He raised his head and caught sight of the Knolls city limit sign. Wow. He must've slept the last twenty miles. He glanced over at Buck. "Sorry, pal, I guess I snoozed a little. I was hoping to help you stay awake." He stretched his heavy arms and reached up to rub his cramping neck. "You doin' okay?"

Buck nodded, his eyes bloodshot and drooping from fatigue. "I'm used to it."

Clarence knew that was right. Since Buck was a fire fighter and first responder who worked twenty-four-hour shifts, he had to do this a lot, but not right after his wife had tried to kill herself. Besides, he'd just finished a long shift a few hours before all this happened.

"Guess you're gonna go home and get some rest now," Clarence said.

Buck turned at the first stop sign and headed toward Ivy Richmond's house. "I don't know." He took one hand from the steering wheel and rubbed it across his beard-stubbled face. "I keep hoping I'm really already asleep and that this is just a bad nightmare."

"I hear you there. Been lots of times I wished the same thing. There's something Ivy keeps telling me, though, and I'm about to decide it's true." Clarence looked out the window at the opalescent morning light. "She says this life isn't what counts. What you *do* counts, and what you *believe* counts, but not what happens to you here."

Buck leveled him a sideways glance and turned onto the street where Ivy lived. "Sounds kind of rough to me. Is that how I'm supposed to get through this thing with Kendra? Just tell myself it doesn't matter?"

Clarence frowned. That didn't come out right. "I don't think that's what Ivy meant. What she's been telling me all these months, while I've been starving on this diet and Darlene's been trying to take better care of her asthma, is that God—you know, Jesus and all—cares a lot about us. It's like He's the big boss, and He knows what's going to happen, even though we don't. You know, like He's got His own plans for us, and sometimes we just need to kind of ride along and see what happens." He wasn't sure how he felt about all that yet, but Ivy's harping was starting to soak in. Somehow a little of what she said made sense to him.

Buck turned into Ivy's driveway and pushed the buttons to unlock the doors so Clarence could get out. "I don't know."

"Me neither, but I'm starting to think there's something to this prayer stuff. When we prayed up there in Springfield, didn't his prayer make things better for a while? Didn't Kendra stop crying?"

Buck thought about the question so long that the front door of Ivy's house opened and Ivy stepped out onto the porch. Her long salt-and-pepper hair was drawn back in a braid, and she wore a red wool sweater pulled down over a long matching skirt. Ivy Richmond cleaned up good for a sixty-six-year-old woman. Actually, she cleaned up good for any age.

"But it didn't last, Clarence," Buck said finally.

Clarence looked across the seat at his friend. "Then maybe we've just got to keep praying." He opened the door and heaved his heavy body out onto the concrete drive.

"Don't guess it could hurt," Buck said. "Lauren McCaffrey used to tell me she was praying for me, back when Kendra kicked me out and I was suspended from the department. Afterward I sometimes wondered if everything turned out okay because of those prayers. But look what's happened now." He spread his hands, then dropped them back onto the steering wheel. "Kendra wants to die."

"But she's not dead. Think about that, Buck." Clarence closed the door and waved his friend off, then turned to face Ivy.

―――――――

Mercy entered the room where Crystal Hollis and her great-grand-mother, Odira Bagby, had been brought the night before. And then she smiled. Since all the rooms here at Knolls Community were private, Mercy had been afraid Odira would have to sleep on one of those chairs that folded out into a sleeper—not a comfortable situation for a woman who had weighed in at two hundred seventy pounds on her last medical visit. Some sweet soul had moved another hospital bed into the room and set it up beside Crystal's so Odira could be close to the little seven-year-old during the night. Probably the night charge nurse, Vickie. She was one of the best additions they had made in this hospital in the past few months—except for Lukas Bower.

Two empty food trays waited for pickup on the tray table, and Crystal lay on her bed with her head propped up, her soft brown hair combed and hanging straight to her shoulders. She didn't have the television on, but her water-blue eyes were open and alert, and they fixed on Mercy as soon as she walked in.

Mercy saw a children's book lying face down on the rumpled blankets of the other bed. Most likely Odira had been reading aloud.

"Good morning, Crystal. Where's Gramma?"

Crystal pointed toward the hallway. "She went to ask the nurse when you were coming." Her serious gaze did not leave Mercy's face. "She wants to see if you'll let us go home today."

"Okay, I'll get the preliminaries over and talk to her when she comes back." Mercy pulled the stethoscope from around her neck and warmed the instrument in her palm for a few seconds. "How have you been feeling this morning?"

"I feel better, Dr. Mercy." Crystal took a deep breath and exhaled to demonstrate. She didn't cough. Her face was back to its normal pale color.

"Good." Mercy glanced at the empty food trays. "Did you eat all your own food?"

"Yes, and some of Gramma's."

Mercy smiled. That would have been a loving sacrifice for Odira. "Then I see your appetite is back to normal." She checked the nurse report on the clipboard at the end of the bed. Crystal had been given another breathing treatment this morning, her coughing had slowed considerably, and her temperature was 99.4.

Mercy was just finishing with Crystal when Odira came in huffing, her face damp with perspiration, with clumps of gray-brown hair clinging to her forehead. "Hi, Dr. Mercy! I was just tellin' Crystal you'd probably be here anytime." Her voice, as always, was strong, but her breathing was louder and more labored than usual. Her face was flushed, and she moved more slowly. "I think she's feelin' better today, don't you?" Odira patted her great-granddaughter on the arm and leaned down to kiss her forehead. "I always did say, in spite of it all, she's a fast healer. How's those lungs sound to you this morning?"

"Much better." Mercy replaced the clipboard and adjusted Crystal's blanket.

"Think we'll get to go home today?" Odira picked up the open storybook and lowered herself slowly onto the hospital bed beside Crystal's.

Mercy watched the woman's movements in silence for a moment. Twice last night, while Mercy had been giving Crystal her treatments in the clinic, Odira had quietly pressed her hand against her chest and winced. Her face was puffy, and her feet bulged out over the tops of her loafers, as Vickie had observed.

And Crystal—observant child that she was—watched with worried eyes. Something was going on here.

"I'd like to keep you here at least another night," Mercy said, patting Crystal's arm.

Odira's expression drooped. "Oh." She huffed a couple more times. "Can't tell you how much I appreciate you, Dr. Mercy, but you know how dangerous it is for Crystal to be in here with all the germs floating around. I've been told hospitals are the worst place to pick up pneumonia. She picks up any little bug so easy, what with her cystic fibrosis."

Mercy nodded. "I'm sorry. I understand your concern. Our staff is always careful to prevent the spread of germs, but where you have illness, you will have contagion. It may help you to know that our hospital is well below the national average for community-acquired pneumonia." She stepped over to Odira's bed, pulling a small bottle out of her lab coat. "Here, I brought this for you." She handed the plastic container to Odira. "It's hand purifier. I want you and Crystal both to rub it on your hands several times a day while you're here, and then when Crystal goes back to school I want her to take it with her and use it."

Odira opened the white top of the container and sniffed. "Not much smell."

"It will kill a lot of germs before they can get to Crystal's face. Usually that's how we contract diseases—by touching contaminated items with our hands, then touching our face or nose or other areas that are susceptible. This should help kill the germs before that happens, if you use it properly." She watched Odira open the bottle and pour a little glob into her hands, then reach over and give some to Crystal.

That simple act could be a potential lifesaver for someone with CF. People didn't realize how dangerous a simple cold could be to this child. Even Mercy had to remember, when Crystal came to see her at the office, not to take the chance of spreading germs that might linger on her clothing from other patients. She always put on a fresh lab coat when Crystal came in because the little girl needed a loving touch.

"And how's Gramma holding up through all this?" Mercy asked, trying to keep her voice casual. She found it hard to believe Odira was close to Mom's age—not old at all. "Are you a little tired?"

"Who, me? I'm just as fine as can be." Odira's words didn't hold as much energy as they usually did when Mercy asked her that. The woman hastened the drying of the hand purifier by waving her hands in the air; then she reached down and thumbed through the pages of the storybook in her lap. She did not look at Mercy.

Mercy continued to watch her. "You know, Odira, it's been a while since your last checkup. We want to make sure to keep you in running order so you can take care of Crystal."

Odira grunted. "Nothin's wrong with me that a nice bed at home won't cure."

Mercy glanced at Crystal and saw growing concern in the little girl's eyes at the continued questions about Odira's health. "Odira, why don't you and I go for a stroll down the hallway? You could use some exercise after being cooped in this room all this time."

Odira turned her uncertain gaze toward her great-granddaughter. "Not sure I oughta leave Crystal here all alone. And what if I was to pick up some disease and pass it on to her?"

The woman was hedging. "We can be careful. I'll call an aide to sit with her for a few moments." Mercy nudged Odira's leg. "Come on, it'll do us both some good." Maybe while they were on their walk Mercy could convince her to submit to an exam. Odira's health now, and not Crystal's, prompted Mercy to keep them here for another day or two. She could not dismiss the nagging question—if something happened to Odira now, what would become of Crystal?

CHAPTER 8

Clarence knew Ivy Richmond's rules for breakfast. At her house everyone ate a nutritious one and nobody skipped. To his great relief this morning was no different. She had fixed a plate for him and covered the food with plastic wrap and placed it in the refrigerator. He was starved. All this counseling stuff could build an appetite.

He watced her unwrap the plate and put a paper towel over the top of the food. All right! Looked like some eggs and cheese on there! Then she shoved the plate into the microwave. With a grimace of distaste she adjusted the heat setting and pressed the on switch. He knew Ivy detested resorting to a microwave, and she seldom used one. Clarence, however, used it often, especially for the low-fat microwave popcorn Ivy kept in the cupboard for him. He hadn't yet figured out a way to keep it quiet, though, so he tried to keep some popped up for a snack late at night. The popcorn helped him resist the chocolate chip cookies. Sometimes.

"Where'd Darlene go?" Ivy asked.

Clarence looked toward the apartment entrance, which was across the great room from the kitchen, and saw his sister stepping inside. Her short, prematurely gray hair hugged her head in a sleek new style, and she wore a pretty pink wool jacket and skirt that made her look like a real woman instead of the sickly, emaciated one who had cared for him for so long. At the sound of her name she turned and looked back at Clarence, grinned and waved, then stepped through the doorway out of sight.

"Gone to hide from the fireworks," Clarence grumbled. He barely saw Darlene lately, she was so involved with her new indexing job, and helping out at church, and volunteering at the hospital.

"Well, I just hope she isn't back on that computer this morning," Ivy said. "I warned her not to overdo it again." She turned from her work and fixed Clarence with a motherly look, hands on her hips. "You could have told us where you were going. Don't you think we worry about you? And then you take off in the middle of the night without even a note or—"

"Sorry, Mom, it won't happen again, but Sis didn't look too worried."

"Cut the sarcasm."

He stifled a grin. Her bossiness didn't irritate him as much as it used to. He'd discovered that she had a caring heart. "I didn't have time to call," he explained. "Buck and Kendra were in trouble, and Buck asked me to help them. So I went. Sorry you were worried."

Sudden reluctant interest kindled in Ivy's dark eyes. He knew how much she hated to be sidetracked when she was in the middle of a tirade. "What kind of trouble?" She pulled a fork out of a drawer and grabbed a napkin from the counter. She looked pretty in that Christmas-red turtleneck and skirt. And she smelled good. Just not as good as the food.

He gave her a superior grin. "Can't tell you. It's privileged medical information."

The microwave beeped, and Ivy took the plate out, uncovered it, and set it in front of Clarence. "I'll hear about it at church anyway."

"Not from me." He looked from her strong-featured face to the breakfast she had fixed him. "This some of those whole-grain eggs?"

"What are you talking about?"

"You know, whole grain. The brown ones. If whole-grain bread is brown, then the brown eggs are whole grain. Stands to reason."

She shook her head. "You need sleep."

"I know." He didn't need her hovering over him, counting every bite he took. The problem with this diet was that he had to pay so much attention to what went into his mouth—and if he didn't, Ivy did. "If you go on, I bet you could still make it for the early service."

"I know."

"You gonna bless the food?"

More interest quickened in her eyes. She pulled a chair out across from him at the table and sat down. "You want me to?"

Clarence thought again about the wild night, the trip to Springfield and back, the heart-deep discoveries he'd made. "Yeah."

Her eyes widened. She leaned forward and laid a hand on his arm. "Clarence, you're not kidding?"

"I'm not stupid enough to kid about God. Not anymore."

And so she prayed. And this time, he paid attention.

"I need to run some tests, Odira, but you have a problem with your heart. We should do something about it as quickly as possible." Mercy preceded Odira out of the empty patient room where she had done an unsatisfactory exam.

The older woman stopped when she reached the hallway, her large, round face crinkled with worry, her rusty gray hair spiked around her face in uneven lengths. She leaned against the wall as if she couldn't help herself. "I haven't had a heart attack or anything, have I?"

"No, but it looks to me like you have congestive heart failure." Mercy resisted the urge to offer the older woman an arm to lean on. She'd learned long ago that Odira was one of the most independent ladies in Knolls. She was quick to help others, but she had to be desperate to accept help for herself. She would, however, accept help for the sake of Crystal.

"What's that mean?" Odira asked, pushing herself away from the wall and continuing down the hallway. "My heart's failing? I'm gonna die?"

"No, we'll do all we can to keep that from happening." Mercy matched her steps to Odira's. "First of all, you have too much fluid in your body, and your heart can't keep up with the pumping process right now. That's why your feet and legs are swelling. It's called edema. I want to put you on a medication to get rid of the fluid."

"Okay, let's do it." Odira stopped and huffed a moment, then went on. "Don't mess with all that testing and such."

Mercy stepped out of the way of a breakfast cart coming down the wide hall and turned to look at Odira. "I want to get a better idea—"

"Cain't we just try the medicine and see if it'll work?" Odira took a couple more heavy steps, then stopped and gave Mercy a hard stare. "You're a smart lady, Dr. Mercy. You've got lots of common sense. I trust you better than I'd trust any of those crazy machines."

"Those crazy machines will tell me more about the extent of your problems than a stethoscope will, and, Odira, you've got to be healthy to take care of Crystal. We have the equipment right here at the hospital to run the tests, and I can arrange to have them done tomorrow, while you're still here."

"But won't they cost—"

"Medicare." Mercy laid a hand on Odira's arm. "We'll take care of the rest. Okay?"

Odira huffed a couple of times, the crinkles around her eyes deepening as she studied Mercy's expression. "Guess I should for Crystal's sake."

"I wish you would."

"Okay, Dr. Mercy, I trust you. Now I've gotta get back to my gal!" She turned and lumbered down the hallway toward the hospital room where an aide sat with Crystal.

Ivy pushed the sleeves of her sweater up above her elbows and stepped over to the refrigerator. "I think we'll go to the late service this morning. Meanwhile I'll make your favorite slaw."

Clarence picked up his fork and poked at the concoction. "I know I shouldn't ask, but what is this stuff?"

"Can't you trust me for once?" She took out a head of red cabbage and red, yellow, and green peppers.

"What if I want to cook it myself someday?"

She placed a small dish of crumbled feta cheese and a bag of sunflower seeds on the table next to her chopping block. "Okay, I use egg substitute scrambled with egg whites, chopped low-fat ham, green peppers, and onions. And fat-free cheese."

Clarence put down his fork and groaned. "Not the cheese, too!"

"Do you know the fat content of regular cheese? You don't need that. Here, I'll give you some sunflower seeds on top. They have the right kind of fat, and these don't have salt."

Clarence jerked his plate out from under the bag she had begun to lower over his eggs. "Sunflower seeds with eggs! Are you crazy? I'm not a bird."

Ivy continued to hold the bag aloft. "Put that plate back down here. You wanted something besides oatmeal for breakfast, and I'm giving it to you. This is healthy. I eat it myself, with a good salsa sprinkled on top. Great for the cholesterol."

Clarence sighed and set his plate back down, then winced when Ivy poured a sprinkling of the seeds over his eggs, but he decided, philosophically, that at least the sunflower seeds would kill the taste of the fat-free cheese on top. But before he could pick up his fork, Ivy plopped something else down on the plate.

"There you go, my own homemade salsa. Dip the eggs in that. You'll think you've tasted heaven."

Clarence studied Ivy's expression for a moment to see if she wasn't playing some mean practical joke to get even with him for staying out all night. She looked innocent enough. He took a deep, sustaining breath and raised a forkful of food to his mouth. He closed his eyes as he shoveled the mess into his mouth and chewed.

"Not bad, is it?" Ivy prompted.

Clarence finished chewing, swallowed, and felt some of the tension ease from his shoulders. Okay, that didn't taste so bad. In fact, it was almost—

"See?" Ivy demanded as she pulled a bunch of grapes from the refrigerator and began to chop her assembled ingredients. "Didn't I say you'd like it? You never believe me, do you?"

He caught the grin of triumph in her expressive dark eyes, so like Mercy's. He couldn't help grinning back. To answer her question, he filled his fork with more eggs. "It isn't exactly chocolate chip cookies," he said, "but I could stand this every so often." He put the next bite in his mouth.

"Now, that's what I call high praise, coming from you," Ivy said dryly. "And speaking of which, did you happen to notice a squirrel in here last night before you left?"

Clarence kept eating. "Hmm-mmm."

"I didn't think so." She reached over and opened the small freezer door on her refrigerator. "But since the squirrels in our trees don't understand proper household etiquette and you do, I didn't think you could have been the one to scatter crumbs all over the packages of frozen vegetables."

He swallowed. "Sorry."

She watched him curiously for another few bites, but he didn't mind. Ivy could get on his nerves, especially when she nagged him to drink more water, eat less dinner, exercise. But even though he was worn out from the long, sleepless night, he felt a warmth he'd never felt before. He couldn't seem to keep a smile from his face.

Ivy kept shooting quick, inquisitive glances at him as she chopped her vegetables. "Clarence, just what *did* you do last night? Are you up to something?"

He took a bite of the multigrain toast and didn't even complain that there was no butter or jam or anything to go on top of it. "Not up to nothing. Don't be so suspicious."

"Don't talk with your mouth full. You're telling me you rode up to Springfield with Buck and Kendra, waited around all night while they got Kendra settled, then rode back with Buck? That's all you did?"

"Yup."

"Then why do you seem so . . . perky?"

Clarence choked on his toast. "Perky!"

"There's something different about you this morning."

Clarence kept chewing and thought about that for a minute. He did feel different. He couldn't say what he felt, exactly, except that he had a feeling of purpose this morning.

That was it. He looked down at himself. He was still fat. He still got out of breath when he walked more than a couple of blocks. He and his sister still lived as Ivy's dependents. But then, he liked to think that Ivy was getting a kick out of bossing him around and whipping him into shape and watching the weight drop off.

But that wasn't why he felt this way. Something had happened last night. He now had some kind of a connection he didn't have before . . . a connection with God? And did that mean he wouldn't have to struggle with depression again?

He wasn't sure. The docs said depression was a physical illness, and even Ivy and Lukas and Mercy got sick sometimes. Their lives weren't perfect . . . but still, they had purpose in their lives. Maybe he did, too.

But he wasn't ready to talk about what had happened. Right now he wanted to hug the knowledge to himself like a secret treasure. He wanted to cherish the newness in his life a little longer before taking the chance of telling someone and being laughed at. He knew God wasn't laughing. He knew God had used him last night. But he wasn't ready to tell a bunch of people about this new experience yet. This would be his own silent communication with God.

"Hiding out?" The cold, rough male voice came from behind Mercy in the hallway, filling her with a shudder an instant before she realized where she'd heard it before.

She swung around and found herself staring up into the glinting, muddy yellow eyes of Abner Bell. He was wild-eyed and stringy haired, and his beefy hands clenched and unclenched at his sides as if he were preparing to wrap them around the next available neck. Abner Bell had always been an unpleasant man. He could cover his temper well when he wanted to, but he usually didn't want to. Some people who didn't know better thought he was attractive. The appearance didn't last long, though, and lots of people in Knolls were afraid of him. One glance at his present expression gave Mercy a chill.

"Where's my wife?" His growl sounded as if it came from the inside of a cement mixer, and his gaze pinned Mercy with accusation.

Mercy resisted the urge to take a step backward from his looming bulk. There was no need to be afraid. Hospital staff bustled up and down the hallway, and trays and dishes still clattered in the rooms.

And then she focused on his question. "Your wife? Abner, what are you talking about? Delphi's—"

"Gone!"

He leaned forward, hovering over her. The rank odor of his breath combined with the hovering threat of his tall frame. Instead of frightening her further, he irritated her. From past experience she knew this man was a moral coward whose main joy in life was manipulating and frightening others. He would not bully her.

His voice rose. "You've been telling her to leave for months, and last night she did. Where're you hiding her? You ain't got any right to sneak a man's wife—"

"Excuse me," she snapped. "I did not 'sneak' anybody anywhere.

What did you do, Abner, get high and start beating on her again?" Her voice raised a few decibels louder than she'd intended it to and caught the attention of several of the staff.

"Whatever she told you was a lie!" He leaned closer.

Instinctively Mercy raised a hand and shoved him backward. "Get out of my face! I haven't seen your wife, so she hasn't had a chance to tell me anything. Now get out of this hospital." She pivoted away and left him standing there. She had more important things to do this morning than listen to some abuser's temper tantrums. Apparently Delphi had finally taken her advice.

But as Mercy walked away she felt the brooding stare of Delphi's husband boring into her back. She said a silent prayer for Delphi. Was she really gone this time? Was she safe?

CHAPTER

At five-fifteen Monday afternoon Lukas sniffed the ham salad sandwich he'd purchased from the vending machine in the Herald Hospital cafeteria. He took a small bite to make sure it didn't taste funny, chewed and swallowed. He took a drink of orange juice, checked the cellophane wrapper on the sandwich to make sure the date was okay, and opened his mouth to take another bite when a public address blared from a speaker directly over his head.

". . . Ottar Ower to the emer . . . oom, please," came a fuzzy female voice. "Octar Bower to the emergency room." He winced at the noise and static, then realized that was his name they were mangling.

He rewrapped his food, took another quick swig of his orange juice, and carried everything with him out the door. So much for dinner. The evening rush was probably beginning, with parents getting home from work and finding their kids sick. The family docs were gone for the evening, and waiting until the next morning would cost a day of work as well as the doctor bill. At minimum wage, no one could miss a shift without skipping a payment of some kind.

The Monday ER nurse, Janice Carter, met him at the front desk. "We have a lady with a traumatic near-amputation, Dr. Bower." Janice was a slender lady in her fifties with short, frosted brown hair and eyes the color of maple syrup. Her temperament wasn't quite that sweet, but she got the job done with a minimum of complaint. Compared to most of the other staff members in this ER, she was an excellent employee.

"Johnson's Poultry again." Janice shoved her assessment sheet toward him. "I haven't completed the vitals yet. Didn't think you'd want me to delay. It's the little finger of her left hand."

Lukas glanced at the paper. "Which room?"

"Trauma. They didn't call in. They just brought her." Janice lowered her voice. "The safety director's with her, so you won't get much information. They always try to make an accident look like it's the employee's fault, but they have an accident out there at least twice a month, and that's just on my shifts."

Lukas followed Janice to the trauma room to find a frightened forty-five-year-old woman lying on the exam bed. She still wore her clothing from work, splattered with pieces of chicken fat where the apron hadn't covered her. She smelled like a butcher shop. A white cloth net covered her hair, and she wore black rubber boots that were still wet from splashing through constantly dripping water and chicken juice. The woman's left hand had been wrapped in several thicknesses of gauze, and blood seeped through the material.

"Hello, Mrs. Morrison, I'm Dr. Bower. Do you mind if I take a look at this?" He indicated the gauze and carefully began the unwrapping procedure. Her hand trembled in his grip. Except for smears of black eye makeup, her face was as pale as a winter sky. "What happened today?" he asked, keeping his voice reassuring and gentle.

Her chin quivered. Her gaze darted toward Mr. Gray, who sat watching silently from the chair by the far wall. She did not make eye contact with him.

When Lukas uncovered the injured finger he found, to his dismay, that near-amputation was the correct assessment. There was a clean slice between the joints of the little finger. Despite the blood that continued to ooze from the cut, Lukas could see the exposed bone deep within the flesh. The tip of the finger was already becoming pale, with a capillary refill of four seconds. A quick test with the point of a needle revealed markedly diminished sensation compared to the corresponding finger. He would have to move quickly. He checked the chart, then turned to Janice, who hovered at the other side of Mrs. Morrison's exam bed. "Have Shirley call an ambulance for us. We need to transfer her to Columbia for this."

Gray straightened then. "Hold on a minute, Dr. Bower." He sounded almost bored. "I have to get clearance from the home office before we can do that."

"If you would do so immediately, Mr. Gray, I would appreciate it," Lukas said. "Meanwhile, we want that ambulance to be on its way. I think the finger is salvageable."

Janice hesitated, giving Lukas a worried frown. "Uh, Dr. Bower, Mr. Amos wants us to call him before we transfer any patients out of here."

Lukas couldn't quite hide his frustration. "That shouldn't even be an issue here. This is a near-amputation, and this hospital isn't equipped to reconnect a finger."

Janice shrugged. "Sorry, that's our order."

"Fine, get him on the phone for me, but I want Mrs. Morrison ready to go as soon as we can get an ambulance here." And he hoped Quinn was not on duty today. He wasn't in the mood for another debate. He turned back to the patient. "Mrs. Morrison, have you ever exhibited any allergic reaction to pain medication or penicillin?"

She shook her head.

"Have you had a tetanus shot within the past five years?"

Again she shook her head, but then she cleared her throat and spoke loudly enough for the safety director to hear as he walked out the curtained entrance to find a telephone. "Never done anything like this before. Never needed a tetanus shot. I'm always careful around knives."

"Okay, then I'm afraid we'll have to give you a shot now," Lukas said. "While we're at it I'm going to have the nurse start an IV in your arm so we can give you fluids, pain meds and an antibiotic to prevent infection. We'll also need to have an x-ray."

As soon as they heard Mr. Gray on the telephone out at the secretary's desk in the central area, Mrs. Morrison reached out with her good hand and gestured to Lukas to come closer.

He bent forward.

"I'll probably get fired for this, but the line was going way too fast." Her voice trembled with fear and anger. "They always do that! It's why so many people get hurt. I'm a leg cutter, and they don't keep my knife sharp enough, and every time I think I'm going to keep up, they speed up the line. They've got those birds flying through there as if they still had feathers on their wings!"

"Can't you tell them—"

The woman snorted. "Griping gets people fired at Johnson's Poultry. We need our jobs, so we keep our mouths shut." She lay back as Janice prepped her arm for an IV. "Don't tell anybody, Doctor. If you do, they'll fire me. Guaranteed." She winced as Janice pierced the skin with an IV needle.

"You haven't told Mr. Gray?" Lukas asked.

The patient shook her head. "He's not going to risk *his* job. The last safety director who reported the company got fired."

"Dr. Bower," Shirley called from the front desk, "I have Mr. Amos on the line." She transferred the call to the phone at Lukas's work station, and he rushed to grab it while she walked quickly away, as if escaping a line of fire.

"Yes, Mr. Amos, this is Dr. Bower. I'm calling as per protocol to inform you of a transfer of a patient who was injured at Johnson's Poultry. She needs—"

"That is not acceptable," came a clipped, nasal voice, which sounded as if it was coming through a speakerphone. "Contact the Johnson's Poultry's company physician to attend to the patient."

"I've already had him paged, but this patient needs to be transferred as quickly—"

"Dr. Jeffries must examine her before she leaves this facility."

"But an ambulance is on the way over now," Lukas snapped back. "She needs a hand surgeon or she could lose a—"

"Not until the Johnson's Poultry physician sees her." The speakerphone disengaged with a click.

At eight o'clock Monday night Mercy finally found a chance to dial information for Lukas's new listing. Surely, even if he had to work today, he would be home by now.

The telephone rang four times, and Mercy braced herself for the mechanical voice of Lukas's answering machine. She hated that thing, but it seemed as if she had a closer relationship with it than she did with Lukas lately.

She was able to at least detect the Lukas-style inflections of voice in spite of the tinny sound of the recording, and she let his words flow over her. Then it beeped.

"Hi, Lukas." She couldn't keep the disappointment from her

voice, hard as she tried. "Sorry I missed you again." She glanced at her watch. "Don't try to return my call, because I won't be here. Tedi's due home from a field trip anytime, and then we've got to go get some groceries before we starve to death." She hesitated, wondering when she would have another chance to talk to him. She didn't even know what his schedule was anymore. "I guess I'll be in touch lat—"

A loud screech snapped at her through the telephone, and she heard Lukas's garbled voice through the line. "Don't hang up!" Another screech, then sudden silence.

"Mercy? Are you still there?" A quickening of welcome rang through his voice.

She felt a smile warm her face, and she relaxed and sat down on the sofa next to the phone. "When are you going to get one of those new digital things that actually record you instead of your evil twin?"

He chuckled. "When this one breaks."

"Sounds like it's time, then. I tried to get your new number yesterday, but you didn't have one at home yet." Did he know how good his voice sounded to her?

"I was sleeping anyway. Were you trying to call me yesterday for any particular reason?"

No, she just wanted to hear him. "Yeah, the rates are cheaper on Sundays. Plus I had a killer of a Saturday night, and I wanted to blame somebody for it. You're the top candidate, since you're not here to defend yourself."

"I can identify. My Saturday shift was pretty rotten, too. Why don't you tell me about it? I have broad shoulders." There was a pause. "Well, in a manner of speaking."

She closed her eyes and pictured those shoulders, and the earnest expression she often saw on his face, and the light that seemed to enter his eyes when he saw her—not that they saw each other very often anymore. "Yes, you do," she said.

"So let me have it," he prompted. "What happened?"

She loved his comfortable, matter-of-fact tone, and she longed to be sitting with him now, talking face-to-face. As she told him about Crystal and Odira, Buck and Kendra, she could feel some of the tension from Saturday night finally ease from the muscles of her neck and shoulders. Even with a hundred fifty miles between them she could feel his presence, could sense his attention and caring. Just talking to him helped her realize that nothing was as bad as it sometimes seemed.

"Mrs. Pinkley wants me to remind you that we need you here." Mercy hesitated. "*I* need you here."

"You do?"

And that was when some of her old doubts—fears she'd thought had been eradicated months ago—resurrected themselves in her mind. *Don't push him too hard. Don't let him know how desperate you are just to hear his voice over the phone.* "Yes," she said. "I'm getting so many walk-ins I don't get out sometimes until seven, and the calls come every weekend now, every day off. Lots of nights. Knolls is growing. I don't have as much time with Tedi, and she's feeling the brunt of it."

"Mercy, you can't do everything. There are other doctors in town. Let them take their share of the overload."

She slumped against the armrest. He wasn't getting the point. Of course, she was trying hard not to make a point. "Some of them do, but—"

"But everyone knows you're a soft touch."

She heard the affectionate humor in his voice. "Yes, and so are you, so if you were here we would both be getting the calls, kind of spread the work out a little."

Another silence for a few seconds, then, softly, "The ER is gone, Mercy. There's no place for me at the hospital until it's rebuilt."

"Then consider joining me at the clinic temporarily. Estelle says construction is ahead of schedule. She's hoping it'll take only another month or so, but I'll be dead by then if I don't get some help."

"Can't you refer some patients to other clinics? Or at least convince Estelle that she needs to hire some extra weekend coverage and find a place for a temporary ER." There was a heavy sigh over the phone. "Mercy, I signed a contract here."

She clutched the phone tighter. "What? But you already have a commitment at Knolls. When did you sign it?"

"Two weeks ago. It's short-term, through the beginning of April, so that'll mean two and a half months more here."

He sounded so matter-of-fact, as if that were the only logical thing for him to do. Mercy laid her head back against the sofa cushion. He hadn't even discussed the matter with her first. Didn't her opinion count with him anymore? Didn't *she* count?

"Mercy? Look, as far as I knew, the projected completion date for the ER was late March or early April."

"It was." She knew he could hear the disappointment in her voice, but why *shouldn't* she be disappointed? Herald was a three-hour drive from Knolls. At this rate, with their crazy work schedules, they would never see each other.

The silence over the line grew tense. "I'm sorry, Lukas," she said at last. "I'm just surprised. You were getting plenty of temp opportunities closer than Herald, Missouri."

"But never in one place, don't you see? I was driving all over southern Missouri, from Cassville to Poplar Bluff. That gets old in a hurry. This way the only traveling I'll have to do is across town."

The disappointment went deeper. "You mean you're not planning to come back here for two and a half months?" She heard the plaintive sound of her voice, and she knew he would pick up on it. *Stop it, Mercy. Nobody likes a whiner.*

"That wasn't what I meant. I'll come down to Knolls, of course."

He sounded so distant suddenly, so detached, and she wondered if that was her imagination, or if she'd irritated him.

The silence was longer this time, and the tension drew taut.

He cleared his throat. "Uh, Mercy? You sound tired. Has anybody tried to reach Cherra Garcias? She's family practice *and* ER, and she's good. She's scheduled for employment at Knolls in a couple of months, and you might get her to come early."

"I don't want Cherra Garcias. I want you," she blurted.

There was a heavy sigh at the other end. "Mercy, I . . . I'm sorry. I didn't think it would get so hectic for you. If I'd known . . . Anyway, I'm really sorry."

She relented a little. "Well, I guess I could give Cherra a call. I hope *she* didn't sign a contract anywhere. Get ready for fireworks, though, because you obviously didn't tell Estelle about your new contract, and I don't think she's going to like it."

"Oh well, cheer up. I could get suspended here before long. It seems that's one of the favorite pastimes around here, suspending and firing people."

Mercy suddenly forgot her own disappointment. "Don't tell me you're in trouble again," she blurted, then bit her lip. This was not a good time to remind him of problems he'd had in the past.

"Nothing bad, just a little disagreement. Our administrator thinks he can rewrite COBRA law and pick the time and circumstances under which we transfer patients. He forced me to hold a patient with a near-amputation until the company doc had a look at it, purely for the purposes of insurance. And do you know that he even called and delayed the arrival of the ambulance for transfer? Seems the company has worker's comp, but it won't pay as much if the company doc doesn't make a visit to the ER."

"And did he?"

"He came in pretty fast. He has a practice in town, and when I called him myself and explained the situation he drove right over. The patient was out in ten minutes from the time Dr. Jeffries came in. I don't like the fact that the ambulance service is owned by this hospital, and I don't like the delay it caused. COBRA law specifies that the transfer must take place in a timely manner. What if Jeffries hadn't come so quickly?"

"Then, knowing you, you would have made other arrangements." Mercy had always admired the patient advocacy Lukas displayed. She wished he was as passionate about making more time to see her. "You could just go straight to the watchdog and call COBRA."

"I hope that won't be necessary." Lukas had experienced his own legal nightmare during a trumped-up investigation by the government agency that regulated hospital emergency rooms.

When he remained silent, she changed the subject. "Something else happened Saturday night," she said. "Delphi Bell disappeared. Abner's looking for her. He came to me in the hospital when I was making rounds yesterday morning and accused me of hiding her."

"Do you think she finally ran away?" Lukas asked.

"I hope so." She thought of Abner's anger, his accusations. Could it possibly have been some kind of an act? What if something even more sinister had taken place? "I hope she's out of state."

Mercy filled Lukas in on news from Knolls, about Ivy and Clarence and their bickering, about the changes taking place at the hospital, and about some of the changes in her own life. "Tedi seems to be enjoying the visits with her father, and so we've started meeting twice a week instead of just once. He comes over and helps her with her math homework on Tuesday nights. He's always been good with math."

Lukas felt his hand tighten on the receiver with an automatic surge of emotion. He sat up in his chair and swallowed. Theo was seeing Mercy twice a week? "That's good." He waited for Mercy to elaborate. She didn't. He prompted. "So Theo's doing well?"

"Yes. He's been attending his AA meetings faithfully, and he's having counseling sessions once a week with our new pastor. He's a completely different person from a year ago."

"That's good." Lukas knew he was repeating himself, but Theo's progress *was* good. He wanted Tedi to be reconciled with her father, and he wanted Theo to grow in his new faith—the faith Lukas himself had almost inadvertently led him to last fall. But the battle Lukas continued to fight in his heart was the Mercy-Theo relationship. It told him more than he'd ever wanted to know about his own selfish tendencies. Jealousy. That's what it was. Mercy had loved Theodore enough to marry him ten years ago. Theo's alcohol and cruelty and desire for other women had taken him from her. Now, with Theo claiming a new life in Christ, would she see in him the man she once loved?

In God's eyes, wasn't that the way their relationship should be . . . for Tedi's sake?

"That's good," he said, and realized he'd said it for the third time.

"Yes, it is." There was a pause. "Well, I'm sure Estelle has Cherra's number. I'll give her a call and see if she'll help us out."

Lukas frowned at the sudden change of subject. He wanted—no, he *needed*—to hear more about this growing friendship with Theo. The all-too-human part of him wanted her to say, without his asking her to, that she was only meeting her ex-husband twice a week for the sake of her daughter, and that—

"Lukas, did you hear me?"

"What? Yes." A movement caught the edge of his vision, and he looked up to see the front door, which he had not bothered to close in his rush to the telephone, easing open slightly. Darkness spilled in with the cold air from outside . . . and kept on coming in the form of the largest black cat Lukas had ever seen.

"What are *you* doing here?" Lukas asked the animal.

"Lukas?" Mercy said. "Is everything okay?"

"Yes, I think so. A cat just walked in the front door."

"A what?"

Then he heard a loud call from outside. "Kitty, kitty, kitty!" The sound was not the cajoling entreaty one traditionally used to entice a cat to come out. It was a strident command. Lukas couldn't fail to recognize Tex's strong voice.

Meanwhile, ignoring her call, the cat peered around the room as if it were his own personal boudoir.

"Lukas, are you still there?" came Mercy's voice.

"Yes, sorry. I just figured out who the cat belongs to. You know Tex, Lauren's cousin? She lives in the other half of this duplex. I've heard her talking about Monster. That's the name of her cat, and now I see why."

"Tex. Is that the paramedic Lauren's always talking about?"

"That's her. Not only is she a paramedic, she's a med student or something." He cast another glance at Monster, who regally marched through the doorless entryway to the small kitchen.

There was a pause, and then Mercy asked quietly, "Is she as pretty as Lauren?"

Even Lukas recognized a loaded gun when he had one pointed at his head. How was he supposed to answer that one? If he said no, then Mercy would think that he thought Lauren was pretty. If he said yes, he'd be lying. Pretty, to him, encompassed the words *petite* and *feminine*. Although Tex was in no way masculine, she was not what most people would call traditionally pretty like her cousin. She had an attractiveness about her prickly personality that one could find appealing . . . but not the way Mercy meant it.

"Tex is fine. She's a good paramedic, and even more outspoken than Lauren."

"So she's a talker?"

"That's right." He heard Tex drawing closer in her search for the missing cat, and then he heard the sudden thump of something hitting the floor in the kitchen. "Uh, just a minute, Mercy. I think the cat's up to something." He covered the mouthpiece of the phone and called, "Tex, your cat's in here!"

There was a sigh at the other end of the line. "Want to trade? Lauren's working for me until the ER's finished."

"She is? And you haven't killed her yet?"

"I've learned to tune out her chatter, and she's been a lifesaver." She paused. "Lukas, I *need* you here."

He shrugged away the sudden surge of elation her words gave him. What she needed was time, whether she realized it or not. She needed time to sort through her feelings and find God's will in her life. And Lukas knew that he, also, needed time. He knew it intellectually. Emotionally he wanted so much more, so much faster.

"I miss you," she said.

"You do?" Yes, she did. He could hear how she felt in her voice. And he missed her, too. And he thought about her so often. . . .

"Lukas, I—"

"Knock, knock!" came Tex's cranky voice from the front door. She didn't wait for an answer but pushed on inside, wearing baggy gray sweats and an old pea-green coat. "Did you say my cat was—oh, sorry, I didn't know you were on the phone."

Lukas waved at her. "I think your cat was in my trash in the kitchen."

Mercy fell silent, sighed, cleared her throat. "I guess I should hang up now. You have company." She sounded disappointed.

"Yeah, I guess so." Lukas was disappointed, too. "Guess I better rescue my trash from—"

"Lukas, isn't there any way you can break that contract?" The words came swift and sudden, and before Lukas could reply she continued. "Okay, I know that isn't fair. I'm sorry. Still I need to talk to you. If you have some time off, would you at least come down for a visit this weekend?"

He would love to see her this weekend. "I work Friday night and Sunday, but—"

"Got him!" Tex came back in from the kitchen, her curly blond mop falling in her face, lugging the giant black Monster under her right arm with a strut of triumph.

"Okay, Lukas. I'll talk to you later."

Mercy sounded hurt, which was exactly what he'd wanted to avoid. She hung up before he had a chance to respond. He watched Tex lug the animal toward the front door.

"Dr. Bower," she announced over her shoulder, "since you've already met the bane of my existence, I'll just stick him in my apartment. Nothing's broken in your kitchen, and I picked up the trash—all empty frozen-dinner cartons. Don't you ever cook?"

He replaced the telephone receiver and tried to paste on a pleasant expression. "Why cook when I can buy Healthy Choice down at the local grocery?" The frozen meals had been Mercy's suggestion.

Tex snorted, opened the front door, and lugged the cat out. He heard a door slam, and then she stepped back in.

She glanced around the small living room. "I told the landlady she ought to paint this place before she rented it out again, but hey, it's cheap." She walked over and plopped down onto the secondhand floral print couch. She pushed back the dark blond hair falling across her forehead into her eyes and blew some tendrils away from her nose. "You don't go in for decorating much, do you?"

"I don't plan to be here long," he said dryly.

She glanced around at the bare walls, and her gaze fell on the one piece of decoration he had brought with him—a handmade Psalm Twenty-Three plaque Tedi had given him for Christmas. In the top right corner was a picture of a dove in flight, signifying the Holy Spirit. Lukas needed that connection to home right now.

He gestured toward the plaque. "A young friend of mine drew that."

Tex averted her gaze from the plaque, as if she'd just witnessed something that made her uncomfortable. She leaned back and crossed her arms over her chest. She had a firm chin, and her jawline was square, especially when she approached argument mode—Lukas had learned that much about her during the few shifts they'd worked together. Her forest green eyes, unadorned by makeup, were wide spaced and inquisitive. Intelligent. As had happened before, Lukas received the impression that her tough attitude and cocky slang were a disguise for a keen mind and a tender heart—but he might be imagining things. Still, she had a good, caring attitude with patients.

"You're a churchgoer, huh?" she asked at last, sounding awkward.

"Yes."

"What persuasion?"

"Excuse me?"

"What flavor? You a dunker or a sprinkler, a shouter maybe?"

"If you're asking my denomination, I'm Baptist."

She grimaced and nodded knowingly. "Aha."

Lukas frowned at her. Aha what?

"Heard you got screamed at by Mr. Amos today."

The sudden subject change kept his thoughts out of balance. "Yes."

"Guy's a jerk," Tex said. "He tries to make everybody think he's got a degree in godhood from some eastern university. Still, I've got to try to get along with him. I don't want to lose my job. It's too far to drive to Sedalia or Jeff City or Columbia every shift."

Lukas sank down in the chair across from her and studied her suddenly grim expression. "But if you're just renting here anyway, and you're a medical—"

"Did you know three nurses have lost their jobs in the ER in the past two months?" She obviously didn't want to discuss her professional status. "And they haven't been replaced. Mr. Amos trumped up some lame excuse about work performance, but everybody knows it's because of the sellout. He's scared he'll lose *his* job if he doesn't cut the budget. The only reason I'm still here is because I'm a paramedic and I don't cost as much as an RN. You can bet Quinn would try to undercut me in a minute if he knew how much I made. He thinks I've got a cushy job."

"What sellout?" Lukas asked.

She gave him a pitying look with her green cat's eyes and put her feet up on the scarred coffee table in front of the sofa. Her old running shoes held a minute crust of Missouri mud, some of which crumbled onto the wood. She didn't notice. "The Brandt Project, an HMO up in Kansas City, bought us out two months ago. They're supposed to be a good company, but I've heard rumors that they like to send their own people in and do a quality check, and they haven't done that here yet. Our brilliant administrator thinks quality means finances. Did you know the man didn't even have medical or hospital experience when he came here? The old company hired him off the street because he had a CPA license. I bet he couldn't even find work anywhere else. That's why this hospital's in the mess it's in now. Poor guy doesn't have a clue. He just tries to make people think he does, with that fake accent and twenty-dollar words and elevator shoes."

Her attention focused once more on the Psalm twenty-three plaque. "If you're looking for a church in Herald, I can't help you. The only one I attended closed its doors after they kicked out all the jerks and hypocrites and there was only one person left."

Lukas didn't respond for a moment. He resisted the urge to point out the fact that she had invaded his home—and an intimate telephone conversation—and plopped down on his sofa without an invitation. He became aware that she was watching him closely, waiting in unaccustomed silence for a reply. But what was he supposed to say?

"Who was the one person left?"

She leaned forward, arms crossed over her chest, gaze locked with his. "My mother."

The obvious wound in her voice spoke volumes of pain through those two words. He had heard the stories before. There were multitudes of people he had met over the years who no longer attended church—who had even turned away from God—because someone who proclaimed Christianity had hurt them.

"You know what church is?" she asked. The wound was obviously still raw. Without waiting for an answer, she continued. "It's a place where Satan sends his best people." The intense bitterness blared through the room, and then she caught her breath softly and had the grace to grimace. She glanced down at her fists clenched in her lap. "Sorry, Dr. Bower, I'm not talking about you."

Lukas paused, then asked, "Does your mother still live around here?"

For a moment she didn't answer. Finally she said quietly, "My mother died six months ago." There was a sparkle of tears in her eyes, which she fiercely sniffed back. "Renal failure. She didn't qualify for a transplant, so I came home and took care of her. Alone."

"Your family didn't help you?"

"My relatives visited a couple of times, but nobody could afford to take off work and stay with us. Besides, I was here." The forceful independence was obvious in her tone. "You know those people she used to go to church with? They never bothered to check on her. They never even knew she was sick until after she died."

Lukas wished there were a gentle way to tell her that Christians didn't read minds any better than non-Christians. "I'm sorry, Tex. I can't imagine how that would have felt."

She sat looking at the floor for a moment, then looked up at him. "So just a warning—don't go trying to preach to me or invite me to your church." She pulled the sides of her pea-green jacket together, zipped up the front, and gave him a half salute as she let herself out.

Lukas noticed she left mud tracks all the way across the hardwood floor.

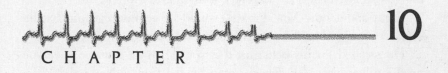

CHAPTER 10

Wednesday morning Lukas pulled out the last set of scrubs from the bottom of his locker and tossed them on the bed as he kicked off his shoes and unbuckled his belt. He'd come in five minutes late to find the night-shift doc already gone and a patient waiting. Three more had come in before he could take time to come to the call room. He'd lost his electricity at home sometime this morning. No lights, no clock, no time to stop at the Dinner Bucket for breakfast and coffee and catch up on the latest tidbits of community opinion about the missing baby and the other missing children. If he hadn't happened to wake up and look at his watch, he wouldn't be here yet.

He picked up the scrub pants and shook them to unfold. They remained folded. He gave them another shake and then caught a glimpse of something little and shiny in the material. He held them up to the light.

Someone had stapled the scrubs. There were at least twenty staples in the thin material, as if some angry child had punched the staple head with rhythmic intensity until the machine had run out of ammunition. What sane adult would do something like this?

He threw the worthless bundle back onto the bed and grabbed his jeans again. He didn't have any other scrubs. The hospital agreement was that they would supply uniforms, and his part of the agreement was that he would present himself in a professional demeanor. He would just have to appear unprofessional today, and if he lost this temporary job because of appearance, so much the better. The next time he signed a contract he would check the place a little more thoroughly beforehand. A guided tour of the ER and a handshake with a fast-talking administrative secretary wouldn't fool him again.

Right about now Mrs. Pinkley would be reminding him that he sounded like a whiny little boy. She would be right.

He reached for his belt, and that was when he saw the envelope on the pillow with *Dr. Bower* typed on the front. "Now what?" he muttered as he snatched the envelope and ripped it open.

The memo was from Mr. Amos, the hospital administrator, reminding him that, in the future, he was to go through proper channels before he ordered an ambulance transfer. Lukas tore the page in half and shoved it into the overflowing trash can.

Thick clouds built a rampart against the sun long after daybreak should have touched Knolls Wednesday morning. Those same clouds had brought rain during the night, which froze as soon as it hit the trees, houses, and streets. Ozark winters were notorious for ice storms, because the temperature, like a dark jokester, had a tendency to hover just below thirty-two degrees. The precipitation didn't know whether to fall as snow or rain, so it just froze. That was Mercy's theory, anyway. This morning at the clinic when the phone rang she was too sleepy and preoccupied to come up with a better explanation.

Since no one else had arrived yet, Mercy punched the button for line one and picked up the receiver. "Good morning, Richmond Clinic."

There was a short pause, an exhalation of breath. "Yeah, could I talk to Dr. Richmond?" It was a deep male voice, slurred and hoarse, and it made her uncomfortable before she even recognized the speaker. For a moment she didn't reply.

"Yeah, anybody there?" he asked.

"Yes." Identification came quickly as she recalled the angry voice in the hospital Sunday morning. Still, she wanted him to identify himself. "May I ask who is calling?"

"Uh . . . this is Abner Bell, but if you tell her she won't come to the phone." He sounded hesitant, not angry as he had been Sunday. He took a breath and released it with a burst of wind over the telephone line. "Just ask the doctor if she's heard anything about my wife, okay?"

Mercy didn't even try to keep the curtness from her own reply. "Abner, *this* is Dr. Richmond. I don't understand why you continue to insist that Delphi would be in touch with me, but I have no idea where she is." And he'd be the last person to hear from her if she did. She hoped Delphi was well out of the area, although where would that be? She had no family, which was probably why she'd endured Abner's abuse as long as she had. Mercy could only guess at the circumstances that would drive the poor woman out into the January cold. If that was what happened. There were other possibilities that continued to nag her.

He took two more audible breaths, then said, "I tried callin' the girls at the café, but she ain't showed up for work. She's gotta be somewhere." Today, unlike Sunday, the man sounded more worried than threatening, and his voice was coarse, as if he'd been up all night. "I really miss her, Dr. Mercy. I know we've got some problems, but I know we could work 'em out if she'd just come back and give it another try."

Mercy resisted the tiny thread of compassion that would automatically surface in a situation like this—a young husband searching for his lost wife. This wife needed to stay lost. Mercy remembered the unearthly glitter in Abner's eyes Sunday, the brooding malevolence she'd felt emanating from him, and the anger it had stirred in her. She'd had a taste of that malevolence when her father was stumbling through the darkness of his alcoholism, or when Theo was drunk and angry with her. That kind of antagonism had nearly killed Tedi last spring.

"If somebody there at your office hears from her, could you call me?" Abner asked.

Mercy bit her lip to control her own anger brought on by specters from the past. Like a poisonous snake, Abner needed to be treated with caution. "I haven't heard from her, Abner." She disconnected abruptly, took a deep breath, and went to unlock the clinic.

She paused before she unlocked the door and tried to will away the tension that tightened her breathing and clenched her stomach into a pit of ice as hard as the frozen ground outside. *Lord, please keep Delphi safe, wherever she is.* Mom had taught her to pray the same kind of simple prayer in the past few months, convincing Mercy that when she was busy with patients and didn't have time to plan out a long, elaborate prayer with all the right ingredients, God would listen to her quick one-liners.

She'd become good at those lately. Too good. She rarely took the time for more, except at night when Tedi did her daily Bible readings. Even that was impossible on those nights when Mercy had an emergency call.

Sometimes she felt as if nobody believed she had a right to a private life.

The telephone rang again. It was the first patient cancellation of the day. Mercy expected many more to follow.

———

Midmorning Wednesday Theodore Zimmerman saw the official-looking envelope through the tiny window of his post office box before he stuck the key into the lock. He recognized the medical emblem, and he knew who it was from. He took the envelope out quickly and ripped it open. He shoved the introductory letter to the back of the sheath of papers so he could study the actual lab test results.

HIV . . . negative. He felt weak with relief as he shuffled to the next page. Until he had begun spending more time with Mercy and Tedi, he'd never considered the possibility that his former lifestyle could come back to haunt him—not until he'd considered the very real, very sweet possibility that he might be able to regain his family. That idea had become a dream and now was a concrete goal. Mercy and Tedi would need more time to get used to the idea, but it was one he couldn't stop thinking about. To have his family back . . .

Chlamydia . . . negative. Gonorrhea . . . negative. Herpes . . . negative. Syphilis . . . negative.

"Thank you, God!" he murmured as he closed his eyes and momentarily leaned against the heavy marble table in the quiet post office. For a week now, he'd worried about the possible results of the blood test he'd had in Springfield last Thursday. He had dated a lot of women in the past six years—since before his separation and divorce from Mercy, much to his regret and shame. That lifestyle continued to haunt him, in spite of the reassurances from so many people that he was forgiven by God.

He uncovered the final page, and his attention suddenly caught on the word *positive* like a dart in the center of a red target. He scanned the line and read "hepatitis B," and his fingers weakened and nearly dropped the sheets.

He shuffled back to the letter, which he knew he should have read in the first place. It was merely introductory, with the news that they had attempted to call him and had received no reply. He didn't have an answering machine. He should have given them his work number, but he didn't want anyone to know about the tests. With the instructions to call their office for a consult and an appointment for retesting, the letter ended.

He stuffed everything back into the envelope and rushed from the post office. Retesting. That meant the results could all be a big mistake. A misreading. It was probably nothing.

———

At Herald Hospital ER, there was a knock at the threshold of the open call room door, and Lukas glanced over his shoulder to see Tex McCaffrey—all one hundred eighty pounds of muscle and wayward blond hair—striding in without his invitation. Typical Tex.

"Dr. Bower, got a couple of kids in room two. Mom's worried 'cause they're groggy. Both of 'em are snoring like a zooful of lions and tigers and bears. Want to check them out?"

Moments later he was listening with concern to Angela Jack's story. Her thin face was etched with worry as she held her three-year-old little boy on her lap. His eyes were shut, his head falling against her right shoulder. "I just can't wake them up, Dr. Bower." She darted a glance at her four-year-old little girl, who lay slack on the bed, drooling onto the pillow, her blond curls splayed out around her. "I tried to get them up this morning like usual, and they went right back to bed. Usually they're up running all over the place trying to make me late for work. Something's wrong."

Lukas turned the bell of his stethoscope to the smaller pediatric side and placed it against the little girl's chest. Her breathing was normal. Heart sounded fine. She stirred for a moment, yawned, and burrowed deeper into the pillow.

Tex came through the curtained entrance. "Dr. Bower, there's a man out in the waiting room who cut himself with an X-acto knife." She frowned, leaned over the little girl and studied her face, then shook her head and straightened to look at Lukas. "Wants to know if you'll just look at his cut real quick and see if it needs stitches. That way if he doesn't have to, he won't check in and get billed for it."

"Did you examine it?"

"Yeah, it's not bleeding much and doesn't look too deep, but you're the doctor."

Lukas sighed heavily and shook his head at Tex, feeling again the frustration of government red tape in the form of COBRA. "You know I can't legally go out and lay eyes on him without checking him in."

"He's paying cash."

"What would you do if you were the doctor on this case, Tex?"

"I'd make sure he had an updated tetanus, then tell him to go on home and clean it up and bandage it."

"I trust your judgment."

She blinked at him, smiled, shook her head. "But I'm not the doc. I'm the paramedic."

Lukas wrapped his stethoscope back around his neck and turned to talk with Mrs. Jack. "The children don't have a fever, and to the best of your knowledge they haven't been nauseated? Are there any medications they might have found around your home?"

Mrs. Jack shook her head. "I keep everything up high in the cabinets, and there wasn't anything out of place this morning. I checked."

"They don't have any symptoms besides the fact that they're very sleepy. I'd like to run a couple of tests on—"

Tex put a hand on his shoulder. "Hold it a minute, Dr. Bower. I just remembered something. I saw a kid in here a couple of weeks ago with the same kind of problem, only it was on an evening shift." She put her hands on her hips and bent down to make eye contact with the mother. "Angela, who's baby-sitting for you now?"

The harried mother did not meet Tex's gaze. "Mrs. Ramey down the street from us."

"Ramey!" Tex exclaimed. "That lush!" She straightened from her work. "Dr. Bower, she was in charge when that little girl disappeared from the park the other day."

"Oh, come on, Tex," Angela protested. "She was more upset about what happened than anybody. She's been out looking for the kid all week when she's not baby-sitting."

"Sure she is," Tex said. "She's got to cover her hide because Sandra smelled whisky on her breath when they showed up to search. And furthermore, Dr. Bower, she got fired from the ambulance service six months ago. She was a part-time dispatcher, and she also kept the books, and she was padding the bills. Besides that, she's a lush."

Angela's mouth tightened in a defensive line. "I never smelled alcohol on her breath, and she's cheap."

"Sure she's cheap." Tex's voice deepened with growing annoyance. "She's not licensed, and she's probably keeping ten kids, from babies on up."

"She's . . . she's good with the kids. They like her."

"Do you want them to grow up to be just like her? Doesn't Johnson's pay better than that?" Tex shook her head and crossed her arms over her chest. "How do you think she keeps them corralled? Were your kids groggy when you picked them up after work last night?"

Angela looked down. "I worked late last night at the plant. Had an extra load of chickens we had to process, so the kids were already asleep when I picked them up."

Tex waved her hand in the air in a there-you-go gesture. "Come on, Angela, you've heard the rumors. Everybody has. She gives them Benadryl when they get on her nerves. A friend of mine heard her talking about it at the store one day. What if she—"

"Oh, Tex, just lay off," Angela snapped. "I'm trying to find another sitter, anyway. She said she's quitting soon, leaving town and everything."

The little girl on the bed stirred and grimaced, then her eyes came open halfway. "Mama?"

As Angela turned to her daughter, Tex leaned toward Lukas and lowered her voice. "Dr. Bower, I just betcha if you checked for—"

"Call lab and order a urine triage and an acetaminophen and aspirin level. Then do a quantitative toxicology screen." Lukas glanced at the children again. "If this really was a drug overdose and it happened last night, it's too late to pump their stomachs. We'll want to keep them here and watch them until they recover."

Tex nodded. "I'll bet that's what it is." She jotted down her notes, then turned back to the mother. "I think you should have a little talk with the police, Angela."

"About what? Nobody can prove anything, and I don't have time for all this. The police aren't worth shootin' around here, anyway. They're like little boys playing with guns."

Lukas slipped out of the exam room and casually sauntered toward the desk at the window that looked into the waiting room. Behind him he heard Mrs. Jack complaining to Tex that she was going to lose her job if she missed another day of work, and he wondered about a poultry processing plant that expected the employees to work late into the night, then threatened to fire those same employees when they had to take their sick children to the hospital. Since the plant supplied the majority of jobs in the town of Herald, most people didn't seem inclined to do much about the situation.

Lukas caught sight of a solitary man sitting in the waiting room. His hand was bandaged with gauze, and as Lukas stepped to the check-in window, the man caught sight of him. Lukas nodded to him, and the man nodded back, watching him closely.

It was frustrating that the very laws that had been written to protect emergency patients from greedy hospitals and health-maintenance organizations could now cost that man at least two hundred dollars just to come in here and be told, possibly, that he didn't need stitches. And he was a cash patient. No insurance company or Medicare or Medicaid card would take care of his bill. Unfortunately, without the laws, some emergency rooms in this country could turn away people who were in dire need and could not pay. It was a question of ethics. So what was new?

The man—a carpenter by the appearance of his canvas coveralls and the sawdust sprinkled across his denim shirt—unwrapped the cloth from around his hand. He looked up at Lukas and held his gaze. Even from this distance, Lukas could see that the cut was not bad. It didn't seem to be actively bleeding and wasn't in a spot of high stress.

Lukas smiled and shook his head, then stepped from the window. No need to take half that man's next paycheck for a couple of Steri-

Strips, and Tex could tell him that. Tex could tell him a lot of things. If he'd had a tetanus shot in the past five years, he was off the hook.

———————

Mercy read the results of the chest x-rays and blood tests that had been run on Crystal Hollis this morning. "They look much improved from Sunday," she told Odira. "She's getting good oxygen, almost back to normal."

"All right!" Odira slapped her knees and chuckled, then got choked and started coughing.

Mercy studied the older woman's plump, lined face as it reddened, then gradually returned to a normal color. Odira and Crystal would be here another day, at least. She couldn't release them yet. The nurses had made sure that Odira was taking her new medication, and they had proof that it was working, but Mercy wanted to retain control of them for a few more hours.

Odira had been a patient at Richmond Clinic for the past thirty years—she'd been one of Mercy's father's favorites, in spite of her occasional tendency toward noncompliance. She had willingly transferred her allegiance to a brand-new physician when Mercy joined the practice immediately out of her residency. She had always encouraged her, always shown gratitude. Mercy adored her and wanted her healthy.

With a gentle tap on Crystal's shoulder, Mercy indicated for the child to lean forward. "Okay, honey, you know the routine. Breathe for me."

Crystal obeyed. Her breathing sounded good. Mercy leaned back and studied the little girl's pale face and blue eyes. Crystal stared back, unblinking.

"I'm concerned about something," Mercy said, still holding Crystal's gaze. "Saturday night you were pretty sick. You got sick last fall, too, after you'd been in school a couple of weeks. I know it's impossible to always stay away from the other kids when they're sick, but, Crystal, have you been taking all your medicines every day when you're supposed to take them?"

For a moment the child's gaze broke from Mercy's. She looked down at her hands, folded together across her stomach.

Mercy touched her shoulder. "Crystal? It's important that you tell me."

Crystal shook her head, then looked back up at Mercy. "No, Dr. Mercy."

"How often do you miss taking them?"

Crystal shrugged. "Sometimes I just wait until school's out, and then I take them before I go home. Sometimes I leave 'em in my desk."

Mercy glanced at Odira. "Her teacher is aware of her physical problems, isn't she?"

"Sure is, Dr. Mercy." Odira turned her suddenly sober attention on her great-granddaughter. "Honey, don't you know you've gotta take that stuff? If you don't, you'll get sick again."

Crystal looked down at her folded hands. "Sometimes the teacher forgets to remind me. It's hard to think of it every time, and she gets busy. Sometimes I take it when I'm alone at recess. The other kids say things. . . ."

"They make fun of you?" Mercy prompted.

Crystal nodded. "They call me 'druggie.' "

"And just what does your teacher say about that?" Odira demanded.

"She doesn't hear them."

And of course Crystal would never tattle.

"Well, then, you just make sure you don't hear them, either!" Odira's voice carried at least to the center of the hospital corridor. "When they try to make fun of you, just remember their sickness is in their minds and spirits, not their bodies. You've got pills and that hand-cleaner stuff Dr. Mercy gave you, and I want you to use it. I want you to stay well." Her voice cracked, and she fell silent.

Crystal looked up. "I'm sorry, Gramma. I'll try harder. Don't cry, okay? I'll be good, I promise."

Clarence concentrated on putting one foot in front of the other. At one mile per hour, the pace wasn't that difficult on Ivy's treadmill, but he knew what was coming. Anytime now, she would turn from that computer and watch him for a moment, then tell him to pick the pace up. No matter how fast he was already going, she wanted him to speed up. So he always started slow.

The woman would make Hercules feel like a wimp.

"Clarence, how did you like those oatmeal cookies I baked yesterday?" she called over her shoulder from her position at the computer in the corner of the great room.

He huffed impatiently. Not only did she want him to exercise, she wanted him to talk while he did it. "What oatmeal cookies?"

"The ones you sneaked out of the freezer while I was gone yesterday afternoon. Don't tell me you didn't eat them, because I counted them before I left."

"Those were oatmeal cookies?" Gross. He thought they were leftover meatballs from the soy and turkey loaf she'd forced down him the other night.

She turned in her swivel chair and looked at him. "They'd have been better if you'd waited for them to thaw."

He grimaced. Ivy considered herself a gourmet health food expert, and he was her guinea pig. She would eventually kill him. "They could've used a little more sweetener." Maybe a few nuts, some chocolate chips, some butter and spices and eggs . . .

"I'll experiment some more." She turned back around to her computer screen. "Listen to this column I'm working on for the *Knolls Review*."

"What kind of column?"

"Weight loss. Harvey's moved to New Jersey, and we have a new editor. Murray is everything Harvey wasn't. I don't know how the paper has survived all these years without him."

"So why does he want you to write a column about fat? You've never been fat."

"I've helped you take it off, haven't I? He heard about the weight you've lost these past few months, and he asked me to do a weekly column on healthy cooking and weight management. You're my human experiment." She turned again to look at him. "Do you realize you've lost about a hundred pounds since spring? Just think of all the people who struggle with obesity out there who will now have a hero to turn to, an example of inspiration—"

Clarence snorted. "Me? A hero?"

She turned back to the computer. "Be quiet and listen to this:

'Fatsos Unite! Get out on those sidewalks and—' "

"Wait a minute! Whad'ya mean, 'Fatsos Unite'?" Clarence growled.

"It's the title."

"It's insulting." She was calling him a hero? Just for starving himself nearly to death all these months?

"Fine, I'll change the title. How about, 'Beware the Enemy'?"

"Sounds like you're getting ready to give them some horror story."

"Oh, just listen. 'Get out on those sidewalks and roadsides and sweat off those chocolate-covered cherries and pumpkin pies and fried chicken from three years ago. Excess body weight is your enemy. Every time you take a bite of something that contains enough fat to smother an elephant, think of it as an alien monster invading your—' "

"Yuck! Do you have to make the article sound so gross? If a little kid read your article, they'd think I had some UFO lurking inside me, ready to jump out and grab them."

She issued a heartfelt sigh. "Fine, I'll scrap it and start from scratch. What I'm hoping to do is reveal the dangers of excess weight, convince obese citizens of Knolls that they can't continue to kill themselves, then use you as an example to prove that it can be done."

Clarence thought about that for a moment. "So you think I'm a hero?"

She turned back toward her work station. "Don't get a big head, but everyone in Knolls who reads the paper will learn how to do it themselves. And just wait until they taste my recipe for low-fat cinnamon rolls. And there'll be more next week."

"Cinnamon rolls? Isn't that like giving an alcoholic a drink of 'low-alcohol' booze?"

"No, because nobody needs alcohol to survive. We all need food. No reason what we eat shouldn't taste good." She glanced over her shoulder at him. "If you've got enough energy to argue with me like that, you're not going fast enough. What's your speed?"

Automatically, without arguing, he bumped the control a notch and hid his smile. He was learning how to bluff Ivy. "I read in your Bible the other day that bodily exercise profiteth little."

She stopped typing and turned around again, her dark eyes questioning. "You must have read my King James version. The NIV translates that into 'physical training is of some value, but godliness has value for all things.' " A smile crept across her face. "You've been reading my Bible?"

"Some." He was getting out of breath.

"You must have read quite a bit to get to that part."

Great, here came the can of worms. Now Ivy would start nagging him about going to church with her. He should have never said anything. He could imagine walking into a crowd of holier-than-thou sourpusses who would try hard not to stare at him but couldn't help themselves, who would whisper to each other about what a horrible sinner he was because he didn't have control of his physical appetites. No, church was not a place for him. He was all for God, but church was the last place he wanted to be.

"Would you like a copy of your own?" Ivy asked.

"Of what, your article in the paper?"

"The Bible."

"Nah, yours is fine. I've just been readin' the parts about food and exercise. You know, you've got that place in the back pages that lists all kinds of subjects, then tells you where to find it." He paused and caught his breath. "I thought I'd find some passages that would make you stop ridin' me so hard."

She sighed and switched off the computer. "I can't get any work done with you jabbering at me. I'll be in the library if you need me, but I don't want to hear that machine slow down."

CHAPTER

As soon as Ivy left the room, Clarence turned the speed down on the treadmill. The woman was a slave driver. How would she like it if *she* was forced to carry all this weight? Since she would be at the other end of the house for a while, he might be able to get away with this. He grabbed the stabilizing bar in front of him and settled in for a nice leisurely walk. Too bad there wasn't a television in this part of the room. Watching a sitcom would ease the monotony. Ivy was not a fan of television, and she only had one in her whole house.

If Clarence had the kind of money Ivy did, he'd have a big screen in the kitchen, a big screen in the bedroom, and maybe even a little one in the bath—

"Hi, Clarence."

The sound of the voice startled him so badly he almost walked off the treadmill. His grip tightened on the handle of the machine, and he looked over to find Tedi coming through the door of the great room from the kitchen. She lugged a big notebook under her arm, and she was wearing her new wire-framed glasses, which made her look too serious for a kid. She walked through the exercise area toward the computer on Ivy's desk.

"Hey there, kiddo. No school today?"

She plopped down into the office chair and set the notebook beside the computer, then turned around in the swivel chair to look at him. "Nope. I've got homework, and Grandma said for me to check on you and make sure you were going fast enough. What's your

SILENT PLEDGE · 133

speed?" She swiveled a complete revolution with the chair.

Clarence glowered in the general direction of the library. "Mile an hour."

She caught herself with her hands on the edge of the desk and swung the other way, her long dark brown hair bouncing back and forth when she changed directions. "Grandma says you have to go at least one point five now for the exercise to do you any good." She stopped and looked at Clarence with solemn dark brown eyes. "I'm supposed to tell her if you don't do it."

"Hey! I thought you were the one pal I had left," he protested. Tedi, with her tender, mischievous heart, could usually be depended on to sneak him a snack when Ivy told him he couldn't eat. She always brought something healthy, like fruit or a slice of bread, but it was more than Ivy would give him when she thought he'd overeaten for the day.

Tedi whirled around in the chair three times without stopping. "Sorry, Grandma said if you don't keep exercising, you could gain back the weight you've lost." She stopped and looked at him again. "It's for your own good, Clarence."

He hit the control up three notches. "Can't get away with anything around here anymore," he muttered.

Tedi grinned. "Grandma never lets me get away with anything. Why should she let you?"

"Well, did anybody ever tell you that you're a lot like your mother *and* your grandma?"

"Yes," she said proudly.

"Thought so." He glanced down at the treadmill control as Tedi spun in the chair again. "You're going to unscrew that thing and go flying off in a minute."

Tedi stopped long enough to switch on the computer, then turned back to Clarence. "Do you have any other brothers and sisters besides Darlene?"

"Nope, she's all I've got."

Tedi's gaze grew somber. "Did your parents die?"

"No, they live somewhere else. What kind of homework do you have?" Sometimes this kid had a knack for bringing up subjects he didn't like to talk about. Unfortunately, she could usually tell when he was trying to change the subject.

"A report about the fire for school. Where do your parents live?"

"About a hundred miles away. Ever heard of Poplar Bluff? That's where they live." He and Darlene hadn't been back since they'd escaped that life over twenty years ago. Mom and Dad had been in touch with them, of course, especially back when Clarence and Darlene were both earning enough of an income to buy their own small homes.

He was starting to get out of breath. He was going to slow this baby down, but he couldn't be obvious. "Now, why don't you tell me about your report."

As Tedi finally took the hint and turned to face the computer screen, Clarence reached over and nudged the control the littlest bit so the slow-down wouldn't be noticeable.

Tedi pressed a few keys on the computer, then turned back to him. "Why don't your parents ever come to see you and Darlene? I've never met them."

"Because they don't know where we are now, and we won't tell them, because they're not nice people." They were like the cartoon characters who got dollar signs in their eyes when they thought they could take advantage of someone with money—someone like Ivy. They'd taken advantage of government aid so long they didn't know how to do anything else. The last time they were in contact, they'd "borrowed" three thousand dollars from Darlene and never repaid it.

Sometimes Clarence worried that he was becoming like them, in spite of all he and Darlene had gone through to pull themselves out of that lifestyle. After three months, they still lived with Ivy in this beautiful house, all expenses paid. Being dependent bothered him a lot. He'd tried to talk to Ivy about their living arrangement a couple of times, but she wouldn't listen. She just told him to think of his sister and keep losing weight. That was the most responsible thing he could do right now. He knew, down deep, she was right. He had to concentrate on getting healthy so he wouldn't lose ground. He still had old habits he needed to break.

"Are you still mad at them?" Tedi asked, spinning again with the chair. She was starting to make Clarence motion sick.

"No, I just don't like them."

"But aren't you supposed to forgive them?"

"What, and let them get their hooks in us again? I don't think so."

"My dad almost *killed* me."

"I know. Have you totally forgiven him?"

She sat still for a moment, the expression in her eyes camouflaged by the glint of light against her glasses. "I don't know." Her voice barely rose above the sound of the treadmill motor.

"You see him a lot, don't you?"

"Yeah, but never alone. Mom's always there."

"I thought you liked your dad."

"I do." She leaned back in the chair and watched Clarence for a moment, then pushed the chair around in another revolution, this time slower. "He's fun to be around when he tries."

"But you don't know if you've forgiven him yet?"

"I don't know . . . maybe. Sometimes I worry he'll lose his temper again, the way he used to." She opened her notebook and picked up her ink pen.

Clarence nonchalantly touched the control again. Just a little slower. Not much. He was getting out of breath, even at the easier pace. And he was sweating like a glass of iced tea in an Ozark heat wave. Most people could go twice as fast and two or three times as far on this machine without a problem. When Clarence first started working out, he couldn't even go a quarter of a mile. He was proud of himself now when he could get in a mile a day. Ivy went four and took less time.

"How fast are you going, Clarence?" Tedi asked into the silence.

He refocused on her to find her watching him, arms crossed, with the same look of challenge on her face that he'd often seen on Ivy and Mercy. He scowled. "One point one."

"If you don't turn the speed back up, I'm supposed to tell Grandma."

Tedi would make a great bossy doc someday, just like her mother. "If Ivy thinks a mile an hour is too slow, let *her* carry an extra two hundred pounds around the house for an hour. Do you think you could carry your friend, Abby, around on your shoulders for a mile?"

"No. I might be able to drag her. She sat down on my stomach one day when I was lying down, and I couldn't breathe."

"Then you know how hard it is for me to walk a whole mile on this thing. Your grandma doesn't understand because she's never been fat."

Tedi thought about that a moment, then got up and came across the room. At first Clarence thought she was going to go tell her grandma on him. Instead, she perched on the exercise bike.

"What's . . . obesity feel like?"

"You mean being fat?" He huffed a moment. "You might as well call it what it is. All this weight on me is fat, not muscle, not big bones."

"So how does it feel to be fat? Mom's been griping because she's gaining weight lately, and I keep telling her she's not getting fat."

"You're right. She isn't." Mercy was perfect . . . even if she *was* gaining a little extra weight lately.

A trail of sweat trickled from his forehead to his chin. "Tell you what, Tedi. You get your grandma's big backpack out of her closet and fill it with bricks until it weighs as much as you do. Then wear it for a week without taking it off, not even to sleep, and buckle it tight so you can't breathe very well. Then shave your head and paint your nose red and wear your clothes inside out so people will stare at you and laugh at you wherever you go, but you have to act like that doesn't hurt your feelings."

He didn't usually talk about his weight this much, although it was something that was always on his mind. But Tedi sat there watching him so seriously . . . and she was a good kid. She was easy to talk to. Just like her mother.

He slowed the speed enough to step off the moving mat, then he switched off the machine. "I'm done for now. I'll hit it again later, and Ivy can stand here and watch me if she wants." Sweat was dripping down his forehead and chest and stomach. His clothes were soaked. He'd have to take a bath pretty soon if he didn't want to run everybody out of the house. He was just glad there was a tub he could fit into—Ivy's previous tenant had been her mother, and there were handicap bars to hold on to when he got in and out.

Tedi slipped her feet beneath the straps on the exercise bike pedals and put her hands on the handlebars. "Doesn't it make you mad when people whisper about you?"

He waited a moment to catch his breath. "Yeah." Sometimes people seemed to resent him for being alive and taking up so much space.

"Me too. Some of the kids at school used to make a big deal about my dad going to jail."

He walked slowly around the treadmill to cool down. "Now, *that* makes me mad. Nobody has a right to treat you like that. If I heard anybody saying anything bad about you, I'd sit on 'em."

Tedi laughed. "That's okay. They don't say much anymore. Abby started beating up on them, and she can hit hard. I think everybody needs a best friend."

Clarence sank onto the straight-backed chair Ivy kept in the exercise area. "Yeah."

She pedaled the stationary bike a few times, her face growing serious. "Sometimes I wish Abby could come and stay with me for a while."

He tore off a section of paper towels from a roll beside the chair and dabbed at his face and neck. "Why? You're over here every afternoon, and you know your mom wouldn't let you two stay at your house alone. You two'd be in trouble half the time."

"Yeah, but Abby would protect me."

Clarence dropped the towels in the trash and leaned forward, resting his elbows on his knees. He didn't like the suddenly quiet tone in her voice. "From what, kiddo?"

She looked down and shrugged. "Last night I saw this old brown car drive by our house a few times. One time it even stopped out in front, and I saw a shadow of a guy just sitting there, like he was watching the house for something."

Clarence studied her somber expression, her downcast eyes, and tried to remind himself what a good imagination she had. Sometimes, when she spent the night here, she woke up screaming from nightmares. "Does your mom know?"

"I don't think so. I didn't say anything to her about it."

"It couldn't be your dad, could it?"

"Dad doesn't have a car, and he doesn't smoke, and this man was smoking."

Ivy's voice suddenly reached them from the other room. "Tedi! Are you doing your homework?" Her voice grew louder and she came closer, and she stepped into the great room, her long salt-and-pepper hair falling around her shoulders in untidy strands. She wore old jeans and an oversized sweat shirt. She caught sight of Clarence sitting down and put her hands on her hips. "Did you already finish your exercise?"

"Grandma," Tedi said sternly. "You need to fill your backpack with bricks and carry it around for a while. Then you'll see how hard it is for Clarence."

Lukas rummaged through the top drawer of his desk in the call room in search of the keys to his Jeep. He'd put them in there first thing this morning, as he always did. He shoved that drawer shut and opened the next one down. No key chain with the plastic praying-hands emblem.

So what had he done with them this morning when he came in? Had he still been asleep? He hoped he hadn't locked them in the Jeep again. That was a particularly irritating habit of his that he couldn't seem to outgrow. At least he had the foresight to keep a key in a magnetized case under the wheel well. He would check on it later.

He stepped out and gazed around the empty emergency room. He saw Shirley, the secretary, typing on the computer keyboard. He heard a floor nurse and the x-ray tech gossiping a little too loudly out in the empty waiting room.

" . . . don't even have any leads. It's like the kids just disappeared. This kidnapper's good, but I tell you"—the voice lowered to a whisper—"I still think those bikers have something to do—"

"Shh! If they heard you—"

"I know, I know."

There was a short silence, then a topic change. "Still, there's lots of dirty deeds going on around this place. Just look at Dr. Moss. He'll probably get away with it, too."

"Maybe, maybe not. I'm glad Tex isn't the judge. When it comes to men, that girl's got no brains. She thinks he's wonderful, and nobody can tell her any different." Another silence. "There's no reason for her to hang around Herald since her poor mom died, but all Dr. Moss had to do was smile at her and tell her what a good girl she was, and now she thinks he's an angel."

"More like the devil," the tech said. "Did you know that man never would look me in the eye? He always focused lower. I say if Tex won't listen to us, let her learn the hard way."

"But she seems so innocent, and I don't think Dr. Moss should get away with this—"

"Dr. Bower, would you check these orders?" came a firm voice from behind Lukas.

The gossipers fell silent.

Lukas turned to find Shirley standing there, holding out a clipboard with a sheet of patient test orders.

"I'm not sure I wrote them down right," she explained.

He read them and nodded. "They look good to me."

Shirley thanked him, then lowered her voice. "Don't believe half what you hear around here."

He heard the gossipers wander down the hallway, and he looked up at Shirley. "So what's going on?"

"I guess you know what happened to the doctor you replaced. He was accused of improper conduct with one of our patients. Of course, he swears he didn't do it. Now we have a war on our hands. Most of the staff believe the patient, but Tex and some of the others are mad about his suspension. I'm staying out of the mess."

"I think that's a good idea."

With charting caught up and signed in the medical records department, Lukas had time on his hands. This was an excellent opportunity to call and let Mercy know he was returning for an overnight visit to Knolls tomorrow after work. He needed some things from the house, and he wanted to drop by the hospital to see how the west-wing structure was coming. He also needed to talk to Mrs. Pinkley about hiring ER medical staff.

And he wanted to talk to Mercy. He wanted to hear her voice up close and personal.

He left the secretary instructions to come and get him if a patient arrived. Then he used his calling card to dial from the call room telephone.

"This is Dr. Richmond's office," came a familiar voice over the receiver. But it wasn't familiar enough. He frowned. It wasn't Mercy's secretary.

"Hello?" the voice prompted again. He recognized who it was then.

"Lauren?"

"Yes." There was a very short silence—something rare when one was speaking with Lauren. "Dr. Bower? Is that you?"

"I'm sorry, I was calling—"

"Yeah, you got Dr. Mercy's office, but Loretta and Josie went out to lunch, and Dr. Mercy's doing rounds at the hospital. We've had so many calls, and you know how Dr. Mercy hates to miss anything, so I offered to take my lunch later."

"That's right, you're working there now, aren't you?" Lauren laughed. Her voice had a musical sound that Lukas remembered well from the months he'd worked with her at Knolls Community Hospital.

"It was my idea," she said. "Dr. Mercy was getting killed with the influx of patients. Obviously, without an ER in town, we have a lot higher acuities, and Dr. Mercy tries to see them all. If the rest of the docs in this town were as dedicated as she is, she wouldn't be working so hard. Did you know Odira and Crystal were back in the hospital? Of course, Crystal was the one who got sick, but when you get Crystal, you get Odira for the duration. If parents were as loving as Crystal's great-grandma is, we wouldn't have nearly as many sick kids in this office." She went on to tell about some of the other cases they'd had since he left.

He grinned to himself. Yep, this was Lauren, all right. She and Tex had few things in common, but one could guess they were related. The McCaffrey family had never met a stranger. In other ways, however, Lauren and Tex were as different as a cactus and a kitten.

"So how are things going up there at the lake?" Lauren asked, pausing for breath at last.

"Just trying to settle in. You know how it's always awkward at first." And the awkwardness in Herald seemed destined to outlast his stay here.

"I wouldn't know about that. I've worked in Knolls all my life except when I was training, and that was twelve years ago."

In spite of the disappointment of not talking to Mercy, it was good to hear a familiar, friendly voice from Knolls—or from anywhere.

"Did you hear about our ice storm down here?" Characteristically, she didn't wait for a reply. "I'm sure Dr. Mercy told you. It was a bad one. They're just now chopping out very fast, so I warned her to be extra careful on the ice. Most of the shops and businesses are closed today and the schools are out, but I bet everything will be back to normal before tonight, because it's warming up now. Theodore Zimmerman called this morning to make sure everything was okay here and to see if Mercy made it to work safely. God sure is working wonders with that man. He's not the same person."

Lukas's attention focused on her words. "Oh really? Theo's doing well?"

"He sure is. I see him at church a lot. Hey, how are you and my cousin getting along?"

But what about Theo? Was he still struggling with his alcoholism? Were he and Mercy seeing more of each other? Was he still working at Jack's Printshop and walking everywhere he went? "Tex is a good paramedic." Was Theo dating someone? "Medicine seems to run in your family."

"Yes, it does. We have another cousin who's a nurse in California, and another who's an EMT in Kansas. We've got about thirty first cousins on our fathers' side. Theresa's dad and mine were brothers, and Uncle Fred started this computer software company and moved to Arizona. He made good money—I mean *good* money—and he's tried to help Tex out so she won't have to struggle through her residency, but she won't take it. She can be so self-sufficient."

Lukas sighed quietly and gave up on the subject of Theo. That discussion would have to wait. "You didn't tell me Tex was a resident."

"Don't bring up that subject unless she mentions it first. She's touchy about it. She was about to start her residency when she had to leave to take care of Aunt Beth."

"But she said her mother died six months ago."

"Right, so you're wondering why she's still hanging around Herald. She cleaned out the house and sold it to help pay the medical bills, but then she didn't move on. You know what I think? I think she's afraid she can't do the job."

"She's good. She can do it."

"*You* tell her that." Lauren fell silent for almost half a second. "You might have noticed that Tex is a little on the outspoken side."

A little? "She has that tendency."

"Don't take it to heart. She's always been that way. She gets it from her mother's side."

"Oh really?" Right. And Lauren got it from the air that she breathed.

"And that wouldn't be so bad if it weren't for the way she grew up. Did you know her parents were divorced?"

"No, she didn't say anything about it."

"The divorce happened when she and I were teenagers. Her mother got custody, so I didn't see her very much after that. And then her mother got involved in this really strict religious group, and that wouldn't have been so bad except their pastor was . . . well, not a very nice man. The guy treated Aunt Beth like dirt, told her she was a ruined woman because she was divorced, and that she'd just have to work her way to heaven, and then he gave her plenty of work to keep her busy. The way he treated her mother soured Tex on religion. As soon as she was old enough she quit going to church, and she hasn't been back. She makes fun of me when I try to talk to her about the *real* love of God."

So that's where Tex's resentment was coming from. "I've been warned not to preach to her or invite her to church," Lukas said.

There was an un-Lauren-like pause. "I miss the way things used to be between us. We were pretty close."

"I'm sorry to hear that, Lauren. Maybe she'll come around."

"Yeah, I hope—oops, I've got another line beeping me. I'll tell Dr. Mercy you called. We miss you. Bye!"

"But wait . . . Lauren?"

The line disconnected. Lukas hung up, disappointed. He didn't have time to dwell on it, though, because the call room phone rang as soon as he hung up. An ambulance was three minutes out. A teenager had been hit by a train.

———

Twenty miles an hour seemed almost too fast on this ice-slicked road, and Mercy was glad for the all-wheel-drive feature of her Subaru Forester. She braked delicately and turned into the small parking area in front of the apartment complex where Odira lived. It wasn't until she actually glanced toward the doorway that she saw the bundled-up figure of a man bent over the sidewalk in front of Odira's door.

In his gloved hands he held a shovel, which he used to stab, slowly and methodically, at the salt-sprinkled ice that coated the concrete. A pile of half-inch-thick ice shards were stacked beside the building, out of the way of faltering feet. He wore green coveralls and work boots with ice cleats fastened onto the soles. His head, face, and neck were covered by a ski mask, but Mercy thought she recognized the fastidious placement of each stab of the shovel as he tried to keep from cracking the concrete along with the ice. He looked up, and she saw the cool, clear blue eyes of Theodore Zimmerman.

Last year at this time she would have been tempted to drive the car up onto the concrete and splatter him. Right now she could have hugged him for his thoughtfulness.

She smiled and waved, parking cautiously beside the spot he had cleared. He paused and leaned against his shovel as she got out of her car. She heard the heavy force of his breathing and saw the mist of his breath.

"In through your nose, remember," she cautioned. "Don't want to freezer burn your lungs in this cold, dry air."

He grinned. "Sure thing, Dr. Richmond."

"How did you know Odira needed her walk de-iced?" Mercy asked as she stepped gingerly to the rear passenger door to start carrying in the groceries in the backseat.

"Tedi told me this morning that you were going to try to get Odira and Crystal home today. Let me guess, that food is for Odira and Crystal." He gestured toward the bags, then leaned his shovel against the side of the building and stepped over to help, still breathing heavily.

Mercy handed him a bag. "You talked to Tedi this morning?"

"Yes, well, actually, I called to talk to you, but you were in the shower, running late, according to Tedi."

"I'm always running late. Why aren't you at the printshop?"

"Jack didn't need me until noon because business is slow right now." Theodore turned and led the way to the door. "I thought I'd see if Tedi was out of school today because of the ice. I was hoping to take the two of you out for early lunch, but she already had plans to spend the day with her grandmother."

Mercy could hear the disappointment in his voice. "Don't worry, you're not being snubbed. Tedi has to do a story on the fire last fall, and if her teacher says it's good enough, he's going to try to get it published in the *Knolls Review*. She wants to put the article on the computer at Mom's, so this ice storm was her big break."

Theo brightened a little.

Mercy dug into her coat pocket for the key Odira had given her to the apartment, then transferred her bag of groceries into Theodore's waiting arms. "I want to get Odira stocked up so she won't have to go out on this ice once she gets home. She'd fall and break a leg before she would ask for help." She unlocked the front door and carried her bag inside, then stood aside for Theo. "Put it on the counter, and I'll snoop around and see if I can figure out where everything goes."

He pulled off his ski mask and reached into the paper bag. "How's Lukas doing? I haven't seen him in a while."

"As far as I know he's doing fine. He's up at a small town at the Lake of the Ozarks."

"Oh?"

"Sounds like he'll be there for the next ten weeks or so." Actually, it would now be nine weeks, three days, and six hours, but who was counting? "I don't know if Estelle knows about the contract he signed, because when she finds out, I bet there'll be another explosion at the hospital. We're going to need him here long before his time is up. I wish he were here now."

"I'm sorry, Mercy." Theo continued to empty the bags, his movements methodical. He placed each can carefully on the counter, as if he was deep in thought. "I know you two are . . . good friends. Tedi talks about him all the time."

Mercy offered no response. What could she say?

"Is he even planning to come back here when the ER's finished?" Theo asked.

"He has no choice," Mercy said quickly. "He's under contract." But did he want to? That question had nagged her several times the past few days.

Theo worked another moment in silence, then asked, "Mercy, is Tedi still having her nightmares?"

"Yes. She climbed into bed with me just the other night, but they're growing less frequent." And Tedi no longer wet the bed, as she had done several times in the months after he hit her. Mercy glanced up at Theo and saw the remnants of guilt written across his handsome face.

She knew he still battled the occasional temptation to have a drink. He was honest about it. But when the temptation struck he called someone for prayer. Sometimes he called her. And those times of temptation were becoming less frequent. Was it possible they were all healing from the past?

"Dr. Jordan says spiritual healing is an ongoing process," Theo said as he reached into the next bag and pulled out a box of macaroni and cheese.

"I think he's right." Mercy found where Odira kept the canned food and filled the shelves with her new purchases. Their new pastor, Joseph Jordan, seemed to have a keen understanding of human frailties—to a point. But he was young and inexperienced. What did he know about divorce? What did he know about alcoholism and child abuse and the struggles of a lifetime? He was barely into his thirties and had been raised in a happy Christian family.

"Now, stop wallowing in guilt and get to work," she told Theo. "You have to get to the printshop pretty soon, and I want to get as much help from you in the meantime as I can."

He folded the next empty bag, rested his hands on the edge of the counter for a moment, and took a slow breath. "Mercy . . ." He paused and held his breath, his jaw muscles working in silent testament to his thoughts, then he blurted, "Do you think it would be possible for me to see more of Tedi?"

She couldn't miss the urgency behind the words, and she had to struggle to quiet her own automatic reaction of discomfort.

"I was going to wait a little longer before I talked to you about it," Theo said, "but it's just . . . I just . . ."

"It's a natural request," Mercy said softly. "What father wouldn't want to see his daughter more than twice a week for supervised visits?"

He turned and made eye contact with her then, and the sudden relief in his expression was obvious. "Actually, the supervision's great. Maybe if we had a little more time together . . ." His gaze sobered and grew more searching.

Mercy's discomfort increased, and she stepped away from him. "I'll go get the rest of the groceries. I don't want the frozen vegetables to—"

"No, I'll—"

The sudden, invasive ring of an old-fashioned rotary telephone shot through the room. She found the origin of the sound and answered.

"Dr. Mercy? Thank goodness you're there." It was Lauren. "Your beeper's here at the office, and I couldn't find you at the hospital. We need you."

"Why? What happened?"

"The police found Delphi Bell. They brought her here. Can you hurry over?"

"I'll be right there."

CHAPTER 12

Sixteen-year-old Chase Riddle was in bad shape, but so far he'd been fortunate. The train had smashed into the front of his truck and sent it crashing backward. The fire department had been forced to do an extrication with the jaws of life, which had taken twenty minutes. Considering that it had taken an extra ten minutes for the rescuers to reach him in the first place, and five more to transport, Chase had already lost thirty-five minutes of his golden hour—that precious span of time during which treatment was most beneficial.

Lukas placed a chopper on standby as soon as he saw the patient, who was on a long spine board with C-collar and head blocks. Four-by-four gauze pads barely covered a bloody laceration on Chase's forehead. He opened his eyes at the sound of Lukas's voice, and he knew his name and where he was, but he didn't know the day. Bruises and abrasions covered his upper torso, and he winced when Lukas pressed against his chest and abdomen.

Lukas went to the secretary's desk and ordered stat trauma work-ups with lab and radiology. "Is the chopper on standby?" he asked.

"Better tell Mr. Amos if you're going to ship the patient out," Shirley warned as she picked up a pen to write the orders.

Lukas suppressed a grimace. "I'm not sure yet. Would you please notify him of the possibility? I'm a little busy at the moment. Who's the surgeon on call today? I need him to evaluate our patient."

"That's Dr. Hemmel."

"Just great," Lukas muttered. Hemmel was the one surgeon Lukas would *not* want for a consult. But rules were rules. "Get him here for me." Lukas returned to the trauma room, where Tex had just finished connecting the monitor leads and was starting the second large-bore IV. Chase was wide awake now, his expression alert and anxious where he lay on the table, fully immobilized. His nose and cheeks were scratched and darkening with bruises. Sections of his short, scruffy blond hair were spiked with drying blood.

"My truck, how's my truck? Dad's going to kill me if . . ." He winced. "My chest hurts."

"I already told you, your truck's been canceled," Tex told him.

Lukas bent over him. "Are you having trouble breathing?"

"Some. It really hurts to take a deep breath. Can't you do something?"

"Yes, as soon as we find out how badly you're hurt." Lukas turned to find the x-ray technician pushing her portable machine into the room. "We'll be right outside the door for a moment."

He and Tex stepped into the hallway while the tech did her job.

"I'm worried about him, Dr. Bower," Tex said softly. "He's confused. He keeps asking me if his truck is okay and if his parents are coming. I've told him at least three times that his parents are on their way and that his truck didn't make it."

"How are his vitals?"

"His heart rate is better following the fluids, and his blood pressure is good, but he does seem to be in a lot of pain, so his BP could be elevated for that reason. And guess what?" Tex's blond eyebrows drew together in a deep frown. "I just found out the CT machine's broken. They're working on it now, but it won't be fixed anytime soon."

"Why am I not surprised?" Lukas said. "Now we'll *have* to transfer. He needs a CT."

After they reentered the trauma room, Lukas did a more detailed neurological exam and was even more uneasy. Chase was definitely slow to respond.

The ultrasound tech arrived with her imaging machine, and Lukas stepped out once more to give her room to work. While he waited, he did another quick search for his keys. They were in the top drawer of his call room desk when he pulled it open—just where he had left them first thing this morning.

Was he losing his mind?

There was a sharp rap at the threshold. "Bad news, Dr. Bower." Tex came striding in. "We've got those x-rays."

He turned and followed her out to the viewing screen. "Why is that bad?"

"See for yourself, but it looks like he's got an upper-rib fracture."

"So would you transfer him if you were the doctor?"

"Absolutely."

After Lukas read the x-rays he agreed with Tex. "Shirley," he called to the secretary, "launch that chopper."

———————

Mercy's ice cleats crunched into the quarter-inch of ice that coated the sidewalk in front of the clinic. Two maintenance men from the hospital hacked and shoveled and sprinkled salt around the entrance, and Mercy could have hugged them. That would have been her next job. At this rate, she might actually avoid chopping ice altogether today.

The men nodded to her as she stopped, removed her cleats, and opened the front door to step into the cozy warmth of the waiting room. She was greeted by pretty chatterbox Lauren McCaffrey.

"Oh good, Dr. Mercy, you're here." The perky RN with long blond hair and a permanent smile to go along with her pointed chin stood and held the inner office door open for her. "Delphi's back in exam room two. We've warmed her up and taken her vitals. Josie's with her now. There's a nasty bruise on her face, and she's favoring her right arm. It looks broken or dislocated to me. You'll want to check it out. I'd have done an x-ray, but she needed warming up worse than we needed info on her arm."

"Thanks, Lauren." Mercy still struggled, on occasion, with the stiffness she felt with this nurse, in spite of the fact that she'd been an answer to prayer when the patient load picked up so dramatically in October. Lauren had always displayed a little more than friendly interest in Lukas, and since he had begun doing temporary work elsewhere, she inquired about him often.

"Guess where they found her?" Lauren asked.

Mercy looked at Lauren and waited.

"You know that motor home that's for sale at the east end of town on Highway Z? She had somehow jimmied the lock and was staying there. Of course there's no heat in that thing. She had one of those skinny little mattresses wrapped around her when the police found her. They said she looked nearly frozen solid, but when they got her here she didn't look that bad. They'd received a call from somebody who lives nearby who'd seen someone going in and out, probably to the bathroom or to get something to eat. I can't believe she looks as good as she does, considering the circumstances."

"Okay, I'll go check her."

"Like I said, Josie's with her." Lauren leaned over a chart at her makeshift desk, then looked up before Mercy could get away. "Oh, I almost forgot. Dr. Bower called for you while you were gone. I told him about the ice storm. You know my cousin works up there in the ER at Herald, don't you? Anyway, Dr. Bower and I had a nice chat, and I'm sure he'll get in touch with you later." She leaned forward and lowered her voice, although there was no one near the desk area to hear her. "He sounds lonely, if you ask me. It sure will be nice when we get our own ER up and running. Then he can come back home, and I can go back to working for him and get out of your hair, and everything will be perfect again."

Mercy frowned as she walked away. Apparently she didn't always manage to hide her irritation with Lauren. Perhaps she should start trying harder—and while she was at it, she should try to demonstrate some of her appreciation for Lauren's efficiency and attitude of caring.

In the exam room, Delphi lay curled on her side beneath three layers of blankets, with her back to the door.

"What's her core temperature, Josie?" Mercy asked as she walked around the bed.

"Ninety-two on presentation," Josie said. "Ninety-five a couple of minutes ago. We managed to get some warm tea down her before she clamped her mouth shut and wouldn't take any more." The black-haired nurse with the large gentle eyes looked down at Delphi. "She hasn't said more than five words since she came in."

Delphi's eyes were squeezed tightly shut, and droplets of tears clung to her lashes. A deep purple bruise circled her right eye, and angry red rimmed her cheek. Except for shivering, she didn't move, didn't acknowledge Mercy's presence.

Mercy pulled an exam stool over and perched on it, facing her patient. She reached out and took Delphi's left hand. It was cold.

The woman stiffened and drew away.

Mercy released her. "Okay, Delphi, you need to tell me what happened so we can take care of you." She reached up to smooth some strands of dirty brown hair from Delphi's face. "Where do you hurt?" She kept her voice and her touch feather light, something Delphi had always responded to after an altercation with Abner.

"I know you left him and you've been hiding out," Mercy prompted.

No response.

"Delphi, I need your help. Abner has been looking for you. He came to see me at the hospital, and he's called here."

The tears multiplied and seeped from behind the closed lids. Delphi's pale, frightened face scrunched up as if in pain. Her mouth came open, and a half cry, half sigh of anguish escaped her cracked, dry lips.

"Honey, all that means is that he doesn't know where you are," Mercy quickly reassured her. "And he won't find you through anybody in this office." Her staff was loyal and dedicated to patient confidentiality as much as was possible in a small, gossipy town like Knolls.

"The cops might tell him." Delphi's eyes opened, her nasal voice barely above a whisper. She continued to shiver. "There was people watching when they hauled me out of the motor home."

Mercy knew Delphi had a point. Although most of the people in the Knolls police force knew about Abner—in fact, most of Knolls knew about Abner—it would take only one set of loose lips to betray Delphi.

"Time for a temperature recheck," Josie said brightly as she shut the exam room door and raised the blankets.

Delphi didn't react as Josie worked, but now that her eyes were open, they fixed on Mercy as if to a lifeline. "He hates you."

"Me?" That thought gave Mercy a quick rush of fear, which she firmly dismissed. Abner pretty much hated everybody.

"I told him once that you wanted me to leave him."

That was not news. Abner had already made it clear he blamed

Mercy. "What shape would you be in now if you'd stayed?"

Delphi studied Mercy's expression for a long moment, then her face scrunched up, and tears trickled from her eyes again. "But he knows I'd come here."

"You didn't come here. The police brought you."

"I did come. Saturday night, after . . . I saw lights in here, and I tried to get in. I called out, but nobody came."

"Oh, Delphi," Mercy breathed. It hadn't been a dream. "If that ever happens again, go to the hospital."

"I don't want the abuse to ever happen again. I can't go back to him, Dr. Mercy."

"I'd like to get you out of this clinic as quickly as possible, just in case." Mercy knew the odds were low that Abner would make a move on his wife in a public place, but she hadn't expected him to hunt her down in the hospital and blame her for Delphi's disappearance, either. Still, spouses seldom became abusive in front of witnesses, because then their behavior would legitimize the victim's accusations.

"All right, Delphi, you're warming up just right," the nurse said. "Some of that shivering's stopped. Dr. Mercy, the owners of the RV didn't press charges, and the police aren't going to come back unless you call for some reason. . . . You know—" Josie stepped to the window and peeked out between the slats of the shades—"like in case you want police protection or something."

"Oh sure, and then they'd park their cars out in the driveway and light a beacon to lead Abner straight here?"

"Didn't think you'd go for that," Josie said. "But my van's parked out back with chains on the tires. All we'd have to do to get Delphi out of here is put her in the back of the van and drive away, in case Abner's out there watching somewhere."

Mercy couldn't resist a teasing grin at her nurse. "You've been watching too many *Mission: Impossible* reruns."

"Not me. That's my hubby." Josie gestured to the patient. "Delphi didn't say anything, but there's obviously a problem with her right elbow. It won't bend past forty-five degrees."

Mercy handed Delphi a tissue and watched as the woman stuck her left hand out from beneath the blankets and awkwardly used it to wipe her face and nose—awkward, because she was lying on her left side. "I hurt my right elbow when I fell," Delphi said.

"Or Abner pushed you?" Mercy lifted the blankets enough to get a look at the arm.

"Tripped me. It's how I hit my face." She winced as Mercy examined her.

There was a deformity at the elbow, but the circulation to the rest of the arm didn't look bad. Her fingers were pink and the pulses were good.

"Okay, Josie," Mercy said, "set her up for x-rays. We may give Delphi a side trip to the hospital for a couple of days."

"No!" Delphi exclaimed. "You said he's already gone lookin' for me there. He knows I got hurt, and if he hears they found me, he'll be back there."

"He won't look in ObGyn." Mercy reached beneath the blankets and pressed the bell of her stethoscope against Delphi's chest. The lungs and heart sounded good. "There aren't any patients, so nobody but the nurse and I will see you. Now let's get those x-rays."

———

"Dr. Bower, did we not have a similar conversation just recently?" came Amos's peevish voice over the line.

"Yes, we did," Lukas said. "And I just received my patient's films. He has three broken ribs, including an upper-rib fracture. We need a CT scan, but our machine is broken. As the patient's advocate, my responsibility is to get him the best possible care."

There was a long pause, during which Lukas heard Chase's parents enter the department and rush to the trauma room.

"Please request an examination from our surgeon on call," Amos said at last. "We will do as he says."

Lukas hung up, relieved. Dr. Hemmel was with Chase now. He must see the necessity for a transfer. Everything would be okay.

———

"Buck? That you?" Clarence Knight leaned against Ivy's kitchen counter and held the telephone to his ear. He heard men talking and laughing in the background of the fire station, but he recognized Buck's voice over the telephone.

"Yeah, it's me."

154 · HANNAH ALEXANDER

"Clarence here. I called to see how Kendra's doing."

"She gets out Thursday morning."

"All right! Then she's doing better?"

Buck sighed and lowered his voice. "I don't know, Clarence. They've got her on all these high-powered drugs, and she sounds like she's stoned out of her mind when I call. Her psychiatrist says she doesn't seem suicidal, but . . ." He sighed again. "I just don't know."

Clarence didn't know what else to say. He'd been looking through this book of Bible verses Ivy kept in the silverware drawer, but he couldn't find any scriptures about suicide. "Well, pal, hang in there. If you want to . . . talk or anything, you know where to find me." But why would he need to do that? He had all those buddies at the station he could talk to. Buck had lots of friends.

"What if she does something like this again?" Buck asked suddenly. "I almost didn't catch her in time."

"Well, I guess something—or Someone—decided to let you know so you could stop her. Maybe that's what'll happen next time, too."

"Why would it? God doesn't know us any better than He knows anybody else in the world, and people are always dying, killing themselves, or killing other people." The frustration wafted heavily through Buck's voice. "I don't know."

Clarence waited. Sometimes, when a guy wanted to talk about something, people could chatter too much to fill the silence, and he could lose his gumption.

"She hates me, Clarence," Buck continued at last. "I've driven up there every day since Sunday, and she won't let me touch her, and if I get too close she jerks away. You don't know how it hurts a guy for his wife to do that."

Buck was right—Clarence didn't know. He had never been married. Even before he got fat, his loud mouth and gruff talk seemed to scare women off before he had a chance to ask them out.

"You've gotta give her lots of time," Clarence finally said. "She doesn't really know what she's doin' right now. She can't see it. Trust me on this. I've been there."

"I don't have any choice. I love her." There was a short silence, then, "Clarence, do you really think God even cares what's going on down here?"

That was a good question—one Clarence used to laugh at. Now he knew better. "Yeah. You know, Ivy said something at the dinner table the other night about God. Sounded pretty good to me. It went something like, 'If you want to find God, you just gotta look.' That's not the exact words, but I think it's close. Didn't make a lot of sense to me at the time, but I don't think He's playing hide-and-seek with us. I think it means if you pray lookin' for God, and not just for your own selfish reasons, He'll be willing to listen to your prayer. So maybe if I pray for you and Kendra instead of myself, then I'm not being selfish, so He'll hear me." And even as he talked about praying, he felt the impact of the words. He was talking about God, here, the One who created the whole planet. "Don't worry, Buck, I think even if we don't know God very well, He knows us."

There was silence, then a masculine, embarrassed throat clearing. "Nobody ever put things the way you do, Clarence. I've got to go. The chief is looking for me. Thanks."

After he hung up, Clarence felt as if he'd lost another ten pounds. He felt the truth of the words he'd spoken to Buck. Somehow, these past few days, as he'd awkwardly reached out to help some people, he felt that God was touching him . . . maybe even talking to him through the silence. In spite of all the struggles with his body, the aches and disappointments and embarrassments, there was some kind of extra energy that ran through him. He didn't want that to end.

Part of him still said he was being stupid trying to talk to Someone he couldn't even see, but that voice was growing more distant all the time. More often he felt like reaching out to other people. So far he'd found that he only had to make that first step and offer to help, and people had actually accepted him.

Clarence had never been shy. Antisocial, but never shy. The poverty in which he and Darlene had grown up—with him and Darlene wearing old hand-me-downs while their parents wore nice clothing bought by the taxpayers—had filled him with resentment from his first memories. He'd watched how the other kids' taunting and teasing in school cut Darlene so deeply she retreated behind a wall of shame and shyness. For Clarence it was a wall of anger. The same anger that made him study to make good grades in school, enough to earn a scholarship to the university in Cape Girardeau. But he wouldn't leave Darlene behind, so he didn't go.

Instead, he'd wrangled and manipulated and worked his way through mechanic school nearby. He could build tractor-trailer rigs from the rubber to the roof, and that knowledge had been his and Darlene's escape.

"You look like a man with something on his mind."

Ivy's voice from across the kitchen startled him. He looked over to find her wearing her old blue sweat suit and running shoes, her streaked hair drawn back in a braid.

"How about a trip to the health club?" she asked. "You could use a change of scenery." She stepped to a cabinet above the sink and pulled out one of the water bottles she always took with her. "I can take a guest with me once a week."

Clarence snorted. "They'd make you pay extra for me. Thanks, but I'll stick to the treadmill. It doesn't gasp and stare when I walk into the room."

She unscrewed the lid from a bottle and filled it with tap water. "Suit yourself. If you want to hide out until you've lost two hundred more pounds, be a hermit. I'd think you'd be sick of Darlene and me after a while."

"Never. You know what they need in Knolls? A fatso club for people who are at least fifty percent above their suggested retail weight when they join. They'd have to build the place with a concrete foundation. You could be the drill sergeant."

She took a swallow of water. "Why don't you do it yourself, Clarence?" She put the bottle down and looked at him, her sharp gaze serious, her dark, straight brows drawn together.

He thought about her words for a minute. Was that something he should do? He could help others who were going through the same thing he had. He could be living, walking proof that there was hope. He could stick "before" and "after" pictures on a bulletin board. Ugh.

"Nah, I wouldn't want to limit myself to just fat people. There's lots of others out there who are hurting, you . . . know." He hadn't meant to speak his thoughts out loud.

Ivy stood still and silent for a moment, as if digesting what he'd just said. "What exactly did you have in mind, Clarence?"

"Nothing, really."

To his surprise, she didn't press, but when he finally found the guts to look at her, he saw a gentle smile playing across her face and softening her eyes.

"The invitation's there, whenever you want to join me." She turned to leave.

———

Dr. Hemmel, a stout, broad-shouldered man in his midfifties, faced Lukas and the Riddles outside the trauma room curtain. "I don't think we have too much to worry about," he said comfortably, patting Mrs. Riddle on the shoulder. "We'll just admit him here over-night and keep a close eye on him. The ultrasound looks okay, and the rectal exam was negative for blood, and his lab counts are normal, so there isn't any evidence of blood leaking anywhere. I don't think we need to get all excited over a bellyache and a few cracked ribs. Sixteen-year-old boys are notoriously tough."

Lukas could not believe what he was hearing. A normal lab he-moglobin result meant little in early blood loss, and surely he knew the significance of an upper-rib fracture. "Um, excuse me, Dr. Hem-mel, we do have a chopper on the way."

Hemmel shrugged. "Cancel it. No need to make the Riddles travel all the way to Jefferson City." He looked back at the parents. "We'll give him a CT scan to be sure. I've given him Demerol for pain, and—"

"Are you sure about that?" Lukas interrupted as he watched the monitor at the head of Chase's exam bed.

Hemmel turned back to him, showing the first signs of irritability. "About what? The Demerol?"

Lukas cringed. He was questioning a colleague's judgment again. With a murmured excuse to the parents, he gestured for Dr. Hemmel to accompany him into an empty exam room. Second-guessing an-other physician did not make him a popular man, especially in front of an audience.

When they were out of earshot, he cleared his throat and turned back to the surgeon. "Dr. Hemmel, are you aware that our CT is broken? I specifically need a CT of Chase's abdomen, pelvis, and head before I will feel comfortable watching him."

Hemmel's expression hardened. "Anything else?"

"Yes, his heart rate is still elevated, and it should have dropped when he received the IV Demerol. And despite the fluid boluses, his blood pressure is dropping. He also needs an angiogram of his chest, which we definitely do not have here. Something else is going on."

"So why did you bother to call me?" Hemmel snapped.

"Because I need a surgeon to rule out the need for immediate surgery. I didn't know I needed to transfer until after I spoke with you."

"And I just told you I disagreed with the transfer."

Lukas was reminded of another grumpy, narrow-minded, antagonistic doctor he'd recently crossed. He was sick of the politics and the ego stroking. "So you agree he doesn't need immediate surgery?"

Dark color flushed across Hemmel's neck and face. He turned and strode out of the room—and out of the ER—without another word.

Lukas returned to the trauma room and came to a stop in front of Chase's parents. "I'm sorry, Mr. and Mrs. Riddle, but I'm concerned about your son. He has multiple fractures, involuntary guarding of his abdomen, and abnormal vital signs, which to me means internal injury until proven otherwise."

"But Dr. Hemmel said the ultrasound didn't show any bleeding," Mr. Riddle argued.

"I know, but an ultrasound isn't as reliable as a CT, and our CT scanner is broken. Chase needs a CT of his head to rule out any bleeding. He isn't acting right. He's confused and slow to respond."

"But surely the Demerol would do that," Mrs. Riddle said.

"He was acting this way before he received the Demerol," Lukas told her. As he spoke the last few words, he heard the unmistakable sound of helicopter blades beating the air on approach. The flight attendants didn't need Mr. Amos's permission to transfer Chase. They weren't owned by the hospital. He could make this call, and he chose to do so.

"Mr. and Mrs. Riddle, your son has an upper-rib fracture. It takes a tremendous amount of force to break an upper rib. Over one-third of patients with that kind of damage die from associated injuries, such as tears of the great vessels."

Mrs. Riddle gasped.

"I recommend we send Chase to a Class II trauma center as soon as possible to ensure his safety." He received permission and prepared for transfer.

———————

Delphi's elbow slipped into place with a satisfying click, and Mercy nodded to Josie. There had been no fractures, but the dislocation was causing Delphi a lot of pain—or had been until Mercy gave her generous doses of Ativan and Demerol. Now the young woman leaned against Mercy's side like a trusting child.

"Good job, Josie." Mercy once more checked the pulses in the arm to make sure they were good. "Now I want a repeat x-ray and then do a splint and a sling. Delphi, I have some friends I want you to meet, but they're out of town right now." She helped Delphi from the table and into the waiting wheelchair so they could take her back into the x-ray room. "Do you remember hearing about that missionary couple who were hit by a car down by the courthouse last September?"

Delphi frowned up at her, eyes slightly glazed from the effects of the drug. "I think so."

"Alma, the wife, lost her leg because of the accident, and they couldn't return to their mission in Mexico. They set up a Crosslines here in Knolls." Mercy realized the futility of trying to explain this to her. With the Ativan, she wasn't likely to remember anything. Still, she needed continued reassurance.

"Crosslines?"

"It's kind of like the Salvation Army, except this service is locally run and operated. Many area churches help support it. Arthur and Alma have connections all over the state, and they can set you up with a new place to live, a new job far away from here." They reached the x-ray room, and Josie reached down with Mercy to help Delphi to her feet.

"How far away?" Delphi asked.

"As far as we think you need to go to get away from Abner." Mercy helped Josie with the follow-up x-ray, then eased Delphi back down into the chair and wheeled her back to the exam room.

"I'd be . . . alone?" Delphi asked moments later.

"No, they wouldn't leave you there alone." Mercy reached for an arm splint and a sling. "As I said, they have friends all over. You would have someone to help you until you were able to make it on your own. Right now, though, Arthur and Alma are in Springfield getting her leg fitted for a prosthesis. As soon as they return I'll introduce you." She placed the splinting materials on the counter and reached down to help Delphi up once more to the table. She felt the young woman trembling, and she reached for one of the blankets. "Why didn't you tell me you were cold again—" And then she saw that Delphi was crying. Her body shook with sobs, her face contorted in misery.

"Dr. Mercy, I'm so scared. What's going to happen to me?"

At the sudden, desolate fear in Delphi's eyes, Mercy sank down to her knees and reached up to frame Delphi's face in her hands. "Honey, look at me." She waited until the woman's eyes opened and focused on her. "I'm not going to let Abner close to you. We're going to get you out of here, and you won't be alone. I'll stake my life on that."

"Hey, I talked to your cousin about an hour ago," Lukas said as he and Tex scrubbed side by side at the sink. They had just treated and released two children with the flu.

"Which one? Seems like I've got about a hundred."

"Lauren, the one who got me into this mess."

Tex snorted a quick burst of laughter. "She's good at that. She thinks she's got the answer to everybody's problems, and she's not afraid to tell you about it whether you want her to or not. For her, everything's wrapped up in church." She rinsed her hands and dried them.

"I don't think that's quite her point." He accepted the paper towels Tex handed him. "Lauren is very serious about her walk with Christ."

Tex shrugged. "Yeah, yeah. Whatever. Hey, if we get out of here before midnight tonight, how about I fix you a decent meal for once? It'll make up for Monster tipping over your trash the other day, and I'm tired of cooking for one."

"Thanks for the offer, but—"

"I won't poison you. I'll even give you the leftovers. You can freeze 'em for later." She watched him a moment, then spread her hands dramatically. "Don't worry, Dr. Bower, I'm not hitting on you. You're not my type. I don't go for Christians, but I do feel sorry for them every once in a while. I'll even go to all the trouble to haul the food next door to your place."

He had to admit, the idea of a freshly cooked meal did sound appealing. But could Tex really cook? "What kind of meal?"

"Spaghetti with meat sauce, salad, and some kind of ice cream dessert. I'll even throw in French bread."

He couldn't help wondering what Mercy might say. "Low fat?"

"I'll pour the grease off the hamburger, then soak up the extra."

Lukas loved spaghetti. He smiled at the memory of the last time he and Mercy had eaten at Antonio's.

Tex punched him on the shoulder. "It's a deal. I cook, you clean up."

CHAPTER 13

As Lukas walked across the unlit hospital parking lot, he caught sight of an eerie glow near where he'd parked his Jeep this morning. As he drew closer he realized it *was* the Jeep. The overhead light was on.

Just great. Was the door ajar? Had the battery run down? He was sure he'd locked it. Here in Herald he always locked his doors.

But when he reached the Jeep he discovered the door was not locked—it wasn't even latched. He jumped in, tossed his bag in the passenger seat, and anxiously stuck the key into the ignition. The engine grumbled and fell silent, then grumbled again. Finally the motor muttered into life and settled into a steady cadence of power. Relieved, Lukas closed the door and gripped the steering wheel.

His fingers landed in ice-cold, squishy goo. He jerked back with a yelp, and the goo stayed with him, stringing across the distance from the steering wheel to his lap. For a moment he sat stunned. And then he raised a hand and sniffed. No smell. He touched the goo and rubbed his fingers together. Surgical jelly. Someone was having a lot of fun. He sure wasn't.

———

The words that Mercy's pastor, Dr. Joseph Jordan, read from the New Testament floated through the warm classroom in the basement of Covenant Baptist Church Wednesday night. Mercy tried to concentrate on them, even though she didn't feel they pertained to her.

" 'A wife must not separate from her husband. But if she does, she must remain unmarried or else be reconciled to her husband. And a husband must not divorce his wife.' "

She tried not to yawn, but it lifted and carried her on a wave of lethargy. No, the reading had nothing to do with her. Her ex-husband had divorced her years ago so he could enjoy his affairs without any interruptions from her. Interestingly, she had spied that same ex-husband sitting at the front of the crowd of thirty or so people scrunched into the classroom built, surely, for no more than twenty.

She yawned again and wished she hadn't come. The Bible study was not boring—far from it. She had been enjoying this study of Paul's letter to the Corinthians, though some of the discussion escaped her. Most of the people in this class had been reading the Bible all their lives, while she'd had only the last three months to catch up. To further muddle her understanding, the past few nights of broken sleep continued to linger. Even the best speaker in the world lost his appeal when her brain felt like a leaky water balloon.

" 'And if a woman has a husband who is not a believer . . .' "

Her eyelids grew so heavy she decided to rest them for a moment. . . . Oh yes, the eye strain could wear a person down. Peace and warmth settled around her like the soft, fluffy comforter on her queen-sized bed at home. . . . It felt so good to relax for just a few moments, to forget about the pressures that were wearing her down at work, to stop worrying about whether Mrs. Robinson's osteoporosis would get worse . . . to stop second-guessing herself about the way she was planning to handle Crystal Hollis and her great-grandmother, Odira Bagby. . . .

At eight-fifteen Lukas gave up on a home-cooked meal from Tex and walked into the kitchen at the urging of his growling stomach. He had some apples in the fridge, and some bread and lunch meat in the tiny freezer section, along with the Healthy Choice frozen dinners. He was reaching for an apple when a loud knock sounded at the front door.

Okay, so she was late. Tex never did anything predictably. The knock sounded again, this time more insistent, and he rushed through the apartment. She was probably carrying a bag of sandwiches from the hospital vending machine in spite of her promise to cook. He had difficulty imagining Tex in a domestic setting.

He unlocked the door and pulled it open, and his breath caught. A tall stranger stood there with a large shopping bag in her arms. She wore a short black dress that hugged a generously proportioned shape and dipped at the neckline, and a soft cloth coat covered her arms and shoulders. Her blond hair curved around her face and over her forehead in gentle waves, and green eyes looked out at him from the depths of an artistic makeup job.

Then she spoke. "Well, are you going to stand there staring all night, or are you going to let me get to the kitchen with this stuff?" She shook her head, rolled her eyes, and barged past him. "It's cold out here."

Lukas stepped out of her way. "Sorry." Why was she all dressed up? Did she think this was a date? It wasn't. Tex was just a neighbor sharing dinner, trying to make him feel at home in a town that had apparently never seen a welcome mat. If she had any other ideas—

"Tonight I'm Theresa," she announced as she marched across the hardwood floor of the living room in her high heels.

Tex wearing heels? And hose? Was this the same woman who'd tracked mud into his apartment a couple of days ago?

"It's what Dr. Moss calls me," she said.

Lukas followed. "Dr. Moss? What does he have—"

"He'll be here any minute." She stepped into the kitchen and dumped the bag onto the counter.

"What do you mean he'll be *here*?" Lukas sputtered.

"Yeah, sorry I didn't warn you. He's going to have dinner with us tonight. I couldn't resist. He called and asked me out tonight after I'd already promised to cook for you. Did you know he has a family practice at Osage Beach?" She reached out and nudged Lukas's arm for emphasis. "*And* did you know he's the one who delivered Marla Moore's baby last week? You know, the one they haven't found yet?"

"*He* delivered Jerod?"

She slipped off her coat and handed it to Lukas. "Sure did. You do have a closet somewhere, don't you? Or you can throw this on your bed. Just remember this piece of wool set me back eighty dollars. How do you like the dress? Got it on sale, but don't tell anybody." She held her arms out and turned around. "What do you think?"

"You look great, Tex. Do you mean to tell me you're interested in a man who—"

"Theresa! Don't forget tonight my name's Theresa." She turned back toward the counter and pulled out a head of lettuce and some tomatoes. "And the gossipers don't know what they're talking about. A man stands up for his ethics—which is more than I can say about a lot of people around here—and the whole staff can't wait to bad-mouth him behind his back. Doesn't that beat all? The guy has some backbone and won't let Mr. Amos manipulate him, and some female patient gets him alone for five minutes and accuses him of making a sexual advance."

"How exactly did Mr. Amos try to manipulate him?"

"The nurses have standing orders from Mr. Amos to delay treatment of any patient with Medicaid or without insurance who presents without a life-threatening injury or illness."

"How do they delay treatment?"

She shrugged and tore the head of lettuce into pieces. "They leave the patient out in the waiting room until they get tired of waiting and go somewhere else. Don't look at me like that, Dr. Bower. I ignore Amos. I always have. Anyway, three weeks ago Hershel had an empty ER but saw someone waiting. When he asked the nurse to bring them back, she refused. So he took care of that patient without the aid of a nurse and wrote her up for insubordination."

"Were you there? Did you see it happen?"

"Nope. Didn't need to. A week later some floozy came into the ER, and that same nurse refused to stay in the exam room with them. The floozy cried abuse, and he didn't have a witness." Tex shrugged. "Mr. Amos had an instant excuse to suspend Hershel, and Hershel's being investigated by the licensing board, so he's got legal fees on his hands. If you ask me, that floozy's on somebody's payroll."

In a cloud of instant depression, Lukas went to put the coat in the closet. Once again, he couldn't escape the fact that greedy, unethical people seemed to lurk in every corner of the world. He knew they weren't just in the medical community, but since that was the realm of most of his experience, he tended toward paranoia on the subject. He'd been shocked when he was in med school by the abundance of information with which medical students were inundated and were supposed to input into their brains. He was even more amazed by the temptations to cut corners, both at the university and in med school. He supposed he should be grateful that such a high percentage of his classmates resisted those temptations. Their patients should be grateful, too. Were they still resisting, or was the pressure of managed care and dwindling finances corrupting more and more people?

As he returned to the kitchen he realized the shallowness of the question. Typical for him, he was labeling people again. In this world of situation ethics, it was sometimes difficult to draw a straight line. For instance, hadn't he just recently sidestepped the rules by quietly checking the injury on that man in the waiting room without making him pay? And in doing so, no matter the sentiment, wasn't he as guilty of breaking the rules as Mr. Amos? In fact, Mr. Amos would most likely have approved. The man had no insurance. Cash patients were notorious for not paying their ER bills—another instance of a few unethical individuals giving the whole group a bad rep.

At the counter, Tex was pulling a package of noodles and some hamburger meat out of the grocery bag.

"Anything I can do to help?" Lukas asked.

"You could slice the loaf of French bread and stick it in the oven." She opened both packages and plunged her hands into the hamburger. "I just washed before I came over, so don't worry, my hands are clean. You've got a pot and a skillet, haven't you? If not I'll get mine."

Lukas glanced down at the cupboards beneath the counter. The apartment had come furnished, but—

She raised her arm to scratch her nose with her arm and left a streak of flesh-colored makeup on the black material. "Well? Pot and skillet?"

He shrugged and bent down to look. Yep, they were there, a little banged up and abused. The nonstick coating had been rubbed away in several places, but they looked usable. He pulled them out and held them up.

She frowned at him. "You don't cook at all, do you?"

"I barbecued hamburgers last fall and set off all the smoke alarms in my house." That was the night Mercy had opened a cabinet door and screamed at the sight of a stuffed rattlesnake.

"Fine," Tex said. "You entertain the guests while I chop the veggies and do the cooking. I hope you have a paring knife, or even a butcher knife. Anything besides a steak—"

"*Guests?*" Lukas prompted. "There's going to be more than one—"

"Dr. Bower, please don't mess this up for me." She crumbled the meat into the skillet. "Where's that knife? You do have a knife, don't you?"

Lukas felt as if he'd been sideswiped by a freight train—an increasingly irritating freight train. He jerked open three drawers before he found a knife. He pulled it out and slapped it onto the counter. "Who else is coming tonight?"

She started to wash her hands at the sink. "Soap? Come on, Dr. Bower, you've got to have soap somewhere. And do you have paper towels? I don't want to get this grease all over—"

"Tex, you're avoiding the question. What are you planning, a full-blown party?"

She left the water running, hands dripping. Her front teeth dug into her lower lip with nervous energy as she gazed down at him in sudden, subdued silence.

"How many are coming?" he asked.

"Only two." Her voice sounded suddenly meek.

He took pity on her and pulled out the drawer with the roll of paper towels. He unwrapped the package and tore off several sheets for her. "Do you think you could call me Lukas tonight? Who besides Dr. Moss is coming?"

"His sister."

Lukas suppressed a gasp. "His *sister?*" Oh no. She was setting him up. "So this is, like, a double date or something?"

She wiped her hands and turned pleading eyes on him from her lofty height. "It's just for dinner. You'll have a lot to talk about. Nancy's thirty-four, just a couple of years older than me, and she's really sad right now. She's recently been divorced, and she's still struggling with the loss. You have such a compassionate nature, I thought the two of you might hit it off."

"But, Tex, I'm not interes—"

"Theresa." The door knocker sounded through the small apartment, and Tex froze, eyes still pleading. "Would you get that? You don't have to kiss her or anything, Dr. Bower—"

"It's Lukas—"

"Just let her talk. She needs to talk. Be nice to her. . . ."

The knocker sounded again, and Lukas went to answer the door. Okay, he could do this. He would think of tonight as a counseling session.

———

Someone jostled Mercy from the left, and a woman's voice floated over her in apology. Opening her eyes took all her effort, but she finally managed. She looked up to see people gathering their books and coats and purses. She heard the rustle of feet and the increased murmur of voices and the clatter of folding chairs being replaced in their compact stacks along the far wall. She'd missed the lesson and the prayer afterward. She'd fallen asleep.

She cast guilty glances at the ladies who had been sitting beside her. Had she snored? They weren't glaring at her. They weren't even looking at her. They were laughing and talking with others around them. Why was she able to fall asleep here in a crowded room, but she couldn't sleep at home without her trusty pill?

She stifled a yawn and reached for her own coat. She needed sleep. Tedi would just have to understand the early bedtime tonight.

Someone stepped up beside her and touched her on the shoulder, and she turned to see Lauren smiling down at her, blond hair cascading around her face and shoulders, green eyes friendly and alert. Disgustingly alert.

"Hi, Dr. Mercy. Can you believe the crowd? You'd think the ice storm would keep everyone away. I wondered if you'd be up for it tonight, after yawning at work all afternoon. You really should give yourself a break and get more sleep tonight." She wore faded jeans and knee boots and a gray SMSU sweatshirt. She could have passed for twenty.

"Thanks for the advice," Mercy said dryly. "I'll try." It wasn't as if she *wanted* to roam the house half the night. It wasn't as if she enjoyed staring at the ceiling of her bedroom until the early-morning hours.

Without waiting for an invitation, Lauren pulled a chair over and sat down next to Mercy. "What do you think of Dr. Jordan—oops, excuse me, Joseph. He likes to be called Joseph. He really knows his material, doesn't he? I could listen to him all night. I even learned something from tonight's lesson, even though . . . well . . . since I've never been divorced. . . . But Joseph explains how relationships go so much deeper than just the rules and regulations, all the way to the relationship between Christ and His church. I feel like I'm learning about the heart of God and discovering some of the reasoning behind the legalism, you know?" She leaned forward and rested her elbows on her knees, and her long shining hair fell forward like a curtain. "I mean, Joseph's right. Who better than the natural parents to raise the children? I just don't know if I could do it. Forgiving would be hard enough, after what you and Tedi went through, but you seem to have already done that," Lauren said as she shoved some strands of her hair back and tucked them behind her ear.

Mercy found herself wondering why this extremely attractive woman had never been married. Men were obviously drawn to her blond innocence, and the patients loved her. And then Lauren's words registered. Mercy sat up straighter in her chair. "Lauren, what are you talking about?" The words came out more sharply than she'd intended.

"I'm sorry. I wasn't implying anything, Dr. Mercy. I was just saying it would be hard if you made the decision to reconcile."

Mercy thought back to the few verses she'd actually heard tonight, and she recalled, dimly, the contents of the study. "*Reconcile?* You're surely not saying I should *remarry Theo*!" She heard the freeze-over of her own voice as she spoke. Obviously, so did Lauren.

"Not me, no, I wouldn't tell you that," Lauren said quickly. "I'm just saying reconciliation would be hard to do . . . if you did. Since you and Theo are both Christians now . . . and Tedi . . ." Her cheeks turned a healthy pink, and she buried her face in her hands. "Oh, there I go again. Me and my big mouth. I'm not saying you and Theodore should get married again, and I'm not sure that's what the pastor was saying, either. It's none of my business, I was—"

"You're right, it's nobody's business." Mercy was suddenly wide awake, and her indignation increased with her level of consciousness. "How could *anyone* expect Tedi and me to return to a marriage like that?"

Lauren looked even more miserable. "But it wouldn't—"

Mercy waved Lauren's words away. "Even if I were masochistic enough to do that to myself, I'd never do it to Tedi. Never!" She was shocked by the sudden revulsion she felt.

Lauren sat back and lowered her hands to her lap. "But that's just the point," she said softly. "If you got back together, your marriage wouldn't be the same. Remember, when you come to Christ, all things are new, and you and Theo have both come to Christ. Your relationship is new."

"Then why would God expect me to return to the *old marriage*?"

Lauren started to speak again, and then her attention turned to someone behind Mercy. "Oh boy," she murmured. "Dr. Mercy, did you know Theo was here? He's coming this way."

Mercy caught her breath and felt a shock of discovery all the way through her body before she even turned around. The anger and revulsion that had risen within her swirled into a confusion of frustration and disappointment. She was tired, irritable, and totally unprepared for the maelstrom of emotions that overwhelmed her. For the past three months she thought she had been doing what the Bible said she must do—trying to forgive Theodore. She thought they had been building a solid friendship from which Tedi could gain a foundation on which to grow. But somehow the anger had found its way back. In all that time she had never considered the possibility that she and her daughter might be expected to plunge back into their past and take the chance of reliving those days again—this time with a man she no longer loved. Would God do something like that to her?

Lauren touched her arm. "Do you want me to stay here or get lost?"

Mercy turned and saw Theo no more than six feet away, his blond good looks and cool blue eyes so familiar as he smiled and waved and made his way toward her past a group of laughing people. For a brief moment an image of a drunken, angry, malevolent Theodore superimposed itself in Mercy's mind. That image was the one she had known longer. It was as if they were two different people. Would the more familiar one ever return?

"Dr. Mercy?" Lauren whispered.

Mercy looked at her and found the strength to shake her head.

"I . . . I'm sorry, Lauren. You go on. I'll be fine." She took a deep breath and braced herself as Theo drew near.

"Okay, see you Friday," Lauren said as she grabbed her gear, said a quick hello to Theo, and left.

Mercy forced herself to meet the gaze of her ex-husband. "Hi, Theodore. I didn't know you were coming tonight."

"Yes, Dr. Jordan mentioned the class during our session Monday. We were talking about the divorce and the subject of forgiveness, and he thought I might be interested in this study." He sat down into the chair Lauren had vacated. He was watchful, hesitant. Had he heard Mercy's outburst?

"Joseph is young, and he's new here," she said quickly. She felt her anger transfer itself to the pastor, who stood talking to a couple near the back door. "He doesn't know how far we've come to get where we are now. If he thinks we can just tumble back into the past—" she began, then stopped herself. Going off on a tangent wouldn't help any. "I'm sorry, Theo. I'm really tired, and I'm going home." She stood up, reached for her coat, and pulled it on.

Theo stood with her. He picked up her chair and folded it, then tucked it under his arm. "I'll walk you to your car. There are a lot of slick spots out in the parking lot."

"Don't worry about it. I brought my ice cleats." She needed to get away, to think, to reassess what was going on, and she certainly couldn't do that in Theo's presence.

He picked up another chair and folded it. "I need to talk to you."

She grew still. "About what?"

"Tedi. You got that call today at Odira's house before we decided on anything."

"Oh." Relief. "Fine." She turned toward the door, and Theo fell into step beside her.

"How many hours are you putting in at the office?" he asked.

"Too many right now, but I don't see what I can do about it."

"I do." He placed the chairs with the others and rushed forward to hold the door open for Mercy. "Learn to say no."

She pressed her lips together, cringing at the phrase she remembered him using when they were married and she had an extraheavy work load. "It doesn't work like that. I can't just leave my patients hanging because I didn't happen to get enough sleep last night." Her commitment to her patients wasn't any of his business, and it would never be again. *Never.*

They stepped into the hallway and walked to the exit in silence. She pulled the removable cleats out of her pocket and bent over to slip them onto her shoes as Theo opened the door. It was cold out there.

"You have a life, too," he said as he stepped out ahead of her, slipped, caught himself, and shuffled aside for her to join him.

"Except for Tedi, my work *is* my life." The sharp metal of the cleats grabbed the layer of ice with a satisfying crunch, and she rushed her steps, aware of Theo struggling to keep up. She hated the sense of déjà vu she felt. They'd argued this way years ago, when Tedi was little. Mercy slowed her steps as she pulled the keys out of her coat pocket and pressed the unlock button. The headlights flashed and the locks clicked as she approached her car.

Theo slid up beside her and caught himself at the door. "I have a lot of extra hours in the evening. Maybe Tedi could come by my place after school. I could keep her until you got off." He opened the door for her.

She sat sideways in the car while she removed the cleats. "Look, Theo, it's cold out here, and I'm tired. I know you want to talk about spending more time with Tedi, and I understand how you feel. Don't forget I felt the same way for five years." Her words—and the obvious, lingering bitterness behind them—seemed to spill out and drift between them like ice crystals in the frigid air.

Theo's labored breathing grew suddenly silent. He nodded and looked away for a moment.

Mercy bent her head. *Why, God? Why is this happening? You can't possibly expect . . .* But then, how was she supposed to know what God expected of them? She'd barely known Him three months. She read the Bible with Tedi at least five nights a week, but that wasn't in-depth Scripture study. How was she supposed to find time to do that on top of everything else?

And right now she was so confused. Part of her wanted to be friends with Theo again, wanted him to be able to be a father to Tedi. Another part of her wanted to tell him to go away. Did he know how badly he complicated their lives, and how much of an inner battle it was to force this friendship?

"Mercy, I know this isn't a good time to talk about all this, but—"

"Why don't you try this a step at a time?" she said as she pivoted in her seat and stuck the key into the ignition. "I'll talk to Tedi, and if she's comfortable with seeing you, you can take her out Saturday for a couple of hours, just the two of you. I'll stay home."

She waited for him to agree and allow her to close the door and leave.

He didn't reply but continued to stand there.

She looked up at him, trying to get a glimpse of his expression in the dim glow that filtered out from the lights of the church building. "Theodore, won't that work for you?"

He sighed and bent his head. "What did you think about . . . what Dr. Jordan said tonight?"

No. She would not discuss this now, when her emotions were already at low ebb and her tongue was getting rowdy. "He likes to be called Joseph."

"Mercy . . ." He leaned down, squinting at her in the dim light. "I mean . . . did you hear the verses he read . . . what he said about divorce?"

"I heard . . . some of what he said. I'm afraid I dozed a little. Look, I'm very tired, and I want to go home. What do you say about Saturday?"

He looked at her for a moment, then leaned down farther, bringing his eyes level with hers. "I was thinking that maybe Saturday would be a good time for the three of us to spend some time together— maybe drive to Branson if the roads are clear. We could make an afternoon of it . . . go to some of the malls, take in a show or—"

"Hold it." She raised a hand. "I thought you wanted unsupervised time with Tedi. That's what I'm trying to do here."

"What did I say to make you think that? I never said anything about unsupervised time. You were the one who brought that up. I want more time with *both* of you."

No. This was not happening. She had fallen into one of Tedi's bad dreams. "You never said anything about a trip to Branson for the three of us." She didn't even bother to keep the irritation from her voice now. "I'll be working Saturday, and I have a load of housework to catch up on, so don't worry about—"

"Okay." His voice came a little louder, a little more clipped. "That's fine. I'm sorry I asked." He held up his hands for a moment, then dropped them and exhaled. "I'm sorry, Mercy. I'm trying, okay? I just don't know how to do this."

She heard the note of entreaty in his voice, and some of her irritation dissipated. Her sense of weariness deepened. He was right. He'd been trying hard to grow and change and to finally be a real father. As for enjoying the time they spent together, Mercy always enjoyed time with Tedi, and Tedi was healing. That was worth a lot.

"Theodore, I'm sorry, too. Just give me more time." And yet, she knew in her heart that even if an eternity passed, she would never be able to love him that way again. Never.

At the look of deep sadness in his eyes, she relented. Slightly. "You have to admit things are a lot better now than they were six months ago."

He thought about that for a moment, then nodded. "Much better. Everything's better."

"Do you need a ride home?" She hoped not, but she had to offer. She just wanted to get away from him right now and forget everything.

"Not tonight. I need to talk to Dr. . . . . Joseph. I'll see you soon, Mercy." He turned and slid across the ice back toward the church.

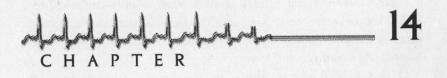

CHAPTER 14

T ex wobbled one too many times on her high heels, and before the spaghetti was done she'd kicked off her shoes and made herself comfortable in her stocking feet.

Dr. Hershel Moss rolled up his sleeves and helped with the food preparation without waiting for an invitation. He stood at least an inch taller than Tex. His soft voice served as a counterpoint to her healthy vocal tones, and his friendly smile did much to add attractiveness to his craggy good looks. He laughed a lot. His was a nervous laughter, as if he wasn't entirely comfortable in the situation. However, he might have just picked up on Lukas's discomfort, because he seemed to enjoy Tex's company—or at least her appearance. He enjoyed it even more when Tex wasn't looking.

Lukas found himself scowling at the man. Why did he suddenly feel like a protective older brother?

And Tex, to his amazement, had suddenly turned into a charming hostess. As Mercy would say, "Who'da thunk it?"

Hershel's sister, Nancy, was nearly six inches shorter than Tex. She had pale blond hair and sad brown eyes that seemed to hold too many unhappy memories. She was dressed in gray slacks and a paler gray sweater that hung loosely from her slender shoulders. Unlike her brother, she did not project a jolly nature. She sat at the table with Lukas at the far end of the kitchen from Tex and Hershel, her arms crossed protectively over her chest.

"I don't make a habit of this, you know," she announced in a soft voice, under cover of Tex's rocking laughter at one of Hershel's jokes.

Lukas turned to her, surprised she'd spoken. "What's that? Let yourself get tricked into a blind date?"

The barely detectable lines around Nancy's eyes deepened in a smile that never reached her mouth. "*Date* is such an ugly word, don't you think? At least it always has been to me. Let's just call this what it is—victimization."

Lukas nodded in sympathy. Time for the counseling session. "So you've had some bad ones?"

She looked away for a moment, thinking, then nodded. "You might say that. The last one landed me in prison for ten years." At Lukas's expression of intrigue, she allowed herself a quick smile. "Some marriages are like that. In fact, I haven't seen very many that weren't that way part of the time."

"Since I'm not married yet, I can't argue with you," he said.

Her gaze settled on his face with interest. "Yet?"

Hmm, a little slip there. He nodded. "I hope to be married some-day, of course. I'm thirty-five, so I guess you could say I've waited a little longer than most."

"Sounds like an intelligent move on your part. Why ruin a perfect record?"

"Okay, everybody, soup's on," Tex announced. "Grab your plates and serve yourselves from the stove. There isn't room on Dr. Bower's table for all this great food I've fixed."

Nancy spoke little throughout dinner, possibly because Tex and Hershel kept the conversation flowing with so much energy no one else had a chance to speak. That suited Lukas fine. Both he and Nancy had been dragged into this unwillingly, and the thought made him relax. She wasn't any more interested in making this a date than he was.

Lukas did not want to "see" anyone. In spite of the Theodore factor, his heart still felt connected to Mercy. Thanks to the battle of chasing a job all over Missouri, they'd only been together a handful of times since October, and still he felt a connection to her, both physically and emotionally, even though they had shared but a hand-ful of hugs and even fewer kisses.

When Tex finished her last bite of lemon cookies and vanilla ice cream—she obviously did not share Mercy's love of chocolate—she pushed back from the table. "Okay, my work is done." She collected plates and stacked them on the counter by the sink while Hershel watched.

And again, Lukas couldn't help noticing how carefully Hershel watched. His gaze took in Tex's every moment. Had he no shame?

Tex, oblivious to the attention, finished stacking the final dish, then looked at Hershel with a grin, beckoning him with her finger. "I only offered to *cook* dinner. I didn't offer to do the dishes. I've got some pictures of our ER staff Christmas party I can bring over from my place. Want to join me on the couch?"

Lukas shrugged away a feeling of discomfort as he watched them walk out of the kitchen. Maybe he was just being sensitive after what Tex told him earlier . . . or maybe she really was as gullible as she seemed. She obviously had a crush on Hershel, but shouldn't she be a little more alert after the incident at the hospital? What if the guy really was a masher?

"Story of my life," Nancy muttered. "Stick me with the cleanup." She stood up and collected the remaining unmatched silverware and glasses and carried them to the sink.

Lukas joined her and ran water in the sink—the apartment didn't come equipped with a dishwasher. "If you'd rather go look at pictures, I can clean this up. I know how. I always had kitchen detail when I was a kid, because I was the youngest." And meanwhile Nancy could chaperone Tex and Hershel.

She gave him a knowing look. "According to Theresa, you haven't had much experience since then, so maybe I'd better stay and help. Besides, I think they want to be alone."

Lukas heard them clearly past the open threshold into the living room as Tex came back from her apartment with picture album in hand: "You've got to see these first ones, Hershel. Quinn was crocked, and Delaney had to take a shift for him, remember? Quinn wanted to fight about it, because he said he couldn't afford to miss a shift. I could use these for blackmail if Quinn had any money to extort, but I wouldn't want to turn my back on that man if I pulled something like that." She grimaced. "I still say he shouldn't be allowed around patients."

As Tex continued to talk, Nancy looked at Lukas, then placed some dishes into soapy water. "So tell me what you're doing in this crazy town if you're looking to get married."

"Biding my time."

"Mystery man? No past, no future, just stuck out here in the middle of nowhere?"

"No, didn't Tex tell you anything about me?"

"She was too busy trying to manipulate my brother for a date. Hershel's wife died a year ago, and he hasn't been getting out much. Tex is determined to change all that. I bet she didn't tell you very much about me, either."

"Not much." *Okay, get it over with. Give the vitals and be done with it.* "I have two brothers in Jefferson City who are computer programmers, I have two nephews, and my dad and stepmom live in Mount Vernon. I live in Knolls, close to the Missouri-Arkansas border. It's about an hour and a half east of Branson."

"So why aren't you there?"

"Our emergency room burned last October. They're rebuilding."

"Did you leave somebody special down there?"

"Special?"

She shook her head in exasperation as she rinsed a skillet and set it on a dish towel spread out on the counter. "I don't know a single man who actually admits he wants to get married unless he has someone in mind."

Lukas tried to remember . . . did he ever express the wish to get married before he met Mercy? He knew he was lonely, but now the loneliness centered itself far deeper within him and made a bigger space in his heart. "Just because you have someone in mind doesn't always mean the relationship will work out the way you want it to."

They worked in silence for a few moments.

Marriage . . . Lukas wished things with Mercy weren't so complicated. He'd never paid much attention to the divorce-remarriage issue throughout the Bible. Now he wished he had. On the one hand, he sensed God's leading in his relationship with Mercy. But then, he knew God hated divorce—it broke a physical and spiritual covenant between two people and tore families apart. Marriage was intended to provide a foundation for children, and now that Theo and Mercy were both Christians, Theo had displayed ample evidence that he wanted back into his daughter's life. He wanted to help raise her. Who better to do that than her own natural father?

"Is she already married?" Nancy asked softly.

This startled Lukas from his thoughts. "What? No. Of course not. We've just been good friends for some time now, and . . ." He didn't want to get into an explanation with a stranger. "It just isn't workable right now." *Drop the subject. Start the counseling session. Isn't Nancy the one who needs to unload?*

"Does she know?"

He ripped some paper towels from a roll and wiped the table off, grimacing at a sudden, loud spurt of laughter from the other room. "Does she know what?" He was getting a little tired of the line of questioning. Tex wasn't going to talk him into anything like this again.

"That you love her and want to marry her." Nancy gave a delicate, ladylike version of Tex's snort. "For a smart man, you don't seem to catch on quickly. If she's not married, and you love her—"

"Well, she's not *exactly* married."

"What's that supposed to mean?" Nancy dried her hands, then fisted them onto her hips. "She's either married or she's not. Is she separated? Is her husband—"

"She's divorced, okay?" Lukas repressed his discomfort. This woman was not the quiet, sad person he'd first thought. Her attitude revealed a well-stocked arsenal of bitterness, and she seemed to be looking for the closest possible target as an outlet. "But her ex-husband is trying to make amends with her and their little girl, and I need to stay out of the way and let her make her own decisions." Didn't that sound simple enough? And yet, why should he even be trying to explain this to a stranger?

Nancy gave him a disgusted look. "And I suppose you haven't even talked to *her* about this, have you? Doesn't she have a choice? Don't you think she's intelligent enough to make an *informed* decision?" The decibel of her voice moved up a notch, and the talk and laughter in the other room went suddenly silent. "Come on, can't you do better than that?"

"Oh no." As soon as Mercy swallowed the medication, she realized she'd taken her sleeping pill instead of her hormones. And it was only nine o'clock at night! "I can't believe I did that," she muttered. Having to depend on drugs just to live a normal life was the pits.

"What, Mom?" Tedi called from the other room.

Mercy shook her head and closed the cabinet door. "Nothing that bad, honey. I just set myself an earlier bedtime than usual." Before she went to bed she'd wanted to have that talk with Tedi about spending time alone with Theo Saturday.

"You took your Ambien already?"

Mercy grimaced. She had taken her medicine early once before. Tedi learned quickly. "I didn't mean to."

"I'd better hide the lunch I packed for tomorrow, then," Tedi teased. "You'll eat it, like you did last week."

Mercy would protest, but Tedi was right. The drug worked fast and always kicked her appetite into high gear. That was why she had trouble losing weight right now, because between the moment she took the sleeping pill and the moment she fell asleep, she turned into an eating machine, and she didn't care what she put in her mouth. That was the way the drug worked on her, for some reason. Ordinarily Ambien was used for short-term sleep disturbances, and so Mercy had no other patients with which to compare this particular side effect. She was just glad she didn't keep a lot of high-fat foods around the house. Crackers worked nicely when she couldn't find anything better. And she loved cheese and potato chips—those baked ones that didn't have the added fat. She preached about healthy eating, and here she was stuffing food in her face at the wrong time of night. Those calories would just sit on her fat cells.

Tedi had grown accustomed to her mother's binges. "Mom, let me fix you a sandwich. I'll make it with lettuce and peppers and alfalfa sprouts on a hoagie bun. By the time you're hungry you'll eat it and get full and you won't want anything else."

"Go for it," Mercy said with a sigh. She stepped to the front window and gazed out at the frozen night. Because of this stupid premature menopause her own daughter had to take care of her now, late at night, when her brain didn't seem to work right, and she got her medications confused.

She was only thirty-nine, for pete's sake! Some of her patients welcomed menopause. She hated the thought of her body entering that change in life. Hormone therapy controlled the majority of the hot flashes and other associated symptoms, but it didn't help her sleep.

It also didn't give her back her fertility. Logically she knew another child would be a bad idea at this time in her life, but she didn't appreciate the choice being taken from her. She'd argued with God about what was happening several times in the past few months, but He wasn't budging.

As she brooded and felt the drug drift into her system and begin the relaxing effects, she saw car lights appear outside and slowly move along the street in front of the house. The pretty reflection of light danced against the panes of the window, against the ice as it broke the light into colors. The reflection looked like a kaleidoscope. The forward motion of the lights stopped for a moment, then moved on, then stopped again. And it hovered out in the darkness.

Mercy frowned and shook her head. Was she suddenly having hallucinations? Had someone parked on the street in front of their house and forgotten to turn off his headlights? She recalled the time she'd taken her first sleeping pill—Tedi had suddenly sprouted another set of eyes from her forehead. For a full week, Mercy had skipped the medication, but the insomnia continued. In the end she had decided that sleep deprivation was more dangerous for her—and for her daughter and her patients—than a simple nighttime dose to help her through menopause.

"Mustard?"

Mercy blinked and turned from the window. "What?"

Tedi held a bottle up. The letters on the label were already indecipherable to Mercy. "Do you want hot mustard on your sandwich, Mom? I'm making myself one, too."

"Yes, mustard. And while you're at it, peanut butter and banana."

Tedi giggled. "Mom, you're already whacked."

"I know." She frowned. Now, what was she thinking about just a moment ago? That was another problem with these sleeping pills—short-term memory loss just before sleep.

Oh well, a little forgetfulness couldn't be as important as food right now. She turned and followed Tedi into the kitchen.

———

Lukas knew he shouldn't be angry with Tex for setting him up, but he wondered if this night would ever end. He and Nancy had joined Tex and Hershel in the living room, and to his everlasting humiliation, Nancy had just finished spouting the details of his dilemma with Mercy. He had a big mouth. Nancy had a bigger one. And he'd thought *Tex* was bad.

What really bothered him was that Nancy had a point—not that he wanted that point spread all over Herald. He probably should have talked to Mercy about Theodore, but it was so awkward. They'd had so little time together. What was he supposed to do, blurt out in front of everyone at the dinner table, "I'm sorry, Mercy, but I can't see you because of some theological complications resulting from your marriage to Theo"? How did one discuss such a personal issue when a talkative eleven-year-old was spilling her guts about school projects and dates with her dad and the divorce her best friend's parents were going through?

"Dr. Bower, I can't believe you never said anything to her about it!" Tex exclaimed. "What are you afraid of?"

Hershel placed an arm around her shoulder. "Now, come on, give the guy a break. He's never even been married, and you expect him to go proposing to a woman with a child when the ex-husband is trying to get her back?"

Lukas cleared his throat. "That isn't exactly—"

"But what irritates me is that he refuses to tell her how much he loves her!" Nancy said. "Doesn't she have a right—"

"Hold it." Lukas wondered if he had the authority to fire Tex. In Knolls, where he was interim director, he might get away with it. Here they were too hard up for help—even loudmouthed, pushy help that set you up with sharp-tongued divorcees. "I'm not sure when my private life became open to public scrutiny, but I think we're blowing this all out of proportion."

"And Lukas has a right to his feelings," Hershel added. "You don't just take a man's emotions out and examine them under a microscope like you women do." He scooted a little closer to Tex.

Tex looked at him quizzically.

"Excuse me." Nancy's voice rose again.

Lukas wondered if that biker gal Birdbrain might make a more appealing date.

"I didn't let you drag me all the way down here for an unwanted date so you could insult—"

"Hey, I resent that," Tex shot back at Nancy. She scooted sideways, forcing Hershel to remove his arm from her shoulder. "I went to a lot of trouble to set you up with him. He's a good guy. He goes to church and everything."

Nancy ignored her. "You know what you are?" She pointed her finger at Lukas. "You're afraid of commitment. You don't think you can handle raising another man's child."

Lukas glared at her and wondered what the repercussions would be if he threw all three of his guests out the door.

"I don't blame him," Tex said. "I wouldn't be a good stepparent, either."

"At least he's smart enough to realize the problem and back off," Hershel said. "Most people jump into the role without giving the kids a thought, and they expect everything to be perfect, and it never works out that way. I think he's showing common sense."

Lukas gazed at each earnest face in turn. Was this for real? They were yanking out and examining his private thoughts like—

"Fine, but the least he can do is tell this poor woman how he feels." Nancy crossed her arms and sat back. "If he doesn't, he's treating her like trash to be thrown away. Use and discard. I know. I've been treated like that."

"But it isn't like—"

The telephone rang from its perch on the wall beside the kitchen entrance. To Lukas the phone sounded like a time-out bell at a wrestling match. He leaped to his feet and rushed over to answer, automatically hoping to hear Mercy's voice at the other end of the line—not that he wanted three eavesdroppers telling him how to conduct his conversation.

"Hello."

"Dr. Bower? This is Carmen in the emergency room. I just thought you might want to know that they found Jerod Moore."

"The baby?" He turned and gestured to the others. "They found him! Marla Moore's baby!"

Tex leaped from the sofa. "All right!"

Hershel laughed and high-fived Tex.

"How is he?" Nancy asked. "Is he okay?"

Lukas relayed the question to Carmen, and to his dismay the three others crowded around him and the telephone to hear the reply.

"They just checked him out here a few minutes ago, and he's perfectly healthy. Two ladies from the Division of Family Services came to get him, and they're taking him to Jefferson City. There's a lady who runs a clinic called Alternative, and—"

"Alternative!" Hershel exclaimed. "Serena Tanner runs that clinic to provide an alternative to abortion. She was the one I called when Marla first had—"

"Shh!" Tex said. "There's more."

"One of the social workers told me that they're hoping this Tanner lady and her husband will be able to adopt Jerod. They can't find any living relatives. So far this sounds like a happy ending, doesn't it?"

"Yes, but where did they find him?" Lukas asked. "What happened?"

"That's the weirdest thing, Dr. Bower. You know that biker gang that's staying down there in those shacks right now? Well, somebody knocked on Catcher's door tonight, and when he stepped out he found Jerod all bundled up, lying beside a Harley. He brought the baby in, and the police tried to give him a hard time. We had quite a stir here for a few minutes, but they let him go. It's a pretty sure bet Catcher wasn't in any shape to steal a baby early last Sunday morning. Uh-oh, I've got to go. They're bringing in another patient." She hung up abruptly.

Lukas sighed in relief.

Hershel laid a hand on Tex's shoulder once again.

Nancy broke the silence. "So, Lukas, are you going to be a real man and tell this woman in Knolls that you love her?"

Lukas made an obvious show of checking his watch. "Wow, I can't believe it's so late. Time sure does fly when you're having . . . uh . . . fun. I'll go get your coat, Tex. Glad you guys could come for dinner, but it's getting late and I have to work tomorrow."

CHAPTER ——— 15

The chirp of Mercy's cordless telephone awakened her Thursday morning. She managed to catch a glance at the glowing digits on her bedside clock as she fumbled for the receiver, punched the wrong button three times, and finally made connection. It was seven o'clock.

"Hello." She pushed the hair from her eyes as she waited for a reply.

No one answered.

"Yes, hello?" she tried again as she folded the covers back and swung her legs to the side of the bed. She would have to get up anyway in a few minutes. Tedi had school today, and patients were scheduled at the clinic, in spite of the fact that this was supposed to be her day off.

Still no one answered, but she heard voices in the background, like a radio or television. And she heard someone breathing, and then a click and a dial tone.

She disconnected and shoved the telephone aside irritably. How rude.

———

Clarence opened his eyes for the fourth time Thursday morning. Daylight at last. The first time he'd awakened had been two o'clock, and then four, and then five-fifteen, and each time at least twenty minutes had dragged by before he could get back to sleep. For him, bedtime was like the beginning of a work shift. Getting enough sleep was a chore. With his bulk it was hard to get comfortable, and after a while most positions put an arm or a leg to sleep. Lots of times he snored so loudly he startled himself awake, wondering if a semi truck without a muffler was bursting through the front door of the apartment. He was glad Darlene slept in a bedroom in the main house.

Darlene was spending more time out lately, getting involved with community and church activities, cooking for Meals on Wheels at the Methodist church once a week, and volunteering at the hospital information desk. Publishers still sent her indexing projects, but she'd cut her work load to a more manageable level. To everyone's great relief, her asthma was under control.

Clarence sat up and looked across the room at a daily inspirational calendar Ivy had given him for Christmas. Yesterday's Scripture portion for the day was "He hath sent me to heal the brokenhearted . . ."

He knew from asking Ivy that the verse meant Jesus Christ was the Healer, but sometimes, when he saw people like Kendra and Buck hurting, he wondered if a little encouragement from a friend might tide them over while they were waiting on Jesus. He thought again about Saturday night and about Kendra's broken heart. Could she be healed? And Buck? Was there a school that taught you how to help people like that?

The thought of a guy his age and weight going back to school seemed crazy. Where would he get the money? He needed to start making a living for himself now, not four or six years from now.

But still . . . there was Saturday night resting in his memory. For a little while he'd been able to help give two people hope. Did a guy have to have a college degree to do that?

With a little less effort than it would have taken three months ago, he stood up and walked over to the dresser. He tore off yesterday's date and verse from the calendar to see what today would bring. The new verse was pretty simple, another one he could memorize easily, although he would never get the address right—he didn't even know what "Thessalonians" meant. The verse said, "Pray without ceasing."

Prayer. When he'd prayed out loud for Buck and Kendra, things had started to change. But to never stop praying? What did that mean?

Part of the message grew clear to him as he thought about it: He was supposed to keep praying for Buck and Kendra and not just stop at that one prayer he said the other night. He could also pray for Odira and Crystal. He didn't know exactly how prayer worked, because it was still a mystery nobody seemed able to explain. But the fact of the matter was that his prayer had helped Buck and Kendra . . . at least for a while.

And so he sat down on the side of his bed and bent his head and closed his eyes the way Ivy did. He'd prayed before. He could do it again.

———

Mercy backed out of the garage and pushed the remote-control button on her key chain to close the garage door. As always on Thursday morning, she wondered how much of her day off she would spend working. She was supposed to meet Buck and Kendra at the clinic this morning at ten, and after that she would go to the hospital and check on Delphi Bell and probably release her if she looked okay. Odira and Crystal were due for release, too, and Odira was begging to go home. And then there were the patients who hadn't been able to make it in yesterday because of the ice—

"See those cigarette butts!" Tedi's outraged voice filled the car, and she pecked at the car window with her fingernails as Mercy backed out of the driveway. "They weren't there yesterday."

"Tedi, what on earth are you. . . ?" Mercy looked in the direction her daughter pointed and saw tan filter tips of three smoked cigarettes lying close together on top of the ice, just inside a stand of head-tall evergreen bushes that grew along the curb by the street. "Yes, I see them. Have you suddenly joined some kind of neighborhood trash patrol?"

Tedi sighed and rolled her eyes at Mercy. "Mom, those are on our property. And there are three of them." She pressed closer to the window. "And they look like the same kind, which probably means that the person who smokes that brand of cigarettes was trespassing on our property long enough to smoke three of them."

"Or those three butts blew from down the street with the hard wind we had and got caught behind those bushes. Are you reading another Jenny McGrady mystery?"

Tedi didn't reply.

Mercy cast her daughter a worried look and reached across to touch her shoulder. "Honey, have you been having your nightmares again lately?" Tedi had a vivid imagination, and events affected her deeply. The situation with her father was better, but she might still be preoccupied with the changing relationship with him.

"Maybe some." Tedi shrugged. "It's probably nothing, Mom. Don't worry about it."

"Okay, but remember you can always tell me if you're worried about something." Mercy pulled out onto the street. She thought of Delphi. "How do you feel about having a houseguest for a while?"

Tedi turned to her excitedly. "A guest? Is Abby going to spend the night tonight? She needs to get away from home. Her mom—"

"No, honey, not Abby. We'll have her over soon, but I'm releasing a patient from the hospital today, and she needs a place to stay until Arthur and Alma Collins return to Crosslines."

Tedi's eagerness turned to curiosity. "Is she a homeless person? Here in Knolls?"

"She's homeless right now, but she won't be as soon as we take her in, will she?"

"Who is she? Do we know her? What happened to her?"

Mercy slowed the car at the end of the street, checked the rearview mirror to make sure no one was driving up behind her, then turned to Tedi and laid a hand on her arm. "Sweetheart, this is very serious. I don't want you to tell anyone that we're even going to have company, do you understand? She could be in danger from her husband, and we don't want word getting out that we know where she is." She held Tedi's dark, suddenly sober gaze. "Do you understand?"

"Sure, Mom. I tried to hide from Dad, too, remember? I know what it's like to be scared and not be able to go home."

Involuntarily Mercy closed her eyes against the sudden pain of those memories. But then a horn honked behind them, and she saw in the mirror that she was holding up traffic. She pulled out into the road to join the line of cars carrying children to school after a day off.

"Did you know that Abby's dad isn't even trying to get custody of her and April and Andy?" Tedi informed her. "She told me that at school Tuesday, and she was crying. Her mom's dumping all the housework on her, and Abby even has to baby-sit her brother and sister while her mom goes out sometimes at night to classes so she can get a better job."

Mercy shook her head sadly. Jason and Lindy Cuendet had separated last fall, and at least half the citizens of Knolls seemed to be making it their business to keep each spouse informed about the other. Jason could smile at the wrong person, and Lindy would hear about it by the end of the day. If Lindy purchased too much on her charge card or took the kids out to dinner, Jason was calling to complain by the next morning. Tedi had a front-row seat for the show and was sometimes an active, though unwilling, participant, since she and Abby were best friends.

"Did you know Grandma volunteered to help out at Crosslines when Arthur and Alma get it set up?" Tedi's informative chatter on the way to school on mornings like this was sometimes the only local news Mercy heard all day. "She's going to do their accounting. And guess who she's talked into helping out at the clinic on Saturdays?"

Mercy frowned. "Clinic? What clinic?"

"Arthur and Alma are starting a free clinic on Saturdays for people who can't afford a doctor, especially for some of the Mexicans who are new in town. They've already lined up all their volunteers, and they start next month."

"Doctors, too?" Mercy turned onto the school drive and waited her turn to let Tedi out.

"Yeah. Grandma sweet-talked Dr. Heagerty out of retirement enough to help out half a day on Saturdays. Grandma's going to work with him." Tedi giggled. "Grandma had to kiss him to get him to help out."

Mercy gasped. "What!"

Tedi glanced around at the car behind them. "Mom, you're going to cause a traffic jam. You know Grandma and Dr. Hugh are seeing each other. And it's not like she hasn't kissed him before. You're just never around whenever they're together."

Why did Mercy suddenly feel as if life was passing her by? "Who else is working at this clinic?"

"Jarvis said he'd help out, but he and Dr. Hugh don't like each other, so Grandma said they would have to split shifts. Either Dr. Hugh could work one Saturday and Jarvis the next Saturday, or one could do mornings and one could do afternoons. They decided to split days. That way it wouldn't wear either of them out."

"Nobody ever called *me* to help out."

"Grandma told them not to. She said you didn't have enough time to spend with your family as it was, and you needed this free clinic as much as anybody did, to take some of the extra work you've had lately. I talked to Dad about it on the phone the other night, and he agrees. He also thinks you should get a partner to help you."

Mercy shot her daughter a quick glance. "He does, does he?"

"Yeah. Are we going to Branson Saturday? He said we might, if you could get off."

"When did he say this?"

"Yesterday morning when I talked to him on the phone."

"Well, I wish he hadn't said anything until he spoke with me. I can't get off that long."

"See what I mean? Mom, you need a break. Can't you at least try?"

Mercy hesitated and chose her next words carefully. "Tedi, how do you feel about a short lunch alone with your father Saturday?" It would be impossible to leave town this weekend, even for an afternoon, with Delphi in such need of reassurance, and Kendra just out of the psyche ward, and Odira and Crystal both fighting their way back to health.

Mercy didn't realize, for a moment, how deep the silence had grown in the car. She looked across the seat at Tedi. "Honey?"

Tedi continued to gaze out the passenger window toward the school grounds. The morning sun glared on her glasses, which in turn reflected against the window and hid her expression. But Mercy could see sudden tension in the line of her jaw and the set of her shoulders.

"Are you just disappointed because we can't go to Branson?" Mercy asked quietly.

Tedi shook her head. "No, Mom," she murmured.

"Is it because you still don't feel comfortable about meeting your father alone?"

"You told me I wouldn't have to." Tedi turned from the window with a look of apprehension on her face. "You said I would never—"

"Okay. It's okay. You don't have to. We'll have our usual date for lunch, and I'll be there all the time. I'll never make you do anything with your father that frightens you." Tedi turned back to the window once more. Some of the tension disappeared, and Mercy heard a sigh.

"I didn't think I'd be scared, Mom."

"I know. He's changed so much, I thought I'd forgiven him, but last night something happened to make me realize I hadn't . . . not completely. I think maybe both of us are afraid he might suddenly change back to the person he was before."

"But that shouldn't happen, Mom. He's a different person now. He's a Christian, so why am I scared?"

"Because you and I both know that even Christians aren't perfect. And I think you and I still need to deal with some things from the past."

"I don't want to hurt Dad's feelings."

"Neither do I, but we have to be honest before we can work things out." Mercy pulled up to the child-unloading zone, frustrated that she had to leave Tedi like this. "We'll talk about it more tonight."

Tedi grasped the door handle. "I think Dad'll be disappointed, though. He told me he'd saved up some extra money, and he asked me what I thought you'd like to do, just the three of us. I was the one who came up with the idea for Branson."

Mercy felt even worse. Theo had undoubtedly been planning to do something special for them for a while, but she hadn't picked up on it. Why couldn't he have left things as they were? "I'm sorry, honey. Maybe if he keeps saving, we can do something later." But she didn't want to spend that much time with him . . . did she?

Maybe her feelings weren't important. She had learned that even when you knew to do the right thing, you didn't always *feel* like doing it.

Tedi opened the door and got out. "Don't forget the play tonight at school. Dad said he was going to be there."

"He is?" Why did it suddenly seem as if Theo was everywhere she looked?

"Bye, Mom." She pulled out her book bag and closed the door with a wave.

Mercy needed to talk to Tedi longer . . . but then she always needed to talk to Tedi longer. Until last night . . . but she didn't want to think about last night, or the idea that she might be expected to remarry Theodore. She couldn't stand the thought.

Why hadn't the thought occurred to her that Tedi would be afraid to spend time alone with her father? She'd lived alone with him for five years and watched his alcoholism and his temper escalate into something uncontrollable and dangerous. But recently there seemed to be a fresh love growing between Tedi and her father, a new relationship that had no connection with the old one. Theo was putting his focus in the right place for once in his life, and his new look on life proved that God could change anybody. Why was that so hard for Tedi—and Mercy—to accept?

The grease-laden smoke of bacon and sausage mingled with the aroma of freshly brewed coffee and the chatter of the breakfast crowd at the Dinner Bucket on Thursday morning. Lukas yawned over his scrambled eggs—he knew better than to ask for egg substitute in this café—and he said a silent apology to Mercy and Ivy for ignoring his cholesterol level. They could give him a good dose of olive oil and avocado when he returned to Knolls, which would be tonight if he could get there. He just needed to give Mercy a call sometime today so she would be expecting him. Nancy Moss would be proud.

He took another swig of coffee and listened to the desultory conversation going on at the table behind him, where four old farmers complained about beef prices at the local sale barn. Because of the hay shortage last year, people were trying to sell off their stock to save money. Things were tight, but hogs were doing well enough.

Lukas checked his watch. He had twenty minutes to get to work, and he wanted to gas up beforehand. He poured an extra squirt of ketchup on his potatoes and raised his fork for the final three bites when the front door of the café squeaked open and four big, black-leathered, puffy-eyed men trooped inside, looking like grumpy bears out of hibernation for a winter snack.

Catcher and Company.

Lukas shoveled a final mouthful of egg and took a slurp of coffee, aware that the only open seats were the four padded stools beside him—two per side at the raised counter. He tried to ignore the discomfort and the resulting shame he felt at their arrival. The word *coward* came to mind, not for the first time since he came to Herald. For pete's sake, he wasn't an undersized little kid anymore. He was a grown man.

Granted, he had made quite a commotion in the ER the other night, complete with shouting and unplugging a television. In the end Catcher had walked out of the hospital in an inebriated state against medical advice. And it was also true that these bikers were still unofficial suspects in the kidnapping of Jerod Moore. Some gossipers had even gone so far as to blame them for the recent disappearance of several children in Central Missouri—not to their faces, of course. These were tough bikers, but no one was going to try to jump Lukas and beat him up right here in the center of a crowded café, not even four big loudmouthed beer guzzlers.

The booted feet stomped in his direction until shadows of the men fell on him. Lukas tried to remind himself that most people didn't recognize him when he wasn't in his scrubs—

"Hey, Doc," came a growl from behind him. A powerful hand grasped his shoulder.

Lukas swiveled on his stool and looked up at the long-haired biker with the sun-creased face and matching black eyes from his most recent fight.

"Hi, Catcher." Lukas nodded to the other three men. One of them was Marin, Catcher's sparring partner who had cut his arm open with a beer bottle last Saturday night. The two others, Lukas realized with deepening dismay, had been in the waiting-room crowd that had been stalking him when Catcher showed up.

"Sutures are holding up great," Catcher said as he straddled the backless stool beside Lukas. The man's breath didn't knock Lukas over with the fumes of booze this morning. He reached up and unzipped the extralong sleeve of his leather jacket, which was constructed specifically for motorcycling. He slid it back over the flesh of his forearm, revealing a nicely healing wound—no bandage, of course.

In spite of the tension, Lukas couldn't deny a glow of satisfaction at his handiwork. "Looks like you're doing a good job with it."

The forty-something waitress in jeans and a white T-shirt walked up behind the counter with four platters of the breakfast special balanced on her arms. "Here you go, fellas." She slid the platters onto the counter at the four empty places. "You're a little early this morning. Coffee's comin'."

As the other three men peeled off their jackets in the overheated room, Catcher reached over and pulled his platter toward him, then leaned closer to Lukas. "Don't suppose you'd yank these stitches out for me right now, would you?"

"Sorry, not yet." Lukas took a final swallow of his coffee and felt the effects of the caffeine surging through his system. Or that might possibly be adrenaline. "I'd like to give this a couple more days to heal, or the wound could come open and make a bigger scar."

"Oh, come on." Catcher filled his fork with bacon and eggs. "You think I care about a little thing like a scar?" He shoved the bite into his mouth.

While Catcher was busy chewing, Lukas checked his watch again, picked up his ticket, and slid from his stool. "I'd give it until at least tomorrow afternoon. Saturday would be better, and don't forget to keep it clean." Before Catcher could argue, he paid his bill and escaped.

But out in the Jeep, when he turned the key in the ignition, the motor refused to speak to him. Nothing but an empty click reached his ears.

He frowned, pulled out the key, and looked to see if it was the right one. It was. He inserted the key and tried again.

Click.

He sat staring at the dashboard for a moment, then closed his eyes and groaned. "This can't be happening." *Not now. Please, not now. I'll be late for work, and Dr. Denton warned me to be on time because he has a flight to catch, and Catcher and his friends could come tromping out and decide they need a little morning exercise, and if I don't remove those sutures for him, he might get mad and turn this Jeep over on its roll bar.*

He jiggled the gearshift and stepped on the clutch and tried one more time. Nothing.

He slapped the steering wheel and wrenched his way out of the Jeep, closing the door behind him with a hearty slam. Of all times to have a dead battery, this could be a worst-case scenario. The hospital

SILENT PLEDGE · *195*

was all the way across town, and although that didn't encompass a whole lot of acreage, that acreage was a long, narrow tract of land that hugged the shoreline. It would be impossible to walk in eight minutes. Herald had no taxi service. Of course, he could step back inside the café and ask one of the farmers for a ride. Maybe Catcher would like to give him a lift. Now, *there* was a thought!

Lukas shoved his hands in his pockets and eyed the big shiny Harley-Davidson motorcycles huddled close together amidst the rusted pickup trucks surrounding the rickety shack that housed the only café in Herald. Then he turned and started walking down the road. He could jog once he warmed up a little. Surely the trip couldn't take that long.

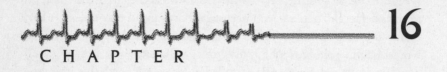

CHAPTER 16

Prayer could make a man hungry. Clarence pulled on his baggy big-man sweats, shoved on his house shoes, and headed toward Ivy's kitchen, where all the warm, comforting smells of breakfast still lingered. And lucky for him, Ivy was nowhere to be seen.

"Chocolate chip cookies, here I come." Four days had passsed since his last three-cookie binge, and he was craving them like a kid craved birthdays. Telling himself he would eat only three cookies, he lumbered to the fridge and opened the freezer door. The cool air reached out and chilled his face like the kiss of an ice cream truck.

The plate of foil-wrapped cookies was gone.

He slumped back in defeat, still staring at the packages of casseroles, ground turkey, and frozen veggies. Ivy always baked chocolate chip cookies for special functions and kept them stockpiled in the freezer for when she would need them. As she had explained to Clarence once, cookies were the only decadent food she ever touched anymore. She used a low-fat recipe—trust Ivy to find a way to ruin even chocolate chip cookies—and she never baked less than three batches at a time. He believed she kept them there to test his willpower. So far he had happily failed the test. Twice a week, usually in the middle of the night, he would sneak into the kitchen when everyone else was asleep and snitch a snack.

Since the ones Ivy made were lower in fat, he doubted if even the biggest ones had more than fifty calories a cookie—he prided himself in knowing the calorie count of every food he put into his mouth. He had to eat thirty-five hundred calories to add a pound, and so even if the three cookies he usually ate equaled two hundred calories, he would have to eat eighteen times that many to gain a pound.

He took the math a step further and decided that, since a normal human being burned seventy to one hundred calories walking a mile, he must burn at least two and a half times that much. He figured he burned off all the cookies every time he walked on the treadmill. Some cookies right now would give him the incentive to exercise.

He closed the door and sighed. He was just slumping back into his apartment when he heard a knock. Someone was at the outside entrance to the apartment—an entrance he never used.

"Clarence!" came a muffled call. "Clarence, are you in there?"

He rushed through the small sitting room and tiny kitchenette to the door that exited onto the side porch. He opened it to find Buck and Kendra huddled together against the cold. Kendra's nose was red, and the flesh around her eyes was puffy, as if her tears hadn't stopped in four days.

"Could we come in for a minute?" Buck asked, glancing through the doorway toward the small sitting room beyond.

"Why, sure." Clarence hustled out of their way and stood aside for them to enter. "Kendra, did they spring you this morning?"

She grimaced as her gaze darted around the room. "It's been over ninety-six hours and it felt like weeks. It's like I was in prison with a bunch of—"

Buck cleared his throat.

She looked up at him. "There are a lot of unhappy people in that place," she ended quietly.

Clarence gestured toward the love seat and chairs that were placed in an area Ivy called the "conversation circle." "Go on, sit down. What's up? Is everything okay? You didn't have any trouble on the road, did you?"

"No, the truck's fine." Kendra perched on the edge of the love seat and looked at Buck nervously. He sat down beside her.

Clarence lowered himself onto the sturdiest straight-backed chair. He didn't use this furniture often. Even after he'd lost over a hundred pounds, these things looked too spindly to hold him. He'd never broken one of Ivy's chairs yet, but something could snap at any time.

Buck leaned forward. "Clarence, you know when you . . . prayed for us the other night?"

How could he forget something like that? "Yeah."

"Would you do it again?"

Clarence blinked, then looked at Kendra. She watched him closely, her beautiful blue eyes wide and . . . hopeful? And Buck, too, looked hopeful. They both seemed to lean toward him as if he had some kind of answer to their problems. He felt like a fraud. All he'd done the other night was open his mouth and speak some thoughts out loud, hoping—no, knowing—God was listening. But Clarence knew he didn't have any power to help them himself.

"Well, sure." Could *this* actually be an answer to his prayer? Maybe they'd made the decision to come and see him while he was talking to God earlier this morning. He thought about the verse for the day on his dresser. If the prayer helped the other night, and if it had helped this morning, then prayer would help again. No reason why God wouldn't be here this time, too.

He cleared his throat as he bent his head and closed his eyes. *God, are you there?* His silent thought seemed to echo. "Uh, first of all, Lord, thank you for answering our prayers and helping us out the other night." A few weeks ago he would have felt like a fool closing his eyes and babbling like this, but he didn't now . . . not much. Ivy had broken him in well. "We're asking more stuff in Jesus' name. Please give some comfort to Kendra and Buck today. They've been through so much pain." As he said the words he felt as if he could feel the pain himself all of a sudden. He knew they felt cut off from the world, alone and wondering what was going to happen to them next. Somehow the loneliness seemed to have transferred itself to him.

To his horror he felt the sting of tears behind his eyelids. He fought to keep them from pressing through. He heard Kendra sniff a couple of times. Should he hurry up and pray so she could get some tissue to wipe her nose?

"Help Buck know what to do to help Kendra. Help him to be strong for her, no matter what it takes. And, God, show Kendra the way out of the pit she's in, because you're the only one who knows. I sure don't. Thanks, God." He opened his eyes to see both of them with heads still bent. Kendra's cheeks were wet with tears. They didn't realize he was done. "Amen."

They opened their eyes and looked at him, and Kendra sniffed again. "It's like you know what to say to Him." She dabbed at her nose with the back of her hand. "That's what it's like. It's like a pit I can't get out of, and nobody knows how to find me here. I feel like I'm just wandering around lost."

Buck reached over and drew her into his arms. Her shoulders tensed, but he didn't let go.

"I've been there, Kendra," Clarence said. "Lots of times. And it was so bad I tried to kill myself, too, but in a different way. But then God sent some people to help. I know God sent them, because they've told me. He'll send somebody for you, too, but I'll be here with you while they're coming."

By the time Lukas reached the center of town, he was ready to wring the gel-smearing culprit's neck. He had a pretty good idea who the culprit was, too. Hadn't he seen the KY on Carmen's desk the other day? Why hadn't he picked up on her nervousness at the time?

She was the reason his battery was dead. She was the reason he was late for work and he was freezing to death. Of course, it was his own fault he hadn't brought gloves and a knit cap. The cold morning air breezing in from the half-frozen Lake of the Ozarks seemed to bite harder now than it did a few moments ago, and Lukas decided not to jog. He didn't want to frostbite his lungs.

He heard the sudden, throttling racket of a motorcycle a few blocks behind him, loud in the morning stillness. The sound echoed from the trees and two-story shops in downtown Herald. Other engines joined in and revved, and then a cacophony vibrated through the air. Obviously Catcher and his crew were roaring out of the café parking lot. What would motivate grown men and women to freeze themselves to death in this cold winter atmosphere? Was this a macho thing, survival of the toughest?

Lukas plodded on. He really wanted to get to Knolls tonight. In spite of yesterday's ice storm, the temperature was probably about twenty degrees warmer, the people were friendlier, and Mercy was there . . . and as far as he knew, no innocent little children had disappeared from Knolls into the hands of some kidnapper.

The racket of the motorcycles grew louder. They were staying in the old apartments down by the hospital, in the same direction Lukas was walking, and until now he hadn't considered the fact that they would come this way.

Get a grip, Lukas. They're just out for breakfast. Once again, he was ashamed of the anxiety the bikers provoked in him. At five feet ten and one hundred sixty pounds he was more accustomed to using his brains than his brawn, but back in college in Columbia he'd formed a habit of working out on weights between homework assignments, and he'd taken up jogging and hiking. He hadn't lost all the muscle to age yet, but he hated the idea of personal, physical confrontation. He always had. Too many bad experiences. Hiking in the woods never bothered him, because he knew the real monsters in this world wore clothing and spoke the human language and drove cars. Or motorcycles . . .

Catcher and crew drew closer, their engines jarring the peaceful quiet of a slumbering town that didn't know what rush-hour traffic looked like or how much noise pollution it entailed.

A shout rang out—it sounded like Catcher's rough voice—and the motorcycles downshifted, grew louder, slowed. Lukas tried not to automatically increase his speed. Funny, last fall he'd run through a burning, collapsing building, and his heart hadn't beat as hard and fast as it was now.

"Hey, Doc!" Catcher shouted over the din of his idling motor.

Lukas slowed his steps and turned to watch them approach.

"Hop on," came Catcher's raspy voice.

"What?"

"You need a ride, don't you? One of the farmers back at that greasy spoon said you were having trouble with your Jeep. Probably your battery in this cold air. Hop on, and I'll give you a lift to work."

Lukas couldn't move, and for a moment he couldn't speak. The man sounded serious. His buddies sat astride their bikes with motors idling, watching Lukas curiously, as if he would be crazy not to accept the offer of transportation aboard a death machine on wheels.

"Don't hurt my feelings, Doc," Catcher warned. He revved the motor and grinned, his straight, white teeth shining in the early light. "What's wrong, never ridden a real one before?"

"Never." He'd just treated patients who'd ridden the real ones. That was enough for him.

"Come on. After Saturday night I owe you." Catcher reached down into the pocket of his jacket and pulled out a familiar set of keys. "Besides, you left these behind in the Jeep."

Lukas sighed in defeat and eyed the offending ignition key. Just great. Cold air and frustration had obviously affected his brain. He took a deep breath and stepped toward the bike—after all, riding with Catcher would get him there faster. And he really needed to get there this morning. But what if they hit a slick spot?

"What damage could a mile on a Harley do?" Catcher asked. "And who's going to take care of your patients if you're not there?"

The man had a point. Dr. Denton had left the ER unattended yesterday when Lukas was only five minutes late for work. He would have no compunction about leaving on time for his flight this morning. And Catcher looked sane enough—for a man whose bruised eyes matched his black leather jacket.

Without giving himself a chance to back out, Lukas took another step forward. "Thanks, Catcher, that's kind of you. Just tell me how to get on this thing."

It was simple. All he had to do was sit there huddled behind the biker's broad shoulders and try not to scream as the icy air froze his bare face and ears into a solid mass of fleshsicle and the rumble of the motor deafened him and tears blinded him. He didn't have time to wonder what would happen if they hit an icy patch and crashed on the blacktop.

They were just pulling into the hospital ER entrance when he realized he wasn't wearing a helmet. An emergency room physician not wearing a helmet.

And it wasn't until after he'd thanked the men and watched them leave that he realized Catcher hadn't returned the keys to his Jeep.

———

Mercy parked in front of Jack's Printshop across from the courthouse on the square. She could have called, but somehow a personal visit for something like this seemed more compassionate. She saw Theodore as soon as she stepped into the shop. He was setting up letters in an old-fashioned printer on display in the front window. A huge gray metal wheel turned at the side, and Theo made a test print and intently checked his work, unaware, for a moment, of Mercy's

202 · HANNAH ALEXANDER

presence. He was obviously enjoying himself. He should have left the real estate business years ago—probably shouldn't have pursued that career in the first place—but when they first got married, he thought he could make enough to retain his pride when Mercy started bringing in a physician's income.

Somehow, nothing had worked out the way either of them had hoped.

As she studied his bent head and intent expression, she felt a rush of sympathy for him. He was trying so hard to please her, to regain Tedi's love—and he really had changed. His heart was more tender. He laughed more. If she hadn't known him from the past, she would think he was a good, kind man.

But didn't that mean he *was* a good, kind man now? Where was her faith? Why did she find it so difficult for her to believe that God could clean the darkest, ugliest human failures—the sins?

He looked up suddenly, as if realizing someone was watching him. When he saw her, the shadowed lines of concentration smoothed out, and a warm smile spread to his hairline. He dropped an ink-stained rag and came toward her.

"Mercy! You're out early this morning. I think this is the first time I've seen you in here." He held his hands out, indicating the red and blue ink not only on them but on a work apron that covered him from chest to knees. "I guess you can see I really get into it. What brings you out of the clinic? I thought you would be buried alive today."

She glanced toward the rear of the shop, where five other employees—and big, handsome, sixty-eight-year-old Jack himself—were busy collating, stapling, and typesetting.

She turned back to Theo. "I just needed to talk with you for a moment."

The smile gradually filtered from Theo's eyes. "Something's wrong."

"I'm sorry. I guess I'll be going with you and Tedi for lunch Saturday." She kept her voice light, and for a few seconds his smile returned and an expression of hope touched his eyes.

Then he thought about what she'd just said, and his shoulders slumped. "Oh." For a moment he didn't speak but closed his eyes and bent his head. "She's still afraid of me."

"She's trying, Theodore. It's going to take time." She was sorry for his sudden misery, and she reached out and laid a hand on his arm. "Maybe you're right. Maybe we should take a Saturday soon and drive to Branson. I can't do it for a while, but it's something we could plan to do in the future."

He straightened and glanced at her hand, which continued to rest on his arm. Then he looked into her face. "I'd like that. Thanks, Mercy."

Stepping back outside into the frigid air, Mercy walked a few steps along the freshly de-iced sidewalk with her head bent, guilt churning inside her as she struggled to dismiss the vision of heartache she'd seen in Theo's expression. He was trying so hard. He sent her money every payday for child support. He was honestly seeking to rebuild a relationship with Tedi. He obviously—

"Now that's what I call a true Christian spirit," came a voice from behind her.

Mercy turned to see Mrs. Alice Eckard walking toward her, her heavily lined face pink from the cold. Mrs. Eckard was an old friend of Mom's from church. She had obviously just stepped out of Gaylene's Pharmacy, next door to the printshop, and carried her small bag of prescription medications in her hand.

"Hello, Alice. I'm sorry, I don't understand what—"

"I saw you in there talking to Theodore." Alice pulled her wool scarf tighter around her neck and sidled closer to Mercy. "Isn't it amazing what God can do with us when we'll let Him? I've never seen such a turnaround in a man's life. Your daughter is so lucky to have parents who are willing to work things out. Some of our older Christians could take lessons from you."

"Thank you, but that isn't—"

"Just think of the power and joy we would have in our own church if we were as open as you are to reconciliation!" She reached out and patted Mercy on the arm. "Well, I've got to get out of this cold. See you in church Sunday, darlin'!" She gave Mercy a thumbs up and hurried away.

———

The mad stapler had struck again. Lukas stood at the side of the call room bed as he took off his jacket and tried to thaw out from his motorcycle ride. He found a pamphlet on drug interaction stapled shut, lying on the desk. He found the trash can turned upside down on the unmade bed, with at least a week's worth of trash accumulated so that wadded paper and empty food containers spilled to the floor. Frustration and anger mounted. Lukas gathered the trash and stuffed it back into the can, then set it outside the door with a thud. Obviously housekeeping hadn't been here in a while. Maybe Amos had fired them, too.

He walked into the ER proper and checked the schedule over the secretary's desk. Alexis had been the night nurse, and Carmen had been the secretary. Brandon—or in Tex's vernacular, "Godzilla"—had been the lab/x-ray tech. According to records that had not yet left the department, they'd had ten patients early in the evening. That meant a light night, with plenty of time for Dr. Denton to sleep . . . which meant he'd probably slept almost until shift change . . . which meant the stapler-toting trash dumper would have had very little time between shif—

"Not again!" The exclamation came from behind him, and he turned to find Tex striding toward him, a long, muscular arm raised toward the entrance. "Would you look at that? Another Worker's Comp."

Lukas looked over to see a man helping a woman through the ER entrance. The man was Mr. Gray, from Johnson's Poultry. To Lukas's surprise, fifty-something, balding Mr. Gray held the attractive young woman by the arm and spoke with her softly. Instead of the traditional garb of the poultry-line worker—stained clothing, rubber boots, and a hair net—she wore tight jeans and a formfitting blue sweater.

"You'd think they would get a clue and slow those lines down," Tex muttered as she picked up a clipboard from her desk. "But no, they'd lose too much money that way. Who cares about the workers? This town is filled with disposable people."

"Then why do you stay here?"

"Because I have a job here. Got to make a living. Mom's illness and funeral left me with a lot of debt, and I'm an only child. Who else is going to pay?"

They watched in silence as Shirley checked in the patient. When the patient gave her name, Yvonne Barrett, the secretary fell silent.

Tex gasped and stiffened beside Lukas. The clipboard in her hand clattered to the desk. She stared at the woman in outraged shock, then turned to Lukas, the strong, well-defined features of her face drawn into an angry scowl. "Do you know who that is?" she hissed.

The name sounded slightly familiar. Yvonne . . . wasn't that—

"That's the woman! She's the one! I can't believe she had the guts to come in here after what she—"

"*What* woman? Calm *down*! And lower your voice."

Tex crossed her arms over her chest and glared toward the front. "She's the one who helped Mr. Amos and that nurse frame Hershel. She's the one who accused him of 'unprofessional conduct.' I'd like to show *her* unprofessional conduct with my fist in her—"

"Stop it," Lukas snapped. "You're the one who's behaving unprofessionally. Am I going to have to call the floor nurse to trade places with you while I see this patient?"

"No way! You're not getting out of my sight. What if this is a setup? You've already had your run-ins with Mr. Amos. Maybe he sent her here to frame you, too."

Lukas couldn't prevent a momentary doubt. Surely nobody was that stupid. Still, he needed to be cautious. "Then, calm down and treat her as you would any other patient. Do the assessment, Tex, then call me."

"Do I have to be nice?"

"No nicer than usual."

She relaxed. "Okay, Dr. Bower." She turned to carry out her task.

"And, Tex?" Lukas called to her.

She stopped and turned back.

He smiled at her. "I'm glad you're on *my* side."

———

"Don't know what we'd've done without you, Dr. Mercy. You're a real angel, I tell you!" Odira's voice once again echoed loudly and deeply enough to damage eardrums, and Mercy felt a glow of satisfaction as she pulled her all-wheel-drive car next to the ice-free space in front of the tiny apartment where Odira and Crystal lived.

Crystal sat in the backseat with her new medication dispenser in her hands. On the ride from the hospital she had flipped up the lid of each small container, called out the day of the week and the time of day on the label, then snapped the lid back down with a click that seemed to satisfy her. She did this several times, never smiling, always serious. She had flipped each of the twenty-one lids at least three times while Odira had talked and laughed and beamed at her with maternal pride.

These were some of the times Mercy lived for. She was glad she'd kept them in Knolls, where friends could visit and where she could be nearby to reassure them.

She got out of the car and walked with them to the apartment. "Now, Odira, no skipping doses on those pills." She waited until Odira unlocked the front door.

"You got that right, Dr. Mercy! I don't want to take a chance on getting down sick and not being able to take care of my gal." She patted Crystal on the shoulder and held the door open for her to step inside first. "We're both going to take our pills like we're supposed to. Ain't that right, Crystal Lee?"

"Yes, Gramma."

"And if you run out," Mercy added, "you will call and let me know?"

"Sure will, Dr. Mercy! We'll be good from now on. We promise."

Mercy said good-bye and left before they could notice the groceries stocked away in the refrigerator and the cupboards. What she had brought would be enough to keep them for a while.

Yvonne Barrett, the pretty line worker from Johnson's Poultry, had a fresh bruise on her right temple caused by a fall into a freezer rack. According to Tex's assessment, the woman's vitals were normal. Lukas resisted the urge to check Yvonne's arm and see if Tex might have set the cuff a little tight for the blood pressure reading. In spite of her bluster, Tex was a professional.

But she was also a good bodyguard. She stood as close to Lukas as she could get without impeding his movements, and she watched every move the woman made.

"They take those lines too fast," Yvonne complained. She didn't seem to notice Tex's overprotective stance. "I was racking chicken halves. Those things just kept coming at me, faster and faster, and some were falling on the floor. That really puts the boss in a bad mood. I'm supposed to have help, but we're shorthanded right now. I tried to keep up, but I couldn't. I got weaker and weaker and just passed out cold. My line boss didn't want me to say anything about what happened, but then she saw the bruise and decided she'd better cover her backside. Accidents like this happen all the time, don't they, Mr. Gray?"

The safety director sat in a chair at the far end of the exam cubicle. At the sudden attention from the other three people in the room, he shifted uncomfortably, turned pink, cleared his throat. "I wouldn't say *all* the time."

"I would," Tex said. "Mr. Gray, everybody on staff knows you by name you're here so often. All those accidents can't be employee error. There aren't that many clumsy people in the whole state, and someday OSHA's going to realize Herald is on the map, and they'll check you out. They'll be after your blood. *Then* who'll be in the hot seat?"

"It isn't that easy," Gray said. "You've never worked in a place like that—"

"Oh yes, I have, and so did my mom. It's just too bad nobody but my mom had the guts to speak out about it, because then she wouldn't have lost her job."

"Tex, I need you to take orders to the secretary." Lukas needed to stop this freight train before it derailed.

Tex looked at him, then looked at Yvonne, and her thick, arched brows drew together in the center. "Uh, Dr. Bower, I can't do that right now."

Lukas gave the others an embarrassed glance, then excused himself and walked out with Tex. "Look, I appreciate your concern for my reputation," he murmured in her ear. "I don't think it's necessary."

"You don't know what—"

"I know how to take care of myself, Tex. I've learned the hard way. I will do nothing to make the young lady think I'm anything but an ethical physician."

"*Lady?* You've got to be kidding."

Lukas stopped and turned to face her. "You don't know for sure what went on behind that curtain. Few people do. You don't appreciate hearing other staff members blame him for the incident with Yvonne, but what if she's innocent? You've got to look at this situation from both sides. You're getting too emotionally involved."

She glared at him.

"Orders." Lukas pointed to the secretary. "She's waiting."

CHAPTER 17

Once upon a time long ago, Thursday had been Mercy's day off. She could barely remember the feeling of freedom. When Lukas was off at the same time, they had gone hiking together in the Mark Twain National Forest . . . back when life was simple and she felt righteous for hating Theo, and she could dream about a future with Lukas without worrying if her dreams were sins. During the summer, when Tedi was out of school, the three of them went swimming at the lake. If only Mercy had then realized how precious those times were.

Now, at eight-thirty Thursday morning, she not only missed her days off, but she especially missed the joy of those first few months of living with her daughter without guilt. Whatever made her think she needed a busier practice? She didn't want a bigger income. She wanted more time for the important things in life. She craved a few hours during the week when she wasn't fretting over noncompliant patients or fighting with insurance companies or taking calls in the middle of the night and worrying if the effects of her sleeping pill would impede her judgment. She loved her patients, and she loved her work, but there was always the possibility of getting too much of a good thing. She was far past that limit.

The clinic telephone rang for the third time as she was preparing to meet with two patients who had arrived moments ago. Several people who had canceled their appointments yesterday because of the icy roads were scheduled to come in later today. Today was still the staff's traditional day off. That might have to change.

"Richmond Clinic." She sat down at the front desk and tried to decipher her secretary's writing in the appointment book.

"Hello, this is Lee Becker. Dr. Mercy, is that you? I'm so glad someone's there." Lee's words spilled over each other in a soft rush of soprano. "Something's wrong with Shannon. If we had an emergency room I'd take her there, but I don't want to risk driving her all the way—"

"Shannon?" Mercy interrupted, suddenly alarmed. "What's happened?" Fifteen-year-old Shannon Becker had been the victim of a rape last fall, and her parents had been concerned about her emotional condition ever since. So had Mercy, especially since she hadn't seen the girl in a couple of months. Shannon had failed to show up for her last appointment.

"She's gotten so weak she almost passed out this morning," Lee said. "I haven't been able to get her to eat much for the past few weeks—she says she's on this diet, but I don't like it. She's lost way too much weight. Now I'm wondering if she's got the flu on top of everything else. Anyway, I gave her some orange juice and it perked her up, but she just doesn't look right. Will you check her out?"

"Give her more juice if she can keep it down, then bring her in as soon as you can." Mercy glanced up at the clock, suppressing a sigh. "I'll probably be here for a while." And maybe she would have to call Lauren in to help. Josie had left early yesterday with the flu.

"Thanks, Dr. Mercy," Lee said.

"Is she still seeing her counselor?" Mercy had recommended weekly counseling sessions for Shannon after the rape.

"Not for several weeks," Lee said. "Dr. Metcalf said she thought Shannon was doing well, and Shannon's been so busy at school there just hasn't been time. I'll give her more orange juice and bring her over."

After disconnecting, Mercy switched on the answering machine so nothing would interrupt her meeting. She walked down the corridor to her office and stepped inside. She took two deep, sustaining breaths and said a quick prayer for strength.

Kendra Oppenheimer had silky golden brown hair, and her eyes were the color of sparkling purple-blue tanzanite. Her delicate features and heart-shaped face only needed a smile. Mercy knew that smile would be a long time coming.

Buck sat slumped in the chair beside his wife. Though he was only in his late twenties, the bags under his eyes suggested an age increase of ten years since Saturday night. With his body-builder muscles and height, he looked like a giant beside Kendra. But the same message of confusion and pain filled both their expressions: What was happening to their lives? To their marriage? What was going to happen to Kendra?

Mercy sat down in the swivel office chair behind her desk and faced the young couple. "Kendra, you look a lot better than you did Saturday night. How are you feeling?"

Kendra drew a slender shoulder up in a half shrug. "Drugged." She rested her hands on the arms of her chair, her gaze slightly out of focus. Her eyelids drooped halfway over those beautiful eyes.

"That's normal." Mercy studied the report in front of her. Kendra was on several different medications to treat bipolar disorder. "When your psychiatrist gets the medicines regulated you should feel better."

"They've already changed the stuff once," Buck said. "That lithium messed her up, so they had to put her on Haldol." He glanced sideways at his wife. "They shouldn't have sent her home so soon."

Kendra's eyes came open wide. She looked at Buck, then away, and her hands stiffened on the arms of the chair. "Maybe I should've just moved in there."

Buck didn't reply, and Mercy felt her heart contract at the pain that raced across Kendra's face. A sense of identification brought back memories of disillusionment and fear that Mercy thought she had released months ago.

"Buck, they wouldn't have allowed her to come home if they thought she was still suicidal," Mercy said quietly.

"I just think I know my wife better than some doctor who never even met her before this week. I just think—"

"You just think life would be a lot better with me locked away." Kendra didn't look at Buck this time but kept her head bent, her full lips pressed together.

"I never said that, and it isn't—"

"You don't have to say it." Kendra's hands gripped the armrests of the chair so hard her fingers turned white.

"Hold it, you two." Mercy had been their family doc since they were married. She'd been through a lot with them, and she felt as if she knew them well enough to speak frankly. "Kendra, you have to understand that your husband loves you, and his only concern is to keep you safe through this."

Kendra looked up at Mercy briefly, and the doubt was evident in her eyes.

"And, Buck," Mercy continued, "you have to remember that your wife is not rejecting you now. She is ill. I think all this springboarded from the grief of losing her father and her disappointment over her inability to conceive. Somehow that sense of loss has metamorphosed into something more sinister, and that's what we're treating."

"He thinks I ought to just snap out of this depression," Kendra said. "He told me that once."

"I didn't say that!" Buck protested. "I just told you to try to get your mind off of everything for a while. I thought if we went on a trip or something, the change of scenery would do you some good."

"You told me I should get my mind off *myself*—that's what you said!" Kendra shot back.

"That isn't how it works," Mercy said. "And Kendra isn't doing this to get attention. The way she feels right now has nothing to do with weakness of character—"

"I know that," Buck said sharply. "I do."

"Could've fooled me!" Kendra shot back.

"Calm down." Mercy braced herself against the unhappy tension in the room. "We have to work together on this. The two of you especially need to realize that the illness is the enemy, and you are allies. Of all psychiatric illnesses, bipolar disorder is among the most responsive to treatment." Mercy leaned forward. "With proper treatment and dedication, and with prayer, we can beat this thing."

"Have you treated something like this before?" Buck asked.

"Yes. Unfortunately, we're finding that about one in seven people in this country suffer from mood disorders." Mercy pulled a pamphlet out of her drawer and pushed it across the desk toward Kendra. "I'm sure they gave you a lot of literature at Cox North, but here's one you may not have yet. Kendra, statistically speaking, probably about fifteen hundred people in Knolls suffer from depression or manic depression."

"How many have you treated here?" Buck asked.

Mercy felt their sudden, concentrated attention, and she couldn't help picking up on the implication. "Believe me, not nearly as many as your psychiatrist. Dr. Guthrie handles this kind of illness all the time, and—"

"And he's a two-hour drive from here, Dr. Mercy," Buck said. "He wants to see Kendra every Monday and Thursday, and that's eight hours of driving a week. If I can't get off for the appointments, that means Kendra will have to drive herself. I don't want that."

Mercy saw a spasm of disappointment pass across Kendra's face, but by the time Buck looked at her it was gone.

Mercy sighed and glanced down once more to study the report on Kendra from Dr. Guthrie. She was taking Serzone for depression, Haldol for the mania, and Ativan for restlessness. To Kendra, all those prescriptions must seem like an onslaught of medication. There would probably still be some quantitative adjustment.

Of course, if Mercy could call Dr. Guthrie for consultations every week . . . she knew it would be possible. On an intellectual level, she knew she could care for Kendra's needs medically. But even as she silently accepted the responsibility, she felt another burden of stress load her down. When would the deluge end?

She cleared her throat. "Kendra, I know Dr. Guthrie has already emphasized the importance of taking your medication faithfully. Do you have a daily dispenser?"

The couple looked at her blankly. Mercy turned and pulled open a door on the credenza behind her. She reached in and brought out a plastic device about half the size of a small paperback novel. The container had fourteen connected snap-on lids, each marking morning or evening for a particular day of the week. The pill box was smaller than the one Mercy had purchased for Crystal Hollis. "I want you to use this. It'll help you keep track of everything at first, when—"

"But that's what forgetful old people use," Kendra complained, staring at the dispenser as if it were a mousetrap with a mouse still inside.

Mercy felt a rush of irritation at the whiny sound of Kendra's voice, but before she could snap a retort, she stopped and reminded herself of the despair and emotional pain the depression could foster.

"Kendra," she said gently, "I need you to work with me. If you want me to help you, I will try, but I can't do this without you." She waited until Kendra met her gaze. "Will you help?"

Once more Kendra gave her that disconcerting stare, first at Mercy's left eye, then the right, then back again. She nodded.

"And I want you to keep in touch with me and call me anytime you notice a change in your emotional or physical reactions. Will you do that?"

Again Kendra nodded. Buck nodded, too. Mercy sat back in her chair. "Buck, during the first few weeks, Kendra and I will be depending on you to catch any warning signs. Kendra's depression can make it difficult for her to follow my instructions, and I need you to make sure she does, especially taking the medication. If her mood swings to mania, the resulting euphoria could convince her she doesn't need treatment any longer. I need you to call me if that hap—"

"So now I'll be living with a prison guard instead of a fireman?" Kendra snapped.

"No, Kendra, you're going to be living with your husband, who loves you and knows what to watch for." Mercy stood to her feet and came around the desk. She sat down in the empty chair on Kendra's right and reached out and took her hand. "We can beat this together."

———

"I've got a brain in there, huh?" Seventy-year-old Mr. Fletcher sat on the exam bed and looked at the CT film Lukas held up to the light. "My wife will be happy to hear that. She says I'm so dense a sledgehammer wouldn't hurt me. Guess I almost proved her right."

"I'll tell you what," Lukas said as he laid the film on the counter and turned back to Mr. Fletcher, "for an extra couple of bucks I'll get you a copy to take home with you. Then you can prove to her you've got a brain."

The man grinned as Lukas helped him to his feet. "That's too good a deal to pass up. Guess I'd better stop messin' around out in the barn when Mildred's at her sister's. Where do I go to pay for the film?"

Lukas directed him to the secretary, then bent down to finish filling out the chart. The Fletchers had been married for forty-five years, and except for those days she visited her sister down in Arkansas, they'd never been apart. He'd told Lukas that five minutes after he'd stumbled into the house with a bump on the head from a falling tractor chain, his wife had called to check on him. She'd said she just "had a feeling" something wasn't right. Then she'd insisted he hurry to the emergency room and get checked out. She was on her way home now.

How would it feel to be that connected to someone who loved you?

"Nice set of wheels, Doc," came a deep voice behind him.

Lukas stopped writing and turned to find Catcher grinning at him through the ER window, his broad, weathered face beaming. Between the thumb and forefinger of his right hand dangled a very familiar set of keys.

"It's outside," Catcher said. "Good as new. I drove your Jeep around some to charge the battery, but you could probably use a new one."

Lukas looked at the keys, then back at Catcher. "A new Jeep?" He reached up and took the keys.

"Just a battery. You don't want a new Jeep, because then you'll worry about messing up the shiny new paint job. Don't ruin a good thing."

"Thank you, Catcher."

"Soon as you can dig her out of the mud she's all yours."

Lukas met the ornery grin with a chuckle.

"Lays rubber nicely." The biker's grin broadened even farther; then he sobered some. "I bought my kid one like yours two years ago when he went off to college. He's still got it, and he treats it better than I treat my baby."

"You have grown children?"

Catcher nodded. "I know, I look too young for that, don't I?" He reached back toward the hip pocket of his jeans. "Better than that, I've got a grandson." With a practiced, fluid motion, he flipped open his billfold directly to a small photograph of a grinning little boy about three years of age. "He's my daughter's kid. She's a paralegal up in Jefferson City. I've been after her for three years to take off and stay home with him, and she finally agreed. They can afford her staying at home. Her husband's got his own auto parts store there. She's six months along with the next baby—a little girl. What do you think, Doc? Isn't he something?" The child had dark brown hair that had already grown down over his ears, and he was wearing a tiny replica of Catcher's black leather jacket.

"He looks just like you," Lukas said. Poor kid.

"Yeah, well, don't worry, he'll outgrow it. That jacket's the closest he's getting to my biker gang." Catcher flipped the billfold shut, but as he did so, a business card fell out and landed faceup on the counter. "No grandkid of mine's going to be splattered across the highway because his grandpa's too stupid to set a better example. I told my girl as soon as she quits her job, that bike out there's going to market and I'm hanging up my jacket." He stopped, shook his head. "Grandkids can sure make you take another look at your life. Guess this is my last big fling. Got any kids, Doc?"

"I'm not married."

"Neither am I—now." There was sadness in Catcher's voice. "Cop work is hard on marriages, hard on families."

Lukas stared at him. "You're a cop?"

"Used to be." Catcher gestured to the business card that had fallen onto the desk.

Lukas picked the card up and looked at it. The man's legal name was Jeff Golhofer. He was a stockbroker and financial advisor with a well-known financial institution. Lukas looked back at the man. "You get around, Catcher."

"Yeah, a little too much. I got the cocaine habit when I was a cop. I tried to blame my addiction on stress for a long time, but I have no one to blame but myself. I was weak. I had to admit I had a problem and make a change in my life. I'm just glad I didn't develop an addiction to money the way I did to drugs. Wouldn't have lasted long as a stockbroker if I had." He grimaced, as if he felt he'd been talking too much. "Well, you'd better get that new battery before you get stalled somewhere again. I might not be around next time. When are you going to rip these strings out of my arm?"

"Come in Friday night."

"What, you're going to make me miss out on party night?"

Lukas chuckled and shook his head, then handed Catcher the card. Catcher slipped it into his pocket, then glanced around the empty waiting room and leaned casually against the counter.

"Don't guess you've heard any more about that kidnapping business, have you?" he asked softly.

Lukas looked up at the man and studied his expression. Was the man being a little *too* casual? "Not in the last hour or so. In a small town like Herald, gossip is as abundant as lake water. Last I heard, the Special Crimes Unit is still in the area, questioning residents."

"Yeah, I know, they've been by to see me a couple of times." Catcher didn't seem upset about the visits. "I told 'em I'd do anything I could to help them, even if it means snitching on my own people. It's not going to come to that, though. Ever tried carrying a baby on a motorcycle? Can't you just see pastel blankets and booties blowing in the wind?" He grinned, but the humor died quickly. "I don't know, Doc, with two kids disappearing in this town, even if that other kid is found, I think the search ought to continue for the kidnapper."

"So do I."

CHAPTER 18

M ercy sank down onto her secretary's chair and took a deep breath as Buck and Kendra walked out the front door of the office. They had orders to call if they noticed any problems. Kendra was supposed to check in by telephone tomorrow and come in on Monday. She had a new appointment with her psychiatrist in Springfield Tuesday. The constant vigilance for the first few days would be comforting to both Kendra and Buck, even though Kendra was still resisting. The overwhelming power of a mood disorder could make its victim feel hopeless. Kendra needed to be reminded repeatedly in the next few weeks that she was not fighting this thing alone. Buck needed that reminder, too.

Mercy checked the telephone recorder and found no new messages. She was just leaning back in the chair to relax for a few moments when the front door opened and Lee Becker walked in with her daughter, Shannon.

Fifteen-year-old Shannon's face held barely more color than the eggshell walls of the clinic waiting room. Her eyes seemed sunken into their sockets. Her blond hair had been cut super short. What shocked Mercy most was the fact that even though she retained a female chest line, her pink sweater hung down over her thin shoulders in folds, and her jeans bagged over hipbones that jutted out like flesh-covered pogo sticks. The child appeared to have tried to erase all evidence of her femininity.

"Hi, Dr. Mercy." Even Shannon's voice sounded lifeless.

Mercy got up and went around through the door to meet them in the middle of the room. "Shannon, what's going on? What happened?" Three months ago this child had been on the verge of blossoming maturity.

"I don't know. I guess I'm coming down with the flu or something. I don't feel too great."

"As I said, she tried to pass out on me at home." Lee's high, clear voice was filled with worry.

"And how long has this been going on?" Mercy asked as she and Lee walked with Shannon back to the first exam room. "How much weight have you lost?"

Shannon blinked up at her and shrugged. "I don't know."

"I've tried weighing her," Lee said. "She won't let me. I figure it's one of those teenage things she'll outgrow. I remember I was pretty self-conscious about my weight at her age."

Before they reached the room, Mercy directed her patient to the set of scales in the wide hallway that stretched between the exam rooms, office, x-ray room, and lab. "Step up on there, young lady. You're not getting out of it this time."

Shannon hesitated and groaned but did as she was told. Mercy operated the balance weights quickly. Before Shannon could step down, Mercy measured her height, as well. The numbers didn't surprise her.

"Not only have you lost thirty pounds, Shannon, but you've grown an inch. That would mean major additional caloric needs in your body, which you obviously have not been getting. Now, let's get you onto a bed." She gently took Shannon's emaciated arm and guided her from the scales into a room. "All this weight loss can't be from the flu."

Lee helped lay her daughter onto the exam bed and brushed motherly fingers across the short, stubby growth of Shannon's blond hair. "You never really regained your appetite after what happened in October, did you, babe?"

The fifteen-year-old lay back against the pillow with a sigh of relief. She ignored her mother's question.

Mercy reached for a thermometer. "Didn't the counselor pick up on this?"

"She never really asked me about it," Shannon said.

"She told us Shannon was doing very well, and she cut her visits down to an 'as needed' basis," Lee explained. "I knew Shannon had wanted to lose some weight anyway, so I didn't think very much about it until the past few days, when she started looking so pale."

Mercy placed the tip of the tympanic thermometer in the girl's right ear and took a reading. Ninety-six. Her skin felt cool to the touch. "I'm going to pinch your arm, but not hard." She pulled the flesh up and compressed it between her thumb and forefinger, then released the skin while Lee and Shannon watched. "Notice that your skin doesn't immediately spring back into place but remains shaped to my fingers for a few seconds?" She pinched her own skin. "This is what your skin should do, Shannon. It lacks turgor, which means you're very dehydrated. Have you had any diarrhea or vomiting lately with your flu symptoms?"

"No, I've just been weak."

Mercy pulled out the blood pressure cuff. "Why didn't you come to me when you realized you were losing too much?"

Shannon blinked at Mercy with washed-out gray eyes. "Too much?"

"You are too thin." Mercy wanted to kick herself for not following up on that missed appointment. And how could Lee have ignored this for so long?

"But, Dr. Mercy, you gave her a clean bill of health last month," Lee said. "We thought she was doing okay."

Mercy looked back at Shannon and once more felt shock at her appearance. Three months ago she'd had plump cheeks and bright, lively eyes. Now there were shadows. "I didn't see Shannon last month." She placed the cuff of the automatic sphygmomanometer and pressed the button to read Shannon's blood pressure. "We've got to get some weight back on—"

"What do you mean you didn't see her?" Lee demanded.

There was a long moment of silence. Shannon still had a hint of that stubborn flash in her eyes, but gone was the healthy blush of a young teenager who was easily embarrassed.

Mercy turned from Shannon to Lee. The stubborn flash and firm chin were obviously a family trait. Lee was an attractive woman whose blond Nordic beauty had reflected well in her daughter. She and her husband and five children had been Mercy's patients since Shannon was five years old. That was when Mercy first went into practice with Dad.

"Shannon's appointment was canceled, Lee," Mercy said. "I remember when Josie told me about it, because I asked her specifically to reschedule an appointment. When she called, she was told that you would reschedule later. No one ever did."

Mercy checked the blood pressure cuff while tense silence echoed between mother and daughter.

"So that's why you didn't want to come in today," Lee said. "Why would you cancel your appointment?"

"I didn't think I needed to come in, Mom, okay?" There was the normal teenage impatience in Shannon's voice and a little defensiveness.

Her blood pressure was on the low side, but the heart rate was normal. This didn't satisfy Mercy. Even though signs of starvation included a slow heart rate, dehydration would reverse the process and mask an underlying problem. Mercy jotted down the numbers, then warmed the bell of her stethoscope in her hand. "I'll want to run more tests, of course. It's going to mean a needle-stick, Shannon."

A brief nod was Shannon's only reaction.

Lee gave a frustrated sigh and sank down on the chair behind her. "Shannon, what am I going to do with you?"

Shannon pressed her lips together and closed her eyes.

"The first thing we're going to do is get this girl into the hospital," Mercy said as she checked Shannon's breathing and heartbeat. "I'll call over there right now and—"

"No!" Shannon stiffened and sat up, eyes wide open now. "Why can't you run the tests here? You can do the needle-stick yourself, can't you?"

Mercy halted her assessment and straightened, unable to miss the sudden panic that careened from Shannon's face. "There are tests I want to run that I can't run here, Shan—"

"But couldn't you take my blood here?" Shannon reached for Mercy's arm and grasped it hard. "Couldn't Mom just take the sample to the lab? Mom, couldn't you do that?"

Lee's chair squeaked as she pushed out of it and crossed to her daughter's side. "Baby, calm down. Dr. Mercy wouldn't—"

"No! No, Mom, don't take me to that hospital!" Shannon's voice rose and reverberated out into the hallway. "I can't go over there!" She leaned into her mother's embrace and burst into sobs. "I can't go back to that place . . . I can't."

Mercy leaned across the exam bed and laid a hand on the girl's bony shoulder as her gaze caught and held Lee's. Knowledge and memory passed between them. Shannon still suffered the deep effects of her experience in October, and Knolls Community Hospital featured a starring role in the traumatizing follow-up. Tears filled Lee's eyes and spilled over. From Mercy's vantage point she saw the contortion of pain and fear and sudden, racking sobs that overwhelmed Shannon. But there were no tears.

"I think it's time we found you a new counselor, honey," Mercy said.

"I don't want a new counselor. I don't want to talk about this over and over and over again. Why won't everyone just let me forget about what happened?"

"Because you're not forgetting the incident." Mercy gently disengaged the girl from her mother's embrace and helped her lie back on the bed. Shannon grasped Mercy's arm with both hands. There were still no tears. That meant at least ten percent dehydration. She had to have fluids.

"Look at me, Shannon." Mercy waited until the gray-eyed gaze reluctantly focused on her. "You're starving yourself, and if you continue this, you'll start having some major physical problems. I have a hunch we may be looking at anorexia nervosa, and it's pretty obvious when it started. The first thing I want to do is get a urine sample. Then I want to put you on a monitor to see if there is already damage to your heart. We'll also take a blood test to see how the chemicals in your body are balancing. Meanwhile, I want to start you on IV fluids. We can do all this more quickly in the hospital, and time is important."

"Then I think that's what we'll have to do," Lee said firmly.

Shannon closed her eyes again and slowly shook her head. "Please, Dr. Mercy, if we stay here I promise I'll be good. You can stick me with all kinds of needles, and I'll drink anything you want me to drink, but please don't send me over there." Her eyes came open to show her desperation, and her hands tightened on Mercy's arm. "Please."

Mercy held her silent gaze. Treating her as an out-patient *could* be done. All the equipment was here. They could set Shannon up, run the tests, hook her up to the monitor, and watch her closely. . . . They even had IV fluids, and a sports drink in their fridge in the break room. Shannon would need to learn to face her bad memories, and she still might have to be admitted, but maybe not right now.

"Lee, can you hang out here for a few hours?" Mercy asked.

Some lines of tension relaxed from Lee's face. "As long as you need."

"Okay, Shannon, we'll try it."

Shannon slumped back against her pillow, and she released Mercy's arm at last. Her face once more convulsed with tearless crying. "Thank you."

———

Lukas glanced at his watch and smiled to himself. In three hours his shift would be over, and he'd be on his way to Knolls. He felt like a man about to be released from prison. Meanwhile, there were no patients, and he had a hankering to study a set of patient files— namely, those of Marla Moore.

The medical examiner had completed the autopsy and found positive evidence of a pulmonary embolism, exactly as Lukas had suspected. There were no illegal drugs involved. Lukas studied the sheets of records and findings. He felt a heavy sadness over the loss of this young life and over the baby who would never know his birth mother. What had brought her here to Herald, alone, with no family to take care of her? What kind of anguish had she felt as she struggled out of the apartment in search of help, knowing her baby was lying helpless inside?

And what had happened to that helpless baby during the hours of his disappearance and his reappearance days later? He had obviously been the latest of several victims, but why had he been returned—and practically to the site of the abduction? Was someone, perhaps, seeking to incriminate Catcher and his gang, or did one of them really have something to do with taking him?

Just as Lukas reached the last page of Marla's records, a shadow fell over his shoulder. He turned to find Tex pulling out the chair at the desk and plopping down onto it, this time the right way. She was wearing a dress. Again.

"What are you doing here?" he asked. "You're supposed to be off."

"I am." She leaned forward. She'd fixed her hair again, although she wore no makeup today. "What do you think of him?"

"Who?" Lukas asked.

"You know who, silly." She looked around, then lowered her voice. "Hershel."

"I can't believe you drove all the way over here to get my opinion." And she'd be sorry if he told her what he really thought.

A smile of pure joy radiated from her face. "I'm on my way out of town anyway, so I thought I'd stop by." She hesitated and glanced around the ER again. All was silent and empty except for Carmen, who sat at her desk talking on the phone. "I'm going to meet him tonight when he gets off work. Do you think I'm crazy?"

Blind might be a better word. Naïve. Gullible. "I don't think my assessment of your mental condition has anything to do with our present conversation."

Tex grinned and socked him in the arm. Hard. Then she grew serious. "I'm surprised my big-mouthed cousin didn't fill you in on my past, but since she didn't, all I'm going to tell you is I haven't always been the best judge of character. Don't tell anyone about him, okay?"

Great. "Okay, I won't tell, but . . . uh . . . Tex, maybe you should move kind of slowly with this one." He felt like an older brother warning his little sister about the perils of dating. Only this sister wasn't so little. He wasn't as concerned about her physical safety as he was about her feelings. Should he say more?

"Thanks, Dr. Bower." She stood up and pushed the chair back. "We'll just have time for dinner—he has a meeting at seven."

Good, then he wouldn't have time to do very much damage. "Tex, you really did just come in to ask my opinion about Hershel?"

Her grin deepened. "You think I'd drive all the way here to get your opinion when all I have to do is step over and knock on your wall at home? I had something faxed here because I don't have a machine at home."

"Oh really? Like, perhaps, application forms for a residency program?"

Her grin held steady. "See you, Dr. Bower."

Mercy watched Lee and Shannon walk out of the clinic seven hours after they'd arrived. Shannon's steps were quick and strong, and her cheeks glowed a healthy pink again. Mercy had warned them the improvement might not last. Shannon had an appointment here in the office tomorrow. Lee would see that the appointment was kept.

The desk phone chirped for at least the twentieth time that afternoon. Mercy jotted a final note for Loretta, yawned, and glared at the phone. How long had Thursdays been her day off? Didn't anybody realize that this was not a twenty-four-hour-a-day office?

And yet, what if this call was another emergency?

Irritably she snatched up the phone. "Yes!"

"I wanna know where my wife is."

Her breath caught, and she felt a sudden rush of outrage. Abner Bell. If he were standing in front of her right now, she would physically attack him. "You listen to me, you sick monster," she spat. "It's none of your business where Delphi is. You're lucky you're not behind bars right now, and you'd better not press your luck, or I'll pull every string I can find to make sure that's where you end up!"

She stopped for breath, gritted her teeth, and concentrated on inhaling evenly and silently, holding the receiver away from her mouth. So much for remaining calm and professional.

"Oh." His voice came in a low, growling tone of discovery. "You've got her."

Mercy felt the strength leave her. "I do *not* have her. Nobody 'has' her. She's not an inanimate possession to be hauled around and knocked around. She's a human being! Don't you understand that concept, Abner?"

There was a long, expectant, tense silence, and his heavy breathing echoed over the distance. Where was he calling from? She glanced toward the door and wished she'd locked it.

"You *know* where she is." His accusation grated across the line.

Mercy slammed the phone down.

CHAPTER 19

Even along the cold, dark, tree-shadowed street that led to Mercy's house, Lukas felt the welcome blanket of Knolls surround his Jeep Thursday night. What he felt had nothing to do with the bright moonlight that outlined the widely spaced brick and wood houses. This good feeling had everything to do with memories.

Lukas had helped Mercy and Tedi move into their new home last summer while Theodore was still in detox. The beautiful gray-bricked three-bedroom house was modern, yet a builder with foresight had left mature maples, oaks, and pines surrounding the house on the one-acre lot and had planted evergreen bushes around the perimeter of the front lawn. The place was such a drastic change from the dilapidated house Mercy had rented for five years that she'd breezed through the move.

Lukas pulled into the driveway and spotted the glowing front-porch light. She must have received his message on her recorder. Good. She was expecting him.

The house looked great, with the wood trim and shutters newly painted and a storm door finally in place. They'd had to take the front door off its hinges to get her new sofa moved in. The movers—volunteers from the hospital—had accidentally broken a box of dishes and glasses and had knocked a deep gouge in the hallway wallpaper. And Mercy had laughed about the damage. She was so happy to gain custody of her daughter after five years of separation and pain, nothing so inconsequential could have marred her joy on that day.

Lukas turned off his headlights and motor and got out of his Jeep.

He never thought he'd thank God for tough-talking, beer-guzzling bikers in leather jackets, but tonight, on his three-hour drive down from Herald, he'd blessed them several times. And he reminded himself how much more he had to mature spiritually. He still made snap judgments about people by the way they behaved or looked. He needed to remember that personality sometimes had little to do with the underlying character of a person. He also needed to remember that God loved all His children, and Lukas could please Him better by doing the same.

He didn't feel the first rush of shy hesitancy until he walked up the three brick steps in front of Mercy's house and approached the door. He couldn't prevent the grin that insisted on spreading across his face any more than he could prevent the way his heart pounded and his palms grew damp. Three weeks had passed since he'd seen her, and even then they'd had barely fifteen minutes to talk before she had to get back to work and he had to leave for his next temporary job.

He found the lighted doorbell and rang it, then held his breath, listening to hear her footsteps, or Tedi's, rush to answer the door. Was she looking forward to some time together as much as he was? He couldn't help himself. He'd thought about her all the way down. They'd been bittersweet thoughts, but for now all he wanted was to see her again. He felt like a man who'd taken a hike into the Grand Canyon without water, and she was a refreshing spring. Traveling from place to place was no fun, and Herald was even worse, but he had to admit to himself that being separated from her these past few months was the worst part of all. What he tried not to think about was the possibility that his whole future would be without her.

No one answered the door. He frowned and rang the bell again, listening until he heard the deep musical chimes inside the front hallway. Yes, the doorbell was working.

He shivered in his long-sleeved chamois shirt. Should have put his coat on, but he didn't think he'd be out here long, and he hadn't expected the weather to be this cold. He knocked on the door, just in case.

No one came.

He reached up to test the latch and see if the house was locked when the sound of a motor and the beam of headlights reached him from down the street. He stepped across the small brick porch to see if it might be Mercy, but to his disappointment it wasn't her car. Instead, he saw a champagne-colored Saturn.

He watched the car slow in front of Mercy's driveway, and once more his hopes rose. He turned and took the steps down to the sidewalk and then felt a quick thrill of joy when he saw the car stop and Tedi wave at him from the front passenger seat. She thrust the door open and jumped out.

"Lukas!" She leaned back into the car. "Look, Grandma, it's Lukas!"

A rush of disappointment overwhelmed him for a few seconds. Grandma, not Mom. Ivy must have bought a new car.

But there wasn't time to wallow in disappointment as Tedi came flying toward him, book bag over her shoulder, long dark hair held back in a clip. And glasses.

Glasses? When did she get—

She hurled herself into his arms and grabbed him around the waist, and the book bag fell off her shoulder and slammed into his side as he reached out and engulfed her in a tight hug.

Tedi. Mercy's daughter. The sweetest, smartest eleven-year-old in the world.

"Lukas, why didn't you tell us you were coming?" Her voice was muffled by his shirt, but he managed to decipher that they must not have received his message. So the porch light wasn't for him. Okay. Tedi sure knew how to welcome a guy.

"It was a spur-of-the-moment decision," he said. "I tried calling."

She continued to hang on. "Did you miss us?"

"I sure did."

"I've missed you so much, and I know Mom has, too. Everybody has! Why don't you just come back and work with Mom until they get the ER built, and then we can see you every day and you can help me with my homework like you used to, and—"

"Lukas!" Ivy came rushing up behind her granddaughter. She, too, grabbed him in a bear hug that threatened to knock him sideways. Her grip was firm and tight, and she laughed as she stepped back and looked up at him. "What a wonderful surprise! I wish we'd known you were coming. You could have come over to my house to wait for Mercy."

"Where is she?" he asked. "Is everything okay at the clinic? I knew she was busy, but—"

"She'll be along soon. You know how she likes to mother her patients, and . . . well, I guess I can tell you. . . ." Ivy lowered her voice and glanced around the house into the darkness, as if someone might be listening. "Delphi Bell needed a place to stay, so she's going to be at my house for a few days. Mercy just wanted to make a last-minute check and see that she was okay for the night."

Lukas nodded. "Oh yes, she told me a little about that on the phone this week."

Another smile crossed Ivy's face. "So you two *are* keeping in touch. I'd hoped you would."

"Yes, we're keeping in touch."

"Not as much as Mom wants, though," Tedi said.

Lukas felt a familiar warmth. "Ivy, you look good." There were no more shadows beneath her eyes, and her face had filled out. He had met her for the first time last spring, when she'd brought her dying mother into the emergency room and insisted on resuscitation measures—her mother was in the last stages of cancer. He had learned at that point how bullheaded the Richmond women could be.

Ivy looked down at her eager-faced granddaughter, and her smile widened. "Why don't you get the front door unlocked, and we'll go in."

"Okay." Tedi reached for her book bag and pulled a set of keys out of the front pocket. "Sorry nobody was here when you arrived, Lukas. I had a play tonight, and Grandma picked me up." She unlocked the door and pushed it open.

Lukas stood back and allowed Ivy to enter first. When he followed, he felt a sweet rush of memories greet him with scents of cinnamon and apples and eucalyptus. He felt so comfortable in Mercy's home. He'd spent a lot of time here.

Tedi stepped over and hugged Lukas's arm and grinned up at him. "Mom's going to be so happy to see you, Lukas. Did you know Clarence lost another twenty pounds? And Darlene hasn't had an asthma attack since you left. And Grandma Ivy's still dating Dr. Heagerty, but she gets mad when I call it dating. She says they're just friends, but I know better."

"Hey, watch it, kid!" Ivy protested. "That's all conjecture."

Tedi giggled and ignored Ivy. "She talks to him on the phone almost every day, and when she sees him she gets all smiley, like Mom does when she sees you." Tedi continued to talk as she led the way into the living room. "Come on in and sit down." She plopped down on the love seat adjacent to the sofa, and Ivy sat across from her, gesturing for Lukas to take a place beside Tedi. He did so gladly.

Ivy gestured toward the green scrubs Lukas wore. "Just get off work?"

"Yeah, I drove straight down. I had my own clothes in the locker, but when I went to put them on . . . well . . . someone had played a practical joke on me." He paused and shook his head. "Another one. I didn't feel like wearing cutoffs down here." And he hadn't wanted to take time to go home. Besides, home was here. As far as he was concerned, Herald, Missouri, *was* a practical joke. "I have everything I need at my house. I just haven't been there yet."

Ivy nodded. "You must have been in a hurry to get here." A teasing tone filled her voice.

"Of course he was, Grandma," Tedi said, sitting back in the love seat and bouncing her legs happily. "He misses Mom." She grinned. "How do you like my glasses, Lukas? Do I look smarter?"

She was so much like Mercy, he couldn't help returning her grin. "You sure do, but you were already the smartest girl around."

"I got 'em two weeks ago. Mom let me pick them out myself. I love 'em, because now the kids at school don't expect me to slide when we play baseball. I usually just sit on the sidelines looking intelligent." She raised her chin in the air and struck a haughty pose but ruined the effect with a mischievous grin.

Ivy beamed at Tedi, then turned again to Lukas. "How are things going in Herald?" She gestured toward the scrubs. "Aside from the practical jokes—and what kind of a person would make cutoffs out of your slacks?"

Lukas spread his hands. "I'm still trying to guess. The natives aren't too friendly. I thought all small towns were the same, but they're not. The only thing Herald has that Knolls doesn't is an ER."

"But we will soon," Tedi announced. "Mom says sooner than anyone expected, and I'm glad, because Mom gets calls and has to go out a lot. Sometimes she even takes me to the clinic with her, although she usually just drops me off at Grandma's."

Lukas gave Tedi a questioning glance. What about Theodore? Why didn't she stay with him part of the time? Surely his working hours weren't the same as Mercy's.

Tedi leaned against Lukas and looked up at him through thick dark lashes. "Why don't you come back and work at Mom's clinic until the new ER's finished?"

Oh no, now he was going to get the guilt trip from Tedi, too. "Because I'm an emergency physician, not family practice."

"But Mom's family practice, and she works in the ER."

Once more, Lukas felt that longing to be firmly ensconced in Mercy's life—and in Tedi's. He looked down into the child's sweet open face and wondered if, indeed, he might not be a good stepdad. Did he possess the maturity? He and Tedi had grown close last summer and fall.

So many questions yet to be answered. They could overwhelm him, and all he wanted to do right now was bask in Tedi's shining smile and see Mercy walk through the door. He felt as if he could do this every day for the rest of his life and never tire of spending time with them.

But how many times would he also see Theodore walking in? He would always be a part of their lives, and Tedi was the connection that would keep him there. This was Theodore Zimmerman's family, not Lukas Bower's.

———

Mercy fought the fatigue that seemed to press her into the car seat with the force of a jet during takeoff. Sleep deprivation did that to people.

Delphi was now safely tucked away at Mom's after a quick getaway from a side door of the hospital, under cover of January darkness. Mercy had been especially careful to make sure Abner would not see them even if he was watching from the parking lot—she'd used Darlene's car.

Lately just the day-to-day routine of life seemed too heavy to man-

232 · HANNAH ALEXANDER

age, and her life was far from routine. She had a tendency to take on the problems of her patients and worry about them too much. She tried to remember to pray for them more often and worry about them less, but sometimes she forgot. Often she forgot. Dependence on God was still such a new concept to her.

Since she'd become a Christian her heart was not only more tender toward her daughter and mother and Lukas, but it was more tender toward her patients. That natural, solid wall she'd built around her emotions as a professional had softened at the top. Sometimes that was a good thing. Sometimes it wasn't.

She turned onto the street where she lived and forced herself to breathe deeply, relax, enjoy the luxury of watching for the lighted windows of her own home, where Tedi may already have popped some popcorn and mixed the lemonade. They could share memories of their day before they went to bed. At least she'd been able to catch the play before rushing off to tend to Delphi. Theo, true to his word, had been there, too.

Mercy frowned, and the weight on her mind grew heavier as she recalled Alice's words today . . . "What a wonderful example of reconciliation!"

The words had continued to haunt her all day. Apparently, Alice wasn't the only one who felt God's will was for Mercy, Tedi, and Theo to become a family again. Lauren had implied that, though reconciliation would take a lot of inner strength, it would be a good thing. And Joseph, their pastor—inexperienced bachelor that he was—also radiated the same message. But none of them had ever experienced the pain of divorce. True, they knew their Bibles a lot better than Mercy did. . . .

Still, she wasn't going to base a life-changing, heartrending decision on the whim of three people, especially people who couldn't even identify with the struggles of her life. There were others she could ask . . . and maybe she should . . . though she didn't even want to think what her reaction would be if they told her to reconcile with Theo. And what, exactly, did reconciliation mean? What would Mom say? What would *Lukas* say?

She caught sight of the lights in the front window of her house, and she smiled, already imagining the buttery fragrance of the popcorn and the blare of the television mingling with Tedi's laughter and chatter. Home. Mom might still be there, making sure Mercy returned so Tedi wouldn't be left alone, but she would leave quickly. She always did.

But the overflow from the porch light outlined two cars in the driveway, one behind the other. Had Mom brought Tedi home? The car in front had a familiar boxy shape. . . .

An old Jeep. She caught her breath. "Lukas!"

Suddenly all the cares of the day dissipated. She braked and pulled into the drive beside the Jeep, pushed the garage-door opener, and eased into the overstuffed garage, barely noticing that the fluorescent overhead light was flickering again, or that more leaves littered the concrete floor of the garage than covered the yard outside.

Lukas was here!

She grabbed her bag and lunged out of the door and up the garage entrance steps and shoved open the door. "Hello! Anybody home?" She tried to control the speed of her footsteps as she rushed across the kitchen floor, through the dining room, and into the living room. There, she stopped with a sudden jolt.

Lukas was looking in her direction expectantly, and as soon as she appeared he stood up, his arms dropping to his sides. His face lit as if an angel had just appeared in front of him. He took a hesitant step toward her, then stopped.

Mercy dropped her medical bag onto a straight-backed chair and rushed across the room to greet him, unable to contain the laughter that spilled from deep inside. She wrapped her arms around him and kissed him on the cheek. He returned the hug with satisfying strength.

Over his shoulder, she saw Mom and Tedi watching. She didn't care. She reached up and grabbed Lukas on both sides of his head and smacked him a nice, noisy kiss right on the lips. She felt a glow of satisfaction when he kissed her back and drew her closer. Tedi came rushing over to hug Lukas and Mercy both at the same time.

"Lukas, why didn't you tell us you were coming?" Mercy asked, disengaging herself from the group hug and turning to the kitchen, where she'd left the back door standing wide open in her rush to reach him.

Tedi followed her. "He did, Mom. We just didn't get the message.

He drove all the way down tonight just to see you, and then he has to go back tomorrow because he's supposed to work tomorrow night. I wish he didn't have to go back at all. Did you know they cut up his clothes up there? Those people aren't very nice."

Mercy grinned at her daughter's garrulous excitement and wrapped an arm around her as they walked back into the living room. "Well, Lukas tells me he has a temporary contract with those people, and that means he has to stay until the contract is satisfied." She sank onto the sofa beside Lukas. She took his arm and squeezed it. "You know I told you about Delphi's disappearance the other day? Well, the police found her hiding in an unheated motor home at the edge of town, where she'd broken in. Unfortunately, word spread. Although our new managing editor for the *Knolls Review* did agree to my request not to print the news. We want to try to keep Delphi away from Abner until we can get her out of town somewhere safe."

Lukas sat forward and turned to her with an expression of concern in his earnest blue eyes. "And Abner knows she's been found?"

She thought about the telephone call at the office today and remembered his grimy, threatening voice, but right now she didn't want to worry Lukas about it, and she would not frighten Tedi. And Mom would call the National Guard if she knew. "It wouldn't surprise me. Theo tells me he's heard about her 'capture' several times down at the shop. You know how fast word spreads in Knolls."

Ivy glanced at her watch and stood. "And speaking of which, I need to get back home and make sure our guest is doing okay. Darlene is out at a meeting tonight—that lady is a gem. She has the sweetest heart and the most gentle disposition, but I can never keep her home long enough for us to spend much time together. Now that she isn't worried about Clarence, she's got her finger in every charitable organization in the city. But that leaves Clarence home alone with Delphi right now, and there's no telling what kind of horror stories he'll tell her about me." She hugged Tedi, winked at Lukas, and waved a hand in Mercy's general direction as she left.

Tedi planted herself between Lukas and Mercy, and that was when Mercy realized there would be no early bedtime tonight.

———

Clarence saw the young woman huddled in the corner of Ivy's

family room, her left arm crossed over her chest as if to protect herself from a blow. Stringy brown hair hung to her shoulders, and fear and pain lurked in her eyes as if they'd been born there. A black bruise marked the skin all around her right eye and cheekbone. Her right arm was hugged tightly against her body with a sling, and under that it looked as though she had half a cast on.

She turned her head enough to look at him as he stepped from the indoor apartment entrance. He was glad when her face didn't register shock or revulsion at his size before she looked away again.

"Hi," he said, stepping farther into the room.

She nodded but didn't look at him again. She didn't look at anything.

"You okay?"

No answer, not even a nod this time, but he didn't take her reaction personally. From what Ivy'd told him, this slightly chunky young woman in her twenties was hurting from the inside out. He could relate—even though he'd never been beaten senseless by a husband.

He walked farther into the room and sank down as easily as possible on the love seat about eight feet from where she sat. He didn't want to scare her off.

He sat there and waited, sending glances at the blank television screen. Should he turn it on? Somehow he didn't think that was what this girl needed, but it sure was quiet in here. And he couldn't just sit here and stare at her all night.

"What's your name?" he asked, figuring that was a good place to start.

Her gaze darted back toward him, startled. She shifted in her seat, cleared her throat, blinked. "Delphina Bell." Her voice came out as a harsh whisper. She cleared her throat again but didn't say more.

Now he knew how Lukas and Mercy must've felt when they first came to see him, when he'd tried to kick them out of his room.

"Delphina? That's kind of an old-fashioned name. Where'd that come from? Named after your grandmother or something?"

She nodded. "Mama's mom. They call me Delphi."

"There, that wasn't so bad. Knew you could talk. I'm Clarence Knight. My sis and I live in that apartment." He jerked his head toward the entrance door and shifted his weight on the love seat.

236 · HANNAH ALEXANDER

"Actually, I'm the only one who sleeps there. Darlene has a bedroom in the main house. Ivy took us in, too." He probably sounded like a jabbering fool, but trying to start a conversation with somebody who'd barely talk was hard. He gestured toward the sling. "Broken arm?"

She looked down at her arm, then shook her head. "Dislocated."

He grunted and nodded. He'd heard Mercy telling Ivy about the husband, and he wanted to reassure Delphi. "Don't you worry, that jerk's not gonna find you here. And if he does, Ivy's mean enough to fight him off. Why, she spouts fire so much she's got singed nose hairs."

Delphi shot him a startled look. Then her face puckered slightly. Tears filled her eyes and trickled down her cheeks.

Uh-oh. What did he say?

CHAPTER

A few minutes before schooltime Friday morning Mercy backed
out of the garage and pressed the remote button that closed the
overhead door. "Tedi, we need to talk."

Tedi yawned in reply and snuggled sideways on her seat within
the boundary of her seat belt, knocking her glasses sideways on her
face as she did so.

Mercy gave her a tender look. The rascal had charmed her way
out of bedtime until Lukas left last night—and had actually hung on
to his arm and walked him to his Jeep. There had been no time for
private conversation.

"Didn't I tell you to get to bed earlier last night? You're the one
who insisted on chattering until midnight. It's time to face the consequences."

Tedi blinked up at her, and a mischievous grin touched her
mouth. "Talking with Lucas was worth it. I got him to help me with
my homework."

"You were perfectly capable of doing the assignments yourself—
and by the way, the next time you ask a man to marry me, you'd
better be out of my reach."

Tedi grimaced and straightened, knocking her glasses farther sideways. She reached up and took them off. "For a grown-up he sure
blushes easily."

Mercy shot her a warning glare, then returned her attention to the
road as she pulled into the traffic of the main highway. "Speaking of
men, I told your father that you won't be meeting with him alone

Saturday. We'll have our usual lunch meeting because I don't have time for a Branson trip right now."

Tedi put her glasses back on and turned to her. "Did your decision not to go hurt his feelings?"

"Yes," she said gently. "But he understands that it's going to take more time to undo years of pain."

Tedi sat staring out the window as Mercy negotiated the heaviest of the Knolls morning rush—not a difficult feat.

"Mom?" Tedi said at last. "You know my nightmares?"

Mercy glanced over at her. "Yes, honey, are they bothering you again?"

"They've changed."

"How?"

Tedi watched the road for a long moment. "They're different now," she said softly.

"Did you have another one last night?"

"No, but I was afraid to go to sleep. That's why I wanted to stay awake with you and Lukas. Well . . . one reason."

"How have they changed?"

Tedi's voice dropped to a bare murmur. "Now *I'm* the monster."

The attack of guilt hit Mercy before she had time to brace herself, and she caught her breath at the force of the feelings swirling inside her. *No, Lord, please, not Tedi, not this innocent child.* "Okay, that's understandable," she said carefully. "I think that just means you're still angry."

Tedi continued to sit and watch the passing scenery.

"Is your dad the victim in these dreams?" Mercy asked. But she knew the answer. Hadn't she had this type of dream herself? Although for her, they hadn't been nightmares.

Tedi nodded.

"It's natural." And it was painful, and Mercy struggled to keep her voice light. Had she somehow, subconsciously, transferred the lingering vestiges of distrust and anger toward Theo to her own daughter in the words she had spoken, in her attitude toward Theo when they were together?

Mercy reached across the seat and touched Tedi's arm.

Tedi didn't respond. That was a sure sign she was still contemplating something. Finally she turned her solemn brown eyes toward Mercy. "Grandma says when we don't forgive others, God doesn't listen to us when we pray. But she also says we can't forgive people without God's help. How can He help me forgive Dad if He can't hear me pray? I thought I forgave Dad, but when the dreams slip up on me like that—"

"You pray anyway." Mercy wanted to pull over to the side of the road and take Tedi in her arms and tell her everything would be okay. *Oh, God, help us both. The guilt is worse than anything else.* "I learned recently that God can deal with all of our emotions as long as we give them to Him. I think that's what Grandma means—first things first. I think we're going to have to work all the way through our anger at your dad—and not cover those feelings up this time—before we can get on with our lives."

"But how do we work through it? I thought we'd done that."

Mercy thought about something Lukas had told her one time. "The Bible says for us to pray for our enemies."

Tedi gave her a reproachful look. "But Dad isn't our enemy."

Mercy pulled up to the school unloading zone, where other parents were dropping their kids off for the day. "I think in our hearts he still is. That's what has to change." *Oh, Lord, what do you mean by reconciliation? I would do anything to keep Tedi from suffering like this. If that means I have to consider Theodore . . . oh, Lord! Please help me!*

Estelle Pinkley sat straight-backed and square-shouldered across the desk from Lukas. Her jaw jutted forward in a firm line. "A contract."

The iron in her deep voice and the steel focus of her gaze made him wince. Lukas had never before been the object of his administrator's wrath. It was not a comfortable position. "Only temporary," he soothed. "Just until the ER here is completed. Signing a contract was the only way I could stay in one place long enough to catch my breath. The Herald administrator didn't want to sign me on any other way."

"And you let him talk you into it."

"I'm sorry, Estelle, but you didn't need me here."

"Who told you that? I don't recall your asking *me* about a contract! We need you here *now*. Do you know Mercy is being deluged with emergencies? There is room in her clinic for another physician, and she needs you. The citizens of Knolls need you. I have a contract that commits you to that position, not Cherra Garcias or some—"

"But the clinic isn't at the hospi—"

"The Richmond Clinic has a direct affiliation with the county, and you have a binding contract with Knolls Community Hospital that supersedes any other contractual agreement. Did you even *keep* a copy of your Herald contract?"

"Yes, ma'am." Her sarcasm stung, but it was justified. Lukas had no organizational skills, and somewhere in his limitless stacks of mail at home he'd lost his Knolls contract—twice.

"Fax me a copy when you get back tonight," she growled. "That place does have a fax machine, doesn't it?"

"Yes, ma'am."

She leveled another steely gaze at him over the tops of her reading glasses, as if she detected a note of false sincerity in his voice.

"I'll fax you a copy," he said.

"Good. If you don't, I'll call your Mr. Amos first thing Monday morning and get a copy from *him*. And then I will explain the situation to him. If there's a way for us to break this Herald contract without putting you into a legal quagmire, I will find it, and I dare Amos to protest. If he does, we will have a dispute on our hands."

Lukas hated the thought of that, but he liked the "we" part. At least she hadn't totally lost faith in him. She wanted him back here.

She continued to glare at him for another few seconds just to relay to him the seriousness of the situation. Then the stiffness of her posture eased slightly. She clasped her hands together in front of her on the small metal desk and rubbed her knuckles, betraying a flare of arthritis pain.

"Estelle," Lukas said, then hesitated. She had interrupted her busy schedule to meet with him today when he had walked in unannounced. The telephone in her secretary's office had buzzed at least five times during this short conference.

Estelle stopped massaging her knuckles and once again directed her full attention to him. "What is it, Lukas?"

"I know it's unprofessional to allow our private lives to influence our jobs—"

"Nonsense," she snapped. "Someone who can totally separate his personal and private lives is schizophrenic and not to be trusted. Speak up, Lukas. What's going on? Are you finally going to be gracious enough to explain to me why you escaped to Herald and left Mercy in the lurch?"

Ouch. "That wasn't what I did."

"It isn't what you *intended* to do." She leaned forward and steepled her fingers together. "My dear Lukas, don't ever forget that I have spent my whole lifetime studying people. I can read faces, predict actions, and many times hear an inflection in a voice that belies the words spoken. I read you before we ever had our first interview last year. It's why I hired you."

"Thank you, Est—"

"I also knew that because of your idealistic spirit, you would encounter obstacles in your life, both personal and professional." She paused to allow him one of her fleeting smiles. "You expect too much of yourself and of others. You're too trusting."

"Not always." He thought about Catcher.

"You're the kind of person who will do what he thinks is the right thing whether it makes sense or not—such as when you came back into this building to rescue Bailey and me last autumn."

"That made sense."

"Yes, but then you removed yourself from Knolls when Theodore Zimmerman straightened out his life and announced his intentions to make amends with Mercy and Tedi."

Lukas stared at her in surprise. Was he that transparent? Even he hadn't realized what he was doing at the time.

Estelle's expression transformed just long enough for him to once again recognize the smile behind her eyes. "Half of me admires your self-sacrifice, but the other half wants to kick you in the pants. We're talking contracts again, even a covenant, if you will, which is something much more binding. Theodore broke that one long ago."

"But if he and Mercy and Tedi were to reconcile—"

"That's where I believe you're confused. I don't have nearly the understanding of God's law as I have of man's law, but I think I know

God's *heart* pretty well. Reconciliation is necessary, but I can't see God demanding a regression. They are two different things."

Lukas straightened and leaned forward. Estelle seldom spoke publicly about spiritual matters, but Mercy had told him months ago what a student of the Bible this lady was. His respect for her grew the longer he knew her.

"But don't you think Tedi is a living, breathing covenant between Theo and Mercy?" he asked. "That's a bond more precious than a piece of paper or a verbal promise or signatures on a line."

"And Theodore broke that bond, too, remember?"

"But that—"

Estelle cut him off with a raised hand. "You're going to say Theodore is a new person now, and that's true. So is Mercy. But think of it this way, Lukas. If they are truly new people in Christ, are they expected to return to a relationship that has been broken for years, broken by the people they no longer are?"

Lukas thought about that one for a moment. He liked the way she looked at things.

"Lukas, isn't it possible that God has brought you here, to this town and to that family, to fulfill a contract Theodore was unable to fulfill? To redeem what was lost?"

He tried not to react to the leap of hope her words instilled in him, but he knew how he felt reflected in his face. Was this how a man felt who had been granted pardon from a prison sentence?

She got up and came around the desk to stand in front of him. As if on impulse, she reached down and placed a hand on each of his shoulders and squeezed gently. "You're a healer, Lukas, and I think you came here to help heal more than just physical bodies. There's something between you and Mercy that has grown stronger and more obvious over time. I can see how you feel about her in your face right now, and I've seen the same in Mercy's, and in Tedi's. Call it an unspoken bond or a silent pledge, but I think there's more to this than just human attraction or compassion. Why don't you give God some time to reveal to you what it is?"

Shannon lay on the same exam bed as yesterday. She wore another pair of baggy jeans and a brown flannel shirt buttoned to the throat. She wore no makeup, and her two-inch-long hair stuck up in uncombed spikes. At Shannon's request her mother had reluctantly left her alone in the room with Mercy.

Mercy checked the IV site and felt a brief glow of pride at the tiny mark she had made with the needle. Not bad for a doc who allowed her nurses to do the needlework most of the time. Shannon had gained seven pounds in the rehydration process yesterday and another pound overnight, thanks to Lee's insistence on fluid replacement drinks and rest. Lee was an attentive, full-time mom. Mercy admired her.

"Okay, Shannon, you've kept your weight overnight, which is good. You look better than you did yesterday morning. I'll talk to your mom in a few minutes, and then I'll let you get to school."

"I'm not going to school today." Shannon's voice held resentment. "Mom wants to keep an eye on me at home. She doesn't trust me now."

Mercy rechecked the test results from yesterday evening. Complete blood count was normal, and blood sugar was good. "I think you'll be able to regain the weight you've lost. She's just very worried about you right now. I don't think she realized the extent of your problem until you came in yesterday." Mercy set the test results down on the exam room table. "Shannon . . . I didn't ask you yesterday about your monthly cycle. Have you been normal? You haven't missed any periods?"

Shannon's gray gaze flicked to Mercy's face in a quick rush of apprehension. "No, why? You don't think I'm preg—"

"No. This is something that can happen when you've lost too much weight. Being irregular with your cycle could still happen, and if it does I want you to tell me."

"Why? What'll you do?" Fear lurked behind Shannon's voice and eyes, and Mercy could no longer ignore it.

"I will continue to do exactly what I'm doing now, but I want to keep record of your physical state so I can give you the proper nutritional support. I'm watching specifically for signs of starvation."

Shannon's stiff, watchful expression did not change.

Mercy pulled an exam stool over and sat next to Shannon. "You need to realize I'm not the enemy. I'm not trying to make you fat. I'm trying to keep you healthy. There is a limit to the weight you can lose before your body begins to shut down, and you're close to that limit. With anorexia nervosa, young women have a distorted view of their bodies, no matter what the mirror tells them, or what their parents or friends—"

"I know I'm not fat." The statement was soft but firm. "I know what I look like."

Mercy stumbled into silence—and into the discovery of something she should have recognized yesterday. It was so obvious. . . .

"Of course you know that." Mercy reached out to touch the short, stubby growth of Shannon's bangs but then drew back. This child desperately needed her physical autonomy. She did not need someone invading her space unnecessarily. Still, they must deal with the problems she had.

"Shannon, why did you lie to your mother about the appointment last month?"

The girl closed her eyes and turned her head away, and Mercy could almost feel her withdrawing, containing herself behind an invisible wall.

She didn't have to answer, because Mercy already knew. "Okay, let me ask you this: If I promised not to initiate another gynecological exam for at least six months—barring new physical complications— would you be willing to come into my office twice a week for nutritional counseling and a weight check?"

For a moment Shannon didn't seem to hear her. Then her eyes opened and she nodded, watching Mercy quizzically.

"I'll have Josie take your vitals," Mercy continued, "and we'll do a blood test every two weeks if we think it's necessary. However, if your weight drops too far again, we'll have to take more drastic measures."

Shannon looked away again, but not before some of the tension melted from the newly angular planes of her face. Mercy caught the telltale sheen of tears in her eyes. Ah yes, the tears were back. She was no longer dehydrated.

"I had to do a deposition last week," Shannon said as the tears accumulated and flowed more freely. "They made me talk about what happened over and over and over again, and I got so sick of it I shouted at them to forget the whole thing! Why are they doing this to me? Don't they know I still dream about what he did to me and think about it and relive that moment every day? Talking about it just keeps it happening, and Mom and Dad won't shut up about it, either."

"And so you're fighting back the only way you know how." Mercy gave her a handful of tissues. She was so tempted to take Shannon into her arms and tell her to cry the pain all away, but the stain that had imbedded itself into this child's soul would not wash away with tears or hugs or comforting words. "Killing yourself slowly won't change the past, Shannon. Neither will starving or cutting your hair to rid yourself of your femininity."

Shannon sat up suddenly and dangled her legs over the side of the exam bed, her back to Mercy. She blew her nose and wiped her face, hunching her thin shoulders. "If I promise to eat my food and drink my milk like a good little girl, will you let me go home now?" Bitterness clung to her voice.

Mercy sighed. "Yes, Shannon, you can go home. Remember to keep your fluids . . ." she began but found herself talking to an empty room. Shannon had slid from the exam bed and escaped without a backward glance.

The fragrance of onions, garlic, toasted cheese, and tomatoes wafted up from the large paper bag Lukas set on top of Mercy's broad desk at eleven-fifty-five. He could hear his stomach growl above Lauren McCaffrey's chatter and the ringing of phones in the outer office. To his relief, Lauren had told him when he came in that Mercy was running on time for once. They would actually be able to share lunch. Eating here might be a mistake, but it was the only way to guarantee any time together. Lately Mercy had few breaks. Lukas hoped today would be an exception.

He'd skipped breakfast so he would have a healthy appetite for lunch, and the plan had worked. He was nearly light-headed from hunger. But hungry as he was, he was even more eager to see Mercy again. Estelle's words continued to echo in his mind . . . *something between him and Mercy and Tedi was growing stronger . . . God's will . . . silent pledge. Reconciliation was not regression. . . .*

Could she be right? Would it be possible. . . ? And if she was, would he have the courage to admit to Mercy the extent of his feelings for her? No . . . not just his *feelings*. His convictions. His assurance. Mercy did deserve to know about all the thoughts that careened through his head . . . but maybe not in a jumbled mess, as they were now. It would be enough just to tell her he loved her, no doubts, no going back. He would not hesitate about that any longer.

He loved Estelle's interpretation of contracts.

As he sat waiting in the cushioned chair in front of the desk, he heard snatches of conversation from Lauren, then Josie, and then from Mercy as she walked down the hallway toward the office where he sat waiting for her.

He relished the sound of her voice.

The door opened, and Mercy slipped in and caught sight of him. The sudden light of greeting that filled her gaze was not as joyful as he had anticipated, not as enthusiastic as she had been last night at her house. Instead, there was a quiet thoughtfulness. Probably a patient case that still drew her attention.

She shut the door quickly behind her and leaned against it. "Can you believe this? Is this really happening?"

Her voice held a sense of wonder, but her dark eyes did not reflect the carefree abandon he had come to cherish when they were together.

"I'm caught up, and you're here, both on the same day."

She wore royal blue scrubs today beneath her white lab coat. Her coffee-colored hair hung loose around her shoulders and down her back and shimmered with health in the streaks of sunlight that beamed through the windows. She'd never looked more beautiful to him. And every time he saw her, that beauty deepened.

"Don't say that too soon," Lukas warned. "This may be the eye of the hurricane."

Without looking away from him, she reached behind her and locked the door with a gentle snap. "They'll have to break in." She smiled at last. "Lukas, you look wonderful. I'm so happy you're here."

He crossed the space between them and caught her in a hug. She smelled wonderful, like antiseptic and soap. She felt even better in his arms. He buried his face in her hair and held tight, unwilling to release her immediately, and he could feel her surprise. He was never one to initiate a frontal attack of affection like this.

"Mercy, I've missed you so much," he said quietly.

He heard her catch her breath—was there just the slightest hesitation?—and then she reached up and drew him closer.

"You can't imagine how many times I've wanted to hear you say that," she whispered. "Oh, Lukas, I've dreamed of holding you just like this."

The soft brush of her words tingled against his neck. He relished her nearness for a final few seconds, then reluctantly released her. "There have been so many times I've picked up the telephone to call you, but you were either at work, or it was too late at night."

"And those were probably the times I was lying awake, thinking of you and wishing I could talk to you."

"I did call to let you know I was coming down last night, but—"

"I know. I didn't get the message." She closed her eyes and shook her head sadly. "It's like we keep missing each other, isn't it, Lukas? You don't suppose . . . is it possible that maybe . . . Someone doesn't want us to be together."

Lukas stared at her, blinked, frowned. "Someone?"

"Someone, with a capital *S*."

He hadn't expected that. All the time they'd been apart Mercy had seemed to miss him, to want him back here in Knolls, even sharing her practice with her. And after what Estelle had said about her . . .

Mercy turned to the paper bag he had set in the middle of her desk. "Did you get this from Antonio's?"

"Yes. Hope you don't mind a little cholesterol today. It's seven-layer lasagna and that triple-death chocolate dessert you love so much."

She grimaced. "You know, I love the low-fat pizza, too."

"Yes, but this is what you got on our first date."

She sighed and shook her head, then stepped toward him and lifted her face toward his as if she might kiss him. "You *are* a romantic. I don't care what anybody else says about you. Thanks, Lukas." Instead of kissing him, she took his hand and linked her fingers with his. "Mind if I ask the blessing?"

Lukas took a last, lingering look into her eyes before bowing his head. Something was still wrong. He could hear it in her voice.

"Dear Lord . . . thank you." The warmth of her words slid into the silence with soft hesitance. And sadness. But sadness about what? "Thank you for this precious friend, who has taught me so much about kindness these past few months. Thank you for his generosity and his wisdom. You knew just what I needed." Her voice wobbled, and she fell silent. Her fingers tightened their grip.

Lukas felt his appetite abandon him. Something was very wrong. He completed the prayer for her and looked up to see tears already making a steady course down her cheeks.

Instinctively he reached toward her. She released his hands and wrapped her arms around his waist as she buried her face against his shoulder.

"What is it?" he asked.

"Oh, Lukas . . ." For a moment she just held him, her body tense from tears.

Lukas felt that old, familiar power she had always had over him, and he felt, with the same familiarity, that sense of helplessness that weakened all his defenses when she cried. That was fine. He no longer wanted, or needed, a defense against her power.

"I've missed you," she said finally. "Last night I was so happy to see you. Tedi—" She raised her head and looked into Lukas's eyes, and the tears sparkled like streams of diamond dust. "You saw how she reacted. She's missed you so much. Both of us have."

"Then, why are you crying? I'm here. If Estelle gets her way, I'll be coming back to help you here at the clinic until the ER is finished."

He thought the possibility of his returning soon would finally bring that joy to her eyes that he loved so much. It didn't. "I made a mistake when I signed the contract at Herald," he said. "I knew after my first shift that accepting a position there was the wrong thing to do. I may be in some legal trouble if I leave before my contract is up, but I doubt if Mr. Amos can face down Estelle Pinkley when she's on a rampage."

Mercy watched him in silence as fresh tears filled her eyes, then she once again pressed her forehead against his shoulder. "Lukas," she whispered, "what do you know about the concept of reconciliation?"

He felt the power of the word like a blast of icy air. "What . . . concept?" he managed to croak.

She sighed. "Do *you* think it's God's will that Theo and I . . . that we try to put our marriage back together?"

Lukas felt as if she had taken a flying leap at him and kicked him in the stomach with both feet. His breath caught. His hands fell away from her shoulders, and he stepped back, staring at her helplessly.

But before he could reply, the piercing cry of a siren reached them. At the same time, the telephone rang at Mercy's desk.

She wiped the tears from her face with the back of her hand, took a deep breath, and snatched up the receiver. "Yes." She listened for a moment. Her eyes closed involuntarily. Her face grew pale. "We'll be ready, but call Air Care for stand-by. She'll probably have to be airlifted out."

She hung up the phone and turned to Lukas. "It's Kendra Oppenheimer. They found her unconscious in the sauna at the health club. Buck thinks she's taken an overdose of her medication. The ambulance is bringing her here."

CHAPTER 21

Lukas stared at the back of Mercy's head as he followed her down the hallway toward the wide back door of the clinic. He was still trying to recover from her question and from the shock and pain it had caused. If she was thinking about getting remarried to Theo, then why the warm welcome at her house last night? Why the telephone calls? Why did she behave as if she still cared?

But he couldn't think about that right now, not with the noisy bustle around him in preparation for Kendra's arrival. He had to take his mind from his personal problems. This was an emergency.

The large receiving room, which had once been used for storage, was now set up somewhat awkwardly for unloading of patients from an emergency vehicle. Mercy had made several obvious improvements to aid in the care of seriously ill or wounded patients. The lab had many more capabilities, as did the radiology room. The place looked as if it had been equipped as a class-four emergency department. Lukas could only pray they would be equipped for this one.

As the ambulance van pulled swiftly into position to unload the patient, Lukas battled his own selfish emotions, telling himself his wounded pride was what made him so upset with Mercy. Hadn't he purposely stayed away from Knolls so she would have the freedom to make her own decision about Theodore? And she was obviously struggling with that decision now. What had he expected? Why couldn't he think about somebody besides himself? If he truly loved Mercy the way a man should love a woman, wouldn't he be able to place her needs above his own?

Before the ambulance stopped rolling, Buck Oppenheimer burst out the back door of the vehicle in a rush. He wore a muscle shirt and snug biker's shorts that showed every ripple in his muscle builder's body. "I found her in the sauna at the end of the weight room." The words spilled out of him in a frightened stream. "She was conscious but could barely lift her head, and she was flat out on the floor. She's stiff as a board, like she's cramping or something. I thought about heatstroke, but I looked for her purse to see if she's taken an overdose of her drugs—"

"No," came Kendra's groggy voice from inside. "I didn't . . ." The complaint dissolved into a mutter of unintelligible words.

Lukas and Mercy stood back as the attendants came around and pulled their patient out of the van. Kendra was lying on a backboard with an IV in her right arm and monitor leads attached to her chest. She was dressed much like Buck. Her eyelids were half draped over her eyes.

Connie, the experienced paramedic with short boy-cut hair, acknowledged Lukas's presence with a brisk nod. "Welcome back, Dr. Bower. Glad you're here." She turned to Mercy. "I guess Buck filled you in on what happened. When we got there she had a heart rate of 130, respiratory rate of 35, and her blood pressure was high but fluctuating. Her temp was 104 at the health club. I didn't tube her, because her airway seems okay at this point. Boy, her muscles are rigid, though."

"Do you have her on normal saline?" Mercy asked.

"Yes. Wide open."

"Good, Connie. Start another IV."

When they moved Kendra, Buck stayed by the cot as if attached by an unseen cord. "What if it's an overdose? All I found was her dosage case in her purse, and it still had medicine inside. All her bottles are at home."

"How long have you been at the club?" Mercy asked.

"About an hour."

"And she's been exercising all that time?" Mercy's voice rose in alarm.

"S-stop . . ." Kendra's voice came in a whisper, and tears dripped down the sides of her face into her hair. Her eyes remained shut.

Mercy stepped to her side quickly. "Kendra? Can you talk to me?"

No response.

Lukas stepped forward and palpated Kendra's legs. Buck and Connie were right—the muscles were very rigid . . . almost too rigid even for heatstroke.

"Push her just inside the door," Mercy instructed them. "That's where we're set up for treatment." She squeezed Kendra's fingers and watched.

Even from where Lukas stood, Lukas could see the capillary refill was sluggish.

"Lauren?" Mercy said. "Where's Lauren?"

"Right here, Dr. Mercy," came Lauren's reassuring voice from the hallway. She rushed into the room carrying ice packs, a fan, and a plastic spray bottle. "Thought you'd want to get the temperature down as quickly as possible."

"Good." Mercy kept her attention trained on the patient. "Kendra?"

Still no response.

Mercy reached over and moved her knuckles against the center of Kendra's chest.

The young woman winced. Her eyes fluttered open, and she looked up at Mercy. More tears dripped down her face. "C-can't move. S-so tight."

Mercy took Kendra's hand in a gentle grip. "It's going to be okay." She turned to Lukas. "Would you help us take her off this backboard? Lauren, get me a blood gas. Buck, you may be right about the heatstroke. Lauren, did Josie go to lunch yet?"

"Yes, sorry, she left about ten minutes ago. You want Loretta to try to find her and get her back here?"

"No, we've got enough help. Let Buck pack her in ice and spray the mist over her. Let's cut those tight clothes off. Sorry, Kendra, you'll have to get some new exercise gear later. Connie, can you stay with us for a while?"

"Sure can, Dr. Mercy," the paramedic said. She turned and gave orders to her EMT partner, Dan, to keep a close watch on Kendra's vitals, then turned back to Mercy. "What can I do to help?"

"Draw blood for a septic work-up and then give her a Tylenol suppository. Lauren, after you get the ABG you can run the lab. It's okay, Kendra. We're going to get you cooled down."

Lukas once again tested the rigidity of Kendra's leg muscles. Heatstroke did cause rigidity, but he'd never seen a case this bad before. "Mercy," he said softly, "feel how tight her muscles are. And look at her—she's not flushed, she's pale. And she's not too dehydrated for tears or perspiration."

Mercy frowned and leaned over Kendra, patting the younger woman on the shoulder. "Kendra, do you feel like you're burning up?"

"Y-yes."

Mercy tested the feel of her arm and leg muscles and looked back at Lukas, her face revealing increasing concern. "You're right. That's lead-pipe rigidity."

Buck placed the ice packs under his wife's arms and in the groin while Connie cut away the outer layer of clothing. Kendra moaned in protest, and Buck cupped the side of her face with his hand. "I'm sorry, but I've got to do this, babe. We've got to get your temperature down fast."

Her tanzanite-blue eyes came open wide when Connie started the second IV, and her gaze reached up to him in pleading. Her teeth were still clenched. "I'm scared, Buck. What's happening?"

He turned to Lukas and Mercy helplessly.

"Spray the mist over her, Buck," Mercy said. "The medications she's taking for bipolar disorder could be causing this reaction, especially with the exercise. She could have neuroleptic malignant syndrome. It's a rare reaction, one we have to treat in a hurry."

"You mean it's not an overdose?"

"No!" Kendra cried through clenched teeth. "I told you—"

"Buck, direct the fan on her," Mercy said, then turned and called over her shoulder, "Lauren, do we have Dantrium and Ativan in stock?"

"I think so, Dr. Mercy. I'll go check. If not, I'll send Dan to the hospital for some."

"No. I know we've got some kind of benzodiazepine here. I want you to give it intravenously as soon as you can get it in, then check on the Dantrium."

"Heart rate's going up," Dan informed them. "One-twenty. BP's rising."

Mercy turned a worried gaze to Lukas. They had to break the fever fast. If this was heatstroke, lowering the body temperature could relieve symptoms. If Kendra was suffering from neuroleptic malignant syndrome, the IV drugs would be necessary to break the muscle rigidity. Otherwise there could be a major dysfunction of all organ systems. Muscle breakdown could lead to kidney failure, even death.

"Connie, keep a close eye on her airway," Mercy said. "Kendra, are you feeling sick to your stomach?"

"No, but I can't move." Her voice rose on a spiral of fear and frustration.

"Just let us know if you feel nauseated. Since you can't move, we'll have to move you."

Tears continued to spill from Kendra's eyes. "Buck?"

"I'm right here. I'm not leaving you." He continued to spray and adjust the ice packs and the fan. "It's going to be okay. I'm not going to let anything happen to you."

Mercy turned to Lukas, and for a moment she reached out and touched his arm, as if for strength. "I can't wait to find out for sure what this is."

"No, you can't. The drugs won't hurt her if it's heatstroke, and they're necessary."

She lowered her voice. "I could turn this one over to you."

"There's no need."

"But you're the ER doctor."

"You're doing great. I'm taking orders from you today, Dr. Richmond."

———

Theodore Zimmerman sat with his fingers twined together like reinforced chain links. He had always hated doctors' offices, feared needles—though he would never admit that to anyone—and resented the lack of dignity a patient suffered sitting in a thin, backless gown. He could almost hear the rattle of the paper on the exam table as it echoed the pounding of his heart.

What was going on? Why the gown? He'd thought he was coming in for the results of his second blood test for hepatitis B. At worst, he'd expected to be ushered into the conference area for a discussion on the best treatments available for the disease. At best, he'd hoped to be told the initial result was a fluke. This naked vulnerability had not been in his plans. Neither had hepatitis.

What he'd hoped—what he'd dreamed about for several weeks— had been the possibility that Mercy would see him with new eyes, that she and Tedi would begin to understand and care for the new Theodore and the different heart God had planted inside him. That didn't seem to be working out any better than his blood tests.

The walls and heavy, ornate wooden doors in Dr. Robert Simeon's office were more solidly constructed than most—an internal-medicine specialist could afford such decor, and his patients expected it. Theodore could barely hear the sounds of ringing telephones, chattering voices, and brisk footsteps. The attractive sweet-faced young nurse who'd taken his vitals simply explained that placing a patient in a gown was standard procedure for examination. And of course, knowing Robert, he would be thorough. Mercy had commented several times in the past about Robert's fund of knowledge and his common sense. He would take every precaution.

For years Theodore had resented Robert Simeon, had even been jealous of his close professional relationship with Mercy. After the divorce he had wondered if Mercy and Robert would take the bond to a more personal level. They hadn't. He should have known Mercy better than that. Robert's style was Porsche Carrera. Mercy's was all-wheel-drive Subaru—with four doors and plenty of storage in case she needed to haul patients home from the hospital or buy them groceries.

At the thought of Mercy, Theodore felt the tension squeeze tighter in his gut. If he really had hepatitis, what would happen to all the dreams he'd been daring, lately, to dream about getting his family back? *God, please let this all be a big mistake. Please give me a chance to make it all up to them.* What if he was truly sick and would be off work for a few weeks or even months? He had good insurance at Jack's Printshop, but how would he pay his bills?

But he shouldn't think like that. Hepatitis wasn't that big a deal. The disease could be treated.

The doorknob turned, and the door swung open on silent hinges, and Theodore gripped the edges of the exam bed. Dr. Robert Simeon strode in, serious and brisk as always. Intimidating. The room grew smaller.

"Hello, Theodore." He placed the clipboard with Theo's vitals on the desk in the corner, then turned around to shake hands. He was about two inches taller than Theo, with thinning brown hair and lines of permanent worry creased into his forehead. His dress clothes were unwrinkled, unstained, his hands well manicured.

"Hello, Robert. Thanks for fitting me in today." Theo spread his hands to indicate the gown he wore. "I'm not sure what this is all about."

Robert pulled a chair across from the desk where he could sit a comfortable arm's length from Theodore. He was a busy internist. Busy internists didn't sit down, did they?

"Theodore, I'll get straight to the point." He gestured toward the clipboard on the desk, and the worry lines deepened. "Both blood tests were positive for hepatitis B. Since you have no symptoms at this time, it's possible the disease is chronic. You could have had it for some time."

"But how did I get hepatitis?" Theo asked. He'd been wondering how he had contracted it ever since he'd received the first positive results in the mail. "Even more important, could I have passed it to someone else? What if Mercy or—"

"Very unlikely after this much time," Robert assured him. "It's been what . . . six years since the divorce? We're talking about a difficult virus to transmit. Of course, Mercy and Tedi might want to be tested as a precaution. Is Mercy aware of this situation?"

"Not yet. I didn't want to worry her." As soon as he knew everything would be okay, he would tell her.

"I understand. My thoughts are this—" Robert leaned forward and steepled his fingers in front of his face—"you were incarcerated for several months during your treatment last summer. Close, continued contact with an infected . . . inmate . . . would increase the likelihood that you would have contracted the disease."

Theodore shook his head. "The treatment center wasn't like a prison. I didn't spend a lot of time with my roommates."

Robert hesitated only for a few seconds. "There are other possibilities. Drug users—"

"No, I never injected drugs."

Robert leaned back in his chair and sighed heavily. His gaze caught and held Theo's, but trying to read the emotion behind those observant eyes was difficult. He said quietly, pointedly, "Intimate physical contact with an infected person can spread the disease."

There was a sudden, intense silence, and Theodore felt his face burn with shame at the impact of too many memories. Dr. Robert Simeon, as well as the majority of Knolls, probably knew about the women, both before and after the divorce from Mercy. Theodore had made no effort to keep secrets—why should he? In his mind at the time, being discreet wasn't a high priority. In fact, he'd been proud of his conquests, eager to flaunt them in Mercy's face, eager to pay her back for not putting him first in her life.

Now he was exposed in every way. "That's possible," he said in defeat. His shoulders slumped and he buried his face in his hands, and once again, as he had many times these past few months, he hated the Theodore Zimmerman who'd lived for himself for forty years. He hated the humiliation he had brought on his family.

"When was the last?" Robert's voice came gently.

Theodore rubbed his eyes and forced his shoulders to straighten. He couldn't bring himself to make eye contact. "In the spring of last year, so it's been over nine or ten months. Julie's married now, and she lives here in town. Do you think she—"

"It could have been any one of them. This disease is unpredictable. There have been none since then?"

"No one since then." And no one again. He couldn't risk passing this to someone else.

The worry lines deepened further in Robert's forehead. "Theodore, since you've reported no symptoms of acute infection, there's obviously been no treatment. Several things concern me at this juncture—the most obvious being your history of alcohol dependence." He stood from his chair and pushed it out of the way on silent wheels. "I need to check for tenderness around the liver, and possibly even a mass. Have you had any recent weight loss?"

Theodore tried to catch his breath. "Some. Why? What do you think is wrong?"

"Chronic hepatitis B can have several complications, and they affect the liver. Unfortunately, with your alcoholism, you can be in danger of cirrhosis, possibly even hepatocellular carcinoma."

The words took a moment to connect in his mind. "Carcinoma." No, this couldn't be. He was too young. "You mean cancer."

"Yes. I would like to do a physical exam to see if I can detect inflammation, but what I really need is a blood test for alpha-fetoprotein. If that shows me anything, then I may want to do a biopsy."

"Biopsy." Theodore cringed. This was serious. Suddenly the fear of needles seemed like a childhood phobia. They were talking carcinomas and biopsies. He lay back on the exam bed and stared at the ceiling, grimacing when Dr. Simeon palpated his stomach. There was pain. Robert frowned. Theodore prayed harder than he had since he first realized what a mess he'd made of his life.

Clarence was just checking on the frozen cookie supply when the swinging door at the far end of the kitchen slid open with a breath of silent hinges. He slammed the freezer shut and turned around guiltily, bracing himself for Ivy's impending wrath.

Instead, he saw Delphi Bell come to a startled stop beside the far counter, the dark bruises on her face caught in the strong rays of morning sunlight that filtered through the kitchen window.

He lumbered backward. "Lady, you like to've scared me out of my shoes!"

Her shoulders hunched forward protectively. She ducked and started to back away, her clean shoulder-length brown hair catching in the shafts of sunlight. "Sorry. I thought Mrs. Richmond was in here, she told me to come, and—"

"No, no, that's okay, Delphina." Man, she was like a timid pet that had been struck once too often. "Come back in. *I* just thought *you* were Ivy, and if she ever catches me touching her cookies, she'll lower my food rations." *Keep talking. Don't scare her away.* "I guess you've noticed I'm not exactly a fashion model. Ivy's tryin' to help me get a few hundred inches off my waistline, and I keep foiling her plans. But, hey, I'm not a total failure. I've lost about a hundred pounds."

Delphi stepped once more into the light, watching him with curious eyes the color of pale winter cedar. She may be wounded and skittish, but she wasn't broken. Her gaze never centered anywhere for a long period of time, but she gave the impression that she was storing away information to take out later and study. She wasn't really pretty, with her long, narrow, bruised face. She might be if she smiled, but Clarence couldn't imagine her with a smile on her face.

"Have you eaten yet?" he asked. When she shook her head, he asked, "Why don't I fix you some breakfast? That way I'll have an excuse for being in the kitchen when Ivy comes to find you. Go ahead and sit over there at the counter on one of those bar stools. I could use a bite myself, and I know a great egg recipe. You like eggs?"

She hesitated a moment longer, still studying him. Then some of the tension left her face. "Yeah, I like eggs. Won't Mrs. Richmond mind if we get into her stuff?"

"Probably." He opened the fridge and took out a carton of egg substitute.

He saw how the red-and-gray-striped shirt of Ivy's fit Delphi too snugly around her thick middle. "Maybe you could go on the diet with me, or . . . oh, hey, you're not pregnant, are you?" He remembered too late what had happened last time he'd asked a fat woman if she was pregnant. "Oh boy, sorry about that, Delphina, I didn't mean . . ."

And then it happened. As he watched her, a brief flash of humor lit her haunted eyes. A smile didn't reach her mouth, of course; that was too much to ask. But the atmosphere changed in the room. Some of her tense watchfulness eased, as if maybe she realized Clarence wasn't the kind of guy to hurt anybody. As if maybe she knew he just wanted to be a friend.

"I'm not pregnant. Wouldn't want a kid of mine linked up with a daddy like—" She broke off and took the stool at the counter, then looked down at her chunky paunch. "A waitress never hurts for food."

"Well, don't worry about that. Ivy'll whip you into shape soon enough. You don't have that much to lose."

"Won't be time to lose it, though."

"Oh? Why not?"

"If you knew Abner Bell, you wouldn't be askin'."

"You're not going back to him, are you?"

She shook her head, and her shoulders slumped again. "I'd rather die."

"Then what—"

"He'll find me." Her tone was so calm, so matter-of-fact. She looked up at Clarence. "He holds on to me like a pit bull holds on to a cat. You say you've got some eggs?"

He leaned against the counter in alarm. "What makes you think he'll find you? He doesn't know—"

"Hide'n watch. He'll hunt me down sooner or later. He's mean, but he's smart. He knows how to work people, and he keeps his eyes open. This time I don't plan to hang around till he shows up."

Clarence pulled a frying pan out of the cupboard and sprayed some no-stick spray into it. As he cooked the eggs, he thought about what Delphi said. He knew she was scared, and he didn't blame her.

"You just stick around me, Delphi," he said at last. "Your husband's a bully, and most bullies are cowards around anybody bigger than them. You just stick with me."

"He has a large caliber gun," Delphi said. "That makes him bigger than anybody."

"Not bigger than the police," Clarence assured her. But suddenly this hiding-out stuff wasn't as much fun.

Lauren came back into the makeshift emergency room with a lab printout. She laid it on the corner of a supply rack. "Dr. Mercy, we've got the results back on the blood tests you ordered. Normal."

Normal was what Mercy expected. "Thank you, Lauren. And thank you for staying. Air Care should be here anytime, so why don't you escape for lunch while you still can?"

Lauren hesitated at the doorway, her expression hesitant, green eyes still alert—obviously leftover adrenaline surge. The pretty blonde was thoroughly professional and thoroughly efficient when they had emergencies to deal with.

Mercy glanced at her watch, then at her peacefully resting patient. "Better get out of here while you can, Lauren, at least for a little break." Their afternoon flow of patients would start in a few moments, and extras had already called, begging to be squeezed in. Typical Friday.

"Okay, but just a short one." Lauren checked on Kendra one more time, then walked out.

Mercy had sent Connie and Dan away ten minutes ago, praising them for a job well done. Buck continued to hover over his wife, holding her hand, murmuring assurances to her. Her temperature had dropped to a manageable 100 degrees. The rigidity in her muscles had eased with the aid of the IV drugs, and her heart rate and respiratory rate had dropped with her blood pressure, all returning to normal levels.

Mercy knew the reaction could hit again at any time, as long as the offending chemical lingered in Kendra's body. She also knew Buck would catch any symptoms the minute anything changed. She stepped over to sit down beside Lukas, who had been beside her throughout, helping with vitals, administering drugs, reassuring Kendra and Buck. Never once had he questioned Mercy's actions. Not once had he tried to take control.

Suddenly she thought about his news earlier. He would be coming down soon to help her, and she felt the sweet peace of anticipation settle over her like a comforter. She laid a hand on his arm and smiled at him.

"It's going to be great to have you back, partner."

He looked at her, and his earnest blue eyes remained serious. He didn't reply.

"Lukas? Is everything okay?"

Before he could reply, she heard the familiar echo of the blades beating the atmosphere. Almost in unison, she heard Loretta greet their first afternoon patient.

CHAPTER 22

The scent of cold lasagna and warm triple-death chocolate dessert greeted Mercy as she entered her office ahead of Lukas two hours later. Her stomach protested in hunger and she craved the chocolate, but she wanted to sleep come bedtime. Lately even a taste of caffeine in the middle of the afternoon could keep her awake half the night. What she craved more than anything right now was time alone with Lukas.

She stepped aside and let him enter. Then she closed the door behind him. "I owe you one, Lukas. If you hadn't helped me catch up, I'd still have a waiting room full of patients. How do you like stale Italian food?"

Lukas didn't look at her. "I can't stay long." His voice sounded suddenly tense again, as it had before Kendra arrived.

"Neither can I. You know how many walk-ins we get on Friday. We'll eat it cold." She set out the food and plastic ware from Antonio's, watching Lukas circle the room like a man looking for a way out of a jail cell. In spite of his nervousness, she drank in the sight of him and noticed the flexing of muscles in his jaw as he clenched and unclenched his teeth.

"Come on, Lukas, you can take time to eat something. I bet you didn't even have breakfast this morning, did you?"

He grimaced.

"Didn't think so. You don't want to pass out from starvation while you're driving back." She nudged a Styrofoam container of lasagna toward the end of her desk and sat down, gesturing for him to join her.

Instead, his gaze circled the room and fell to rest for a moment on the picture she kept of him on her desk. He looked back at her, then away again.

"I could heat the food for you," she said.

"No thanks."

She felt a tingle of irritation. If he had a problem, why didn't he just blurt it out? That was what he usually did. Why was he suddenly so silent?

The tension stretched between them for another moment, and she heard Lauren ushering a patient down the hallway to an exam room. The afternoon would fill up quickly. They were running out of time.

She had to explain some things to him before he left. He deserved to know what was going on in her life, and in her heart. "Lukas, we're having a Bible study at church on Wednesday nights. In spite of my schedule, I've been trying to attend as much as possible. I wish I hadn't."

He turned to her, caught off guard by surprise. "Why?"

"Because the last one—through which I slept—had a lot to say about divorce." There. Now she had his attention. He took a step toward her, expression tense again. "Imagine my surprise," she continued, "when I discovered that—at least according to some people—not only am I expected to forgive my ex-husband, now I'm supposed to remarry him." She'd rehashed the entire concept over and over in her mind, and still she felt her resentment building. She watched Lukas's gaze waver, and then his shoulders slumped and he walked over and sat beside her.

"And that isn't something you want?" he asked softly.

Her resentment peaked. "Of course not!" She caught her voice on its spiral and lowered it. "I thought you knew me better than that. I thought you understood how I felt about him. How could you even ask—"

"Okay, I'm sorry." He raised his hands in a self-protective gesture, but suddenly the tension in him melted, and the light sparked once more in his eyes. A smile tugged at the edges of his lips. "Mercy, why are you suddenly letting someone else tell you how to live your life? You've never done that before."

"I've never been a Christian before, either." Her resentment disappeared as quickly as it had attacked her. "You're the one who's always spouting about the need to do God's will. I can't live my life for myself any longer, and I don't want to. I want to do the right thing."

"And you think that's remarrying Theodore?"

"How am I supposed to know? I haven't read the Bible all my life, like you have, or like most of the people in the Bible study class." She dropped her voice. "Lauren seems to think I should—"

"Lauren?" Lukas exclaimed. "Since when do you listen to her?"

Mercy shushed him and gestured toward the door. "Our voices carry."

"Good, then Lauren will learn it's time to try to mind her own business—*again.*" The heat in his voice reached around Mercy and warmed her. He leaned toward her and lowered his voice. "This is between you and God. It's nobody else's business. Lauren doesn't have a right to tell you to return to a painful relationship just because she reads the Bible a certain way."

"But that was the way the pastor taught the lesson."

"How do you know? You said you were asleep."

In spite of the subject, Mercy couldn't help smiling, and Lukas smiled back. Impulsively she leaned forward and hugged him. He slowly, tentatively, raised an arm and placed it across her back. She didn't let go. Instead, she rested her forehead on his shoulder. His other arm came around her, and she basked in the warmth of his closeness, in the joy of hope.

She knew better than to trust in emotions, but being held by him felt so good, so right. He had an undeniable power in him that drew her. The Spirit in him had always drawn her, and the love he had for God. He was the one who had first brought her face-to-face with the reality of God and had caused her to recognize the need within her for that same God. And, she'd argued with herself since Wednesday night, if Theo also had the same Spirit of Christ in him, and God wanted her to return to him, why wasn't she drawn to *him*?

"I get so confused sometimes, Lukas."

His embrace tightened around her shoulders. "I know. I do too." His baritone voice was soothing. "But usually I get confused when I try to second-guess God's next move, when I forget that He's busy working in the present of my life, and not just the future. That's when I have to learn, all over again, to wait on Him. It isn't because He's slow and can't keep up with me, but it's because I still have something to learn from the situation I'm in. He's so patient, Mercy. Be patient with Him, and with yourself. Give yourself some time. Wait on God."

Mercy basked in the flow of his words. Was it possible that everything could be so simple? Did she already know which lesson God wanted her to learn, what part of the healing that still needed to take place?

Voices reached them from the hallway once again. Another patient. They were getting busy, and time was passing. Lukas had to go soon.

"Lukas, I want to do God's will. At the same time I'm praying that remarriage to Theo isn't in His plans for me. Is that sacrilege?"

"No. In Gethsemane, Jesus prayed that He wouldn't have to go to the cross."

"But He went anyway."

"And I think He knew He would have to, but still He shared His heart with God, just as you are doing."

"But I don't see how I could go through with remarrying him." She raised her head and looked into Lukas's blue eyes and saw the tenderness there, the sincerity and vulnerability, and she was caught. She could not force herself to draw away from his comfort and his touch. What if this was her last chance to spend time like this with Lukas? What if he, too, decided that she and Theodore belonged together because of Tedi? What if he'd already decided? What if. . . ?

"Lukas, why have you stayed away for so long?" She asked the question on impulse, and she felt him go still, heard his breathing stop for a moment. She knew the answer from his silence. "I couldn't remarry Theodore because he broke our marriage covenant repeatedly," she said, "For the past few months I believe God has been doing something very special between you and me." She watched his eyes and caught a brief glimpse of longing before he closed them and drew back. And she knew she wasn't jumping to conclusions, wasn't imagining the emotions. She knew Lukas too well. God had allowed them to spend that much time together, to learn each other's thoughts. *God* had allowed that.

"In fact," she continued, "I believe that ever since you and I met, He has been leading us in that direction."

Lukas opened his eyes and looked at her a long moment. He nodded, and she felt the joy swell inside her.

"And so," she continued, "even though God may be telling me to wait on Him, I don't think it's wrong for me to be honest, to share my heart with Him, and tell Him that I love you. If Jesus could admit His reluctance to go to the cross—an act that was necessary to pay for our sins, to cancel our estrangement from God—then we can admit anything to Him. I'm telling Him, and I'm telling you, that I love you, Lukas."

Without taking his gaze from her face, he sighed and stood up. He reached down and drew her to her feet, and then he pulled her against him in a tight grip that enveloped her and sang through her whole body.

"And God knows I love you, Mercy," he said softly into her hair. "I want what's best for you, and for Tedi, and I know that isn't my decision to make. I just know what I want it to be."

More voices reached them from the hallway, and then a discreet knock. "Dr. Mercy?" came Lauren's hesitant voice.

"Yes, Lauren, I'll be out shortly." Duty called. She drew back and looked once more into his eyes, and she saw the promise there—the reassurance that he loved her enough to do what was right for her. And she knew that was a reflection of God's love. It was enough.

On impulse she kissed him, and he returned the kiss in a reflection of all the love she felt for him. In that kiss, the promise was repeated. She would be able to trust.

———

Lukas found his copy of the contract with Herald Hospital as soon as he arrived for his Friday evening shift. He faxed it to Estelle with the promise that he would talk with Mr. Amos. He compiled a concise one-page letter to Mr. Amos with his resignation, explaining the conflicts and taking responsibility for them.

Saturday morning when his shift ended he drove to the drugstore in downtown Herald and purchased a greeting card for Mercy. It was the first of its kind he had ever sent, and he signed, stamped, and addressed the card before he could change his mind. The front of the card was decorated with roses, and in the center were printed the words, *You are so special to me.* The inside was blank, and he had written, *Mercy, I'm praying for you. I'm also praying for us. I can't say for sure what God's will is right now, and that is because I know what I want so very much for it to be, and I'm trying hard not to confuse my will with His. Please don't make any hasty decisions, and I'll try hard not to pressure you. Love, Lukas.*

He dropped the card in a mailbox on his way home and then wondered at his own audacity. Had he done the wrong thing? By just sending the card, was he attempting to influence her?

At one o'clock Saturday afternoon, Mercy refolded her napkin and placed it next to the fine china on the table at the Victorian. "Theodore, that was wonderful. Thank you for the treat." A waiter appeared silently at her side and refilled her water glass, then stepped over to refill Tedi's, then Theo's. The Victorian was the most expensive restaurant in the county. Theodore had obviously decided to use some of the money he had saved for Branson.

This refurbished old home had several dining rooms, each with its own individual, elegant decor and colors. Their table was set in an alcove overlooking a tiny indoor garden that thrived amongst rocks and waterfalls.

Theodore thanked the waiter and picked up his water glass. This was his fourth refill. There was something on his mind, some tension in his behavior. Was he simply craving more than water, or was he upset about something else?

"I heard Jack's wife talking about this place at work," he said. His voice carried the tension. "You know Marty, don't you? She says this place has the best food in the area. I think she's right. Tedi, don't you want some dessert?"

Tedi looked at him curiously. "No thanks, Dad. I'm stuffed."

"Mercy? You neither?"

Mercy shook her head and turned to study Theo's face more closely. That was the second time he had asked them about dessert. He had unfolded and refolded his napkin at least three times, and there were beads of perspiration on his forehead in spite of the fact that the room was a little cool.

"No, thank you. That was a very filling meal. Theodore, is everything okay? Are you feeling well?"

He put his water glass down quickly, looked across the table at Tedi, then back at Mercy. "I'm fine."

"Are you sure? You barely ate half your salmon."

"Yeah, Dad, and you didn't even ask for a doggy bag," Tedi said. "You always do that at Little Mary's when we don't eat everything."

Mercy thought about her talk with Lukas yesterday, and suddenly Theodore's discomfort transmitted itself to her. Was he trying to gather the courage to make some kind of a declaration? Or maybe that wasn't his intention at all. Just this week he had discovered that his own daughter was still afraid to spend time alone with him. That had to be bothering him. She knew how much that kind of distrust would hurt her. Maybe she just needed to tell him to quit trying so hard.

Impulsively she laid a hand on his arm and felt the muscles tense beneath her fingers. "Thank you," she said again.

He jerked his head in a nod, cleared his throat, picked up his glass for another sip of water. "Um, actually, I may not be feeling that great." He took another sip and set the glass down. "I—"

The waiter materialized beside him with the check, and Theo opted to pay him immediately. While he was distracted, Tedi bumped Mercy's leg under the table and rolled her eyes, as if to say, "What's bugging Dad?"

As they stepped out the front entrance of the restaurant, Mercy turned to him. "Thank you again, Theodore. I've always wanted to try this place, and I just never seemed to have the time for a leisurely meal. This worked out perfectly." She glanced at her watch. "I need to get back to the office for a few minutes. I want to check on a couple of patients. Why don't we drive you home?"

He hesitated, and Mercy noticed a slight pallor of his complexion. Maybe he really wasn't feeling well. It was flu season, and she'd had countless patients in this week with strep and bad colds, even a couple of cases of pneumonia.

"I think I'll walk," he said.

Tedi nudged Mercy's arm, then stepped toward Theodore. "May I walk with you, Dad? Mom can pick me up at your apartment later."

Mercy and Theo stared at her in surprise, and an expression of joy crossed Theodore's face. "Are you sure? I thought you didn't—"

"I'm sure." She stepped forward and took her dad's hand. "I just had to have time to think about it."

Theo looked up at Mercy, and she couldn't miss the spark of wonder and relief in his eyes. At last Tedi had taken that first step back toward trust.

Sunday afternoon at Ivy's house, Mercy volunteered to help her mother with kitchen duty. It was the only way she was going to catch Mom alone. While Clarence entertained Tedi, Darlene, and Delphi in the family room with fat jokes and diet tips, Mercy stood at the sink and chopped eggplant, zucchini, and yellow squash for a stir-fry.

"That's a new knife, so don't cut yourself." Ivy stirred some brown rice into a pot of boiling water on the stove.

"Thanks for the warning."

"So what's up?"

Mom was right. The knife sliced through the eggplant like water. "Does anything have to be 'up' for me to spend time with you?"

"No, but since you chased Clarence out of the kitchen with the threat of violence, I thought you might have a reason. I realize it's hard to keep him away from food, but—"

"I didn't threaten violence. I threatened to haul him down to the office to weigh him if he ate any more snacks before lunch."

"For him, that's violence. What's up?"

"I'm taking an opinion poll." Mercy cut the ends off the zucchini and chopped it, peeling and all. "Do you think I should remarry Theodore?"

"No. Next question?"

"That's it? No discussion?"

"What's to discuss? You're going to marry Lukas and live happily ever after." Ivy stirred the rice and cast her daughter a look of sympathy. "Been listening to the gossip, have you?"

"What gossip?"

"The usual. Seems like half the town was suddenly at the Wednesday night Bible study, and the other half was driving by afterward when you and Theo had a long heart-to-heart talk on the way to your car."

Mercy plunged the point of the paring knife into the yellow squash all the way up to the hilt. "Why should I be surprised?" she muttered.

"Beats me. You've grown up here. Too bad I missed the Bible study, though, because I could've given Dr. Joseph Jordan and those interfering busybodies *my* interpretation of the Scriptures—I tell you, he's a good pastor, but he's too young. No experience. Give me a man at least in his forties if you want solid, experienced teach—"

"What's *your* interpretation?"

"Well, I know what I think isn't exactly a popular teaching, but according to Leviticus, Theo should be dead right now."

"You didn't happen to write your own version of the Bible, did you?"

"Honey, I've been a Christian almost six years now, and because of your situation I'm studied up on divorce and remarriage. In the Old Testament, a person who committed adultery was stoned to death. So if Theodore was living with the Israelites in the desert, he'd have been dead six or seven years ago. That means you'd be a widow, and Tedi would be an orphan. According to the apostle Paul, young widows should remarry to keep out of trouble." Mom shrugged. "Works for me."

Mercy shook her head at her mother's "interpretation." Then she finished her chopping, rinsed her hands, and set the knife down carefully. Mom certainly didn't mince words. Suddenly Mercy felt her mother's arms come around her from behind in a gentle embrace.

"Have you asked God what to do?" Ivy asked.

"Yes."

"Then wait for His answer. He will give it to you, heart to heart. And don't forget how much He loves you and Tedi."

The warmth of Mom's breath and the assurance of love in her voice made tears prick Mercy's eyes. And God loved her more than that. How many times would she have to remind herself?

"Don't compare God to your earthly dad, Mercy."

"It's hard not to," Mercy said. "I used to see God as this big, controlling person who could suddenly lash out at me in anger at any moment. I guess I still see Him that way sometimes."

"He isn't like that. He'll protect you. Trust Him."

Theodore Zimmerman sat in Dr. Robert Simeon's office Monday afternoon, this time with his clothes on. He faced the doctor across the wide oak desk. He'd learned not to panic at the worry lines that framed Robert's strong, even features, because by now he knew those frown lines appeared every time the man was concentrating.

"The numbers are high," Robert said, passing a sheet of faxed paper across the broad desk and pointing to the test results.

Theodore looked at the paper. "What does that mean?"

"Alpha-fetoprotein is, as the name implies, an enzyme that should not be found in the human body after birth. Its presence signifies that something in your body is growing at a fast rate, as a fetus would grow. When we find high levels such as yours, we look for tumors."

Theodore realized that this time he should have panicked. "You mean cancer."

"Yes. I would like to do an ultrasound on your liver to see if we can find evidence of a mass. If we do find something, our next step will be a liver biopsy, and then a metastatic work-up to see if the tumor has spread to other—"

"Wait!" Theo caught his breath, willing his heart not to pound out of his chest. "Robert, what you're saying is that I really do have cancer? Liver cancer?" Just like that, he'd gone from a healthy man getting his life together after forty years to a man with death lurking in his body?

Robert bit his lip in worrisome concentration for a few seconds. He leaned forward, as if he might somehow be able to focus a sense of comfort across the broad expanse of his desk. "I don't want to make a final analysis at this point. I know how stressful it is to wait on news like this, but there are other tests, taken in stages, that will be more conclusive. I'm sorry if I seem to be rushing you, but I always attack suspected cancer aggressively. Time is important here, but so is a systematic, sensible approach."

Theodore forced himself to speak. "What do we do next?"

"I want to set you up for an abdominal ultrasound immediately. Now. Today. Afterward, if that shows a mass, I want to refer you to a friend of mine in Springfield, Dr. Walt Huffman, who is a gastro-enterologist. He will do a biopsy. I spoke with him this morning, and he is willing to take you on short notice, possibly on Wed—"

"Whoa! Wait a minute, Robert." Theodore felt as if the breath had just been knocked from his lungs. "That fast? Couldn't you do the biopsy before you refer me to Springfield?"

"Yes, but if the ultrasound shows a mass I'll have to refer you anyway. Springfield has a lot more experience with liver biopsies."

"So you already expect to find a mass."

"I have you scheduled at the hospital for an ultrasound in thirty minutes." Robert looked at his watch. "Twenty-five." He leaned forward on his elbows, his expression grim. "Then we'll know for sure. If this is cancer it can be a vicious enemy, Theodore. I told you I want to be aggressive. It's the only way we can fight. Do I have your permission to proceed?"

Theodore thought about Saturday afternoon with Tedi—it had been his first quality time alone with her in many months. He wanted more times like that. Many more times. "Yes. I want to go for it."

———

At two o'clock Tuesday morning Clarence sat in the center of Ivy's sturdy sofa in the family room, switching channels mindlessly on the only television in the house. For his own safety, he left the volume on "mute." Besides, he'd watched TV at this hour enough times that he knew the pitches by heart. He could choose between the Home Shopping Network—"Oh, sure, I've got that kind of money to spend on a set of mixing bowls"—or the Fitness Channel. Oh, and there was the Cooking Channel, where pork fat rules. "I'll show you some pork fat," he muttered. He hit the button again and discovered a couple of kids who couldn't be more than twenty, wearing Spandex and smiles, swearing how their new little box of wheels and bars could melt off the tummy in five minutes a day without dieting.

Clarence grabbed a pillow and threw it at the set—after all, they were called *throw* pillows, weren't they? How did these people live with themselves? They couldn't be naïve enough to believe all their own hype, could they?

From out of the shadows past the set, there was movement, and a figure bent forward to pick up the pillow. Clarence nearly shouted in alarm, until he recognized the slightly tubby form of Delphina Bell, dressed in a pair of jeans and a sweater Ivy had given her yesterday. Delphi didn't step into the room but stood there holding the pillow in front of her, as if it might be a shield. How long had she been watching him? Had she heard him talking to the TV? Did she think he'd lost his mind? Or was she scared because she thought maybe he'd lost his temper? For Delphi, watching a man lose his temper must be harder than watching him lose his mind.

"Come on in, Delphina. I'm not going to bite. I'm not that hungry yet. What's the matter, can't you sleep, either?"

She shook her head and took a tentative step closer, as if she might run like a scared rabbit any second. "I thought . . . I heard some noise in here."

"You did. It was just me. Don't worry. I'm harmless unless you get between me and my chocolate chip cookies." He pressed the remote and the TV screen went black. Unfortunately, so did the whole room. He flipped the switch back on, but then the mute had disengaged, and exercise music blared through the room—and possibly the whole house. He fumbled for the power switch again and plunged them once more into darkness and silence.

Through the silence he heard a sniffle. Oh man, he was as clumsy as a dog climbing a tree. "It's okay, Delphina, really," he said in his gentlest voice as he stumbled toward the end of the sofa and reached for the lamp. He switched on the light without knocking it over and saw her still standing where she had been, though because of the light she was no longer hidden in the shadows.

Her head was bent forward, and her face was scrunched up as if in pain. Her fingers dug into the gold-and-blue pillow so deep Clarence thought she might pull out the stuffing.

"Hey, lady, you okay? Come on over here and have a seat. Sorry I scared you like that. Come on." He gestured for her to join him on the sofa—at the other end of the sofa, so the huge dent his weight made in the cushions wouldn't pitch her over into his lap.

She hesitated a moment, then slowly stepped forward and perched at the edge, still clutching the pillow.

"There you go. Now, why don't you tell me why you can't sleep, and then I'll tell you why I can't sleep."

She sniffed. He grabbed some tissues from a pretty floral-and-gold dispenser on the coffee table and handed them to her. She took them and blew her nose, keeping the pillow in her lap. She started crying again.

"You're afraid he's going to find you, aren't you?" Clarence asked. She nodded.

"Well, I've been reading up on domestic violence in one of Mercy's textbooks, and it looks to me like you're okay as long as you're with other people, you know? The typical wife beater wants everybody to think he's a good guy, so he's not going to come crashing through the door here when there's a bunch of other people with you. It'd make him look bad. What he tries to do is let everybody think you're making all this stuff up."

She shook her head and wiped her nose again. "I don't think he cares what other people think. Not anymore. Not since last fall."

"Why? What happened then?"

"He got drunk and passed out, and I pounded his head into the concrete."

Clarence tried not to show shock on his face. He didn't think he was doing a very good job, but luckily she didn't look at him. She just stared across the room, hugging the pillow to her chest.

"They had to fly him to Springfield," she muttered. "I wish he'd've died."

Clarence hoped his eyeballs didn't go flying out of their sockets. He sat perfectly still and waited for her to keep talking. Which was the only thing that was going to save this conversation, because he couldn't think of a single word to say. He just hoped Ivy didn't let Delphi use any knives or other pointed objects around the house. He'd better make sure she didn't ever get mad at him.

But he had to remind himself about what she'd been through. And she was just sharing her thoughts with him. Oh yeah, nice little thoughts about how she'd tried to kill her husband, and how she still wished he were dead.

"I've got to go see Dr. Mercy tomorrow," Delphi said. "She's going to check me out and do a chest x-ray to make sure this cough isn't pneumonia or something. Then I'm getting out of this town. I can't stick around." She turned to look at Clarence. "Next time he gets ahold of me, he could kill me, or maybe somebody else. He gets crazy, goes wild. One minute he's brooding and the next he's crying. Then he'll fly into a rage and knock everything off the counters and ram his hand through a window. I know. I've seen it all. He's crazy."

Clarence stared at her in the lamplight, trying to think of something intelligent to say. But what do you say to an abused woman who'd tried to make her husband's skull a piece of the garage floor?

"Will you take me?" came Delphi's timid request.

Clarence watched her a few seconds longer. "Huh?"

"To see Dr. Mercy tomorrow? Mrs. Richmond says you've got an appointment, too, and she and Miss Knight will both be out of town. Dr. Mercy said she'd loan you her car."

Clarence shook off the goose bumps that had accumulated at the back of his neck. He had to stop making judgments. How did he know what Delphi's life was like? How would *he* like to be a scared young woman with a mean, crazy man for a husband? "Sure I'll take you, Delphina. Don't worry, I'll be there."

Business was nonexistent at Herald Hospital Emergency Room Tuesday morning, which was why all the staff except for Lukas were taking a break to celebrate Carmen's birthday. He had been invited, as well, but he thought it might be a good idea for *someone* to watch the phones and hang around in case of emergency. Consequently he was the one who answered Mr. Amos's call. And the call was for him.

"Dr. Bower, it is provident that I caught you." The disembodied voice was less harsh and angry than the last time Lukas had spoken with him, though it was far from friendly. His nasal twang was more evident, like a country boy attempting to speak with a British accent. "I received your missive in yesterday's delivery."

"Yes?" Missive?

"As per your request, I have perused your contract. As I understand section five on page two, either party may render this contract null and void if both parties agree to do so."

"I see. And do they?"

"I think it would be in the best interest of both parties, don't you agree?"

"I certainly do, Mr. Amos." Relief, sudden and overwhelming, flowed through Lukas. "When do you think this . . . agreement might take effect?"

"It so happens that I am in receipt of a curriculum vitae of a Jefferson City physician who expresses his wish to escape to the country. At this time he is not employed, and I believe it would behoove me in this matter to allow you to step down."

Lukas shook his head. Why couldn't the man just say, "I've got a replacement for you, so good riddance"?

"I've taken the liberty of viewing your work schedule," Amos continued, "and Friday appears to be your final day this week."

"That's right. I'm not down for another shift until next Tuesday." He'd been looking forward to the long weekend. Was it premature to hope that he could pack his Jeep Friday and—

"I believe I can arrange things so that Friday will be your final time with us, Dr. Bower."

He sounded irritable, but why? If he had a replacement, why be cranky? Of course, when was Mr. Amos not cranky? Lukas certainly wouldn't want to be a hospital administrator. "That sounds good to me, Mr. Amos."

"You may tell Mrs. Pinkley to expect you in Knolls next week." Yes, definitely peevish.

Hold it . . . Mrs. Pinkley? "You know the Knolls hospital administrator?"

"Of course. Her acumen and wisdom are legend among hospital administrators in this region . . . and I had the privilege of speaking with her via telephone yesterday afternoon."

Aha! So Estelle *had* called about the contract! He'd told her he would handle the matter, and he had. He should be annoyed by her interference. He wasn't.

As soon as Mr. Amos hung up, Lukas dialed Estelle's direct number.

"You didn't trust me," he accused as soon as she answered.

"Of course I trust you, Lukas." She didn't pretend to wonder what he meant. "I just needed to speed things along. I felt it would be easier for Mr. Amos to see reason if I explained the difficulties we were having down here without you."

"You bullied him."

"I did not. In fact, I even gave him some advice about a pending court case."

"A court case?" Could she be talking about Hershel Moss? Or perhaps someone was suing the hospital for substandard care? They could have fifty court cases pending and Lukas wouldn't know a thing about it.

"According to Mr. Amos, I can expect to see you here on Monday?" Estelle asked.

Lukas smiled and felt a warm sense of peace cover him. "Yes. I'll be looking forward to seeing you." He said good-bye and hung up, and the next patient who walked through the door heard Dr. Lukas Bower laughing out loud with relief and joy. Come next Monday, he would be working with Mercy.

"Three pounds down since Friday." Mercy carried Shannon Becker's clipboard over to her desk and sat down facing her silent patient. "Your mother says you still aren't eating."

"I know." Shannon's shadowed eyes looked huge in her drawn, parchment-colored face. "I'm sorry." She didn't meet Mercy's gaze but stared out the window at the winter grass and gray-brown trees.

Mercy couldn't avoid the irony of the situation. Poor Clarence, who had struggled so hard to lose weight, had gained two pounds as of a few moments ago. On the other hand, Shannon seemed unable to force herself to eat. And emotions held the power over both patients. Depression. If she could only help them gain better control of those emotions, she couldn't help believing the rest would fall into place. Shannon would regain her weight and be a chattering, happy teenager again. Clarence would feel like a man again. But she couldn't work miracles; only God could do that.

Mercy had to constantly remind herself that she was not expected to control these people. She couldn't have prevented Kendra from overexercising at the health club, she couldn't have prevented the violent rape of Shannon's body and spirit, and she didn't even know Clarence when he'd gained all that weight. All she could do was pray for them and let them know she cared. And she had to know when to get firm and when to let go.

The time had come to get firm with this one.

She pushed the chart aside and got up from behind the desk. This girl didn't need to feel as if she had been sent to the principal's office. So instead, Mercy sat down beside Shannon and moved her chair around so they could face each other.

"I'm sorry, honey, but I'm afraid this isn't going to work." She kept her voice soft and nonthreatening but made it clear she would not back down. "You're trying to starve yourself to death, and I can't let that happen. If you lose much more weight, you could be setting yourself up for osteoporosis, even heart damage. You could lose sensation in your hands and feet, and that's just the beginning."

Shannon gripped her hands tightly together in her lap and didn't look up. "I tried to eat, Dr. Mercy. I've been drinking water, lots of water. I just . . . can't."

"Yes, I know. And I know why. If I were a fifteen-year-old girl in your situation, I also might try to remove all evidence that I'm a female so no one would look at me like that again. I might cut off all my hair and wear my dad's baggy shirts and jeans and forget to take a shower or brush my teeth for days at a time. I might withdraw inside myself and refuse to trust anyone again."

Shannon nodded, and she looked up at Mercy then. A look devoid of hope filled her eyes.

The girl's despair brought a quick sheen of tears to Mercy's eyes. "I can't let you do that."

Shannon studied the tears for a moment. "You're going to make me go into the hospital, aren't you?"

"Not in Knolls. I can't help you, Shannon. You need to go to a place that deals specifically with emotional disorders. I've already spoken with your mother about sending you where you can get some good help, and she agrees."

Shannon didn't move. She didn't blink. "Where?"

"There's a hospital in Tulsa that has a good cure rate." Mercy couldn't help hoping that if they caught this thing early enough, Shannon wouldn't have the long, painful recovery period that other patients sometimes suffered. A 75 percent cure rate was considered good, and that took an average of seven years.

At first the girl didn't even seem to have the energy to show alarm. "It's a long way from home."

"It's a five-hour drive from here. And the healing process will take time and a lot of effort from you and your family. Are you willing to give it a try?"

Shannon bent forward until her forehead rested on her knees. Mercy could see the sharpness of her shoulder blades and the outline of her rib cage. Her shoulders heaved and she sniffed, and Mercy wanted to take the child in her arms and comfort her.

"I don't really want to die, Dr. Mercy," came the muffled reply at last. "It would kill my mom and dad, too. I don't want to do that to them. And my brothers and sisters . . . I don't want to die. I just don't want to be raped again."

Mercy sat back. Finally the heart of the problem. "I'll tell you what, Shannon. You go to this hospital and get healthy again, and I'll personally see to it that you attend a complete self-defense course. Then the next time some dirt-bag tries to mess with you, *he'll* end up in the hospital. Okay?"

After a long hesitation, Shannon straightened and looked at Mercy and wiped her face with the ragged sleeve of her dad's old work shirt. "I'll try it."

"And I'll be praying for you all the way through it, Shannon," Mercy said softly.

I'm going home . . . I'm going home . . . Lukas had to force himself to concentrate on the monitor in the trauma-cardiac room. Mr. Bennett, a chubby man in his late fifties, lay on the exam table, hooked up to oxygen via nasal cannula. He was in obvious pain in spite of the four baby aspirin and the nitroglycerin Tex had given him as soon as she established an IV. He was due for another nitro under the tongue.

His wife stood beside him and held his hand. "His face was white and he was sweating just before we left to come here, Dr. Bower. It's his heart. I know it's his heart. His father died of a heart attack when—"

"Dad was seventy when he died," Mr. Bennett snapped. "Relax, woman. I'll be fine."

Lukas reread the chart with Tex's assessment. The patient smoked two packs of cigarettes and drank a six-pack of beer daily. His blood pressure upon presentation was 180 over 95. Tex had already drawn blood, established an IV, and ordered a portable chest x-ray.

"Mr. Bennett, we're running an EKG to see what your heart is doing right now," Lukas said. "The lab is running a cardiac enzyme level on your blood. When we get the results of that we'll have a better idea about how we're going to treat you."

The gray-haired patient started shaking his head before Lukas finished talking. "Can't stay, Doc. My mother's flying in tonight for a family reunion this weekend. My brothers are driving in from Sedalia and St. Louis, and aunts and uncles will be here Friday. It's a big deal with—" He grimaced and caught his breath, squeezing his eyes tightly shut.

"More pain? Is it your chest?" Lukas asked.

The man nodded, eyes still shut.

Lukas gave him another nitroglycerin tablet under the tongue. If the pain didn't improve, there was morphine waiting.

"He woke up like that," Mrs. Bennett said. "He said he was sick to his stomach, and he was breathing in short gasps. Did I tell you he's diabetic?"

"No, but that's helpful," Lukas said, concentrating on his patient. "Mr. Bennett, have you had other episodes like this recently?"

"Yes, he has," Mrs. Bennett volunteered before her husband could answer. "At least four times in the past few weeks, although nothing like this. He woke me up this time on purpose. He never does that. You know how these tough guys are."

"The doctor doesn't want to hear my life history," Mr. Bennett complained.

"Actually, I do." Lukas continued to study the monitor. It showed occasional irregular beats, but they were decreasing in frequency. "How's the pain now, Mr. Bennett?"

The patient took a couple of deep breaths and looked up at Lukas. "Better."

"Gone completely?"

"It will be. I can't stay."

That wasn't good enough. "Let's wait for the test results to come back."

———

The lines of wood grain on Dr. Robert Simeon's desk had begun to coalesce into flickering flames that taunted and waved at Theodore, manipulated by the shades of sunlight that slanted in through the broad bay window. Winter wind blew the bare branches of a hawthorn tree outside. Theodore watched the movement with intense fascination, watched the chickadees and cardinals as they skittered from branch to branch, watched the ethereal floating of the clouds against the milky blue of a Missouri winter sky. Nothing kept his imagination hampered for longer than a few seconds, and the clouds grew darker, mocking and sinister.

Worry drew Theo's gut into a tight knot of memories and fears. He hadn't even had the courage to tell Mercy about his appointment with Dr. Simeon during their lunch date Saturday. He'd walked away like a coward. But then, Tedi was there. And he still didn't know for sure . . . not for sure.

The tension drew tighter as the door opened and Robert stepped through with his ever-present chart. Robert's frown was deeper than usual, his movements slower, his head bent in thought.

"Hello, Theodore." Preoccupied, he didn't offer a handshake.

Theodore couldn't move, couldn't speak.

Robert walked around to his chair and sank down into it with a sigh. He placed the chart carefully on the desk and aligned the edges so that it lay perfectly straight. "I'm sorry to say this, but we need to do a biopsy."

Theodore nearly moaned out loud. He wanted to shout. He wanted to cry and beg God to please not let this happen. He swallowed. "You saw a problem with the ultrasound?"

A nod. "We found a large lesion in the liver."

"So it really is cancer."

"I'm sorry."

"How bad?" Theo saw the flicker of discomfort in the doctor's eyes. "Look, Robert, you can tell me. It isn't like I'm going to sue you for a misdiagnosis at this point."

Robert shot him a sharp look of reproach.

Theo felt immediately ashamed. Don't take your frustration out on the messenger. "I'm sorry. That was uncalled for. It's just so . . . this is such a shock. I've been praying about this. I went to my pastor and talked to him about my condition, and he prayed with me. I just can't get it out of my mind. The wondering is the worst thing."

"No, it isn't." Robert leaned back in his leather swivel chair and rolled his head from side to side as if to stretch tense neck muscles. "You'll have to trust me about this, because I've seen this happen a few more times than you have. I've had patients who jumped to conclusions at this point and decided they were going to die, and they gave up. They started to grieve when they should have been fighting back. At this stage of the procedure, we don't jump to conclusions."

Theodore allowed the steady cadence of Robert's voice to calm him. Of course he was right. "You aren't saying the test could be wrong, are you?"

"No. Something is there. Ultrasound is not diagnostic enough in this situation for us to—"

"But it's cancer."

"Theodore—"

"Please, Robert."

"I want to do a biopsy immediately. It's some form of cancer, but we don't know what, or how to fight it yet. Having no previous films with which to compare, I have no idea of the rate of growth, but I do know that the sooner we attack it, the better your prognosis. Dr. Huffman can see you in Springfield tomorrow afternoon at three."

Theodore didn't hesitate. "I'll be there." But first he was going to do something even more difficult. He had to tell Mercy and Tedi about this.

———

Thirty minutes after Mr. Bennett's initial tests, the results were back, and Lukas studied them in relief. There was no evidence of an MI on the EKG, and the lab was normal except for an elevated glucose level of 215. The portable chest x-ray showed no obvious congestive heart failure.

"I feel fine now, Dr. Bower," the man said. "I told you, I've got to get out of here."

"I'm sorry, but I can't let you go," Lukas said. "I've put a call in to a cardiologist at—"

"No, you don't understand." Mr. Bennett reached down and started ripping lead patches from his hairy chest. "You've got to let me go. I'm not staying. I'm walking out of here."

"Leonard, stop it!" his wife protested, rushing to his side from the chair where she had been sitting. "You can't leave here if the doctor doesn't say—"

"Wanna bet?" He pulled the plastic oxygen tube from his nose. "If I start to feel bad again, I'll come back. I'll be good and dump the cigarettes and pour out the beer. I won't run and play with my nieces and nephews. I'll just watch from the house, but this is probably the last family reunion we'll ever have, and I'm going to be there." He reached for the IV.

"No, don't!" Lukas grabbed his hand to stop him. "You'll bleed."

"Then take it off now."

"Okay, I will. Settle down, Mr. Bennett. I can't force you to stay here against your will, but it's definitely against my advice."

"Fine, let me sign out. I thought you said the lab and EKG looked good."

"EKG is only diagnostic in early heart attack about forty to fifty percent of the time, and it takes six hours for the lab to be positive for an MI. At best, this could be unstable angina, which can lead to a heart attack with no warning. I don't think your family would want you to risk—"

"You don't know anything about my family." The statement was matter-of-fact, with no malice or anger. In fact, Mr. Bennett didn't seem upset at all, just determined. "I missed the last two family reunions because I was too busy. My brothers complained, my mother was mad at me for six months, and this time I can't miss it. Now, will you take that needle out of my arm?"

Lukas did so reluctantly. "Okay, Mr. Bennett, but please come back and see us when the pain hits again. I don't doubt that it will."

"Then you'll be seeing me again."

———

Clarence sat in a deep funk, listening to the classical music and waiting for Delphi at the Richmond Clinic. It was a miracle he'd even been able to fit behind the steering wheel of Mercy's car this afternoon. He'd gained two pounds! After all that suffering and starving and getting gas from high-fiber foods and exercising every time Ivy cracked the whip, he'd had nothing to show for it for two weeks. Nothing to prove he'd been good Saturday night and only eaten half a cookie on his food raid. Nothing to prove he'd choked down so many oats for breakfast and salads for lunch he should be growing a mane and tail and whinnying like a horse—or braying like a Missouri mule.

Mercy had reassured him that he'd hit a plateau and he just

needed to keep working until he pushed through to the next level. She also reminded him that he'd already lost nearly a hundred pounds of actual fat, and that progress had taken less than a year—in fact, the majority of his weight had come off in the past three months. That helped some. But he wished she would leak that news to the teenager who sat at the other end of the waiting room staring at him and snickering and jabbing his buddy, or the old woman with the pinched lips and eyes the shade of dog droppings who had moved to another chair when he sat down next to her. This was why he hated going out in public.

He could only blame himself. He was the one who'd stuffed the food in his own mouth, and he wasn't going to whine and say "not my fault" and play the victim game like so many others did.

The waiting room door opened, and Clarence looked up automatically to see a big hulk of a man shadowed in the threshold. He had stringy hair that fell into muddy, bloodshot eyes and at least three days of beard on his face. Cold air breezed in through the entrance, but he took his time and studied the room before he stepped on in and closed the door behind him. Then he looked at Clarence.

Clarence shivered. It had to be the cold air. What he felt couldn't be from the lifeless, soulless look in the man's face, or the way he seemed to stare right through Clarence into the wall behind him. The man gazed around the room again, then sat down in one of the chairs near the entrance. He didn't even walk over to the window to tell Loretta he was here.

The smart-aleck teenager cracked another joke to his friend, and the two of them snickered. The telephone buzzed at the secretary's desk. The waiting continued.

Clarence shifted uncomfortably in his dinky chair, glad these didn't have arms on them. He'd gotten stuck in a chair like that one time. Nearly tore his pants off getting out of it. He could imagine the attention *that* would draw from this crowd. And what if this weight gain wasn't just a plateau? What if he gained the whole hundred pounds back again, or even more? Then he wouldn't fit into any chair. He could get so big, Buck would have to haul him in the back of his pickup truck to get him anywhere.

What was Ivy going to say when she found out he'd gained two whole pounds? Would she preach a sermon? Threaten to stop baking chocolate chip cookies? Put a pedometer on the treadmill so she could keep track of how far he walked each day? This was turning out to be a rotten day.

———

"Your elbow looks good," Mercy assured Delphi as she pulled the sleeve of the pink cotton sweater back down. "So does this bruising around your eye. A little makeup will cover the chartreuse skin until it clears." She gently pressed the cheekbone. "Any pain?"

Delphi didn't wince. "Not much."

"That doesn't tell me a lot," Mercy teased. "You have a high pain tolerance. I had a friend like that when I was in school. Jackie fell on the ice and broke her shoulder and never went to the doctor to check it out. She just thought she'd pulled some muscles, and that the pain would go away. Six months later she went on a canoe trip with some friends. About ten miles downriver, she came to the obvious, painful realization that something was still wrong with her shoulder. When she finally did have it x-rayed, there was so much damage it took a long time to heal, and she had to have physical therapy for several months." After a short pause, Mercy touched Delphi's shoulder until they had eye contact. "Jackie would have been a lot better off if she'd asked for help as soon as she fell and hurt herself. All of us need to ask for help from time to time."

Delphi looked away. "You've helped me, Dr. Mercy. Like you said, I'm okay now."

"Physically, you're fine. I'm not concerned about that. What I am concerned about is the rest of your life." Mercy walked over and picked up a business card she had received recently. "The day the police brought you in here last week, I told you about Crosslines." She handed the card to Delphi. "You were pretty drugged, so I doubt you remember me mentioning it. A couple by the name of Arthur and Alma Collins run it. They were missionaries in Mexico until last fall, when they were hit by a car. Alma lost her leg. They've been in Springfield this past week, while she's been going through therapy so she can be fitted for a prosthesis."

Delphi studied the card as if it were a poisonous spider. "What's that got to do with me?"

Mercy sat down on her stool and looked up at Delphi. "They can help you. Have you given any thought about what you're going to do for the rest of your life?"

Delphi shrugged. "I guess I'll see if Clarence can give me a ride out of town someplace. I can't stay here, not with Abner around."

"And you expect Clarence to just dump you in another town with a bunch of strangers? I'm sorry, but that isn't an option." Mercy realized her voice was suddenly sharp, impatient. She sighed. The subject of Abner brought up old feelings of frustration. "I know I've asked this many times before, but if you would just admit to the police—"

"No." Delphi slid down from the exam bed and reached for the thick, soft green jacket Ivy had given her several days ago. "It won't do any good, just make Abner mad. They can't stop him, Dr. Mercy." She pulled the jacket on carefully, as if her elbow still felt a little stiff. "Guess I'd better get out of here, or Clarence will get tired of waiting."

"What about Crosslines?" Mercy followed her patient out into the hallway.

"I don't know. I'll think about it," Delphi called over her shoulder as she reached for the knob of the dividing door between the treatment rooms and the waiting room. She pulled the door open and stopped with a jerk in the threshold. She cried out and stumbled backward, and Mercy saw terror in her eyes.

Abner Bell stood at the other side of the threshold.

"No, get away from me!" Delphi swung around and ran past Mercy, thrusting her sideways in desperation.

"Delphi!" Abner grated. "Get back here! I'm just going to talk to you." He lunged after her, but Mercy stepped in the way, which made him hesitate.

"Oh no you don't, buster!" Clarence came hurtling through the doorway after him. "Hey, don't you—"

The man rounded on Clarence with an elbow and smacked him in the shoulder, but instead of letting go, Clarence shoved forward with the force of his whole body, knocking the air from Abner's lungs in a grunt. Someone in the waiting room screamed.

"Call the police!" Clarence yelled. "Somebody call the police!"

Abner twisted away with a frantic motion, stumbled away from Clarence, turned, and fled out the front.

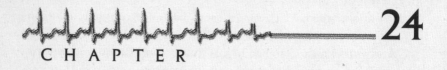

CHAPTER 24

At six-thirty Tuesday night Mercy turned out all but the security lights in the office and switched on the answering machine. Clarence would be here any moment to pick her up.

Poor Clarence. After Delphi panicked and ran out the back entrance to the clinic, he went in search of her, driving up and down the streets and alleys in Mercy's car, blaming himself because he'd allowed Abner to get close to her. But who would have expected Abner to be so bold? Clarence hadn't even known what the man looked like. The police had come, taken statements, and finally admitted there wasn't a lot they could do, since Delphi had never filed a complaint. Abner hadn't attacked anyone except Clarence, and it could be argued that was self-defense. He hadn't even threatened anyone. And he had disappeared before the police arrived.

But how had he known Delphi was here? Had he been lurking somewhere nearby, watching the clinic? A quick check this afternoon revealed he hadn't been to work at the iron foundry in a week and a half; therefore, Abner was no longer employed.

Shivering, Mercy rechecked the front door to make sure it was locked while she waited. She stepped over to the front window to stare past the glare of her reflection into the evening sky. In late January it was always dark when she left the clinic, even when she finished on time. The moon was high in the sky, and a scattering of the brightest stars were visible in spite of the streetlamps and the glow of the hospital lights a block away.

Her gaze shifted to the shadowed forms of the ER construction workers who hammered and welded and climbed ladders with masculine precision, their silhouettes coalescing and mingling in the floodlights that surrounded them.

Three months ago Mercy had stared out this window at a very different view as fire burst from those walls and threatened to consume Lukas Bower, Estelle Pinkley, and a host of others who were caught in its embrace. When her anguish had become too great for her to bear, she had learned, at last, with Alma's gentle guidance, to place control into the hands of Someone infinitely more powerful than she. Soon afterward she had placed her whole life in His hands.

So why, in the past few weeks, couldn't she leave control with Him? Why did she continue to worry? Where was the peace she remembered claiming as her own?

Another shadow moved into her vision, striding across the parking lot to the sidewalk in front of the clinic, and she gasped and retreated into the darkness. It wasn't Clarence. With quickened breathing she watched his movements, unable to forget the image of Abner in this office today, or of Delphi's desperate flight.

But it wasn't Abner. As the man came closer, Mercy recognized Theodore's tall form, his clean-shaven face and short blond hair backlit by the streetlights. His ears were bare to the cold, his hands jammed into the pockets of his coat. He slowed and stopped halfway to the clinic door, obviously noticing that no cars were parked nearby. In appearance, the Richmond Clinic was quiet for the night.

His shoulders slumped forward and his head bowed. The glow of lights from behind him etched the outline of the even features of his face, and for a moment she thought he was crying. But it must be a trick of the shadows. What would Theo have to cry about?

Mercy couldn't prevent the concern that compelled her to unlock the door and step out into the chill air. "Theodore?"

She heard him catch his breath. He stiffened, then looked across at her. He straightened his shoulders and stepped toward her. "Mercy."

"What are you doing here? Are you okay?"

After a brief pause, he said, "I heard about the excitement you had over here today, and I thought I'd stroll over and have a look around, make sure everything was okay." There was tension in his voice. "Where's your car?"

"Clarence has it. He's supposed to pick me up. You heard about Abner?"

"It's all over town. I heard about what happened at the printshop a couple of hours ago." He took another step forward. "I was worried, Mercy."

She smiled up at him. "Come inside out of the cold until Clarence gets here, then we can take you home. You walked all the way across town to make sure I was okay? That's very sweet of you, but wouldn't it have been easier to call?"

He didn't answer as he followed her into the clinic and closed the door behind them. He sighed and turned distractedly to look around the dimly lit waiting room, and the scent of ink and solvent from the printshop mingled with the antiseptic smells of the clinic.

"You can relax," Mercy said. "We're the only ones here, and the burglar alarm is in place except for the front door. Bill Peterson will try to patrol the area every hour or so, but there's no reason for Abner to return to an empty clinic. He's looking for his wife."

Theo nodded and turned back to her, still obviously distracted. Mercy watched him curiously. He'd behaved the same way last Saturday at lunch.

"Theodore, something else is wrong. What is it?"

He opened his mouth to speak, then stopped and shook his head. He reached up and rubbed the back of his neck. "Could you and Tedi meet me for lunch at Little Mary's tomorrow?"

When she hesitated, he said, "Please, Mercy, I need to talk to you, I . . ." He broke off and turned away from her to look out the window.

"Okay," she said slowly. "What's going on? Can't you—"

"I have cancer."

He remained standing with his back to her, and she saw the sudden jerk of his shoulders, as if from a sob. And they jerked again, and again. There was a quick gasp, and he dipped his head and raised a hand to his face. Mercy felt the shock of his words race through her like a jolt of electricity. For a moment she couldn't think, and before she could gather her wits to reply, she saw headlights coming down the street. The outline of her car was highlighted by the spillover glow from the hospital. Clarence was coming to pick her up.

Theodore sniffed and straightened, making an obvious effort to control his emotions. "Robert Simeon did an alpha-fetoprotein test. The numbers were high. An ultrasound shows a mass in my liver. I'm going in for a liver biopsy tomorrow afternoon."

Mercy felt the sadness and shock wash over her, as if he were already dead, and the reaction surprised her. "Hepatocellular carcinoma?"

"That's what Robert thinks." There was a long pause as they watched Clarence pull into the drive to the right of the clinic. He stopped the car and turned off the headlights. The interior light came on. He opened the door and heaved his huge bulk from the seat.

"I tested positive for hepatitis B," Theodore said. "Robert says the disease must be chronic." He turned to Mercy then. "I went in for a comprehensive blood test two weeks ago, because I wanted to be sure . . . I thought if you and I were to . . . if there was ever a chance for remarriage, I didn't want to infect you with . . ." He hung his head. "All the affairs . . ."

Quick tears of pity and pain stung her eyes. "Oh, Theodore," she breathed.

"I'm sorry. I'll never be able to tell you how sorry I am. I wish I could make those years up to Tedi, but I think I'm running out of time."

"No. Stop talking like that." Past the outline of his shoulder, she saw Clarence lumbering up the walk. There were so many things she wanted to say, so many reassurances she wanted to give him, the same she would give to one of her own patients—there was hope, they could fight this, it didn't mean he was going to die—but she knew he needed privacy to talk about the cancer, and Clarence was reaching for the door and turning the knob.

"Tedi and I will meet you tomorrow," she assured him as Clarence came barreling in.

"She needs to be prepared—" Theo began, then fell silent.

"Man, it's colder than springwater out there!" Clarence announced. "I sure hope Delphi found a place to stay warm. Hey, Theodore, how you doing? I guess you heard what happened. I can't find her anywhere. I thought I'd grab a bite to eat, and if she still hasn't turned up, I'll borrow Ivy's car and look some more after dinner."

292 · HANNAH ALEXANDER

A giant splotch that looked and smelled like Betadine stained the right leg of Lukas's jeans when he pulled them from his locker Tuesday night at the end of his shift. He groaned and held them up to the light, then looked around the room suspiciously, as if the perpetrator might still be hanging around, watching for his reaction. "You know," he called to the absent prankster, "you should have to graduate from kindergarten before you can work in a hospital. Obviously, that isn't the case here." He threw the jeans onto the bed and reached into the locker for his jacket. He would have to wear his scrubs home again.

He knew he shouldn't allow himself to get angry. He was leaving at the end of the week, never to return. He should be joyful. He should celebrate at this extra reminder of the annoyances he would no longer be forced to endure. But he didn't feel like a party.

He shut the locker and marched from the room into the ER, where shift change was still taking place. Day personnel were giving report to night personnel. The lab-radiology tech hovered in the doorway that connected the ER to the lab, gossiping with Carmen, the day secretary. The ambulance crew was still here from the last run they had made from the nursing home two blocks away. Quinn and his new partner were completing reports at the counter.

"Excuse me," Lukas said.

No one acknowledged him. The low office buzz continued.

He cleared his throat and raised his voice. "I said, excuse me!"

Okay, that worked. A sudden hush fell over the room. The staff looked at him in surprise. Now was an unfortunate time to start having second thoughts about displaying a temper tantrum. Still, he needed to say this.

"Someone likes to play practical jokes in the doctor's call room," he said. He looked from Sandra, to Quinn, to Carmen. Carmen looked away. He remembered the surgical jelly on his steering wheel. "I overlooked the trash upended in the bed, and the stapled scrubs, and the ruined lunch." He looked toward the temperamental lab-radiology tech, and then Jane, the night nurse. "I didn't say anything, until now, about the vandalism of my Jeep, or my good slacks with the legs cut off."

Carmen gasped, and her mouth came open. She shot a look of

accusation toward the doorway, but Lukas couldn't tell whom she was looking at.

"I want to warn whoever is pulling these pranks that if anything else happens while I'm working here," Lukas said, "I will report the incidents to the police. You shouldn't find it too hard to deprive yourself. I'll only be here three more days. Then you'll have the joy of picking on my replacement. I believe in turning the other cheek, but I'm running out of cheeks."

Suddenly embarrassed by his outburst, and his poor choice of phrasing, he left without another word.

———

After delivering Theodore to his apartment, and Clarence to his waiting meal, Mercy drove toward home along an avenue occasionally pooled by the amber glow of streetlights. She couldn't push thoughts of Theodore from her mind, and compassion for him overwhelmed her. More overwhelming, however, were her fears for her daughter. How would Tedi react to the news that her father had cancer? After all the hardship that had been heaped on her this past year, how would she handle it if Theodore died?

The next few days would tell for sure how advanced the cancer was. The biopsy tomorrow would be conclusive, and further testing would show them if the carcinoma had spread. Unfortunately, if the cancer *had* metastasized, his prognosis was not good. Robert Simeon wouldn't tell him until the work-up was complete, but his life expectancy would be from three to six months.

She turned onto her street and drove more slowly. She was in no hurry. Tedi was spending the night with Abby, and the house would feel empty without her. In spite of the emptiness, however, Mercy could use that time alone. There seemed to be so many people in her life these days, and so many needs she couldn't scramble quickly enough to meet. She felt pressed in from all around. Before Tedi came to live with her, the loneliness had been so intense at times that she purposely stayed at the hospital with patients in the evenings. She had worked shifts in the ER, both as a means to supplement her income to support two households, and as a diversion. Now the loneliness was a memory. Though she never needed a break from her daughter's lively personality, she sometimes wished the two of them could leave town for a few days and life could slow down.

The dark silence of the house felt oppressive as Mercy stepped into the kitchen from the garage and pressed the button to lower the overhead door. The only light came from the front porch, which she always left on when she would be coming home at night.

She turned on the light over the kitchen sink, then walked into the study, where she and Tedi had a habit of curling up together at night to read the Bible. She switched on the lamp beside the sofa and sat in her familiar spot. For a moment she allowed the silence to cover her. Slowly the sounds of the house drifted in . . . the gentle hum of the refrigerator, the hushed movement of air from the central heating vents, the ticking of the wall clock.

Her gaze fell on the black leather-bound Bible, and she reached for it, wishing she were more familiar with its contents—but glad, especially now, that she was intimately involved with its Author. That was Whom she needed.

She bowed her head as the events of the day overwhelmed her and tears stung her eyes. "Oh, God, help us," she breathed. "Help Theodore. Why is this happening to him, now that he's getting his life together, now that he's trusted you?"

She was still humiliated by her recent discovery that she had not completely forgiven Theodore over the past few months. What kind of an example had she been to Tedi? Sure she had compassion for him now that he was sick, but if he were proclaimed healthy tomorrow, if all this had been some big mistake, how would she feel?

"Lord, forgive me in Jesus' name. Show me again how to love the unlovable, as you love me. Please don't leave me stuck in this confusion forever."

She recalled what Lukas said Friday, about getting confused when he tried to second-guess God's next move.

"Please, dear Lord, give Theodore your strength and your blessing. Touch him—touch us all—with your healing. Give Tedi peace and faith in you, and take her fear and bad memories away. She's just a little girl, God. Please don't make her suffer any more than she has already." The thought of Tedi's suffering made the tears flow more freely. "Please protect her tomorrow when we tell her about the cancer."

She waited, and listened, and didn't fight the tears but allowed them to wash through her in a healing stream as she cried for Tedi, and for Theodore. Delphi came to her mind, and fresh tears flowed for her. Was she hiding somewhere in the cold darkness, afraid to seek shelter because Abner might find her? And Shannon . . . and Kendra . . . so many hurting souls in the world. So many lost, hurting people. How could she take care of them when she couldn't even see to her own daughter's spiritual needs?

One by one, Mercy prayed for them and then did what was so hard for her to do—once again, she turned them over to the care of Someone more powerful and more loving, more able to forgive, than she. With the prayers came a soothing balm of comfort. By the time she was finished her back ached and her head pounded from the flow of tears, but something within her had changed. She was where she needed to be, talking to God. And she was doing what He wanted her to do—wait. And while she did so, she would try to make it easier for the others who waited with her. She couldn't do this alone, but she didn't have to. The faith that had felt so shaky a week ago now flowed through her with power. God wasn't going to let her go.

Someone was pounding on a semi truck with a tire tool, and the noise was starting to bug Clarence. If they didn't stop soon, they'd damage something. He tried to shout at them to stop, but when he opened his mouth, no sound came out. When he tried to walk across the big garage, his legs wouldn't move.

The pounding grew louder, more insistent, until it awakened him with a start. He jerked and felt the bed shudder beneath him. And the pounding continued . . . more like tapping. On a window. He frowned into the darkness. Was it hailing outside? Were they having a sleet storm?

"Clarence!" came a muffled hiss from the back window of the bedroom.

"Huh?" He squinted outside and saw a shadow looming beside the bushes. A human shadow. The tapping came again. "Okay, yeah." He rubbed his face to wake up a little better, then threw the blankets back and struggled out of bed. He always wore shorts and a T-shirt to bed, so he wasn't indecent.

He stumbled through the dark room and peered more intently at the shadow. And then he gasped and rushed to the window. "Delphi?" He unlocked the pane and rolled it open. It was her! "Go around to the back door and—"

But she had already levered herself through the window, bringing with her a rush of icy air. Clarence wanted to hug her.

"You're okay! You're safe! Where've you been? I looked all over for you—"

"Shh!" She turned around and fumbled with the window and locked it. "Don't tell anybody I'm here, okay?" she whispered. "It's cold out there! Can I stay here in the apartment with you until morning? I've got to get out of town, but—"

"But everybody's worried about you."

"Shh!" Delphi placed her finger to her lips. "Don't turn any lights on. What if he's followed me? What if he knows I've been here? He knew where I was today, and I don't want to take any chances. Please, can't I just stay on your couch tonight?"

"Sure you can, Delphi. Let me just get a blanket from the closet, and we'll get you all set up. Are you hungry? There's some food left in the fridge from dinner. We kept a plate for you, just in case."

For a moment, Delphi didn't respond but seemed to be peering at him through the darkness. Then she threw her arms as far around him as she could get and held on with all her might.

CHAPTER 25

Mercy awoke Wednesday morning at six o'clock, thirty minutes before her alarm was set to go off. For a moment she thought about trying to go back to sleep, but she knew she wouldn't be able to doze off again. In spite of continued concern about Theodore, she had slept well for once. She needed to pray again. She also needed to talk to Lukas. She needed to hear the comfort and love in his voice and feel that connection to him, however many miles separated them.

She reached over and took the cordless phone from its base, punched Lukas's auto-dial number, then settled back into her pillow. Four rings later she heard a groggy "Hello" and felt a brief moment of doubt.

"Lukas? It's Mercy. Sorry to call so early, I suppose this could have waited until—"

"No, that's okay." The sleepiness dissolved from his voice. "Mercy." Lukas Bower was the only person in the world who could make her spoken name sound like a symphony. "Did you get the card?"

"You mean the one I'm looking at right now? The one I put on my nightstand so it would be the first thing I see in the morning?"

There was a masculine chuckle over the line. "I hope that's it."

"Yes." She glanced at his illegible signature and remembered the rush of joy she had felt when she received the card; when she had to read it through three times to decipher all the words it had only served to sweeten the pleasure. "Actually it was the message you wrote that made me decide to call you."

"It was?"

"Well . . . not the only reason, but I need your advice again."

There was a brief pause that echoed the seriousness of her tone. "Is it the same kind of advice you needed Friday?"

She closed her eyes and took a deep breath. "It's still about Theodore, but this time it's worse. He has cancer." Without skipping details, she told him everything Theodore had told her last night.

When she finished, Lukas breathed the words "Oh no. Has he had a biopsy?"

"He's scheduled to have one this afternoon in Springfield. We're meeting for lunch today at Little Mary's Barbeque so we can tell Tedi."

"How's Theodore handling it?"

"He's in shock. I didn't get to talk with him last night for very long."

"Mercy . . . he doesn't have any other family in the area, does he?"

"No."

"Then he's alone."

What an awful word. *Alone.* "I . . . think so." She felt a fresh surge of compassion. How would it feel to be alone, with no loving family around, no one to care if you lived or died? All of Theo's old friends were drinking buddies or women who might have given him hepatitis B in the first place. He had avoided them for months. His parents were both dead, and his younger half brother lived in Florida and didn't want anything to do with him.

"I was going to call you later this morning." Lukas paused, as if a thought had just occurred to him. "Friday is my last day at Herald. I plan to pack the Jeep and check out of this town as soon as my shift is over. How would Theo react if I called him?"

Mercy felt a surprising surge of relief, and for the first time she was able to acknowledge an unspoken sense of responsibility she had felt for Theo since she'd talked to him last night. "I think it would help, Lukas. He needs to know . . . someone cares." She considered the impact of his words. "You're really coming home Friday? To Knolls?" To her?

"Yes." Another thoughtful silence. "Theo probably shouldn't stay alone after the biopsy if he's released from the hospital."

That hadn't occurred to Mercy, but Lukas's words forced her to consider it now. Where *would* Theodore stay? He would probably be kept in the hospital for an immediate metastatic work-up, but what would happen to him afterward? And why did she feel as if she were suddenly Theo's caretaker?

"Lukas, can I trust you not to condemn me if I say something horrible right now?"

"I could never condemn you. What is it, Mercy?"

"It keeps occurring to me that . . . that Theodore—"

"Brought it on himself," Lukas finished for her. "And now we're feeling responsible to deal with the consequences, and it isn't fair."

She felt a rush of warmth, and she wasn't sure if it came more from embarrassment at her judgmental attitude, or pleasure that he cared enough to know her heart so intimately. "How did you learn to read my mind so well?"

"You're having a natural reaction. I've always had the same tendency, and I have to watch it. I have to remember Who's in charge, and Who gives out the grace."

"I don't want to feel this way."

"There's a parable I read a few days ago in Matthew, chapter twenty. Maybe it'll help."

"Tell me about it." Mercy glanced at the clock and realized it was almost time to say good-bye. "Better make it quick. Neither of us can afford to be late for work today."

"Okay. Briefly, it's about a man who hired workers from the town marketplace to do some field labor for him. He hired some the first thing in the morning, then a few more a couple of hours later. Then he needed more help, and so he hired more workers throughout the day. When it came time to pay them, he gave them each the same amount—the equivalent of a day's wages."

"Even the last ones he hired?"

"Yes."

"But that's not—"

"Fair? That's what the men said who'd worked all day. But the employer reminded them that each of them had agreed to work for a day's wages, and it was his money to give. They just did what they were hired to do. Who had a right to complain?"

Mercy sat up in bed and swung her legs over the side. "So since we belong to God, and we've agreed to live for Him, we should be willing to just do what He tells us to do and stop griping to Him about the job and the wages and what the other guys get."

There was a thoughtful silence. "Theodore stands to lose so much, Mercy. He may not get to see his daughter grow up."

Mercy closed her eyes. She couldn't imagine how that would feel. "I know. I keep thinking about that, too."

"I'll be praying for Tedi." The very sound of his voice relayed his caring spirit.

"Thank you, Lukas. She's just beginning to trust her father again. She's still struggling with forgiveness, and if something happens to Theodore now . . . it could affect her deeply."

"That sounds like someone speaking from experience."

"I can't help remembering. . . . I don't want Tedi to go through what I did." For Mercy, the anger toward Dad had come early, when she was about ten or eleven. By the time she was a teenager it had become a hardened knot of bitterness that prevented her from having a normal relationship with him. And then had come the guilt that clung to her in adulthood. When her father died six years ago, she was still struggling, and the guilt came in spite of the fact that she and her father had worked together in his practice—when he could work, when he wasn't on a binge. When he was alive, she never quite outgrew the resentment at what his alcoholism had done to his family.

"Mercy," Lukas said quietly, "there's a difference. Theo has changed, and Tedi will have a chance to work through this. She'll still have trouble, she'll still struggle, but she has your faith, and hers, to depend on."

Mercy allowed his assurance to settle over her as if God was speaking the words. And in a way, He was. She had no doubt that God had used Lukas to impact her life, to teach her about Him, to lead her to Him.

"Lukas, do you know how much I love you?"

"I might be able to guess. I know how much I love you."

The sound of those words overwhelmed her with joy in spite of the worry.

She heard an alarm in the background over the telephone, and she heard Lukas groan.

"Time for me to get up," he said. "But I'll be back in Knolls Friday night. Meanwhile, I'll try to call Theodore later this morning. Would you please let me know the results of his biopsy?"

"Yes. Lukas, I'm so glad you're coming home."

"So am I."

Mr. Bennett was back in the ER Wednesday morning, less than twenty-four hours from the time he had signed out against Lukas's advice. Today he wouldn't be signing out. His ECG showed acute myocardial infarction—he was having a heart attack. His wife, his mother, and two of his brothers had tried to crowd into the cardiac-trauma room before the ER nurse directed all but Mrs. Bennett to the waiting room. The echo of helicopter rotors reverberated through the ER as the big bird landed outside.

Mr. Bennett moaned. His face was pale and perspiring, and there had been no improvement this time with nitroglycerin. Lukas had him on morphine and a Heparin drip, and still the pain was bad. Even the big guns—the clot buster—seemed to have little effect as it filtered through his blood system.

"I shouldn't've played with the kids," he muttered to his wife, who stood holding his hands, obviously frantic with worry.

"Hush," she said. "Just hang on. Dr. Bower has you all set up at Jefferson City. We'll get you there in time."

The chopper grew silent, and the flight team came trooping through the front door with their equipment. There was nothing more Lukas could do for this patient except pray.

As Theodore stared into the lively brown eyes of his daughter, the aroma of barbeque and the chatter of the cooks and waitresses in the homey café seemed to disappear. He wanted to capture her expression of enjoyment as she licked the barbeque sauce from her fingers and dabbed at her mouth with a napkin. How much more time would he have with her?

Funny, as much as he'd worried and as hard as he'd prayed since Robert Simeon gave him the news about the cancer, nothing had upset him more than Lukas Bower's telephone call this morning about ten-thirty. Lukas had been kind and encouraging, and he had promised to pray. Then he had invited Theodore to stay with him if he didn't feel well enough to be at home alone after the biopsy. What he didn't say—what he'd obviously been careful not to say—was that he expected Theodore to get worse. Lukas and Mercy expected this liver cancer to be bad; Theo could tell it in their voices, and he could see the concern in Mercy's eyes.

"Dad, if you don't eat your sandwich you won't get dessert." Tedi's teasing admonition dragged him back to the present.

He winked at her. "I'll take it home and eat it later." Her appetite had been hearty. Not only had she eaten a mixed-grill sandwich, but she had devoured her red-cabbage-and-pepper salad and downed a glass and a half of pink lemonade. Mercy, he noticed, had eaten three bites of salad and finished a glass of water. Their gazes had met occasionally throughout the meal, and he still read the concern in her eyes. It told him so much more than he wanted to know.

Mercy took another drink of her water, set it down, and pushed her food away, catching his gaze once more. It was time.

He glanced with distaste at his untouched food, then pushed backward a few inches from the table. "Tedi, your mother and I need to talk to you about something."

She stopped eating, and the liveliness of her expression grew serious. "Okay." She picked up her lemonade glass and took a swallow, then set it down quietly. "What is it, Dad?"

"I'm going to Cox South in Springfield for a test this afternoon."

Her expression didn't change. "Are you sick?"

"I guess so. The doctors tell me I am. I've got hepatitis B, and it's affecting my liver. They're going to do a biopsy."

Tedi's eyes widened a fraction. "They think you've got cancer?"

"Yes." He looked at Mercy, and she reached out and laid a hand on his arm. Comforted by the gesture, he continued. "After the biopsy, they'll probably want to keep me in the hospital a couple of days and do more tests to see if the cancer has spread."

This time she didn't answer right away, and he wanted to weep at the change in her eyes, the sudden tension that froze her facial muscles, at the careful breaths she had suddenly begun to take.

"Can we come and see you there?" Her voice was softer.

"I'd love to see you, but your mother—"

"I can get away tomorrow." Mercy's mellow voice washed over him in a wave of concern. "We'll come as soon as school's out."

For the first time in months . . . no, in years . . . he felt as if he actually had family who cared for him. He was becoming adept at battling sudden tears. He swallowed hard and prayed that he could make this as easy as possible for Tedi.

"Are you scared, Dad?" Tedi asked.

He had to be honest. "Yes, but I don't want you to worry."

"I'm not going to worry. I'm just going to pray. You are praying, aren't you, Dad?"

"Yes." He smiled. If only he had her faith. "I've done a lot of praying."

"We will be, too," Mercy said. She gave his arm a final squeeze and released it. "And we'll bring you home from the hospital when it's time."

He stared at her in silence for a moment. "You don't have to do that, Mercy. Joseph Jordan is going to drive me there, and he offered to come and get me—"

"Would you rather have your pastor take you home from the hospital, or your daughter?"

He stared into Mercy's dark eyes, so much like Tedi's, filled with compassion, and he wanted to hug her. "My daughter, of course."

She smiled. "Then stop arguing." The door opened, and six people walked into Little Mary's Barbeque. Mercy glanced at her watch. "We'd better get out of here before the noon crowd descends."

As Theodore paid the bill and walked out with Mercy and Tedi, he felt a mixture of joy and regret. After all this time, his relationship with his family—with his daughter—seemed to be going so well. What would happen now?

———

Lukas stood staring out the front ER window at the cold shoreline of the Lake of the Ozarks. He had received the news just a few moments ago that Mr. Bennett had been taken immediately into surgery when he arrived in Jefferson City. He'd had quadruple bypass and was doing well in the intensive care unit. The nurse who passed on the information was not amused when Lukas asked about the rest of the family. Apparently the reunion was now being held in the ICU waiting room.

Lukas couldn't prevent the second-guessing that always accompanied a case like this. Should he have tried harder to convince Mr. Bennett to stay yesterday? Could he have done more when the man returned with a full-blown MI this morning?

Outside, an icy wind rippled the water into tiny waves that splashed against the rocks and brown grass along the shore. He felt it spit at him through the cracks of the poorly fitted windows. He felt it in his heart. Some days were like that, when none of the news was good, when no one seemed willing to listen to medical advice. At least Mr. Bennett was still alive.

Lukas turned back toward his desk and saw Carmen watching him surreptitiously. She looked away and pounded a few keys at her computer while he sat down and picked up a chart. Then she stopped and glanced at him again. Finally he turned his swivel chair in her direction. "What is it?"

She slumped and looked away, her gray dark-lashed eyes brooding. She shook her head and sighed, then looked back at him. She glanced around the room and out into the hallway, then rolled her office chair closer to his desk and leaned forward. "Dr. Bower, I didn't know they were doing all that stuff to you." She spoke softly, and it was apparent she didn't want anyone to overhear her.

For a moment his thoughts were so far away, he didn't realize what she was talking about.

"I mean, I knew about the surgical jelly—but I didn't do it! I didn't know they were cutting your slacks and ruining your clothes, and I didn't know about all the other stuff until I heard them laughing about it in the break—"

"*They?*" Was there a practical joke committee at this hospital? "Carmen, was it more than one person?"

"No, but everybody knew about it."

"Who was it?"

She glanced away, pressing her lips together uncertainly.

"Was it Quinn?" Lukas asked.

She blinked in surprise. "Quinn? No. He hangs around here all the time, and everybody wishes he'd leave. He's always got these big plans about how he's going to make a bunch of fast money and get out of Herald. Nobody ever listens to him anymore."

"So who chopped the legs off my slacks, and why are you covering for them?"

"Because until you came storming in here spouting fire about it, I didn't realize he'd done all that damage—"

"It was a he?" Aha, a clue! There weren't that many male nurses or techs in this hospital.

Carmen put her hand over her mouth and rolled her eyes. "Okay, fine, it was Brandon Glass. You know, the night tech in lab who does double duty in x-ray."

Oh yes, Lukas knew the guy. He was the one Tex called Godzilla. He was the one who always griped when he got too busy. Somehow this surprised Lukas. Brandon didn't strike him as the kind of person to be a practical joker—he had no sense of humor.

"Don't take it personally, Dr. Bower. He did the same thing to Dr. Moss."

"And I heard from Tex that Dr. Moss handled the situation much more graciously than I did."

Carmen rolled her eyes. "Dr. Moss had a bad habit of *handling* everything, if you know what I mean."

Lukas tried not to react, but he could feel the heat of embarrassment flush his neck.

Carmen shook her head. "Poor Tex. Everybody in the hospital but her knows Dr. Moss is a lech."

A lech. Yes, that was a good word for what Lukas had witnessed the other night.

"You know, a groper. He was always 'accidentally' putting his hands where they shouldn't be, and if someone complained, he apologized and acted all innocent and everything or, even worse, tried to make them feel sorry for him because his wife died last year and he had 'special needs.' What a loser. I wasn't around him much, because he was fired a couple of days after I started working here, but I know the type. He was probably just too scared to try anything with Tex. She was the only one who was surprised when that patient complained." Carmen made a wry face. "Tex is a great paramedic, but she doesn't know squat about men." She paused, then added, "Except with Quinn. She got his number real quick. She never liked him."

"He's not a groper, too, is he?"

"Worse than that." Carmen glanced around at the still-empty emergency department, then rolled her chair closer to Lukas's desk and lowered her voice further. "You know that night you had to run the code on Marla Moore? Well, Quinn was making a telephone call—right in the middle of all that! What a jerk! Like human life didn't mean diddly to him. And then after Marla dies he comes out acting all upset and—"

"He was on the phone!" Lukas came halfway out of his chair. "We had a patient dying, and Quinn walked out and left us to make a telephone call?"

Carmen crossed her arms over her chest. "That's right. That shows you what kind of a paramedic he is. I guess I should've said something to you about it then, but everything was so new to—"

"Who was he talking to? What did he say?" Lukas sat back down in his chair, but he'd lost all interest in keeping his voice down.

"Well, I was pretty preoccupied at the time, but I remember hearing him call the person's name . . . something like Raymond or . . . no, that's not it. Maybe it was Raynell. No, wait a minute . . . it was Ramey! That's it, Ramey. Then he caught me staring at him, and he lowered his voice and I couldn't hear anything else he said, and I had more important things to do, but I know I heard him say something like, 'Ramey, it's Quinn. I need you to do something for me.' I'm not sure that's exactly what he said, but something like that. And that was when he saw me. I'm sorry, Dr. Bower. I should have told somebody. Like I said, I was so—"

"Ramey," Lukas said. "Where have I heard that name before?"

Carmen shrugged as she rolled her chair back to her desk. "The only one I know of around here is Mrs. Ramey, who baby-sits my sister's kids, and she's in her sixties. Why would Quinn risk somebody's life to call a baby-sitter?"

Lukas no longer had any interest in confronting the practical joker. He wanted to confront Quinn. But first, there were others he needed to talk to.

CHAPTER 26

Late Wednesday afternoon Theodore opened his eyes in the recovery room and saw a blurred vision of a man in scrubs. He blinked and raised his head, and recognized his gastroenterologist, Dr. Huffman, standing at his bedside.

"Mr. Zimmerman, the biopsy was positive, as I'm sure you've already suspected." The doctor's words were sympathetic.

Theodore pushed against the mattress and tried to sit up, but he still felt woozy.

"No, lie still for a while longer. Relax. You'll be with us a day or two. You don't need to rush."

The man's voice was kind, soothing. He obviously intended to be reassuring, but Theo felt no comfort. He'd already read the studies on advanced hepatocellular carcinoma.

The doctor explained their plans for a metastatic work-up the next morning. Theodore nodded, but he didn't listen. He already knew the routine. In the morning he would have more tests to see if the cancer had spread. Between now and then he would have to combat his panic and fear. He would call his pastor. He would call his boss. He wanted to keep his thoughts at bay for as long as possible.

"Do you ever pray with your patients?" he asked suddenly, interrupting Dr. Huffman's descriptive monologue about the next day's schedule.

The doctor hesitated for a moment, obviously caught off guard by the interruption. Then he relaxed and smiled. "Yes, I do. Would you like me to pray for you, Mr.—"

"Theodore. Please call me Theodore. And yes, I would like you to pray with me, if you don't mind."

"Of course." Huffman was a young man, possibly in his middle thirties—young enough that his wide blue eyes betrayed a sympathetic heart, and a knowledge of what was to come. He reached out and touched Theo's shoulder, closed his eyes, and bent his head.

Finally, as the doctor's voice drifted through the room in peaceful prayer, Theodore felt the comfort. It was far more complete than human hands or heart could convey. There was no doubt about Who was in control.

Wednesday night at seven o'clock Lukas picked up his jacket from the hastily made bed in the call room, pulled the remainder of his dinner from the tiny fridge beside the desk, and turned to leave. He didn't get far. He found Tex standing just outside the open threshold, hands jammed into the pockets of her pea green jacket, head bent in obvious dejection.

"Hi, Dr. Bower." She slumped into the room, blond curlicues of hair falling across her face. Her nose was red, and her face was pale and pinched. Her green eyes were bright and moist.

Lukas stared at her in surprise. "Tex? I thought this was your day off."

"Oh, I'm off, all right." Sarcasm sharpened her husky voice. She wore an old, worn black sweat suit beneath her jacket, definitely not her work scrubs.

"What's wrong?" Lukas asked.

She walked over and sank down onto the only chair in the room, then leaned forward and rested her elbows on her knees, chin in her hands. "You got a minute?"

"Sure." He tossed his jacket and leftovers onto the bed and sank down beside them.

"I got fired." She tried, and failed, to make the words sound casual. Her voice wobbled.

For a moment Lukas didn't understand the news he was hearing, and he couldn't reply. Fired? He must have misunderstood what she—

She looked up at him and frowned. "Don't tell me the news already reached you."

"Of course not. Did you say *fired?* Why? You're the best nurse they have."

The statement seemed to mollify her, and some of the misery lifted from her expression. "I'm not a nurse, I'm a paramedic."

"You're a doctor," he said. "You graduated from med school, didn't you?"

She rolled her eyes. "Fat lot of good it'll do me without a permanent license. Mr. Amos telephoned me this afternoon. The wimp didn't even have the guts to meet with me face-to-face. I'm surprised he didn't get somebody else to do the job for him."

"What did he say?"

For a moment he thought she wasn't going to answer. She straightened and leaned back in the chair and reached up to tug her fingers through her hair. "Somebody saw me with Hershel and complained."

"They saw you? Where?"

"Remember when I went and met him for dinner the other evening? Well, we just happened to run into somebody from Herald, wouldn't you know. She's been in here a couple of times for migraines, and you know what a cesspool of gossip this place is. Everybody makes it their business to keep up on all the latest. So when she saw me, she let out a big gasp and stomped out of the restaurant. I guess . . . well . . . Hershel might have had his arm around me at the time."

And when didn't Hershel have his arm around her? "And Mr. Amos heard about it."

"Of course," Tex said bitterly. "I told Amos it was my business who I saw when I wasn't at work. That went over like a lead balloon."

Lukas thought again about the conviction that had been growing within him about Hershel Moss. Granted, it was wrong to listen to hospital gossip—particularly since Lukas had learned from painful personal experience that the rumors were often started with malicious intent—but something about what Carmen said earlier rang true.

"And he said . . ." Tex took a breath and blew out sharply, disturbing a few curls that had fallen into her face. "He said my bedside manner stunk." Fresh tears misted her eyes but didn't spill over.

"I don't believe that," Lukas said. "How would the man know anything about your bedside manner? He never leaves his office. And besides, he wouldn't use the word 'stunk.' "

She shrugged and nodded her head, as if he had just made a logical point.

"You have a great bedside manner," Lukas continued. "You know how to put the patients at ease, you know how to do not only your own job but everyone else's, including mine. I've never heard any patient complaints about you, and believe me, if there's something to complain about, the patients around here will do it."

The tears dried, and some of the misery disappeared from her expression. "Well, that's the gist of what he said." She straightened her shoulders, and with a hint of her old chutzpah, she pressed her lips together in a clumsy impersonation of the hospital administrator. " 'I'm sorry, *MSS* McCaffrey,' " she intoned in a grave, nasal twang, " 'but you lack the high quality of people skills we seek to employ at this facility. And furthermore, your predilection toward controversy maintains an agitated environment among the staff.' "

Lukas chuckled and was rewarded by a flicker of mischievous humor in her eyes. Tex might be emotional right now, but she was tough. She would bounce back. "In other words," he said, "you speak your mind. Sounds like good doctor material to me."

The barest of smiles touched her lips, and then she slumped back in her chair and sighed. "You really think I'd make a good doctor?"

"You're already a doctor. Get enrolled in a residency program. Go now, when there's nothing to hold you back." He paused for a half second. "And do it before you become more emotionally involved with Hershel."

She gave him a sharp glance. "I'm not—"

"Don't try to fool me, Tex. You haven't exactly been subtle about it. You know what you said the other day about your . . . Let me see, how did you say it? You haven't always been the 'best judge of character,' right?"

She stared at him so hard he was tempted to scoot away. But he held the stare. "I'm sorry, Tex. I'm not the best judge, either, but I've had enough experience with mashers in the past—both male and female—to recognize one."

He saw the flash of pain in her eyes and then a follow-up of anger. Time to do a little more explaining.

"Tex, I was fired from a job and kicked out of my residency program a few years ago because of a vindictive nurse who had a lot of pull with administration—her father was the director of internal medicine. She had a baby out of wedlock and convinced them I was the father—believe me, I had nothing to do with it, and that was what made her mad. I had to take the hospital to court to restore my good name, and I still didn't get my job back. After that I learned to recognize the users in this world. Maybe I became a little too wary after that, but Hershel strikes an odd chord. I don't like gossip, but don't dismiss too lightly what the women around here are saying about him. I've seen the way he looks at you . . . and touches you."

Tex slouched once more in her chair, and the tears welled in her eyes again. She sniffed and irritably wiped at them with her hand. "It figures, Dr. Bower. What man in his right mind would want a klutz like me? Sometimes I think all I'm good for is—"

"Any man in his *right* mind would be glad to have someone like you, Tex. Don't blame yourself that there aren't very many of those men around." He waited while she struggled to compose herself for another moment. "If you need a recommendation for residency, I'll give you one."

Her chin quivered, and she wiped at another tear. "You really think I could—"

"You're a natural, and don't let Mr. Amos tell you different. What would he know? He's an accountant who doesn't even know how to keep good help."

She looked down at her clasped hands. "You make it sound easy." There was a strain of hesitance in her husky voice.

"Doing a residency isn't easy. It's one of the most difficult experiences you'll ever have in your life."

"No." She became suddenly quiet and reflective, like a pebble falling into a pool of deep water. "Watching your mother die is the hardest."

Lukas understood exactly what she meant. "It's a different thing, Tex. You have no control over death, but you have the freedom to decide what to do with your life now. Didn't your mother sacrifice a great deal to send you to school?"

She nodded, her firm jaw jutting forward a fraction as if she was making a concerted effort to control her emotions.

"Then turning your back on the opportunity won't honor her memory."

She winced and closed her eyes.

"What's keeping you here?" he pressed.

For a moment she didn't speak. The telephone buzzed out in the ER, and the secretary answered, and the nurse and the lab tech laughed and flirted with a maintenance man out in the hallway. "I guess I just thought . . . maybe it really was possible to have a good relationship with a man. I thought Hershel was interested in more than friendship."

"Believe me," Lukas said, "any man worth the sacrifice wouldn't let you *make* that sacrifice. You've come too far to quit."

She bit her lower lip and stared into space for a moment. Then she nodded and met his gaze. "You say you'd give me a recommendation?"

"Anytime."

She continued to hold his gaze. He could tell by her expression that she wasn't convinced, that she hadn't decided yet. She gave him a noncommittal nod.

"I'm serious."

She looked away. "Thanks, Dr. Bower. That means a lot coming from you."

"You're welcome, Tex. And whether you like it or not, I'll pray for you to make the right decision."

She gave him a wry frown and a shrug, and stood up to leave. "Suit yourself."

Lukas thought once more about Quinn. "Can you answer a question for me?"

"Sure."

"What was the name of the baby-sitter you suspected of drugging Angela's kids?"

Her forehead wrinkled. "You mean Ramey?"

Bingo. "Didn't you tell me she worked for the ambulance service for a while?"

"Yes, she was bookkeeper and part-time dispatcher. They caught her drinking on the job, and when they checked her out they discovered she was padding the bills."

"Remember the day Angela brought her kids in? She told us Mrs. Ramey was quitting, leaving town. Did she?"

"Nope. I saw her at the store the other day, hauling about six kids up and down the aisles with her." Tex shook her head sadly. "I can't believe so many parents in this town still trust her with their children after that little girl disappeared from the park. I did tell you, didn't I, that Ramey was her baby-sitter?"

"Yes. Do she and Quinn know each other?"

Tex's eyes narrowed with increasing interest. She made no move toward the door. "Yeah, he was working there when she got the boot, but I don't know if they were friends or anything. If you'll notice, he and I aren't exactly bosom buddies. What are you getting at? What's going on?"

"I'm not sure yet, but Carmen told me something interesting. Remember the night Quinn walked out on us when we were coding Marla Moore?"

"I sure do." Tex scowled. "The jerk."

"He made a telephone call to somebody named Ramey."

Tex's mouth dropped open. "In the middle of the code!"

"That's right."

"That's crazy! We needed him! What did he call her for?"

Lukas repeated what Carmen had told him. "My question is, what would have caused him to leave so suddenly and make a phone call? What happened just before that?"

"I don't know. Why don't you ask his ex-partner? Sandra got fed up with him and changed shifts. I talked to her just a few days ago."

"I think I'll do that. Meanwhile, Tex, why don't you check out your possibilities about returning to residency?"

She nodded, preoccupied, and turned to walk out of the room. "Yeah, Dr. Bower, I'll check into it." She stopped suddenly and turned back, her green eyes widening. "Of course! The baby disappeared! Jerod Moore. That's what you're thinking, isn't it? You think Quinn called Mrs. Ramey to steal the baby as soon as he had a chance to get away from Sandra to make the call." Her excitement grew. "It's perfect! You think Quinn and Ramey stole that baby!"

It was late Wednesday night, and Theodore couldn't sleep in spite of the pain medication the nurse had given him an hour ago. Every time he closed his eyes he saw Tedi's face, or he heard her voice, or he smelled Mercy's perfume. His senses threatened to overwhelm him in their intensity, and he wondered if this was what happened with all terminal patients.

Yet he resisted the idea of impending death. Earlier he thought he'd come to grips with the possibility, but tonight, in the silence and the darkness, he knew he wasn't ready. Spiritually, yes. Emotionally, no. How could any man bear the thought of leaving his family to face life without him?

He picked up the telephone beside his bed and dialed the number Mercy had given him earlier. He knew it was late, and he waited tensely for the telephone to ring two . . . three . . . four times before a groggy male voice answered.

"Hllmph."

Theo's heart pounded harder, and his throat threatened to close with an overwhelming surge of emotions. He swallowed and closed his eyes. "Lukas?" He sounded like a strangling man. "I know it's late. This is—"

"Theodore," Lukas said, his voice suddenly clear and filled with concern. "Are you okay? Are you at the hospital?"

Lukas's concern overwhelmed him. Theo allowed a sob to escape, and then another, and his shoulders heaved, and the force of the movement shook the bed, and pain shot through him from the wound at the biopsy site. While he cried in a wash of physical and emotional pain that he couldn't hope to resist, he heard the soothing sound of Lukas speaking to him, and then praying for him, and then seeking to calm him. And as the healing voice reached his heart, he knew this was the call he was supposed to make. Lukas belonged to God; he could be trusted.

"I'm sorry," Theodore said when at last he could breathe again. "When you called me this morning, you told me you would be there for me." He sniffed and grabbed at a facial tissue on his nightstand to mop up the tears.

"I meant it."

Theo took another breath. "Lukas, just do one thing for me."

"Tell me what it is, and I'll do all I can."

"Please . . . take care of Mercy and Tedi for me." Tears threatened again, but Theodore swallowed them back. "When I'm gone, be a father to my daughter, the kind I never was. Watch out for them, and—"

"Hold it, wait a minute." There was alarm in Lukas's voice. "Theo, why are you talking like this? Are you on pain medication from the biopsy? Sometimes that can really mess with your mind. Why don't we just talk for a while and give you a chance to calm down."

"I've been reading the medical journals," Theo said. "I've read everything I could get my hands on about hepatocellular carcinoma. I know the statistics. I know the cancer has metastasized. I have a few months, at best."

"No. That isn't how you're supposed to look—"

"Lukas, please. What I need from you is assurance. That's all I ask. Just promise me that you'll take care of—"

"I promise, but I can't allow you to write yourself off like that. There's time, Theo, and only God knows how much time. Just make the most of what you have—whether it's months or years or decades—and let Him take care of the rest. You're still Tedi's father."

"But you promise to be there when I'm gone, whenever that may be?"

There was a heavy pause. "Yes, Theodore. I'll be there."

"For both of them?"

"Yes."

Theodore lay back against his pillow and felt his body relax at last. "Thanks, Lukas, that's what I needed to hear. I think I'll say good night now."

CHAPTER ———— 27

Thursday afternoon Clarence steered Ivy's Saturn to the curb in front of the new Crosslines house and switched off the ignition. He pulled out the keys and dropped them into his shirt pocket, then realized he would need them for the remote locking system, so he took them back out. After spending two years operating nothing more complicated than a TV remote, driving Ivy's new car still made him nervous.

He glanced sideways at his passenger. Delphi's profile was etched in sadness, her eyes still shadowed with remembered pain, her mouth drooped like a broken bow. She was just about to leave everything familiar and enter a world filled with strangers, and Clarence wished there was something he could say that would help her. He would go with her if he could—but she was going to have a hard enough time by herself. She didn't need to lug a four-hundred-pound gorilla around with her.

She was tough. She could take care of herself if given a chance. That's what he was doing here—making sure she got that chance.

"You'll like Arthur and Alma," he said, his heavy voice bursting through the silence of the car. "They'll take good care of you."

Her expression didn't change.

"It's going to be okay," he said more softly. "You'll see. Alma told me this morning that they've got some friends in Sikeston who have a home for battered women and children. They're always finding jobs for people and helping them back on their feet. You might even get to take some classes at a trade school. You'll be able to start a whole new life."

She sighed at last and turned her head to shoot a cynical glance at him. "What's in it for them?"

He couldn't help smiling. Last spring he'd asked Lukas Bower the same thing. He still remembered what Lukas had told him. "Glory."

She frowned. She obviously didn't appreciate irony. "People don't help you for nothing. There's always a price."

"Dr. Mercy didn't charge you anything, did she? And neither did Ivy. They've taken care of my sis and me for months, and they never let us pay them back."

The cynicism didn't waver. "You jump their hoops. You've lost all that weight."

"That was for me, not them. I would've died if I hadn't lost it. But they would've still taken care of me. It's the way these people are."

Delphi sat watching him, searching his face. "It's the way *you* are," she said after a moment. "Why do you do it?"

That was a question he hadn't really asked himself, because he'd been so excited that he was *able* to help. But he knew if he hadn't been willing to receive help from Lukas and Mercy and Ivy in the first place, he wouldn't be here now. And he knew Who had led him here.

"Ever heard of Jesus Christ?"

She rolled her eyes and reached for the door latch. "Sure, from those people who sent me back to Abner the first time I tried to escape. They didn't want me, so they told me it was 'God's will' that I go back and make my marriage work."

"I think maybe they were talking about a different god. Lots of people don't want to help or get involved, so they use 'God's will' as an excuse. I know. I've been there. The way I look at it, those people are the ones who really 'take God's name in vain,' like it says in the Bible."

"Maybe."

As if from force of habit, before Delphi got out of the car she glanced in the rearview mirror, then looked in each direction along the street. "You sure you didn't see anybody following us? You couldn't miss that old brown piece of junk he drives."

"I drove around a lot before I came here, and I watched to see if anyone followed. I didn't see anything, Delphi. Come on, let's go inside."

The front door of the Crosslines house opened when Clarence and Delphi were halfway up the walk, and Arthur Collins came striding out, a smile of welcome on his tan-creased face. The winter sun highlighted the red tones of his graying hair. He reached out and shook hands with Clarence with a hearty grip.

"You're just in time. Alma can't wait to meet our guest and show off her new prosthesis. I predict that in two weeks, a stranger won't be able to tell she doesn't have two flesh-and-blood legs like the rest of us." His full attention turned to Delphi, who hovered beside Clarence in sudden, quiet watchfulness.

Clarence awkwardly made the introductions, then touched Delphi's arm and urged her forward. "Come on, these people don't bite." He watched her hesitate, and he leaned forward and said quietly, "They don't use God's name in vain, either. I would've been the first to notice if they did."

Delphi looked into Clarence's eyes as if she were searching his soul, then she looked at Arthur, who led the way back toward the house. She stepped forward reluctantly.

Alma greeted them at the doorway in her wheelchair. "Clarence, darlin', it's so good to see you again." Her customary smile of pure light radiated out and embraced him, then moved to shine on Delphi. "Hello, young lady. You've got to be Delphi Bell."

No response.

Alma wheeled closer and reached out to gently touch Delphi's tense arm. "I know you must be scared and wonderin' what's going to happen next, but, honey, you've come to the right place. We're goin' to do whatever it takes to help you back on your feet in a safe, new home. You'll see. Are you hungry? I've got some snacks out in the kitchen. Want to come and get to know us a little better?"

For another moment, Delphi stood still. Then Clarence reached out and touched her shoulder. She turned to look at him, and her gaze caught his with a silent plea.

"I don't think I'll leave just yet," he said. "Alma, you got any chocolate chip cookies? One little snack isn't gonna hurt me."

The relief in Delphi's eyes cushioned his next blow. There were no cookies. He would have to settle for homemade rolls and apple butter. He could live with the disappointment.

Lukas finally reached Quinn's former ambulance partner at home Thursday afternoon, nearly twenty-four hours after he'd spoken with Tex. She was a hard lady to track down.

Sandra's quiet, gentle voice was hard to hear over the telephone as she informed him why she no longer worked with Quinn. "He didn't care about the patients, Dr. Bower. You should have heard the way he talked about them and even laughed about them sometimes after we left the emergency room."

Lukas didn't have any trouble imagining that. "I heard enough when you brought Mr. Powell in a couple of weeks ago," he said. "Do you remember Mrs. Ramey, who worked in the ambulance office for a while? Were she and Quinn friends?"

"Yes." She sounded surprised at the question. "They really hit it off, not that their relationship was anything romantic. She's old enough to be his mother."

"Did they spend time together after hours?"

"Dr. Bower, are you conducting some kind of an investigation? I don't want to get anybody in trouble. I just don't want to work with him anymore."

"Don't you think the people in this town deserve good, caring paramedics?"

"Well . . . yes, but—"

"Don't worry, I'm not doing this in an official capacity. In fact, tomorrow is my last day at Herald Hospital. I'm going back home to southern Missouri. Could you tell me a little more about Quinn and Ramey? This is really important to me, Sandra. Believe me, I'm not trying to hurt anyone."

She hesitated a few seconds longer, then seemed to relax. "Well, okay. They went riverboat gambling together a few times up in Kansas City. They'd come in laughing and talking about it the next day, and since he spent the whole night gambling, I could barely keep him awake for runs."

"Gambling?" Lukas was scarcely surprised at this revelation. "Did Quinn ever say anything about how much money he lost?"

There was another hesitation. "Yes. How did you know? He tried to borrow money from me a couple of times, but I told him he made more money than I did, and he'd just have to learn to spend more wisely."

Lukas smiled at the thought of timid, soft-spoken Sandra making Quinn back down. She might be shy, but she was no pushover. "Did Quinn and Ramey stay in contact after Ramey was fired?"

"Yes, I saw them together a couple of times, and once we stopped at her house on our way back to the ambulance barn after a run. That was just a little over a week ago, so I know they're still friends." Sandra paused, then said, "I'm surprised he's still around."

"Why? Did you turn in a complaint?"

"No. I just didn't think he was planning to stay in town very long. All the time we worked together, he kept bragging to me about how he was going to quit his job and get out of here."

"If he didn't have any money, how was he going to do that?"

She gave a soft laugh. "Oh, he was always talking about how he would strike it rich on a riverboat someday." She paused. "He didn't, though. All he did was lose money there. A couple of weeks ago, he must have lost big time. He was a real grumphead on one run, muttering about how he'd be stuck here for the rest of his life if he didn't do something drastic. He was real morose."

"Drastic? What do you think he meant by that?"

"How should I know? Hitch a ride on a freight train? Rob a bank? We're talking about Quinn, here. Anything's possible. Dr. Bower, can't you tell me what's going on? Why all the questions? Is Quinn in some kind of trouble?"

"I don't know yet, Sandra. You say anything's possible. . . . Do you think Quinn might have participated in Jerod Moore's kidnapping?"

There was a quick gasp and then a long, shocked silence. "I don't know." She nearly whispered the words.

"If there was a police investigation, would you tell them what you've told me?"

"Of course . . . I know I *should* . . . it's the truth."

"How well do you remember the night Marla Moore died?"

"I'll never forget that night. That was so horrible. I noticed that Quinn was upset, but since all of us were, I didn't think much about it. After all, it looked like he'd messed up the intubation."

"How upset was he? Can you remember what he said?"

There was a short silence over the line, then a gentle sigh. "He was really nervous, couldn't sit still. He made me drive back to Marla's apartment, and the police were all over the place. He acted worried about the baby, asking everybody if they'd seen him. When he got back into the van, he kept saying, 'What have I done, what have I done . . . what have we done?' I felt pretty guilty myself. I mean, we should have realized earlier that there was a baby, but Marla was in such bad shape . . . I didn't even consider that it might be . . . Dr. Bower, he might have taken the baby!"

After Lukas ended his call to Sandra, he telephoned the police.

———————

" . . . metastasized . . ." Dr. Huffman's gentle announcement pierced Theodore's heart like a giant syringe. He laid his head back and closed his eyes and forced himself to remain calm. He'd prayed all morning to prepare himself. Every time he woke up last night he'd asked God to help him come to terms with what could happen. What hurt him now was not fear or pain about his own death, but regret. He could have spent so much quality time with Tedi . . . he could have been a good husband to Mercy. The loss of all those wasted years ate at him. Even though he had made peace with God—or rather, accepted the peace God had offered him—and even though he knew his eternity would be spent in heaven, he still felt the waste here on earth. What kind of time frame would he have for atonement? A few months? There was no way he could show Tedi how much he loved her in just a few months. All he wanted to say would take a lifetime.

"Theodore?" Dr. Huffman bent over him, concerned. "Are you okay? Do you need—"

"I'll be fine," Theodore said. And he would. These past few days, he felt as if he'd been scrambling to retain his hold on this world. It was time to let go. He needed to look forward to the next one, and he needed to trust God to take care of those he was leaving behind.

"Do you have children, Dr. Huffman?"

"Yes, I have a seven-year-old daughter and a five-year-old son."

"My daughter's eleven." Theodore sought Dr. Huffman's face hovering over him and saw the compassion that drew faint lines of sadness around his eyes. "There are few things more precious than spending time with them. A career isn't as important. Running tests on people like me . . . that's not nearly as important." He didn't realize he was crying until he felt tears trickling down his face.

"How about another prayer, Theodore?" Dr. Huffman asked.

"Yes." Theo reached out and touched the doctor's arm. "Thank you." Something about the human contact kept his thoughts from veering into depression or fear—kept him focused on the prayer. As Dr. Huffman appealed to God in a soft voice, Theodore closed his eyes, leaned his head back, and sent up a silent entreaty. Immediately he felt the impact of God's presence, and the total peace and comfort that presence gave him. His nearness to death, and his acceptance of it, placed him closer, spiritually, to God's throne. And the Spirit of God hovered near to give him comfort, assurance, and a reminder that, past the pain, a promise was being fulfilled. Theodore had to keep his heart focused on that promise.

By seven-thirty Thursday night, a blanket of clouds had moved in from the west, warming the atmosphere to a toasty thirty degrees, and Lukas was grateful as he stepped out of the hospital and walked toward his Jeep in the dark parking lot. He would load all he could tonight, and by the time he got off tomorrow he was out of here.

Except for one detail—the police wanted to question him about Quinn. He didn't know if they would be able to come by the ER tomorrow and get his statement, or if they expected him to drive all the way back up—

"You work long shifts, Doc." The deep voice reached him suddenly from the blackness just past his Jeep, and he stumbled to a stop. Then a big figure stepped from the shadows.

Lukas relaxed. "Catcher." Maybe the tension about Quinn had been a little unnerving. "Actually, twelve-hour shifts are normal for a rural emergency room."

"Tomorrow's your last day?"

"That's right."

Catcher shoved his hands in the pockets of his jeans and stepped over to lean against the Jeep. "Hope you have a good ride back down to Knolls."

"Thanks, Catcher. The weather's supposed to . . . be good." Wait a minute. "How did you know I was going to Knolls?"

The white teeth gleamed in a sudden, broad grin. "You've been an employee at Knolls Community Hospital since last April, but in mid-October you started doing temp work for a company called Evans Locum Tenens after an explosion knocked you out of a job for a few months. In Knolls you're a local hero because you went back into the burning building after the explosion to rescue a—"

"How do you know all this?" And why? And what else did he know?

Catcher shrugged and gently thumped the left back tire of the Jeep with the toe of his boot. "Had to check you out."

"For what?"

Catcher didn't speak for several seconds. He cleared his throat, kicked the tire again, and watched Lukas through the darkness. "If you hadn't followed that lead about Quinn, probably nobody would have suspected him or Ramey of taking the baby."

"But what do you—"

"After you called the police today, the Missouri Special Crimes Unit dug a little deeper. Quinn and Ramey are in custody, and Mrs. Ramey's been spilling her guts."

Lukas stared at him, lips parted. "So they actually took Jerod?" And why would a vacationing, booze-guzzling biker know so much about the kidnapping? Unless . . .

"Ever heard about the baby black market?" Catcher asked. "There've been three other kids missing from central Missouri in the past couple of weeks, including Rachel Anderson, the little girl from the Herald City Park."

"And Quinn and Ramey took the other children, too?"

Catcher looked away and shrugged. "That's just an educated guess. No one's confessed to that yet. Give 'em time."

"But they brought Jerod back."

Catcher didn't reply.

"You're still a cop, aren't you?" Lukas said.

There was a long, thoughtful pause as the black-garbed biker studied Lukas in the darkness. "Can we claim doctor-patient confidentiality?"

"Okay."

"Have you ever heard the term 'officially unofficial'?"

"Yes, but—"

"I blew it big-time, man." Catcher looked down and shook his head. He reached up and scratched at his unshaven face, and for a long moment the only sounds they heard were the voices of staff who had stepped outside the doors of the hospital to smoke. "I should have been down at the apartments in my right mind when Jerod Moore was taken that night. I let down my guard."

"You were supposed to be watching?"

"Nope, but I should have been, shouldn't I? I gathered my gang and came into town the day after little Rachel disappeared. While the rest of them went about their normal business, partying and scaring the town to death, I did some checking. Last week, after Jerod disappeared, I looked up Mrs. Ramey and asked a few pointed questions. Scared her, I could see it in her eyes. She must have told Quinn. That's why we got Jerod back."

"So she really did take Rachel?"

"The jury's still out on that one. I think she helped set it up. Then she pretended to be upset because one of her 'precious little darlings' had disappeared. Made a big show of looking for the kid."

"What about the other children?"

A slow grin of satisfaction spread across Catcher's tanned face. "That's what the police are working on now. Like I said, Ramey's spilling her guts."

"Why did you come and tell me about this?"

There came the grin once more. "Ever since I found that baby beside my bike last week, I've been worried what might happen to my own grandson if these creeps got away with what they're doing. Who knows what kid would be next?" He reached forward and clapped Lukas on the arm. "I just think the good guys should know when they've done the right thing."

CHAPTER **28**

L ate Friday afternoon Lukas was thinning out his paper work and packing the personal paraphernalia that had gathered over the past couple of weeks on the call room desk—since all the physicians used the same desk from shift to shift, there wasn't much accumulation. He'd just completed a chart on his most recent patient when the secretary sent him a call.

Expecting word on one of his morning's patients from a receiving physician in Jefferson City, he picked up. "Emergency room, Dr. Bower speaking."

There was a hesitation. "Lukas." The female voice was soft, wobbly, as if near tears.

He recognized who it was immediately. "Mercy? What's wrong?"

She sighed. "I just got a break between patients, and I needed to call you and . . . and hear your voice."

"Why, Mercy? What's happened?"

"I spoke with Theodore this morning."

"Is he still in the hospital? Did he get the results of the tests?"

"Yes. It's bad, Lukas."

Lukas paused and braced himself. "How bad?" In spite of the emotional struggle Theodore had caused him over the past few months, in spite of everything—or perhaps, partially, because of the situations in which they'd been thrown together through a common interest in Mercy and Tedi—he felt a kinship to Theo.

"They found spots in his lungs and adrenal glands yesterday," she said. "They did a bone scan this morning, and there's a spot in his ribs."

Lukas slumped backward in his chair. Not only had the cancer spread, it had spread to more than one place in his body. Poor Theo.

"He's been reading all he can about hepatocellular carcinoma," Mercy continued. "He realizes there isn't much time left."

Lukas felt a great surge of sadness, and he shook his head. *Lord, why? He's barely had a chance to live for you, and now you're allowing him to be taken from his daughter. Why?*

"Tedi and I are taking him home with us this evening," Mercy said. "He refuses to stay another night in the hospital. He won't discuss chemotherapy."

"None at all?"

"None. He knows they can do little for him." She sounded exhausted, as if her emotions had been stretched too far to snap back. Lukas couldn't imagine how he would react if he were in her situation . . . or in Theodore's. How did it feel to face a future of intense illness and death? "How does he sound emotionally?"

"He's calm, but very sad. He told me he's at peace with it. And he told me that was because of you."

"Me? I barely had a chance to talk with him Wednesday."

"You told him about Christ soon after he came out of detox last fall, when the rest of us would have nothing to do with him. You gave him the opportunity to have his life changed forever, when he was desperate for change."

"That opportunity came from God, not from me." Lukas recalled with shame how unwilling he'd been to talk to Theodore and how resentful he had been when just a few spoken words had given Theo new life. Deep down, he'd wanted Theo to suffer longer and struggle harder, because he knew Mercy still had not come to grips with the thought of an Almighty God caring about her.

"Are you still coming to Knolls tonight?" she asked.

"Yes. The Jeep is packed and tanked. I'll try to be out the doors as soon after seven as I can, but you know how undependable quitting time is in the ER."

"Would you stop by my house on your way home?" Mercy asked. "Theodore wants to see you, and Tedi and I *need* to see you. I don't know—" Her voice broke—"I don't know how Tedi's going to take this."

Lukas gripped the receiver in empathy. "I'll be there as soon as I can, Mercy. My heart and my prayers are already with you."

———————

Ten minutes after a meager dinner Friday evening, and for the fourth time in two days, Clarence found himself driving Ivy's car along the quiet street past Mercy's house. He knew Mercy and Tedi weren't back from Springfield yet, but ever since he'd delivered Delphi to Arthur and Alma's place yesterday, he'd felt restless. It was as if Delphi had transferred her fear of Abner to him. It hadn't taken much, after that run-in with him at the clinic the other day. That had shaken him. Seeing him there had obviously shaken Delphi.

What more was Abner Bell capable of doing? After Delphi arrived on the scene last week, Clarence had read a few things about domestic violence. But some of that stuff didn't seem to hold true with Abner. Abusers supposedly put on a good show in front of other people and did the damage behind closed doors. Abner wasn't putting on a good show.

And what about that "old brown piece of junk," as Delphi had called it? When Clarence thought about what she said later, he remembered Tedi talking about an old brown car driving past their house last week. And what about the suspicious-looking cigarette butts in their front yard? Delphi had said something about Abner wasting all their money on cigarettes and booze. So Abner was a smoker.

Clarence should have taken Tedi's fears more seriously. He would stop and talk to Mercy as soon as she got home tonight. Meanwhile, it wouldn't hurt to hang around the area, just in case.

———————

Lukas checked his watch at six-thirty, when the last patient was cleared out from the after-work rush. Now if he could just get past seven before the Friday-night party crowd descended, he was free to leave. The weather was good, so the roads would be fine except for the occasional drunk driver. If he'd asked, he believed Catcher and friends would have given him a motorcade escort all the way to Knolls. He would almost miss them.

To his dismay, at a quarter to seven he heard the emergency room door slide open. He stiffened and craned his neck to look over the counter. He relaxed when he caught sight of a familiar tall, muscular form with a mop of curly blond hair. It was Tex.

"Hi, Dr. Bower!" She stepped into the ER proper, strolled past the unoccupied secretary's desk, grabbed the empty chair, and pulled it over to his desk. In customary Tex fashion, she turned the chair around and sat straddled, leaning her elbows against the padded back. She wore her usual pea green coat over jeans and a sweater. She was also wearing a warm smile that lit her face and transformed her whole appearance.

Tex McCaffrey was, after all, as pretty as her cousin.

"Excuse me," Lukas teased. "Do I know you? This isn't the same person who was bawling her eyes out in the call room just recent—"

"I was *not* bawling my eyes out," she said. "At least . . . not when I left here. You gave me a lot to think about. Hey, I got your message on my recorder about Quinn. Way to go, Doc!" She raised her right hand in the air for a high five.

Lukas slapped her hand and returned the smile. "Thank you. So you've been doing some thinking about residency?"

She grimaced at him and gave a dramatic sigh. "You're like a bulldog, you know it? You sound like my mother. In fact . . ." She reached into the deep right pocket of her coat and pulled out a tissue-wrapped object about the size of her fist. "I think my mother would have wanted you to have this." She held the gift out to him. "Go on, take it. I won't have anywhere to put it where I'm going."

Lukas looked at the object, then into her eyes, suspicious. "Where are you going?"

"Hey, I'm offering you a going-away gift, here. At least have the decency to unwrap the thing and see what it is before you start grilling me."

Hesitantly, Lukas took the parcel from her. It was surprisingly heavy for its size. He removed the layers of white tissue paper to uncover a sparkling crystal replica of a bird with wings spread as if preparing for flight.

He looked back at Tex.

"It's a dove," she said.

"I know what it is." Did she know what it symbolized? Did she remember the picture and the Twenty-Third Psalm he'd had hanging on his wall in the apartment?

"It's Austrian crystal," she said.

"It's beautiful." He held the crystal up to the light and stared in wonder at the prism points of color that filtered through it. He couldn't possibly accept a valuable gift like this. He knew Tex didn't have a lot of money. "You bought this for me?"

"Nope. It was Mom's. She saved her money for months after she saw it in a shop at Lake of the Ozarks. I helped her pay for it when I landed my first job as a paramedic."

"This was your *mom's*?" He placed the crystal bird carefully on the desk. "Tex, I can't take this. Your mother wouldn't want you to give this treasure away to someone you worked with less than a month. You can't—"

"I'm going to finish my education, Dr. Bower," she said quietly. She didn't look at him but fixed her gaze on the dove for a long moment. "I can't go hauling my stuff all over the country while I figure out where I'll have my residency, and I won't have the money to keep renting here. I don't want to take a chance on losing this, and I got to thinking yesterday . . . you've done what I want to do. You've already spread your wings, and you didn't let anyone stand in your way. You've helped me realize I can do the same thing. That's what this bird represents to me." She looked up at him then. "Please. I want you to have it."

"Do you know what the image of this dove represented to your mother?" he asked.

She took an impatient breath. "Yes. You don't have to worry, my mother read me all the Bible stories and took me to Sunday school and church for as long as I remember. I already told you about that, Dr. Bower. Church isn't—"

"I'm not talking about church now, I'm talking about God. Sometimes there's a big gap between the two subjects, and I'm sorry about that. Not every church will hurt you the way yours obviously did."

Tex sat and held his gaze for a moment. "That's what Mom always told me."

"But what about your relationship with God? That's the most important thing."

"I'll think about it, okay?" She glanced at the clock on the wall. "Dr. Bower, it's almost seven, and you haven't written that recommendation for me yet. You want to sit here arguing about a piece of cut crystal, or do you want to get on the road to Knolls so you can see your lady?"

Lukas rewrapped the gift and stood. "Thanks, Tex. I'll hold this for you until you get your medical license. Then I'm giving it back."

She shrugged. "Suit yourself." She grinned at him again, then stood up. When he stood, she reached out and grabbed him in a bear hug so hearty it threatened to squeeze the air from his lungs. Then she glanced at the clock again. "You've got three minutes to write that recommendation."

Five minutes before eight on Friday night, lights from the familiar twin water towers of Knolls greeted Mercy, Tedi, and Theodore through the darkness on Highway Z. Theodore leaned back in the passenger seat and sighed. "Home," he murmured. "For as long as I can remember, those towers have always been there to welcome me home."

Mercy glanced across the seat at Theo. In the lights from the dash, his skin looked pale and tightly drawn. "Are you doing okay?"

"I've felt better." He closed his eyes. "You know, last week I was feeling pretty good until Robert Simeon told me I was sick. You think this was all just the power of suggestion?"

She returned her attention to the road. "You'll be uncomfortable from the biopsy for a couple of days," she said. "Give it some time to heal. You'll start to feel better." What she didn't need to mention was that he was destined to be sick again.

"Yeah, Dad, and the best place to do that is our house," Tedi said from the backseat. "You'd better take advantage of it. We've got the guest room all set up and ready to pamper you, and since I'm out of school for the next couple of days, I get to do the pampering."

Theo smiled. "A guy couldn't ask for a better doctor."

By eight o'clock Friday night, Clarence felt like a paranoid idiot. He passed Mercy's house for the fifth time that evening to find her porch light still on. It was still dark inside. Anytime, she and Tedi and Theodore would arrive home from Cox South Medical Center in Springfield and go inside. Then, just for the sake of completeness, Clarence would go up and knock on the front door and make a fool of himself by warning Mercy about what Tedi had told him. Was he crazy to jump to the conclusion that Abner Bell had been casing their house?

He was three blocks away when he passed an old brown car parked along the curb, away from the direct glare of the streetlights. No one was inside.

Suddenly he didn't feel like such an idiot. Maybe he would take one more cruise through the neighborhood, see if there was anybody out and about on the streets—or maybe in an alley somewhere nearby. He knew what to look for.

Theodore eased from the backseat of the car with Tedi's gentle—though unnecessary—guidance. His side was sore, and if he moved wrong it felt like a giant wasp was stinging him in the abdomen, but he was strong enough to stand on his own and walk up the sidewalk to the house without help. Still, when Tedi carefully placed her arms around him, he relished the connection with his daughter. He leaned on her shoulder for support.

"Are you okay, Dad? Do you need the crutches?" She looked up at him with such sweet concern, he never wanted to let her go.

"I'm fine, Tedi." He repositioned his hold on her shoulders. "If you'll walk with me I think I'll make it inside."

She turned and strolled through the garage with him in the dim glow from the automatic garage-door opener. "I hope you like oatmeal with honey and almonds and blueberries for breakfast. Grandma makes it a lot, and she showed me her special recipe with all the right spices. I'll make it for you in the morning." She stopped at the steps that led into the house while Mercy opened the door and led the way inside.

Theodore made a big show of depending on Tedi to help him up the steps, but he knew that she knew he would have no trouble making it into the house himself. This was the sweetest contact he'd had from his daughter in such a long time, and he didn't want that contact to end. If he could only let her know through his touch, through his tone of voice, how special he thought she was. If only he could cram a whole lifetime of a father's love and pride into the few short days . . . or weeks . . . or maybe months he had left to—

Mercy switched on the light to the pantry through which they entered, and then she stopped suddenly, causing a traffic jam behind her. She swung toward Theo as he was taking his last step into the kitchen from the garage. Her eyes were wide with shock as she reached forward and grabbed Tedi by the shoulders. "Out!" she cried. "Get back—"

"No!" came a roughhewn male voice from somewhere beyond her in the darkness of the kitchen. "I'll put a bullet through you before you can reach the garage floor!"

Tedi cried out in fear and stumbled backward against Theo. A big, stringy-haired, wild-eyed monster stepped from the shadows holding a black .357 Magnum.

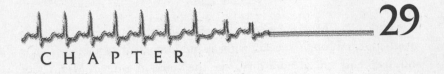

C H A P T E R 29

Clarence drove around the block one more time, keeping his speed below fifteen miles per hour, studying every dark spot between the houses, and the bushes, and beneath the trees. He couldn't stop thinking about that car. He didn't like it. Maybe he should just call the police now, if he could figure out how to use the car phone Ivy kept in her glove compartment . . . or maybe he'd use the pay phone at the convenience store over on the highway after he checked Mercy's house one more time.

He eased up to her front curb and braked, saw the front porch light still on, and stopped. Then he caught sight of another light—a dim one filtering out from the small window in the garage. He saw the telltale glow of the automatic overhead door. That was a timed light, and it hadn't switched off yet. They must have just arrived home.

He glanced up and down the street. Could that jerk be hovering in the shadows, watching him, or maybe watching the house? With a pricking at the back of his neck, he opened the car door and heaved his bulk up from the seat. Might as well warn Mercy before he called the police. And while he was at it he could use her phone. He stepped past the evergreen bushes that gently shielded the house and stepped into the glow from the porch. Funny, none of the lights came on inside. He would have thought that, by now—

The faint sound of a deep, angry male voice reached through the darkness. He stopped walking and frowned, unable for a couple of seconds to pinpoint the source. It came again, and he caught his breath. The sound was coming from inside Mercy's house.

He'd better figure out how to use that car phone, and fast.

———————

"You've got her somewhere, I know it! Where is she?" The shout reverberated through the air with an undercurrent of mania, rough and deep and spiked with fury, like the voice of a devil. Mercy saw in their attacker's eyes a blackness more deadly than the gaping end of the weapon he pointed at her.

"Abner, I don't know what you're talking about. What are you doing with that gun?" Mercy's question was instinctive and sharp, and Abner's gaze lashed out at her, then at Theodore. His angry stare settled, like a curse, on Tedi.

Instinctively Mercy moved to block his view. The sudden movement was another mistake.

His grip tightened on the handle of the gun so hard his hand shook. "Stay there! Don't move!" The aim switched from Mercy to Theo. Abner's gaze centered on Theo's face with a brief show of panic. He obviously hadn't expected Theodore to be with them. "Get away from that door! Now!" he shouted.

Dread rooted Mercy to the floor, and her heart beat so hard she felt the adrenaline surge through her body. She felt Theo's hand come to rest on her shoulder and nudge her forward. "Do what he says, Mercy." His voice was soft and conciliatory, which helped to slow her runaway panic. As she stepped forward, the soothing tone continued.

"Look, I don't know who you are," he said to Abner, "but I think you've come to the wrong house." He maneuvered in a smooth motion to place Tedi behind them as he eased alongside Mercy. "My name is Theodore—"

"Stop right there!" The aim readjusted, this time back at Mercy. She froze again, and she heard Tedi's breath catch behind her. Behind . . . as long as she stayed blocked from Abner's sight. . . .

"It's okay," Theo said, his hand still resting on Mercy's shoulder, "we're stopping." There was silk in his voice, a tone Mercy remembered him using to make many a sale in real estate. Theodore had prided himself in his ability to charm people—usually it was individuals of the female persuasion, but he'd had quite a bit of success with both genders when it came to manipulation.

Mercy prayed hard that this special talent—which she had hated for so long—would now be resurrected.

"We might be more comfortable if we all sat down at the dining room table to sort this thing out," Theo said. There was a barely detectable quiver in his voice. "Or we could go into—"

"You shut up!" Abner gestured toward Theo with the gun. "I don't want anything from you. I just want one thing here." The aim once more went to Mercy's face. "I want her to tell me where she took my wife."

Mercy fought desperately to control another burst of panic. "I didn't take her anywhere," she said with total honesty, taking her cue from Theo's calm, conciliatory voice. "I don't know where she is, Abner." She struggled to keep her voice steady and resist the anger that continued to build momentum within her. How dare he endanger her daughter like this!

"Liar!" he snarled. "You're lying! You're the one who turned her against me. You're the one who filled her head with ideas, made her think I was dangerous!"

She clenched her teeth and stared pointedly at the gun. He didn't think a .357 Magnum was dangerous? "I know she left town a day or two ago." *Keep talking, defuse the situation, give him a chance to back down.* "But I was so preoccupied with other patients that I didn't have time to speak with her." She breathed deeply in a desperate attempt to quiet the fury that boiled within her and threatened to spill over. She could not control the situation. The best she could hope for was the ability to control her own emotions, and that was proving to be enough of a challenge.

"I don't believe you!" He waved the gun wildly and took a lunging step toward them. "You're the one she ran to! You're the one who told her to leave!"

He leaned toward Mercy until the smell of his smoker's breath wafted toward her.

"You trying to tell me now that you didn't even give a rip about her?" He gave a harsh burst of laughter that crackled through the kitchen.

As if he'd reached an invisible line on the floor, he seemed to

336 : HANNAH ALEXANDER

catch himself and back away, like a trapped animal coming into contact with the bars of the cage. He paced a few feet across the kitchen while Mercy desperately tried to recall a helpful de-escalation technique she had used in the past with violent patients.

She swallowed and cleared her throat. "I care very much for my patients, Abner, and I have a lot of them right now." She paused as he swung around and paced back the other way, always keeping his hostages in view, his eyes darting around the room, a muscle beside his right eye jerking. "You happen to be one of them, and I'm wondering if you might be in the most need of my help right now." She hoped the insincerity wasn't obvious in her voice.

He narrowed his eyes and raked her with a gaze of suspicion as he continued his pacing. "You never helped me! You'd like to see me rot!"

"I was the one who discovered your cerebellar hemorrhage last October. If I hadn't acted quickly, you wouldn't be alive."

"If you hadn't poisoned Delphi's mind against me, she wouldn't've tried to kill me!" His voice continued to grate like a cement mixer, and he kept the gun pointed toward her.

She noticed, however, that the aim had dropped. If he pulled the trigger now, he would hit her somewhere in the abdomen. Was he lowering his guard slightly, or just losing control? That gun looked like a small cannon. It had to be heavy. "I can't tell you something I don't know, Abner, but I can find help for your problems. It's never too late—"

"My problem's standing in front of me!"

His breath once more engulfed her in stale smoke—but no alcohol fumes. He hadn't been drinking. She should have picked up on that immediately. Drugs, then. He wore a jacket, so she couldn't tell if there were track marks on his arms. She'd tried talking to him once about drug rehab, and he had stormed from her office in a typical rage. Questioning him now wouldn't be a good idea. Still, if she could talk him down from his anger high . . .

"You obviously care about your wife," she murmured gently. "You've gone to a lot of trouble to find her, and you've contacted me several times in your search." Did he realize the trouble she had taken to make sure his search was not successful? "It seems to me that someone who cares that much might be willing to take the next step toward reconciliation."

He continued to watch her, his muddy brown eyes cold and spooky.

"Would you be willing to talk to a counselor about—"

"No!" His trigger finger flinched as he spoke, and she held her breath, aware once again of Theo's tightening grip on her shoulder. "You sound just like Delphi—you never know when to shut up!" He turned aside again and muttered under his breath, "Just like Delphi . . . just like those stupid women at work . . ."

Mercy heard the continuing fear in her daughter's audible breathing behind her, and she banked down her own anger and frustration once more. She needed to keep her thoughts clear. She wanted Tedi out of this house before he lost control. She couldn't keep her gaze from the deadly weapon in his hand.

He stopped and turned, like a snake coiling to strike. "If you didn't help her get away, who did? I saw the fat man take her to your office that day. He was driving *your* car. Try explaining that!"

She didn't hesitate. "Abner, didn't you know your wife was injured? And she was sick. She had a dislocated elbow and a bad bruise on her face." It was difficult to keep the blame and accusation from bleeding through in those words. "She'd been out in the weather during that ice storm we had last week, and she didn't have a coat. She needed medical attention."

"Nobody ever called *me*! You *knew* I was looking for her, but you never called me to let me know she was okay!"

Mercy closed her eyes and bowed her head to keep from revealing the loathing she was unable to completely suppress for a moment. He'd been the one to cause his wife all that pain and suffering. The man was vile.

Once more, she looked up at him. "I am constrained by a pledge of doctor-patient confidentiality. You surprised us the day you came in looking for her, Abner. That frightened Delphi, and she ran out the back. Were you watching the clinic for her?"

"Yes," he hissed. "And I've been watching your house." His movements grew more agitated and his voice more coarse, and for the first time he stepped past that invisible line on the kitchen floor and towered over his hostages, holding the gun inches from Mercy's chest. "I know what time you get home at night, and what time your lights go out after dark!"

His voice deafened her, and she could hear the weakening of his control.

"I know the license plate number on your Subaru." His hand wavered as he held the gun, and he brought his other hand up to steady it as he brought his gaze into focus, first on her face, then on Theo's, then past them. "I know where your little girl goes to school."

Mercy exhaled and gasped as if she'd been kicked in the stomach, and she saw a flash of satisfaction in Abner's eyes.

"Oh yeah," he grated. "I know how to get what I want from you." He leaned closer, peering over Mercy's shoulder. "Get out of my way." He moved to step past the wall of protection Mercy and Theo had made with their own bodies. "I can make you talk."

He raised his elbow to shove Mercy aside, and as he did so the barrel of the gun pointed toward the ceiling.

With a sudden explosion of movement from behind, Theo lunged forward and grabbed Abner's beefy right arm with both of his. "Run!" he cried. "Tedi, run! Mercy, get her out of here! Get her—"

The gun fired with a scream of sound and blinding light, and ceiling tile scattered across the room. Mercy whirled around as Tedi jerked open the door behind them and pressed the button to open the overhead door. The light came on and the motor engaged, but as Tedi raced down the steps, Abner shoved Theo aside with a roar of fury, hitting him hard in his weakest spot—the biopsy site. Theo fell with a grunt of pain against the counter.

Mercy saw the gun come back down and take aim at Tedi, and she lunged for Abner's arm, kicking up with her right knee. "Run, Tedi! Get away!"

The gun fired wild again. Abner shrugged Mercy aside as if she were no more than a spitting, scratching kitten. He shoved the gun barrel hard against her cheek. She felt the cold metal against her flesh. Still listening to the sweet sound of the garage door opening, she ducked and rolled at the same time Theo hurled his whole body forward and rammed Abner sideways. Both men struggled and fell against the far counter. Once more, the gun fired.

A third shot echoed through the night, and Clarence gripped the handset. "Just get somebody here fast! Somebody's shooting in the house! Get the police!"

The operator ordered him to stay on the line.

"Sorry, can't do it." But he laid the phone down on the seat of the car without disconnecting. He didn't know how. Didn't have time. He turned in panic toward the house and heard the overhead door engage and start its slow climb upward. Before the door reached the halfway point he saw a hunched shadow burst out into the night.

He recognized that compact form. "Tedi!"

She changed directions and raced toward him, her breath coming in ragged gasps. "Clarence! Help them! He's got Mom and Dad and he's shooting!" Her voice plunged past the edge of hysteria. "He's shooting!"

Clarence grabbed her by the shoulders and shook her gently. "Okay, I'm going. The police are on their way. You just run! Go across the street to the neighbors. Now!" He nudged her in that direction, then turned and ran as fast as he could toward the house. There was no time to wait for the police.

Theo felt the shaft of horrible pain in his chest and he knew there was a raging animal somewhere nearby, and he knew Mercy would have to fight that animal alone. He could do nothing to help her. His helplessness was complete. *God, protect her.*

Tedi was safe. That's why the animal raged. With the knowledge came satisfaction that no pain could touch. Theo had been her shield. For once in his life, he'd been her father. And his own Father was waiting. He sensed the presence, the strength that came from outside his own will. He felt the love and acceptance, and he knew God was holding him with a love more powerful than anything he could have imagined. God would never lose his grip.

The darkness grew, but where he was going was never dark. Theodore Zimmerman would never experience dark again. His way had been prepared.

Mercy saw the gun on the floor beside Abner's outstretched hand, where he lay panting across Theo's prone, silent form. She had to get to that gun, kick it across the room, or grab it and run. For the moment, Abner looked dazed, and blood trickled from his nose and mouth where Theodore had struck him repeatedly.

She couldn't take the time to check to see if Theo was okay. She couldn't hear him breathing, only Abner, and the monster was becoming more coherent with each breath. Still praying for her daughter's protection—and her own—she stepped over the toppled bodies, placing her full concentration on that gun.

She had to get to the gun.

She rushed past the end of the counter and bent down . . . and she encountered the creeping depths of Abner's muddy gaze on her.

In a final, desperate move, she reached for the gun and brought it up, gripping the barrel with both hands. Abner snaked out his hand and grabbed her by the ankle. His fingers dug deeply into the flesh, and she cried out. He jerked harder. She lost her balance and fell against the refrigerator, but she did not lose her grip on the gun. She wanted to throw it across the room, get it far enough away from him that he could not regain control before she could escape. But first she had to get away from him. She kicked at him with her free foot, but he held on as if he had her encased in concrete. She drew the gun back and slammed its heavy grip into the side of his head with a dull, sickening thud.

He grunted and relaxed his hold, and she scooted backward across the floor. He shook his head and growled like an angry bear. He turned his gaze of fury back on her. "You better be ready to use that thing." He gave a low, inhuman laugh. "If you don't, I will."

Mercy scrambled to her feet and ran to the counter that separated the kitchen from the dining area. If she could just climb over . . .

He pulled himself up and staggered toward her. Going against every instinct she had ever learned, she gripped the gun in her hands with her finger on the trigger. "Stop!" she cried.

He kept coming.

She aimed far above his left shoulder and fired. The sound exploded in front of her, and the recoil knocked her backward. He hesitated but started after her again. His animal instincts had taken over his mind. She fired again, unable to bring herself to aim for his head or chest.

He growled in angry pain as a splotch of red stained the sleeve of his arm. In one swift move he reached out with his good arm and grabbed for the gun. Mercy squeezed the trigger one more time, and he stumbled backward as another explosion of blood surfaced from his shoulder. There were no more bullets. She flung the gun away and tried to run past him.

His big hand came out and grabbed her by the throat and closed on her like the mouth of a crocodile.

She kicked out at him and punched his face and tried to scream, but he was oblivious to all but the work of his one powerful hand. He blocked her air and blood flow, and the light in the room began to go dim.

She cried a silent prayer for help. She couldn't let him kill her. She couldn't leave Tedi behind . . . but darkness overwhelmed her and she couldn't catch her breath. *God, please! Not like this . . .*

The grip broke free from her throat, and the force of it shoved her sideways.

A new, deep, angry voice filled the kitchen. "Get away from her!"

Two giant male bodies went tumbling to the floor in a confusion of mass and sound, and Mercy fought to catch her breath and stay out of the way of the fight. As her vision cleared and oxygen once more filled her lungs, she saw her four-hundred-twenty-pound rescuer pinning Abner to the floor.

"Mercy, you okay?" Clarence called to her over his shoulder.

"Yes," she choked.

"I've got him. Help's on the way, and Tedi's with some neighbors."

The sounds of multiple sirens reached them through the open garage door and grew louder with reassuring sound. Mercy fell to her knees at Theodore's side, and she saw the wound in his chest. She bent over him and cried.

———

Fingers of flashing red and blue strobed into the night sky as Lukas turned from the highway onto Mercy's street. He immediately tensed, as he always did when he saw the telltale signs of a nearby emergency, and then he forced himself to relax. He knew the Knolls ER was still out of commission, but the ambulance service wouldn't be bringing patients to Mercy's house now.

It wasn't until he rounded a curve and drew closer that he discovered with shock that the focus *was* Mercy's house. An array of police cars and ambulances surrounded the area along both sides of the road and in her driveway. A small crowd of bystanders hovered at the periphery of the scene.

Heart pounding, Lukas pulled over and parked a block away. He tried not to panic as he got out of the Jeep and ran along the street toward the nearest uniformed officer. Before he could reach the man, he heard his name shouted from the interior of one of the ambulances.

He looked over to find Tedi jerking away from the tech and racing toward him across the yard. "Lukas!" Tears streamed from her eyes, and her breath came in hiccuping sobs.

Lukas held his arms out, and she ran into them. She grabbed him tightly around the waist and pressed her face into his chest, and for a moment, crying took all of her breath. While Lukas held her and tried to comfort her, his mind raced out of control.

"What happened?" he called to the policewoman walking toward him. "Where's Mercy? Is she—"

"Dr. Richmond is still in the house with the investigating officer," she said as she came nearer. She frowned and peered at him through the red haze of the flashing lights. "Aren't you Dr. Bower from the emergency room?"

"Yes."

The woman stepped closer and laid a sympathetic hand on Tedi's shoulder. "This girl's father saved her life tonight."

"He's dead." Tedi's voice was muffled by Lukas's thick wool shirt. She raised her head at last and looked up into his eyes, and tears still streamed down her cheeks. "Abner Bell tried to shoot me, because he was mad that Mom helped Delphi get away from him." Lingering terror echoed through her voice. "Dad jumped in the way, and Abner shot him. Lukas, he's dead!"

Lukas closed his eyes and drew her head once more against his chest. He buried his face in her hair, and he felt his own tears of shock and grief fall silently.

"Don't ever leave us again, Lukas." Tedi tightened her grip around his waist. "Please don't leave us again."

He kissed the top of her head. "I'm not going to, Tedi. I've already promised your father."

One more time he heard his name called, and he looked toward the house. Mercy came walking through the open garage door between Clarence and a police officer. Her slacks and sweater were stained with blood, and there were cuts and bruises on her throat and the side of her face.

"Tedi, here's Mom," Lukas said softly. Together they turned and opened ranks to embrace Mercy, and the three of them clung to one another and cried.

EPILOGUE

On Sunday, February 14, Lukas eased slowly into Mercy's driveway and parked his car. Weather was unseasonably warm, and the roads were clear, so he didn't need the four-wheel-drive capabilities of his Jeep. And besides, this was a special occasion. A very special occasion.

He sat in silence for a moment, staring at the front door of Mercy's house. He was a little early—he'd intended to be. Mercy wasn't expecting him so soon, and she was probably still rushing around, getting ready for church, fixing breakfast for Tedi, and urging her to eat while eating nothing herself.

Lukas reached up to tug at the unaccustomed tightness of his shirt collar. It was buttoned all the way to the top, and there was a tie knotted there—he'd actually remembered how to do the knot. Mercy might faint when she saw him. He grinned to himself, then felt the cold wash of trepidation wipe away the smile.

Before he could chicken out, he reached for the door handle, opened it, and stepped out, fighting the tide of panic that made his breath come faster and his pulse pound in his ears. Was it too soon? Barely two weeks had passed since Theodore's memorial service. Was this appropriate?

Theo had made the initial request. Theo was the one who wanted Mercy and Tedi loved and cared for. If this was wrong, Mercy would say so, and they would wait. But he didn't think the timing was off. He'd prayed about this. In spite of the natural reaction of nerves that any man in his right mind would have at a time like this, he felt sure that this was good. It was right.

He stepped to the front door and reached up to ring the doorbell, but the door flew open before he could push the button. Tedi stood before him with a dazzling grin, her dark brown hair still damp from her shower, her glasses slipping down her nose.

"Hi, Lukas, you're early. You look great!" She paused to admire him for about two seconds before she released the knob and turned to swirl in front of him. She wore a satiny sapphire dress that fell in soft folds around her shoulders and seemed to radiate highlights of her hair. "What do you think? Isn't it gorgeous?"

"It's beautiful." She looked so much like Mercy.

"It's my favorite color."

Lukas knew that. "It's perfect."

"Grandma bought the dress for me yesterday. Don't you love it? Mom's still in the bedroom putting her clothes on." She lowered her voice and leaned toward Lukas conspiratorially. "She was griping this morning because her clothes are too tight."

Lukas returned the grin as he stepped inside and followed Tedi to the sofa. He knew Mercy was frustrated about her weight. He'd overheard her just yesterday complaining to Lauren that she had gained another five pounds and that she was going to stop getting on the scales. She looked good to him—if she was gaining girth, it had settled in all the best places. So far in their relationship, though, he'd remained silent on the subject. He'd discovered long ago that women had a very touchy attitude about the subject of weight, no matter what their size.

As soon as he sat down on the sofa, Tedi scooted next to him and caught his arm in a loving embrace. She had always been affectionate with him, but in the past two weeks he'd spent most of his evenings here after working with Mercy at the clinic all day, and Tedi had hardly left his side. It was as if she was making up for the months they'd lost together while he was doing locum tenens work out of town. He knew there would be plenty of opportunity to make up for the loss, but he couldn't help the regrets. Still, if he'd been faced with the same decision again, he would probably make the same choices. Theodore and Mercy and Tedi had needed their time to heal as a family.

"Guess who's dating?" Tedi pushed her glasses back up on her nose and gazed up at him with adoring eyes.

"Dating? I don't know . . . your grandma?"

"Oh, Lukas, that's old news. I mean Darlene! She's been going out with Mr. Walters, my teacher at school. Did you know his wife died two years ago? He goes to the Methodist church over on Lincoln. They've been out three times in the past two weeks, and he's had dinner with us at the house once. It seems kind of weird having your teacher eating dinner with you, but it's okay. And you know what else?"

He leaned back and gazed down at her, charmed by her grin and by the light in her eyes. Theodore's death and the events of that Friday night had left a deep wound in her, but Lukas knew she would heal. There would be scars, but there had been time to forgive. Now Lukas intended to be here for her when she struggled, when the nightmares visited her, when the doubts came. He wanted to be here for her for whatever she faced.

Tedi waited for Lukas to answer until she looked ready to explode with the news. "It's about Clarence. Can you guess?"

"He's lost more weight?"

"No, besides that."

"*He's* dating . . . he's joining the police force . . . no, wait, I know! He's opening a gym."

Her hands tightened threateningly on his arm. "Lukas," she warned. "Get serious."

"I am serious. Why couldn't he do all those things? He's a hero, you know. He saved your mom's life." Under that tough, thick facade truly beat the heart of a hero.

"Clarence is going to work for Arthur and Alma at Crosslines," she blurted at last, unable to contain her excitement.

"He's going to *work* for them?"

"Just volunteer at first, but he's really excited. He told me all about it yesterday. You'd think he'd just won a million dollars."

A warm alto voice reached them from the hallway. "For Clarence, this is even better."

Lukas felt his breath catch, and he turned to find Mercy stepping into the living room in a slender cloud of soft white silk that draped over her beautifully shaped curves in perfect harmony with her movements. Her dark hair was swept up and away from her face to fall gracefully over her shoulders. And her gaze held a special light as it rested on him. To him, Mercy was the most beautiful woman in the world, the one by whom all others would be measured. She set the standard, with her thick dark brows, high cheekbones, firm chin, and the multitude of changing expressions that radiated across her face at any given moment. At this particular moment there glowed a depth of affection . . . even more . . . a depth of love.

He stood up, feeling awkward in the presence of perfection. "Wow."

The light of her gaze deepened as she smiled. "Thanks, I needed that. Wow, yourself." Her admiring eyes traveled from his eyes to the toes of his shiny black wing tips. "Must be a special occasion."

"It is." He watched her, fighting the old feelings of awkwardness.

"Want some orange juice? You're early. I didn't think—"

"Uh, actually, I meant to get here a little early." He shoved his right hand into the pocket of his suit coat and grasped the velvet-covered boxes nestled there. He stepped back from the sofa and gestured for Mercy to be seated. "I needed to talk to both of you before church this morning." He studied Mercy's face to see if she guessed what he was going to say. He saw a slight widening of her dark eyes. A question.

She sat down beside Tedi.

He cleared his throat and took out the boxes. The one for Tedi was covered in pale pink velvet. The one for Mercy was red.

He held the pink one out for Tedi. "A valentine gift for you."

The excitement that had filled her eyes since his arrival now radiated from her with an almost tangible force. "All right!" She took the box from him and opened it in one fluid movement. Her mouth opened in a gasp, and she cried out at the sparkle of tiny precious stones set in the shape of a heart on a ring of gold.

He bent on one knee in front of the child he hoped would be his daughter someday. "Tedi, this ring is a symbol of promise from me to you. I promise that as long as I live I will be there for you. I will love you and protect you as a father would his own child. I will never ask to take your father's place in your heart, but maybe I could share a spot—"

"Oh, Lukas, I love you!" She lunged at him with her arms open wide and nearly knocked him to the floor. She gripped his neck in an iron grip, her face suddenly wet with tears. "I love you, Lukas." Her voice trembled.

He looked over her shoulder to find tears of joy in her mother's eyes, as well.

Tedi straightened as he caught sight of the box that had not yet been opened. "Is that an engagement ring? Are you finally asking Mom to marry you? Is this a proposal to both of us?"

He laughed. Nothing like being welcomed with open arms. "No, it's a promise ring, too." He turned to Mercy and handed her the red velvet box. He watched her eyes as she opened the box and caught sight of the narrow gold band inset with tiny heart-shaped rubies, emeralds, sapphires, and diamonds.

"Oh, Lukas," she whispered, reaching for the ring. Almost reverently, she took it out.

Lukas forgot to breathe as he continued to kneel and watch the two most important women in his life try on their gifts—his promises to them. The fits were perfect.

Mercy held her left hand up to the light and cast him a look of awe. "How did you—"

"The lady at the jewelry store gave me a ring sizer, so while you two were otherwise engaged last week, I did some checking in your jewelry boxes."

"You thought about that all by yourself?"

"I had a little help from Ivy. But I designed them all by myself."

Her expression held new respect. "And the promise?" There was a hint of hesitation in her voice. "What does it signify?"

"That with God's help I will be here for you." He caught her gaze and held it, and reached forward to touch her face, unable to resist. "That I'll love you and pray for you every day. I won't leave as long as you need me."

Her dark, fathomless eyes shimmered again with tears. She laid her hand over his. "What if I told you I would need you for the rest of my life?"

He smiled with relief. "I'd tell you that it would be my greatest joy to be here for you."

"Wouldn't that be easier if you were my husband? Isn't that what marriage is all about?"

"Is that a proposal?"

She nodded, all the joy and hope and fulfillment of months past culminating in one clear gaze.

"I accept."

"All right!" Tedi tackled them both from the side and nearly knocked Lukas sprawling. "We're getting married! We're getting married!" She kissed them both on the cheek and then jumped up to run into the other room. "We can announce our engagement in church this morning! This is the best Valentine's Day ever. Wait till Grandma hears." Her voice faded down the hallway. "I'll call Abby as soon as we get home, and . . ."

Lukas drew Mercy closer to him. He wanted to stay like that forever. "I love you, Mercy. I'll always love you. That's a promise."